W9-CIP-773

MASTERS OF DARKNESS II

EDITED BY
DENNIS ETCHISON

TOR
HORROR

A TOM DOHERTY ASSOCIATES BOOK

MASTERS OF DARKNESS II

Copyright © 1987 by Dennis Etchison

First printing: January 1988

A TOR Book

Published by Tom Doherty Associates, Inc.
49 West 24th Street
New York, NY 10010

ISBN: 0-812-51764-4
Can. Ed.: 0-812-51765-2

Printed in the United States of America

0 9 8 7 6 5 4 3 2 1

He had been looking for people—had heard their voices and come expecting to find someone, but he was not prepared for what he had found.

Most startling was their color. They were white: bone, chalk, dead white. They looked as if, instead of flesh, they were made of porcelain.

They were unnaturally thin and tall, with elongated necks and arms. When they moved—as now, they moved toward him—they undulated.

Charles didn't dare run—he felt too weak to escape them, and the idea of being caught by them was far more horrible than merely confronting them. So he held his ground, braced himself, and prayed they would not touch him with their dead-white hands.

MASTERS OF DARKNESS II

Tor Books edited by Dennis Etchison

MASTERS OF DARKNESS I
MASTERS OF DARKNESS II

to
STUART DAVID SCHIFF
exemplary editor

ACKNOWLEDGMENTS

Masters of Darkness II and Preface copyright © by Dennis Etchison.

"Up Under the Roof" © 1938 by the Popular Fiction Publishing Company, for *Weird Tales*. This version revised by the author for *Worse Things Waiting,* © 1973 by Carcosa. Reprinted by permission of the author's estate and Karl Edward Wagner.

"The Other Room" © 1982 by Stuart David Schiff. Reprinted by permission of the author. Author's Note © 1987 by Lisa Tuttle.

"A Garden of Blackred Roses" © 1980 by Charles L. Grant. Reprinted by permission of the author. Author's Note © 1987 by Charles L. Grant.

"Cottage Tenant" © 1974 by Ultimate Publishing Company. Reprinted by permission of the author and his agent, Kirby McCauley Ltd. Author's Note © 1987 by Frank Belknap Long.

"The Hounds" © 1969 by Damon Knight. Reprinted by permission of the author. Author's Note © 1987 by Kate Wilhelm.

"Zombique" © 1972 by H.S.D. Publications, Inc. Reprinted by permission of the author. Author's Note © 1987 by Joseph Payne Brennan.

"Taking the Night Train" © 1981 by Thomas F. Monteleone. Reprinted by permission of the

CONTENTS

PREFACE

Masters of Darkness II is a second "authors' choice" anthology offering readers the rare opportunity to enjoy what the masters of this field consider their most outstanding short works.

As in the first volume, I have asked some of the most honored authors of horror/dark fantasy to select a personal best or a favorite that somehow did not reach a wide audience on original publication, if necessary restoring or correcting the text, and to compose an afterword explaining how or why the piece came to be written. A number of the stories appear here—and only here—in their final form, having been previously subjected to abridgment, censorship or editorial error; others, such as Frank Belknap Long's "Cottage Tenant," have been newly revised especially for this edition. Once again it is my aim to bring you outstanding examples by writers working at the height of their powers, gathered together in a volume that can be called definitive. These books, then, constitute a unique reference, an historical record of the true and complete versions of stories that are justly famous or deserve to be, and a collection that should fascinate and entertain any fan of the dark and fantastic.

You will note two entries by writers now deceased. Manly Wade Wellman agreed to participate and made his selection shortly before his untimely death in 1986. Because of this, Wellman's story and the accompanying remarks are taken from the Carcosa edition of *Worse Things Waiting*, compiled in 1973 under the author's supervision and known to reflect his intentions. I wish to thank Karl Edward Wagner, publisher of Carcosa, and Frances Garfield Wellman for their cooperation in allowing me to begin these pages with "Up Under the Roof."

The late Richard McKenna (1913–1964) is the only writer in either of two volumes to be represented without the opportunity to revise or comment on his work. Though his contribution to this field is singular, his genre works have regrettably remained out of print for several years, and the chance to correct this unfortunate state of affairs cannot be refused. With gratitude to Mrs. Eva McKenna, who very kindly chose her husband's first published story for reprinting here, I am therefore proud to close with an authentic masterpiece, the unforgettable "Casey Agonistes." One of a handful of contemporary classics, this story of a modern-day Hanuman provides an incomparable summation of my ambitions as editor. If you have not read it before, I envy you your first meeting with Casey and his defiance of the encroaching night.

Once again my job has been to stand aside and allow accomplished professionals the right to select, edit and have final say about their own work.

Of course, arriving at the list of contributors has been my responsibility, and once more that much has proven exceedingly difficult, with so many talented artists now practicing in this New Golden Age of the Horror Story. The challenge is made that much greater by limitations of space that do not permit the representation of every important writer in even two volumes, as well as by my disinterest in observing the artificially contrived boundaries between genres that so often define publication. It is my thesis that such commercial considerations do readers as well as writers a disservice by subdividing literature into separate and sometimes opposing camps, discouraging catholicity and precluding access to a larger and potentially appreciative audience. For example, Damon Knight and Kate Wilhelm have often written profoundly disturbing stories that in no way reassure with the presumption of salvation through technology that permeates science fiction; yet how many fans of horror and the supernatural will have encountered "Strangers on Paradise" or "The Hounds" prior to opening this book? If my moderately eclectic approach can help in some small way to introduce a greater number of readers and writers to one another, this undertaking will have been worth the effort.

These are uncertain times for the art of the short story, considering the present nature of the marketplace. Yet I remain committed to what Truman Capote maintained is, "when properly practiced, the most difficult form of writing extant." As writer and reader, I have been loyal to it for more than a quarter of a century, and it has served me well. I hope that the fine examples presented here will deepen your respect for the form while satisfying your hunger for the deliciously outré, and whet your appetite for other splendid works by these very remarkable writers.

—Dennis Etchison
January 1987

UP UNDER THE ROOF
Manly Wade Wellman

WHEN I WAS TWELVE YEARS OLD I LIVED IN A SHABBY old two-story house, built square below and double-gabled up above. The four gables contained an upstairs room apiece, each facing in a different direction and the entire four making a cross, with a hall and a stairwell at the center. The front and side rooms were ceiled and plastered and painted, for use as bedrooms, but the unfinished rear chamber held only a clutter of trunks, boxes and broken furniture. That part of the upper floor was hot and dusty in the summertime, and it was left open right up to the peak of its gable. Directly above its doorway to the central hall gaped an empty dark triangle, that led to the slant-sided cave above the bedroom ceilings. Because it was so full of lumber, this unfinished room was called the garret, though it was not a real garret. The real garret was that dark space, up under the roof.

I was the youngest person in the house by more than a generation, and my youth seemed to offend everyone bitterly. I was constantly reminded of my childish stupidity and inexperience. Nobody felt that years would make me any wiser, and in time I grew to share that opinion. I tried never to make a statement or venture a suggestion that had not been voiced previously by one of my elders. Even at that, I came in for plenty of snubs and corrections, and repeated admonitions that little boys should be seen and not heard. So I learned to keep my own counsel. The downstairs parlor was full of books, and I read in them a great deal, including nearly all the volumes of an old *Encyclopaedia Britannica*. This taste for reading attracted some curious attention on the part of my guardians; occasionally one of them would say that I must be trained for the law or the ministry. I was never consulted as to my own ambition, which would have shocked the entire household. I wanted to be a deep-sea diver.

That summer was a hot one, and my room, in the gable on the right or northern side of the house, had only one window. The sun's rays fell directly on the outside of the room's sloping walls, which were only the plastered-in pitches of the gable, and which offered little insulation. Even by bedtime, my room did not cool down. I slept poorly, bothered by strange and vivid dreams. Sometimes I started awake in the darkness, sweating and tingling, and lay there as I listened to the rustle of the cottonwoods in the yard and the creaking of the old house timbers.

After a while, I am not sure exactly when, I began to hear something else at night.

Awareness of that sound grew upon me, first slowly and faintly, then with a terrifying clarity, over a number of hot, wakeful nights. It was something up above me, between the ceiling and the peak of the roof, something big and clumsy and stealthy. I remember telling myself that it was a rat up there, but the moment the thought came into my head I knew it was a very silly thought indeed. Rats skip and scamper, they are light and swift and sure. This movement was huge and weighty, of a bulk that I judged was far beyond my own; and it moved, I say, with a slow, unhandy stealth that had a sustained rhythm of a sort. It did not drag or walk, but it moved. Years afterward, I was to see through a microscope the plodding of an amoeba. The thing up under the roof sounded as an amoeba looks, a mass that stretches out a thin, loose portion of itself, then rolls and flows all of its substance into that portion, and so creeps along. Only it must have been many, many thousands of times larger than an amoeba.

Before long, I was hearing the noise of that motion every night. I would wait for it, lying awake in bed until the moment it made itself heard and humped itself across the ceiling above me. Always fear came with it, fear that did not diminish with time. I would stare into the hot gloom, my tongue would dry up between my teeth, and my fingertips would smart as though they had been rubbed sore. On my back would sprout and fan and winnow little involuntary wings of chill, that made my spine shrink and quiver as though ice came and mingled with the marrow. The ceiling, I knew, would descend some night. It would descend upon me like a great millstone being lowered, and then it would crumble about my bed. Something huge and soft would wriggle free of the broken bits. . . .

There could be no talking about any of this, I

knew very well. Long before, I had learned that nobody in the house would listen or care. As I have said, I was scorned and disliked by all those others. Once, when a neighbor boy of fifteen gave me a terrible beating in the front yard, everyone watched from the parlor windows, but none stirred to help me, not when I thought I would fall dead at my enemy's scornful feet. When he got tired of pulping my face with his knuckles, he turned away at last, and I dragged myself in and was tongue-lashed on all sides for an hour. Today I cannot remember exactly what was urged against me, only that the tears I had not shed for pain welled forth under the scolding. Things like that made me hesitate about asking for help or anything else. One morning at breakfast, I did dare to inquire if the others had ever heard anything strange, up under the roof; but I was only reprimanded for interrupting a discussion of local politics.

That night the noise was louder and more terrifying than ever. It began somewhere above another of the rooms, and then it trundled along my ceiling, slower and still slower, until it paused immediately above my bed. At that moment it seemed to me that the lath and plaster were no tighter or stronger than a spider web, and that the bulk up there was incalculably more dire than the very prince and father of all spiders. I was certain that it crouched there, almost within reach of me, that it gloated and hungered, and that it turned over in its dark sub-personal awareness the problem of when and how to come and take hold of me.

I could not have stirred from my bed, could not even have cried out for help.

The thing and the fear of it were with me always, night after night and week after week, until a day late in the summer, a dark and rainy day when it did not wait for nightfall.

I was alone in the house that day, and I had grown tired of hearing the rain and the dank swish of soaked leaves outside. I looked at the books in the parlor, but I had exhausted all that interested me. Then I remembered a stack of illustrated magazines, very old, in a corner of the lumber room. I climbed the stairs and opened the door. The lumber room was ugly and close, and a sort of brown light reflected from the unpainted joists and the insides of the shingles overhead. I found the magazines and began to paw through them.

Up to then, there had been no sound except for the weary rain outside. But as I leafed through one of the magazines, there came a slow, muffled *bump-bump-bump* from above me, from that dark opening that led into the space above the ceiling. I knew that something sly and heavy was there, looking down upon me.

In one scrambling moment I had fled into the hall and downstairs and to the front door. I grabbed the knob, then I stopped and thought.

It was no swelling of courage that made me pause before rushing out, only a hopeless but sensible consideration of what must follow. I could leave the house and go into the rainy street and mope there until someone came back. Then I would have to come back, too, and in time night would fall and I would have to go to my room and go to bed in the dark. Then whatever made the noise would come down. It would wait no longer, for it had seen me and my tortured terror. It would flow to the floor and come in at my door and creep up on my bed. Then I would know how it looked, and what color it was, and what it wanted with me.

All these things I pondered, and from somewhere came a cold determination that stiffened my limbs and my neck like new sawdust poured into an empty doll. I left the front door unopened, and walked back through the house to the foot of the stairs. There I paused, and tried to lift my foot to the bottom step, but I could not.

After a while, and I think it was a fairly long while, I turned and walked to the back porch. There, upon the wood box, lay a handaxe. It was dull and rusty and wobbled upon its helve, but I took it in my hand and went back in, and this time when I came to the steps I mounted them.

It was a slow journey, one step after another, with long, tight breaths between. The old boards creaked under my shoes, as if aghast at my rash ascent. I gained the upper hall, and now I did not hesitate, but went back into the lumber room.

The brown light had darkened since I had first come there to find the magazines. I stood in the middle of the floor and made myself look up at that triangular opening, and that took a mustering of all my will power, but there was nothing to see there. I stuck the handle of the axe down into the waist-band of my knickerbockers, and dragged a heavy, dust-laden old bureau across and pushed it close against the wall beside the door. Upon that I placed a broken-backed chair, and upon the chair a candle box, set precariously on end.

Finally I climbed up on the bureau, up on the

chair, up on the box. My chin rose level with the threshold of the black cavern, and it was like gazing into a pool of ink.

I peered and listened. With both hands I got hold of a cross-timber and drew myself slowly up. The candle box tipped over and fell from beneath my feet, striking the floor boards with a crash like an explosion. But next moment I had dragged myself up inside the loft. The roof peak came so low above my head that I could barely rise to my knees.

The axe still hung in my waistband, and I was heartily glad I had brought it. I pulled it out and tried to hold it in my mouth, like a pirate's dirk. But it was too big and heavy, so I kept it clutched in my right hand. Then, crawling on my knees and my left hand, I went forward on top of the rafters. Every inch took me deeper into darkness, and when I reached and made my way past a big rough chimney I might as well have been in a coal mine for all the light that came to me.

But if I could not see, I could feel, and so I groped my way. First I went straight to the front of the house. I kept the axe poised for a blow as I felt all along the boards, and into the corners. The dust made me want to cough. When I had explored that area, I dragged myself around. I could see some feeble glow of light when I looked toward the far end, past the obstruction of the chimney. Crawling back, I explored gropingly the space above the south bedroom. Last of all I made myself venture into the loft above my own room, where I had always heard the noise.

I found nothing.

Those are the three words I always finished with

when, grown-up enough to be listened to, I told this story in later years. And one or two listeners have spoken of the undefined and sometimes malevolent psychic forces that now and then afflict children on the brink of adolescence. But I knew then, and I know now, that there was something, or that there had been something, that was a mortal peril until I drove myself to face it. If I had done anything else that day, it would have come looking for me that night. And I do not want to guess what would have happened then.

But from that time forward, there was not the slightest murmur of sound up under the roof. I slept so deeply that I had to be shaken and shouted awake in the mornings. And I never knew real fear again, not even in the war.

AUTHOR'S NOTE

During many years of writing for a living, I finished and saw into print a number of stories about ghosts and devils and other things people say can't exist. Most of us, as I think, have the sixth sense of wonder and want to hear, even to believe, stories of wondrous terror. Montague Summers insists that you must believe in ghosts to tell good stories about them, but M. R. James, who wrote better and more frighteningly than he, says only that he is ready to consider evidence of ghosts. If I may intrude into such splendid company, I'll confess that I have felt strongly persuaded now and then.

"Up Under the Roof" is as close to autobiography as I have ever come. I experienced every bit of this story, as a boy growing up in Kansas, left alone in a hostile old house by grown-ups who could give a damn about a child's fears. One memorable day in that house, I conquered my fears, just as I've told it here.

—Manly Wade Wellman

THE OTHER ROOM
Lisa Tuttle

IT WAS SOMETIME PAST MIDNIGHT WHEN CHARLES Logue mounted the front steps of the house he still thought of as his grandfather's.

His grandfather had been dead thirty-five years: Charles had never known him. The house, unlived in, had been his own property for ten years. Still Charles thought of it, when he thought of it, as his grandfather's house.

The house had been built solidly of wood in the days when families required a lot of room. The front porch was long and deep, and there had once been a screened veranda above it. Grandly pillared and gabled, it was an imposing, old-fashioned house in a once-gracious neighborhood now gone to commerce. It had been stripped, gutted and subdivided to hold small businesses in the early sixties.

Charles Logue stood on the porch, remembering evenings spent reading comic books on the splintering wooden steps in the last light of the day, until his mother or grandmother scolded him for ruining his eyes and sent him running across the street to join in a game of kickball or fox-and-hounds. He remembered the sound of cicadas, the sudden flare of fireflies in the deep shadows under the oak trees, the smell of freshly-cut grass and baking cookies.

The keys jangled together—an adult sound—as Logue found the correct one and unlocked the front door. He entered uncertainly, trying to recall the present floorplan. The old one was still clear in his mind, and he knew he would have to superimpose new walls and spaces over the rooms of his memory.

There was a health-food store and a lawyer's office on the first floor; upstairs, he knew, was a record store and something called "Woman/Space." It might have been much worse—next door was a beauty parlor/fortune-telling operation, and a few houses down was a gift shop Logue had heard was a cover for more illicit business.

Something—broken glass?—ground and slipped beneath his feet as he walked slowly into the high-ceilinged hall, gazing at the health-food store's display window. Bands of white light from the street revealed dim shapes, boxes of tea, bags of nuts and bottles of vitamin tablets. But Logue didn't see the present display, nor the ghost of the parlor once in that space. He was caught up in his misery again, thinking the thing he could not forget, the central fact of his existence for the past year:

His daughter was dying.

There had been room and time for hope, once. There had been an operation that was supposed to save her. But it hadn't. It hadn't helped at all. There was nothing any of them could do but watch her, every day, draw a little closer to death.

Already she had gone so far that it was hard for the living to talk to her, hard to pretend or to say anything that had meaning, impossible to comprehend her experience.

There was the barrier of physical pain, and the agony of observing, without being able to lighten or share, her suffering; there was the fuzzy, sense-numbing wall of drugs around her; but highest and sternest of all the barriers was Death, which she approached steadily, leaving her family and friends helpless in the distance.

He sat for hours beside her bed, holding her bony little hand until his arm was numb, trying to pull her back by sheer force of will. He tried to pray. He would have made any bargain with god, devil or doctor, but everyone told him there was nothing, now, that anyone could do. Nothing he could do but hope for a miracle or wait for the end.

Beyond tears, beyond hope, standing in the heart of the old house, Charles Logue pressed his hands to his face and shuddered.

Charles Logue first came to the house when he was eight years old, at the end of a long journey, late at night. The reason—although his parents did not tell him—was that the old man was dying. It was a uniting of the family, a last chance for togetherness and forgiveness at the end.

Under ordinary circumstances Charles's mother would have noticed he was "coming down with something." But in her own excitement and worry about her father, she was impatient with the boy's whining and fidgeting, and saw them as signs only of childish restlessness with a long car trip. To keep him entertained, she told him stories about her childhood in the house they were now going to, including the information that the house contained a secret room, accessible through a hidden door.

"I won't tell you where it is," she said mysteriously. "I'm not sure anyone in the house remembers it nowadays—I discovered it myself when I was a girl. You can have fun looking for it, and using it as a hideout."

The prospect cheered Charles almost to the point of forgetting his discomfort, and he passed much of the trip in fantasies about finding the room and putting it to good use.

It was very late indeed by the time they reached the house, and Charles was bundled off to bed in a room filled with the lurking shapes of strange furniture. He wasn't made to take a bath, or even to brush his teeth, and he was put to bed—the grown-ups talking all the while over his head, oblivious to him—in his underwear, then left alone.

He lay quietly for a few moments, hearing the voices and footsteps move away from him and down the stairs. He gazed at the rectangle of light which was the doorway, blinking his eyes, which, like the rest of him, felt sore and hot.

Irritably, he kicked the covers off. The rasp of the sheet against his bare arms and legs annoyed him, and the air was so close he could hardly draw a satisfying breath. He got up and padded softly to the door.

The upstairs hall, he saw, was long and narrow, lit by a chandelier which hung above the landing at the turn of the stairs. It hurt his eyes to look at it—it seemed all fiery, faceted crystal, shooting light in all directions—so he turned his face away from the stairs to the winding hall to the left. It made a sudden turning after a few feet, and he could not see past the projecting corner.

As he stepped out into the hall, Charles suddenly wished he had not left his bed, however uncomfortable it was. His body ached, his throat hurt too much to swallow, and now, after having been so hot, he was shivering uncontrollably.

He called for his mother in a plaintive voice. But there was no reply. No one came. Charles realized that he could hear no one in the house, which surely meant that, wherever his parents had gone, they could not hear him, either. He could call until he had no voice left, and no one would come. Helplessly, because he felt so very sick, Charles began to cry.

But not for long: he was a brave, sensible boy and knew crying wouldn't bring his mother if she couldn't hear him. He would have to go look for her.

He turned to the stairs again and stopped short. They seemed to be moving, like the steps on an escalator he had once been afraid of in a department store. They crept back and forth between shadow and light. They taunted him with hidden teeth: step on me and I'll suck you under and chew off your legs.

Charles moaned softly, closing his eyes against the dizzying back-and-forth motion. He dared not go near those treacherous stairs. He leaned against the doorframe, calling for his mother in a hopeless whisper. Tears seeped from his eyes and rolled down his face.

Gradually, through his pain, Charles became aware of voices. Soft voices, muffled by a wall, but they were somewhere nearby, upstairs. He stopped sobbing and held his breath to listen, to be sure. It might not be his mother, but that didn't matter —any grown-up would do. Someone to take him back to bed, make him comfortable, and climb safely, carelessly down the stairs to fetch his mother back to him.

He turned and began to make his way down the hall, away from the stairs and the light. His legs were weak, so he leaned against the wall for support. He could feel the voices through the wall, a slight vibration, but when he paused to listen he could not make out any words. But the voices went on rising and falling, a comforting, natural sound. Behind this wall he would find a room with people sitting and talking together.

Yet when he finally came to a room, the door gaped on black emptiness. Charles stared, disbelieving, into the silent darkness. Where were they, those people he had heard through the wall? Had he missed a previous door?

Shoulders slumping, head reeling with dizziness, Charles turned back and pressed his ear against the wall. Yes, the voices were still there. They were clearer now: he heard a woman say his name.

Excited now, he hurried, certain he had only missed the first door in his weariness. But he came back to the room he had started from without finding, in the long, empty stretch of corridor, any entrance to a room where people sat together and talked about him.

There had to be a door, Charles knew. He did not see how he could have missed it, open or closed.

Unless it was a hidden door.

He remembered then, with another surge of excitement, that his mother had told him this house had a secret room, behind a hidden door. That must be it!

He retraced his steps, leaning against the wall now less from weakness than from the hope of finding some difference in the surface, some bump or indentation or crack which would indicate the hidden door.

And at last he found it, just as he had imagined.

There was nothing more than a light depression, a smooth dip in the wood about the size of a grown man's thumb. Charles put his own thumb in the spot and pressed. There was a clear, distant click, and then a long, straight crack appeared in the wall, expanding as the door swung open.

The room was surprisingly large for a hidden room, Charles thought as he entered it. It was long and furnished like a waiting room or hallway with wooden chairs and dark oil paintings in heavy gilded frames. The floor was a dark, polished wood, and a rug patterned in maroon and brown made an aisle down the center of it. Covering the far wall —or perhaps hiding a doorway—was a straight, heavy curtain.

Charles gazed around at this unexpected room and, suddenly, felt frightened.

"Charles."

A whisper in the empty room.

"Who's there?"

Behind him he could hear the smooth, latching sound of a door falling shut. The faint echoes of his high, frightened voice hung in the air. The heavy curtain ahead of him moved slightly, although the air was perfectly still.

He could not go back, Charles told himself. He must be brave. He had come here to find someone, and he would. He had heard their voices. His mother knew about the secret room—perhaps she was waiting for him on the other side of that curtain.

Bravely, he walked the length of the room, and took hold of one corner of the stiff, heavy fabric. As he raised it, he felt a gentle waft of scented air against his face. Breathing it in made his heart beat a little faster, but he didn't know why. It was a sweet, slightly musky smell, strange to him, but exciting.

The newly-revealed room was enormous, with an immensely high, airy ceiling that made Charles think of churches. The room was filled with a pale, blue-white light that seemed to have no particular source but simply was, like the air. The walls and floor were made of a highly polished white stone which had within it flecks which caught the light in a silver gleam.

There were people in this room, and the sight of them terrified Charles.

He had been looking for people—had heard their voices and come expecting to find someone, but he was not prepared for what he had found. These people were certainly not his relatives—they did not look like any people Charles had ever seen before.

Most startling was their color. They were white: bone, chalk, dead white. They looked as if, instead of flesh, they were made of porcelain.

They were unnaturally thin and tall, with elongated necks and arms. When they moved—as now, they moved towards him—they undulated.

Charles didn't dare run—he felt too weak to escape them, and the idea of being caught by them was far more horrible than merely confronting them. So he held his ground, braced himself, and prayed they would not touch him with their dead-white hands.

"Dear boy."

It was a woman's voice, gentle as music. He looked up into a narrow, elegant face. It wasn't human, but there was something beautiful about it all the same. Charles stared at her, his fascination winning over his terror. Her face seemed to glow with a faint light, and her long, narrow eyes glittered like blue ice.

"Come with me, dear boy, and rest yourself. I'll make you comfortable."

Before he could think to pull away, she had rested her pale hand on his head, and immediately Charles felt soothed and cooled. He was no longer feverish or sore, and his initial terror of these strange people had been lulled. They looked strange, but they seemed so kind. . . .

"Let the boy alone!"

It was a loud, coarse shout, completely out of place in this ethereal room. Charles was vaguely irritated by it. As he turned in the direction of the sound, he saw a large, angry man bearing down upon him. The man, like his voice, was equally an intruder here. He was an ordinary man, old and fleshy. His face reminded Charles of an old hound dog, and he wore a red and white striped robe that was garish in this place of muted colors.

Charles shrank away from the stranger, against the woman who had offered to comfort him.

With surprising strength, a bony, freckled hand pulled Charles from his refuge. "Get out of here, boy!"

Then the ugly old face swooped in close. "Who are you, boy? You look familiar, somehow."

Charles craned his neck to see how the white people were taking this intrusion. There were perhaps a dozen of them gathered around, all standing quietly, with no readable expression on their thin, still faces. He turned back to the old man. "My name is Charles Logue, sir."

"Charles. Logue. My name is Charles, too." His voice quickened with eagerness. "Logue . . . are you Elaine's boy?"

"Yes, sir."

"But what are you doing *here*?"

"We came to see my grandfather."

"Bless you, son, I'm your grandfather. I mean how did you come *here*?"

"Through the secret door. My mother told me there was one. I heard voices through the wall, and looked until I found it. They said my name."

"*My* name," the old man said softly. "You shouldn't be here, boy. It's no place for you. You go on back now, and find your mother."

"You come with me," Charles said.

The old man closed his eyes and shook his head quickly. "Go on, now."

Charles looked up. The lady who had offered him comfort was smiling at him. He had a glimpse of small, pointed teeth, like a cat's.

"Please," whispered Charles to his grandfather.

The old man straightened to his full height. "Let the boy go," he said. "You have no business with him."

The encircling crowd did not move or speak. The old man bent down and spoke softly to Charles: "We'll walk toward the curtain. The first chance you get, you must run for it, without looking back and without waiting for me, understand?"

Charles nodded and put his hand trustingly into his grandfather's. They began to walk, slowly, and the white people gave slightly before them. But they moved at a snail's pace—Charles realized that his grandfather did not want to touch, even to brush against, these people, and, not understanding why, he grew more frightened.

Finally they came near the curtain. The white people did not seem anxious to be close to it, and moved away, making a gap in the circle through which Charles saw he could escape.

His grandfather gave him a push, then, and Charles ran as he had been told to, without pausing or looking back. As he slipped behind the heavy curtain, he heard a woman's voice right at his ear, as if she ran at his side, saying, "You'll come back. When you understand, you'll come back to me."

Now a grown man, standing in the house he owned, Charles Logue was afraid to go upstairs. He didn't know which he feared more: finding the room, or not finding it.

Thirty-five years before, when he had recovered from his long illness, young Charles had begun to search again for the hidden door. The adults had told him that his grandfather was dead and buried in the ground—and what a pity they'd never met —but Charles knew better. He knew where his grandfather was, and he meant to find him, to save him, somehow, from the strange people who kept him prisoner.

But no matter how many times he walked the

length of the hall, no matter where he pressed or knocked or scratched, he could not find the door again. His efforts were noticed, the object of amused speculation by the adults, and finally his mother had taken pity on him and told him that the secret room was downstairs. She had even showed him what she called the secret room—a stuffy little cave beneath the stairs, accessible through a door at the back of a closet.

It made no difference: Charles knew what he had seen. He refused to believe it had been only a dream and, for the rest of the summer that he stayed in the house, Charles continued to look in vain for the door, the room, his grandfather.

Would it be any different this time, Charles wondered. Could it? Leaving aside the question of dream or reality, why should he succeed now when he had failed so many times as a child? Was it enough that he was an adult now and fully aware of what he proposed to do? That he was willing to sacrifice himself to save his daughter? He would try to leave the room with his daughter, but if a life was called for, he would give up his. All he asked was the chance.

He pressed his hand to his forehead, checking his fever like a key or a weapon. Would it be enough to get him in? But his hands were cold, and he could not tell if his face burned or not.

Coming down with this virus, three nights before, tossing restlessly in his bed, Charles had had a dream. In the dream he had gone again to that hidden room and there had seen his daughter, surrounded by those thin, white people. The look of mute terror on her face as she sought to find a

familiar human being in that place had torn his
heart, and he had woken crying and calling her
name.

He knew she was there—he had heard her speak
to them. He had seen the blue shadows of that
room in her eyes. He'd heard her initial fear turn to
a weak fascination as, in a drugged half-sleep, she
begged them to touch her with their cool, white
hands and take away her pain.

I come with pure heart and clear intentions,
thought Charles, only half ironically. His mouth
was dry. Please, let me save her.

He began to mount the stairs. The banister was
new and ugly, but the steps beneath his feet seemed
to be the same ones he had climbed as a boy, so old
that a shallow depression was worn in the center of
each broad step by years of footsteps.

He heard voices above his head. Dimly, through
a wall, he heard them.

Charles froze, holding himself perfectly still and
silent, and listened intently. The murmur of voices
came again, a distant, familiar rhythm.

He let out his breath in a sigh and continued to
climb. He had been right to come here, after all.
They had let him hear them; they would let him
find the door again.

But the upper hall was not empty, as it should
have been. He was not alone. There were others
here, dark figures moving swiftly toward him, harsh
human voices; he scarcely had time to realize that
something was wrong and he was in danger before
the sudden, intense pain took him into a suffocat-
ing blackness.

When he came to, he was standing in the antechamber with the dark oil paintings on the walls and the wooden chairs lined up beneath them. So he must have found the door, although he did not remember how or when.

His head ached abominably, and his shirt was wet—with blood, it seemed. He didn't stop to reflect on it, but hurried toward the tapestry hanging at the end of the room.

As he lifted one corner of the heavy curtain that rich, strange, musky scent came to him again for the first time in years. He breathed it in, feeling pleasure and nostalgia so sharply that he wanted to weep. He still did not know what the smell was, but it was beautiful.

The other room was just as he remembered it. His eyes went to his daughter at once, picking her out easily amid the strange, pale people. She sat on the floor beside a chair, and the person in that chair encircled her loosely with a bone-white arm.

Charles called out her name, and she turned her face towards him. The helpless, drowning look she gave him nearly broke his heart. She was almost past saving; she would have to be pulled away. But he would; he would do it, he would make her leave, thought Charles, and, hunched against the pain growing in his side, he began to walk towards her.

"You've come back at last. I've been waiting."

It was the woman who had spoken to him during his first visit. She had not changed at all. She was still beautiful in the nonhuman way of stone or statue or insect with her dead-white, faintly glowing skin, her frozen eyes, her oddly elongated limbs. The sight of her made him shiver with something much more profound than cold or fear.

Before he could think to avoid her, she touched his side and then his head with the white branch of her hand.

"Let me make you comfortable," she said.

The pain vanished instantly. Despite himself, Charles felt weakly, slavishly grateful to her. He had not realized how badly he was hurting until the pain had gone.

"Come sit with me and let us talk together," she said. "It's what we've both been waiting for since you were just a boy."

Charles could not imagine why he had ever wanted to run from her. She was so beautiful, and her touch was so soothing. Her voice was music that he wanted to listen to forever.

He knew now why he had come here, why he had dreamed of coming back and searched for the hidden door for so many years. His daughter—sad little thing—had never been more than incidental in his decision.

He put his large, rough fingers into her smooth hand and let her lead him away.

AUTHOR'S NOTE

When I write a story, the house where it is set (and, somehow, most of them are set in houses) is as important to me, as compelling to my imagination, as any character.

I grew up in Houston, in a house without a past. My parents bought it while it was being built, in 1952, so it had no history. It was new and clean and modern and absolutely ours, without ever being so individual that it really stood out from its neighbors. From an early age I read fairy tales, fantasies and ghost stories and I dreamed of finding a secret room, a passage to another time or place, a mystery at the heart of an ordinary house. But I never did, except in my dreams, and probably I should be glad of that. "The Other Room" comes out of that childhood longing, although given a much darker adult interpretation.

—Lisa Tuttle

A GARDEN OF BLACKRED ROSES
Charles L. Grant

I. Bouquet

A COMFORTABLE FEBRUARY WARMTH EXPANDED throughout the house as the furnace droned on, and the cold outside was reduced to a lurking wind skittering through leafless brown trees, the ragged tail of a stray dog tucked between scrawny haunches, and glimpses of bright white snow through lightly fogged windows. Steven paused at the front door, his left hand on the knob, his gloves stuffed into his overcoat pockets. The girls were in their rooms, either napping fitfully or lying on the floor staring at the carpet, hoping for something to do. Rachel was in the kitchen, arranging in a Wedgwood vase the flowers he had slipped out of old man Dimmesdale's garden. He glanced into the living room, at the fireplace and the logs stacked neatly to be charred into ash; up the stairs at ancient Tambor's tail poking around the corner while the rest of his dark brown-and-tan bulk slept in front of the furnace's baseboard outlet; then down to his hand on the knob. Barely trembling, as he waited.

"Steven, have you gone yet?"

The voice was muffled but the apology was evident. In the beauty of the roses, she had forgiven him the act of stealing. He grinned, rubbed once at a freshly shaven jaw, and slipped on his gloves. There would be no need now for penance.

"No, not yet," he called. "Just going."

"Well, look, on your way back would you stop in Eben's for some milk? I want to make some pudding."

"Chocolate?"

"Butterscotch."

His grin broadened; the peace was complete. "Shouldn't be more than an hour," he said.

"Love you."

"Me, too."

The door opened and he was on the stoop, his face tightening against the cold, his breath taken in small, metal-cold stabs. Using his boots to clear the way, he kicked a narrow path down the concrete walk and past the barberry hedge. There were no cars yet on Hawthorne Street, it was too soon for the returning commuters, but the snow at the gutters was already turning a desecrating brown, though the fall had stopped only an hour before. He wondered what it was about the physics of weather that caused flakes to drift here an unbearable white, and there become slush that could only be described, and charitably so, as unspeakably evil. It seemed to be automatic, needing neither cars nor trucks nor plows to make the transformation. It was, he decided finally, not physics but magic, the word he used when nothing else made sense.

Several women and not a few young children were already out, shovels scraping against stone as they pushed aside the several inches accumulation amid temptations of snowballs and snowmen, and the lingering grey threat of another fall. He waved to several, stopped and spoke with two or three, laughed when a missile struck his back and he was delayed for a block fighting a roaring action against an army of seven. But finally he broke and ran, waving, and warning that he would be back. The children, pompously waddling in overstuffed coats, shrieked and scattered, and the street was suddenly quiet.

No place like it, Steven thought with a smile that would not vanish. Then he looked to his left across the street, and the smile became a remembering grin. Where else, he wondered, except on our Hawthorne Street would there also be a house that belonged to a man named Dimmesdale, the damned and adulterous minister who rightfully belonged in *The Scarlet Letter*? He paused, then, a momentary guilt darkening his mood as he stared covetously at the garden the old man had planted at the side of the blue Cape Cod. While the rest of the street's gardens were brittle and waiting for spring, Dimmesdale had discovered a way to bring color to snow.

Magic, Steven thought: no two ways about it.

The flowers were mostly roses, and at the back of the houselong garden a thicket of rosebushes with blossoms so deeply red they seemed at a glance to be midnight black.

The night before, as he and Rachel were returning from bridge at Barney and Edna Hawkins's apartment over the luncheonette, Steven had bet his wife he could steal a few of the flowers without being caught. She had grown angry at his sudden

childish turn, but he had sent her on in stubborn
defiance and had crept, nearly giggling, along the
side of the house until he had reached the rear of
the garden's bed. There, with a prickling at the
back of his neck (though he refused to turn
around), he had risked the stab of thorns to break
off and race away with a double handful.

Rachel had not spoken to him when he finally
returned, out of breath and grinning stupidly, and
he had placed the roses in the refrigerator. And the
next morning he found her standing over them,
each lying neatly and apart from the others on the
kitchen table. Her brushed black hair was pulled
over one shoulder and she tugged at it, and worried. When he had brought out the vase, she'd
glared at him but did not throw the flowers away.

"Amazing," he whispered to the silent house;
and when he returned from the office with the
papers he'd wanted and had run the gauntlet of
children again, Rachel was waiting for him in the
living room, smiling proudly at the roses displayed
in the bay window.

"You're incorrigible," she said, dark lips brush-
ing his cheek.

"You love it," he answered, shrugging out of his
coat and tossing it onto a nearby chair. "Where are
the kids?"

"Out. I chased them and the cat into the yard
when Sue decided to fingerpaint her room."

"Ah . . . damn," Steven muttered.

Rachel laughed and sat on the broad window
ledge, her blue tartan skirt riding to her thighs, her
black sweater pulled snug. "Watercolors, dope. It
came right off."

"You know," he said, sitting by her feet and

lighting a cigarette, "I don't know where they get it. Honestly, I don't. Certainly not from their father."

"Oh, certainly not," she said. "And I'm too demure and staid. It must be in the genes."

"Gene who?"

"The milkman, fool."

"As I thought," he said, holding his cigarette up as though it were a glass of wine, turning it slowly, swinging it gently back and forth. "It's always the husband who's the—"

The scream was faint, but enough to scramble Steven to his feet and race out onto the back porch. His daughters were running toward him, arms waving, hair streaming; four girls, and all of them crying. Rachel came up behind him as he jumped the steps to the ground and knelt, sweeping his girls into his arms, listening through their babbled hysteria until, finally, he understood. And rose.

"Keep them here," he said quietly.

Rachel, who had heard, was fighting not to cry.

He walked across the yard, his legs leaden, his head suddenly too heavy to keep upright. Oblivious to the cold wind blowing down from the grey, heedless of the snow tipping into his shoes.

Tambor. A Siamese that had been with him since before he had met and married Rachel. Seventeen years, fat, content, extraordinarily patient with the babies who yanked at his crooked tail, pounded his back, poked at his slightly crossed eyes, and pulled his whiskers.

Tambor. Who loved laps and the bay window and the hearth and thick quilts. Who dug into paper bags and under rugs and as far as he could get into anyone's shoes.

He was lying beneath the crab apple tree at the

back of the yard. The children had cleared the snow away from the knees of protruding roots, and the grass was still green, and the earth was still warm. Steven knelt, and was not ashamed when the tears came in mourning for nearly two decades of his life. He buried Tambor where he lay and, as an afterthought, took one of the roses and placed it on the freshly turned clayed dirt.

"He was old," he said late that night as Rachel hugged him tightly in their bed, her head on his chest. "He was . . . tired."

"I expect him to be there in the morning, big as life, with the rose in his mouth."

Steven smiled. Tambor ate flowers as much as his own food.

"I don't want him to die," she whimpered, much like his daughters. "He introduced us."

"I'll get Dimmesdale to bring him back. He's sure spooky enough."

"Not funny, Steve," she said; and, after a minute: "What are we going to do? I want him back."

"So do I, love."

"Steve, what are we going to do?"

There was nothing he could say. Rachel had hated cats when they'd met, but Tambor had sat in front of her in the apartment, his crossed blue eyes regarding her steadily. Then, as she'd reached out politely to stroke his cocked head, Tambor had gently taken her finger into his mouth, released it, and licked it, and Rachel had been besieged and captured in less than a minute.

To replace him was unthinkable.

Yet, the following morning as he trudged glumly down the street to fetch the morning papers, Steven could not get the idea out of his head.

The children were inconsolable. They'd moped over breakfast and refused to listen to his multivoiced rendering of the Sunday comics. When he suggested they go outside and play, they pointedly used the front door and lined up on the sidewalk, watching the rest of the neighborhood, but not joining in.

Lunch was bad, supper was worse, and his temper grew shorter when Rachel took the remaining roses and threw them into the backyard.

"They're too dark," she said to his puzzled glare. "We have enough dark things around here, don't you think?"

And as he lay still in bed again, Rachel sighing in her sleep, he listened to the wind scrape at the house with claws of frozen snow. Listened to the shudder of the eaves, the groan of the doors, and tried to remember how it had been when he had brought Tambor home for the first time. How small, how helpless, stumbling across the bare apartment floor with Steven trailing anxiously behind him, waiting for the opportunity to teach him of litter boxes and sanitation.

The cry made him blink.

Sue, Bess, Annie. Holly. Damn, he thought, someone was having a nightmare again.

Sighing, he waited for Rachel to hear and to move, and when she didn't, he threw back the quilt and stuffed his feet into his slippers. A robe on the bureau found its woolen way around his shoulders and he slipped into the corridor without a light.

A baby crying, wailing plaintively.

He looked into Bess's room, into Holly's, but each was silent.

A baby. Begging.

The other two rooms were equally still.

He pulled the robe tightly across his throat and, after a check to see if Rachel had awakened, he moved downstairs, head cocked, listening, drawn finally into the kitchen. He stood at the back door after flicking on the porch light and peered through the small panes into the yard beyond.

The crying was there.

We were partners, Tambor and I, he thought; friends, buddies, my . . . my conscience.

Remembering, then, the look on the cat's face when he'd crept into the house with the roses in his hands.

Tambor?

You're dreaming, son, he told himself, but could not stop his legs from taking him to the hall closet, his hands grabbing boots and coat and fur-lined gloves. Then he rushed back into the kitchen and yanked open the door.

The crying was there.

And the snow.

Silently now, sifting through the black curtain beyond the reach of the light.

"Tambor!" he whispered harshly.

A shadow moved just to one side of him. He whirled, and it was gone. A faint flicker of red.

He stumbled across the yard to the crab apple tree, pulling from his pocket the flashlight grabbed from the kitchen and aiming it at the grave. It was, in spite of the snow, still cleared; and the rose still lay there, its petals toward the bole.

"Tam, where are you?"

The crying.

He spun around, flashlight following, and in the sweep the darts of red . . . eyes reflecting. He slowed, and there was only the falling, sifting, gently blowing white.

Something else . . . something crouched beyond the cleared space of the grave. He knelt, poked at it with a stiffly trembling finger and saw another rose, one of those Rachel had thrown away. And, still kneeling, he suddenly looked back over his shoulder and saw the shadow, and the steadily gleaming twin points of red.

Big as life, Rachel had said.

One rose . . . big as life.

Two. . . .

Suddenly, choking, he threw the flashlight at the now glaring red, at the eyes that told him they did not like being alone. Then he fell to his hands and knees, digging at the snow, thrashing, casting it aside in waves, in splashes. Another rose, and another, as he made his cold and slow way back toward the light, the porch, the safety of the house.

The crying was louder, no longer begging.

The snow was heavier, no longer drifting.

And just before the porch light winked out and the shadow grew, he wondered just how many roses he had stolen from the garden.

2. Corsage

A sea of clouds in shades of grey. Breakers of wind that scattered spray. And Barney Hawkins —short, large, nearly sixty—stood by the fence and chewed on his lip. As he had been for an hour, and as he would be doing for an hour more, for the rest of the day, if he didn't make up his mind one way or the other.

He was the owner of the only luncheonette on Hawthorne Street, and he was proud of it, and of the fact that what he called the "nice kids" had chosen his corner establishment for their base, their rendezvous, their home away from school. With long hair and short, short skirts and jeans, they had somehow decided that the red false-leather booths and the green stools lining the white counter were peaceable places undisturbed by disdaining adults and scornful police. He never bothered them, never tried to be more than a friendly ear, except when he tried to show them by his example that romance both capitalized and small was something that did not belong in the modern world. They might argue, then, through a barrier of what he called reality; but as he tolerated their flowers and their causes, so they tolerated his cynicism and his acid.

And he wished that tolerance extended to his wife.

Just that morning a quartet of boys had been huddled over a small tape recorder in the back booth, poking at it apprehensively, looking at one another and at Barney, but not touching it.

Brian was a junior, and the bravest of the lot, and as Barney stared over their heads through the plate-glass window into the drizzle beyond, he listened with half an ear while the boy made his case.

"Look, I was there! And there ain't nothing there at all. You guys don't understand these things, do you? I mean, if there's nothing there, then there's nothing there. That's all there is to it."

"Brian, you're a . . ." The speaker looked toward Barney and grinned. "You're a jerk." It was Syd, bespectacled and tall, somewhat respected, and definitely feared for the brains he had, and used, but seldom flaunted. He pushed back his wire-rim glasses and poked at Brian's arm, then at the recorder. "I was there, understand? And I got it all down on tape. Tapes don't lie. I wouldn't fool you."

The other two only nodded; for whom, Barney could not tell.

"All right," Syd said finally. "You want to hear it or not? I haven't got all day. My dad's coming home this afternoon and I got to be there."

Barney pushed reluctantly away from the counter when Edna called him from the back. Shaking his head, he took a swipe at the grill with a damp cloth and pushed aside the bright blue curtains that kept the wrong eyes from peering into the sanctuary he used when things out front got a little too sticky, lovey, and loud. Edna, her dimming red hair bunned tightly at her nape, was seated at a battered Formica table, a cup of cold tea cradled in her wash-red hands.

"What's up?" he said, taking the chair opposite, hoping she wouldn't want, for the thirty-fifth time, to do something silly and candlelighted for their anniversary.

She pointed to the pay phone on the wall by the curtain. "Amos called again."

"For God's sake, now what? Didn't I pay for that damned parking ticket last Saturday, for crying out loud?"

Edna's smile was weakly tolerant, and he scratched a large hand through his still blond hair. Amos Russo might be the best cop in town, he thought, but there were times when he could be too damned efficient. And Barney could not convince him that he was not the father of every stray kid who wandered into the shop.

"Well, is it the ticket?" he asked again; and when she shook her head, he groaned. "Then who's in trouble, and why the hell doesn't he call their parents?"

"It's Syd," she said, lowering her voice and glancing toward the front. "That's why I called you in here instead of coming out." Her voice had scaled into a whine, and only by staring at the greasepocked ceiling could he stop himself from wincing. "It's Syd. The nice one."

"Syd? My God, that kid's got more brains than any twelve of those kids put together. What could he possibly do to rile Amos?"

"He's been prowling around the Yardley place."

"So who hasn't?"

"And he insists that someone is living in there. Amos wants you to tell him to stop bothering the police."

"No," Barney said, straightening and glaring. "No one lives there."

"Now, Barney . . ."

He tightened his lips and stared over her head. The last people, he remembered, to ever live in that rundown firetrap was a young couple who moved in about ten years ago. One weekend they and their van showed up, and two months later the windows were blank and no one knew what had happened. It wasn't the only house in the world like it, he thought, and wouldn't be the last: a relic from an age when high ceilings and wall-sized fireplaces were considered quite romantic and necessary —but to heat such a place now, to replace the outmoded wiring, the plumbing, put on a new roof and drains . . . he himself had once considered buying the house when he was younger, but the money had not been there and the dream soon faded.

Like all the dreams he had had when he was young, of wealth and power and a vast legacy for his children.

Now, there was only the luncheonette and the apartment above it. And children . . . none.

"I'd like to burn the place down," he said.

"Barney!"

He almost laughed at the shock in her face, and the quick resignation that he would never understand. Then, before the fight could begin—as it always did when he tried to explain what reality was—she reached down into her lap, lifted her hands and placed on the table three deep red blossoms wired together. He stared at them, at Edna, and she smiled as she held the flowers to her left shoulder.

"Pretty?"

"Where'd you get them?"

"Dimmesdale's."

"You're not telling me he gave them to you!"

Her smile drifted, returned, and faded. "No. I . . . I took them."

"For God's sake, why?"

"Because they're better than plastic, damnit!" she snapped.

Again he stared, then pushed himself to his feet. "I'll talk to Syd. He's as crazy as you are."

She doesn't know what love is, he thought sadly; she reads too many books and sees too many movies.

He stepped back through the curtain, stopped, and heard the voices.

Edward, it's cold!

It's only the fog, dear. Nothing to fear, nothing at all. Up from the river. Something to do with temperature change and moisture in the air, things like that.

I don't like it. And I'm tired of waiting.

We won't have to wait long, I promise you. Besides, it's peaceful, you have to admit that.

It is. Yes. It is. Quiet, like just before the sun goes down. Would you light a fire? We can sit while we're waiting, and look at the flames.

A click, and the voices changed.

Andrew, it's cold.

Shall I light a fire?

Yes, and draw the curtains, too. I don't like the fog.

Oh, I don't know. I rather enjoy it. It cuts us off, and it's as though we had no problems, no one in the world but you and me. I kind of like it.

It reminds me of graveyards.

You have no romance in your soul, Eloise.

Enough to marry you, didn't I? Kiss me once and light the fire.

All right. But I still like the fog.

And yet again.

I love you, Simon.

It's a beautiful house.

Are you sure you had no one else in mind?

No one, no one at all. It was built just for you.

Do we have to wait long?

Charity, I love you, but you have no patience.

Let's stand on the porch, then, and look at the fog.

I'd rather stay inside and look at the fire.

The four boys had been joined by two girls in cheerleader jackets and short skirts, high white socks and buffed white shoes. They were giggling, and the boys were laughing silently. Barney glared, then rushed around the counter and slammed his hand down on the table, hard enough to jolt the recorder, pop the lid and send the cassette skittering. He snatched it up and jammed it into his pocket, at the same time backing away and ordering the kids out.

There were protests, though muted, and one of the girls stopped at the door and looked back at him.

"Mr. Hawkins, you ain't got no soul," she said.

He grinned tightly. "I do. I just know what to do with it."

"Well," she said as Syd returned to tug at her arm, "you won't have it for long if you don't loosen up."

They vanished, then, into a rusted Pontiac that howled angrily away from the curb toward the football field. He watched a plume of exhaust twist into the rain, blinked, and wondered what in hell had made him react that way.

"Barney?"

He felt the bulge of the cassette in his pocket. Edna moved to stand beside him, one hand on his arm, lightly.

"Syd," he said, "has a perverted sense of humor. He's been sneaking around the neighborhood at night, taping people in their houses. People doing . . . getting ready to do . . . things. He's been using the fog for cover."

"What fog?"

He blinked and looked down at her, stepped back suddenly when she shimmered slightly and her hair brightened, her face softened, and her figure lost the pounds it had gained. Quickly, then, he began untying his apron.

"Why," he said, "the fog. You know what a fog is, don't you? Last night, the night before, I don't know when. Syd's been—"

"Barney, there hasn't been a decent fog around here for . . . for weeks." She stepped toward him, her hand outstretched. "Come on, love, we have sandwiches to get ready before the game is over."

"I don't want them back in here."

"Barney, you're being ridiculous."

He snatched his arm away and tossed the apron into a booth, snatched down his overcoat from the rack by the register, and grabbed the cassette. "I'm going out for a minute," he said as he left. "I'll be back in time, don't worry."

"Barney! Please . . . don't—"

He stood outside and saw her through the window, her hands clasped in front of her stomach, and was more than somewhat startled to see the hatred in her face.

Now, an hour later, he could still imagine the uncharacteristic hardening around her eyes, the tight set of her mouth, and the way she stared when he had walked away.

He shuddered and pulled at his collar. Only a few degrees cooler and the rain would be snow. The road was slick and black, and there were puddles skimmed with thin ice. He hunched his shoulders and wished he had brought his hat, wiped a hand over his face and looked out over the lawn beyond the fence. To the Yardley house.

He had been inside that Victorian mockery of a rich man's mansion only once. And once had been enough, more than enough. It had been with Edna, before they were married and while they still watched sunsets and sunrises and delighted at the way young birds learned to fly. They had crept in through the back door, each carrying a blanket, had made their way to the front of the house and set the blankets atop each other on the floor before the hearth. Edna brought a single candle from which she dripped wax to set it on the mantel. It cast shadows, and as he undressed her, she made stories of them, turning men into knights and women into Guineveres; and when they had done and lay sweated and sated, he tried, tenderly, to tell her what she had done wrong, and they had fought. In the shadows. While the candle burned to the end of its wick.

In the three and a half decades since that night, neither had mentioned it, and Barney only tried to keep boys like Syd from thinking there was something . . . special . . . about a house that overlooked the river.

Finally, he pushed at the gate in the middle of the fence and walked slowly to the porch. As he expected, the front door was locked, and all the windows were grey with dust. He moved down the side steps and made his way through the sodden weeds to the back. Looking through the rain to the blur of the river and the hillside beyond.

There was no fog. There was obviously no one in or near the house. He began to feel foolish, and wondered whom Syd had enlisted to make the tape. But since, he thought, he had come this far he might as well lay all the ghosts to rest so the kids could come back, so they could come back to the store and learn what he knew, and what he had lived.

He tried the back door and, when it opened,

hesitated only long enough to pass his fingers over his face before stepping over the threshold and closing the door behind him. The light was dim, and he hurried through the kitchen and down the long narrow corridor to the living room. And it was as he remembered: empty and dusty and more damp than his bones could take. There was a fireplace on the back wall, and he knelt on the hearth and passed his hand over the blackened stone. Cold. And iced.

He jammed his hands into his coat pockets. The left curled around Syd's cassette, and there was reluctant admiration for the thought behind the prank. He knew, then, that it had all been planned; that the kids would know he would listen and become angry at the soap-opera dialogue and the shy giggles of the girls. He licked his lips and laughed.

Stopped.

His right hand felt velvet.

He pulled out the roses Edna had taken from the garden, stared, glared, and tossed them angrily into the fireplace, the curse on his lips dying unborn when he looked at the windows.

And saw the fog.

Tried the doors, and all of them locked.

Raced through the house, tripping over dust, throwing his weight against glass and none of it breaking.

It was cold, and he was sweating.

He stood in the middle of the living room, shaking his fist at the windows, the fog, the roses in the fireplace, and the single lighted candle that glowed on the mantel.

Dropped to his knees and opened his hand.

And the shadows of mournful vengeance pulsed in the corners and *sighed*.

3. Blossom

When Syd gave the rose to Ginny, she was obviously unimpressed and perhaps even a little scornful. It would not matter then, explaining to her (and somewhat embellishing) the risks he had taken in sneaking it out of Dimmesdale's garden. Had he been caught, the police in general and Russo in particular, would have followed tradition and forced him into a public restitution for his stealing; and how, he wondered, do you replace a rose?

He glanced across the classroom aisle and watched with weary bitterness as Ginny toyed with the petals, poking at them with her pen and jabbing at them once. So far as he could tell, she had not lifted it to enjoy the scent, nor glided a finger over the velvet to close her eyes at the touch. He saw her shrug. And when the last bell rang, he sat there until the room had emptied. He, and the rose . . . lonely on the floor where a half-dozen feet had trampled it to a pulp.

His first reaction was self-pity: while not exactly homely, neither was he quarterback-handsome. And to get Ginny, in any sense of the word, was apparently and finally impossible. He loved her. And he could not have her.

Then, as quickly, he became vindictive: he'd pour the blackest ink he could find over her collection of snug cashmere sweaters, tangle forever that cloudsoft sable hair, use a razor and define in blood the gentle lines of her face.

He snorted, knelt on the floor, and used his handkerchief to cover the rose and lift it into his hip pocket.

Another time, another ploy, he thought as he walked home; but Ginny seemed so cold not even the equator could warm her.

After turning onto Hawthorne Street, he quickened his pace. His mother would be more than annoyed if he were late one more time. It was bad enough that his father had taken a job that required him to travel over two dozen days a month; should he himself now be absent, he knew his mother would cry. Not loudly. Standing in front of the living room window perhaps, or by the stove, or just in the middle of the upstairs hall . . . tears, not sobs, and as quickly wiped away as they appeared. And were denied when he asked. When he left for college in the fall, he wondered how she would be able to stand the empty bed in his room.

Someone called him then, but he was in too much of a hurry to do more than lift a hand in blind greeting. The only time he stopped was at Dimmesdale's house, where he stared boldly at the flourishing garden, the Cape Cod, delighting as he did so in the brightness of the afternoon, the shimmering new green of leaves and grass, the fresh cool bite of the early spring breeze. And then he blinked, thinking he saw a figure behind one of the first-floor windows. Certainly a curtain moved, but there was a window opened and he decided it was wishful thinking. Wishful . . . he gnawed on his lower lip, one hand guiltily at his hip pocket, and he whispered: "Ginny. I want to be like one of her candies."

How many boxes had he sent her over the past

four months? Anonymously. Painfully. Watching her share the chocolates and the creams with everyone. Or nearly so.

"A wishbone would be better," a voice said behind him, and he spun around, angered and embarrassed. Flo Joiner stood looking at him through green-tinted glasses and ruffled black bangs, her lips in a slight smile, her arms folded around books held protectively in front of her breasts.

"I don't like people who do that," he said, walking again, and cursing silently when she kept his pace.

"Sorry," she said, "but when you waved at me, I thought you wanted to walk me home. I didn't know you were going to have a séance."

"A what?" The sun was in his eyes and he squinted as he stared down at her.

"A séance. You know. Disembodied heads and tambourines and stuff like that. I thought you were holding a private séance at the creep's house."

"How do you know he's a creep?"

She laughed and blew at her bangs to drive them up and away from her glasses. The habit annoyed him; Flo thought it made her look cute. "Anyone who lives the way that old man does has got to be a creep. But . . . sometimes wishing works, I guess. Right?"

"No," he said, stopping as she did in front of a low white ranch house. She took a step up the walk, turned, and asked if he would like something to eat, cake or whatever. "Never say whatever," he said with a grin that apologized for his brusqueness. "It puts evil thoughts in a senior's head."

"Oh, really?" she said with a smile he couldn't

quite read. "And yes, wishing does too sometimes work. My dad said he wished for a new car and got it. My brother wanted a new glove and he got it, too. I'm not telling you what I'm going to wish for."

"You guys are just lucky, that's all. I never saw so much luck in one place in my life."

Flo shrugged as though she weren't interested. "Probably. Besides, my stupid brother says you got to have a flower first. Something from the creep's garden." She lowered voice and head then, and stared at him over her glasses. "But not the roses, Sydney, definitely not the roses."

"Are you trying to imitate someone?"

"You'll never know, Sydney, you'll never know."

"Oh, for God's sake, Flo!"

Once again, irritatingly, she laughed, and Syd waved her a curt good-bye.

Once in the house, he yelled for his mother, raced up the stairs, and dumped his books on the bed before changing his clothes. The handkerchief he set very carefully on the windowsill and gazed at it a moment, scratching thoughtfully at his waist, his jaw, the back of his neck. Then he was downstairs again and in the kitchen, kissing his mother quickly on the cheek while he looked over her shoulder at the pot of split-pea soup simmering under steam on the stove.

"Ugh," he said.

"You know you love it," she laughed and aimed a slap at his rump.

He sprawled on one of the kitchen chairs and nodded when she lifted a bottle of ginger ale, watched as the carbonation gathered and leaped, foamed and dripped over the side of the glass. His mother moved back to her cooking, and for a long and peaceful while they listened to the sounds of the neighborhood winding down toward supper.

"Do you have any homework?"

He grunted.

There was a card from his father propped against a salt shaker in the middle of the table. He turned it around and stared at the picture: a Hopi Indian summoning spirits for the tourists. He thought it disgusting and turned it back, not bothering to read the message done in red ink.

"He'll be home on Saturday."

Syd grunted.

In spite of the bubbles, his soda tasted flat.

"Mom, I'm wondering . . . I've been thinking for a long time that maybe . . . well, maybe I shouldn't go to college this fall, I mean, what with Dad—"

"Don't," she said, turning from the stove, her face pale with anger. "Don't ever say that! Never say that in this house again."

"But, Mom—"

"It's that Ginny girl, isn't it? You want to run away and marry her or something. Always going out with her four or five times a week, coming home late at night even though you know you have school the next day, sneaking in and thinking I'm asleep so I don't know how late. How stupid do you think I am, Sydney?"

He saw the tears brimming in rage and shook his head, in slow defeat. "All right," he said sullenly. "I'm sorry. I just wanted to save you and Dad some money, that's all."

"No," she said, anger fled and her voice suddenly soft. "You just don't want to leave me alone."

He allowed her to hug him tightly as he sat there, his head pushed into her small breasts; and he was

ashamed and annoyed that an image of Ginny
sprang instantly into his mind, chewing thoughtfully on her precious chocolates and smiling at . . .
someone else. His mother began rocking him,
crooning wordlessly, and he wondered if she suspected how much he loved her, and how much he
needed someone else to love, suspected that his
dates with Ginny were solitary walks in the park,
along the back streets, along the river. He wondered, and suddenly cared that she did not know.

Later that night, when supper was done and the
dishes washed and his mother was working her
needlepoint in front of the television, he walked
down to the luncheonette to see what was happening, and on the way home a few minutes later
plucked   four   huge   golden   mums   from
Dimmesdale's garden, saluted Flo's house as he
passed it on the run, and gave the flowers to his
mother. As she cried. And he stood awkwardly in
the middle of the room, waiting, then mumbling
something about his homework and retreating to
his room.

The following afternoon he saw his father's car in
the driveway. Their reunion was, as always, noisy
and emotional, and he whooped through an improvised dance when he learned that his dad had been
transferred to the home office and would no longer
travel. His mother grinned, he grinned, and for the
first time that year they went out to dinner.

And in the restaurant he saw Ginny sitting with
her parents. When she spotted his staring, she
smiled and held it. He choked and dared a smile
back.

In school the next day she passed him a note. He
did not read it, did not want to—the last time she

had done it was to beg him for an introduction to his ex–best friend. He stood in the hall after class and held the folded paper dumbly in his hand, and didn't even notice when Flo asked him a question, saw the note and took it, opened it and read it with one eye closed. When she had done, her lips were tight and, he thought, she looked rather saddened. She handed it back to him and left without speaking. He knew why when he followed, unbelieving, the words that directed him to meet her after supper, in the park, and alone.

No, he thought; not me, it's a mistake.

But he showered twice when he finally made it home, tried on four pairs of jeans and three shirts before he achieved the effect he thought she would like.

When he left, his mother and father were sitting in the living room, holding hands on the sofa and watching a blank-screened television.

Hot damn, he thought, and smiled.

The park was small, scarcely two blocks long and three blocks deep, but once inside he walked hurriedly through the trees and across a small baseball field, around an even smaller pond and back into the trees again. The wind had picked up somewhat, and the leaves and brush whispered at him as he passed, stroked at his arms and face, scuttled underfoot like small furless animals. Here the sounds of the street were smothered in shadows, and the shadows themselves were tantalizing and deep. Yet he refused to allow himself to fantasize. Whatever Ginny wanted to do was all right with him. Just talking with her would be the improvement he had searched for, prayed for, wished . . . his hand slapped at his hip pocket. The handkerchief with the rose was still at the window, but he grinned when he realized he would need no talisman this time. Be yourself, his mother had told him often enough; and so he would be, if that's what Ginny wanted.

She was standing when he found her, almost despairing that he wouldn't, leaning against the curved trunk of a birch, dressed in powder-blue cardigan and tartan skirt, her hair feathered down over her shoulders. He stopped until she noticed him and nodded, and held out her hand. He took it, felt its cool, its soft, felt her press against him and lift her head, her face, her lips to his.

Lord, he thought; and thought no more until they were sitting side by side against the tree, staring through the foliage at the first glare of stars.

"I've wanted you for a long time," she said finally, quietly, almost shyly.

"Me, too," he said, grimacing at the brilliance of his response.

"I thought you were the one who was sending me all those chocolates."

"I was," he admitted, looking away and smiling. "I knew you liked them."

"You'll get me fat."

"Never," he said seriously. "Ginny, you'll never get fat."

In silence they listened to a mockingbird's sigh.

"Ginny . . . why did you send me that note?"

"I don't know. Suddenly, I just felt like it."

She took his hand and nuzzled it. Her lips were soft, moist, and he thought of the rose.

"I'm glad you liked the candy."

She laughed and lay her head on his arm. "I couldn't live without it."

He grinned as she kissed his palm, and wondered how long she would keep him there, in the park, beneath the trees, on the grass.

"Ginny, do you . . . this is dumb, but do you believe in wishes?"

"You're right, that's dumb. You're the smartest kid in the class. You should know better."

"No, I mean it." He felt his face grow warm as she stared at him, her eyes moist, her lips gleaming darkly. "You know, the other day I was so mad when you . . . well, I wanted you so much I even wished I could have been one of the chocolates or something."

"Now that," she said, "is not so dumb. It's not. It's beautiful."

Her tongue flicked over his thumb. Kissed it. Moved to his lips and he drew her down on top of him.

A rustling in the branches above them. The feel of grass on the back of his neck. And suddenly, as she wriggled over his chest, he thought of poor Flo and the sad look on her face.

Something drifted down to his cheek, and he thought of the mums he had given his mother . . . and his father's car parked in the drive.

The Joiners' luck.

The blackred rose. In his handkerchief on the windowsill. Crushed. Dead.

"You're sweet," she whispered as she took the first bite.

4. Thorn

The window. Framed on the inside by pale white curtains. Framed on the outside by two spikes of juniper.

The cobbler's bench. Roughly hewn and edged with splinters.

The man on the bench seated before the window. Dressed in a preacher's black jacket, black trousers, black shoes. His hair a trapped cloud of angry grey. His eyes only shadows. His mouth just air.

Watching: the eldest and the youngest pass to the opposite side of the street, while those in between quickened their pace but kept to the sidewalk; the traffic pass in pendulum waves; the wind, the rain, the sun light to dark.

Listening: the laughter stifled, giggling bitten back, footfalls and running and not a few dares; the snarl of dogs, the spitting of cats, the wingbeats of birds that deserted his trees; and the wind, and the rain, and the sun light to dark.

And when the moon had gone and the street was a grave, he stood and stretched and moved out to his garden where he grabbed with powerful hands what remained of the flowers stolen during the day. He carried the debris into the kitchen, down the cellar stairs, and dumped it all on a pile in the corner.

Then he turned to the center of the floor where strings of artificial suns glared brightly over beds of new-growing flowers. Violets, pansies, mums, and lilies. He considered them carefully, and the promises they would bring.

But sooner or later someone would come inside.

A young boy on a lark, a man simply curious. Perhaps even a girl who was braver than most.

No, he thought; there was still too much laughter.

Around the furnace, then, and into the corner where the lights did not reach and the warmth would not spread. He blinked slowly, forcing his eyes to adjust until they could barely discern a row of low bushes like miniature Gorgons, with twigs instead of snakes and buds instead of fangs. He took a deep breath of the swirling dark air, released it slowly and dropped to his knees.

His fingers moved with ritual slowness over the buttons of his shirt and parted the edges to expose his chest. He leaned over, and touched a forefinger to his skin, probing, tracing, then taking his nail and digging into the flesh that would never form scars. There was no pain. Only the practiced identification of smooth sticky wetness. With the fingertip, then, he touched at his chest, at the letter drawn there, and on each waiting bud (with the sigh of a name) he placed one shimmering drop (with the remembrance of a name), and sat back and watched as the buds drank in the blood . . . and the dark . . . and the air never warm.

Were roses.

Blackred.

Blackred . . . and waiting.

AUTHOR'S NOTE

Sometimes, too often for my ego, I sit down to write a story and don't get anywhere. There's a beginning, and there's the last line (which, for me, is essential before I even start), but there isn't a middle, or even a two-thirds of the way through. Which leaves me with a lot of paragraphs floating around, sounding great, portending great things, and doing absolutely nothing because all they do is sound good. They don't mean a thing.

In 1972 I noted in my journal: *The Power of Love, different colors for different kinds.* And there, miserably alone, were great-sounding paragraphs with no place to go. I was trying to write a series of linking stories, thematically similar yet each capable of standing on its own. The problem was, I didn't know what I was doing, and even if I had known, I wouldn't have known how to go about it.

Then, in 1975, Kirby McCauley asked me for a story for his anthology, *Dark Forces.* He wanted me to be different, be experimental if possible, and since, in that year, I was having a hard enough time just being what was for me conventional, the idea terrified me. But I tried. I tried several times, and each attempt was a disaster. Until I found that notation in my journal. And at the same time, I also finished rereading, for the hundredth time, *The Scarlet Letter.*

I don't know how or why the connection was made. But it was. And along with a smidgeon (i.e., the title) from e. e. cummings, "A Garden of Blackred Roses" was born.

I also note, from the superior vantage point of hindsight, that this story was also the blueprint for *Nightmare Seasons* and *The Orchard.* I didn't notice that until just now, actually, and in a way it's comforting. It tells me, on the one hand, that even great-sounding paragraphs are never entirely wasted. But on the other, it also says I'm nowhere near finished growing. Thank God. Because I have an awful lot of stuff floating around here I don't know what to do with yet. Maybe sometime soon. Maybe a few years from now. And maybe, if I'm lucky, never.

—Charles L. Grant

COTTAGE TENANT
Frank Belknap Long

"WHEN WE WERE CHILDREN," CREWSON SAID, TRYING hard to sound thoughtful and wise, "the old English nursery rhymes and tales of Greek gods unaging seemed just the right kind of reading for eight-year-olds. No one would have dreamed of putting them on a restricted list. But I'm afraid that today—"

He broke off abruptly to stare at Susan Jane, who was two years short of eight, and at his son, Timothy, whose recent birthday had made him nine. They bore a remarkable family resemblance, and though his son was the better looking, Susan Jane could hardly have been thought of as plain.

He avoided looking directly at his wife until Anne Crewson said, "That's nonsense and you know it. Complete, absolute total nonsense. What would you have them read—sociological tracts?"

Instead of replying instantly, Crewson allowed his thoughts to stray. It seemed such a pity, in a way. No young married couple—he still refused to let the years alter his perspective in that respect—could have achieved more harmony and fulfillment. If just one "fly in the ointment" could have been set aside. They had an attractive white cottage overlooking the sea, with flowering plants and bright shells in the sun parlor, and the wide half acre of lawn that sloped down to the sea was a miracle of smooth emerald enchantment, with a pathway of white gravel leading to the wharf and a small cabin cruiser riding at anchor close to the end of it.

They were both employed as well, Anne as second in command at a tourist-frequented village antique shop and himself as a junior high school principal. But somehow they could never seem to agree concerning what was best for the children.

It wouldn't have mattered much if Timothy didn't say things at times which alarmed him. He was doing that now, raising his eyes from the book he'd been reading in a sprawled-out position on the floor to comment on what his mother had just said.

"I don't believe any of these stories," he said. "The fall of Troy wasn't like it says here. No one saw what came out of the sea—just a stupid, big wooden horse. All right. There were soldiers inside the horse and they set fire to Troy and burned it down. But the Greeks couldn't have done that without help. They were told what to do every minute."

"Oh, sure," Crewson muttered sarcastically, his concern blotted out for an instant by irritation. "But how do you account for the fact that Virgil and the Greek dramatists didn't view it that way at all? Poets are supposed to be inspired, perceptive far beyond the average. How could they have written about the fall of Troy as they did if they had suspected there was something hidden and hideous about the sea where the Greek ships rode at anchor? This isn't the first time you've let yourself take that tale apart in a silly way—but the time has come to put a stop to it."

To his surprise, Crewson found himself quoting: "'Troy has perished, that great city. Only the red flames now lives there.'

"That's poetry, Tim boy. Great poetry. And when I was your age those stories meant a lot to me. But kids today—well, that kind of reading seems to do more harm than good. Perhaps because life has become too complicated in too many different directions. I don't know. But if a more realistic kind of reading could be substituted, I'm sure I wouldn't be so worried about you, and that means a lot to a father."

"Darling, just let him say what he pleases," Anne protested. "All children have strange ideas at times. They exaggerate just one aspect of experience out of all proportion. It's part of the growing-up process."

"It's nothing he could have experienced," Crewson retorted. "He wasn't there."

"Neither was Virgil."

"What does that mean? What are you trying to tell me? That if a boy his age lets his imagination run riot, he's doing something we should encourage —if only because it's harmless, and can be chalked up to the marvelous imagination of children? There was nothing childish about Virgil. You'd realize how ridiculous all this is if you'd put Timothy's meanderings into an adult frame of reference."

"You're better at that than I am," Anne said. "What frame do you have in mind?"

"One of simple plausibility. Timothy is sure that

something monstrous and long-haired came up out of the sea and took possession of the Greek intelligence. Not one person in ten thousand, child or adult, would have hit on so freakish a conjecture. No—not one in a million. Its very freakishness makes it grotesque. And it disturbs me.

"Besides," Crewson added, "to have taken possession of the Greek intelligence in the Homeric Age would have required some doing even for a sea monster. Ulysses survived every encounter with monsters on land and sea, remember?"

It was a poor attempt at humor and Crewson knew it. But he was beginning to feel that if he didn't dismiss lightly what his wife had been saying he might end by taking one small part of it seriously. He had never come close to accepting Jung's theory of archetypal images, and only a Jungian would have been willing to concede that Timothy might have dredged something up out of his collective unconscious that was both deeply buried and unusual.

Solely to keep himself from dwelling on that, Crewson set his lips in tight lines, swung about and crossed to the door of the sun parlor in three long strides.

"Where are you going, Daddy?" Susan Jane asked.

"Just for a walk on the beach," Crewson said, wrenching the door open. It always seemed to stick on damp days, and there had been a gray overcast since morning. The fog that had drifted in from the sea had thinned a little, however, and there was a brightness where the sun was trying to break through. If the beach stayed the way it was, he told himself, it would be just right for the kind of stroll he enjoyed most. The tang of the brine in his nostrils, a good visibility for two or three yards ahead, and enough scattered seashells underfoot to keep him occupied in a pleasantly active way. Not that he shared Timothy's interest in collecting shells of all shapes and sizes. But he did like to stop occasionally, pick one up and send it skimming out across the surf line.

An unusual shell or a stranded spider crab or jellyfish gave him a boyish kind of thrill—just why he could not have said. Certainly they were abundant enough on every stretch of New England coastline in the wake of a slight storm, and should have been familiar enough to a New Englander born and bred to stir no interest at all.

"Supper will be on the table in just twenty minutes," Anne said. "Why did you have to pick this time to go for a walk?"

"I always seem to pick the wrong time for just about everything," Crewson said. "I'm truly and honestly sorry, Anne."

"Oh, forget it," Anne said. "Perhaps I married you for that reason. I'm a strange woman in many ways. I guess you've discovered that by now."

Crewson shut the door very quietly behind him. He walked down the white gravel path to the wharf, and then struck eastward across the narrow stretch of beach that fringed his property for close to half a mile in both directions.

The fog had cleared surprisingly fast and he could see not just two or three yards ahead, but as far as the bleak, ragged ledge of rock that ran out into the bay where Richard Forbes's sailboat was anchored. It was a trim, handsome craft, and had much in common with Forbes himself, who prided himself on his popularity with women. Crewson had often found himself wondering how much the attractive blondes and redheads—only rarely a brunette—Forbes took on brief excursions around the bay appreciated the absolute perfection of the boat's lines and the dent its cost had made in the playboy's income. Probably not excessively. Forbes had kept them too busy.

The sailboat was on Crewson's property, but the water was unusually deep on both sides of the rock projection, and he had been only too happy to make Forbes a present of that mooring facility.

Halfway to the rock projection Crewson paused for an instant to stare down at an enormous horseshoe crab that the recent blow had cast up on the beach in an upside-down position. It was wringing its legs furiously in its efforts to right itself, and he was moved by pity to bend down, pick it up, and toss it far out beyond the small waves that were lapping at the sand a few feet from where he was standing.

A strange thought came into his mind—what Timothy had said about the Greek ships riding at anchor in an age remote from ours, but not in the least ancient to a horseshoe crab. For uncounted millions of years horseshoe crabs had survived unchanged, passed over by an evolutionary process that had brought about the rise and fall of dinosaurs.

He had just started to walk on when he heard the screaming. Two voices seemed to be screaming in unison, one unmistakably that of a woman and the other even more unnerving, because it wasn't often that a man screamed in just as high-pitched accents of masculinity.

He had no doubt at all that the screams were coming from the anchored sailboat. The beach was unoccupied by human forms as far as the rock projection, and when screams drifted ashore across a short stretch of water, they had to come either from someone thrashing about or from a boat. And there were no desperately struggling forms anywhere in the water.

Crewson had always believed that it was a mistake to break into a run unless someone in need of help was in immediate, critical danger. A swift stride could lessen the danger of stumbling, and when the distance was very short the loss of a few seconds was more than offset by a gain in purposeful assurance.

He moved swiftly enough, keeping parallel with the surf line, but avoiding too close an approach to the narrow ribbon of sand that the waves had left wet and soggy.

He was soon within wading distance of the boat, with the rock ledge stretching out in front of him like the fanlike crest of some enormous lizard half buried in the sand.

The tide was receding, but that did not mean that he could reach the anchored craft solely by wading. But the distance he might have to cover by swimming would, he felt, be so short that untying his sneakers and kicking them off would needlessly delay him.

The screams had stopped, but before the water reached to his knees other sounds came to his ears—a creaking and a shuffling, followed by a groan that made him pause for an instant to stare at the boat's rail. He could see nothing and continued on until the water rose to his shoulders.

He was less than thirty feet from the boat when the depth of the water ruled out further walking. He surrendered to the buoyancy of the tide and swam toward the almost stationary craft with a breaststroke, feeling that an overhand crawl would have been an absurdity.

So short was the distance that he was at the rail, grasping it firmly and heaving himself across it, before the froglike movements of his legs had made more than a slight swirl in the water.

There were two people in the sailboat, both of whom he recognized.

Richard Forbes was dragging himself across the foredeck, one hand pressed to his side and the other grasping the loose end of a coil of rope that kept unraveling like a snake in his clasp. His features were distorted with what could have been either stark terror or dazed incomprehension. It was impossible for Crewson to tell. His jaw sagged and his eyes had a slightly filmy look.

Slumped on the deck a few feet from him was perhaps the most strikingly beautiful of the dozen or more women who had accompanied Forbes in a sailing cruise around the harbor and often farther in coastal waters in the past year and a half.

Helen Tanner was thirty or thirty-two but she had the rosy-cheeked complexion of a girl of seventeen. Only now most of the rosiness had vanished and she looked haggard-eyed and drawn. Her pale blond hair, dampened by the fog, clung to her brow in such a way that, quite suddenly and appallingly, made Crewson think of Medusa's coils. She had seemed to be bearing up fairly well, but the instant Crewson looked directly at her, her expression changed and she screamed once shrilly, and then fell silent with a look that might well have turned Perseus to stone.

It was a terrible, fathomless look, as if she had gazed on something so monstrous that it had drained away all that was womanly in her.

But still, despite all that, she seemed to want desperately to tell him what had happened to bring her to such a pass. Her lips moved, twitching spasmodically, and she raised herself a little more and her hand went out toward him.

He moved forward on his knees—getting to his feet had seemed less urgent than reaching her before she collapsed—and took firm hold of her hand.

"What is it?" he breathed. "What has happened here? Did—did Forbes try to attack you?"

She shook her head. "No, no—oh, God, no. He's badly hurt. Can't you see? It tore at his side . . . clawed him."

Forbes's voice came then, as if from a great distance, as if the air surrounding him had changed into a swirling vortex carrying him far away in space and time. There was a deadness in his voice, a hollowness. Yet it seemed laden with anguish as well.

"It was like a mist at first—a mist that crept in over the rail. I thought it was just the fog—coming back again, getting quickly denser, as fogs often do."

Crewson released his tight grip on Helen Tanner's hand, swung about and stood up, a little surprised by the steadiness in his legs. He was grateful for the slight swaying of the boat, for it enabled him to cross to Forbes's side in a somewhat lurching way. Otherwise he might have given

Forbes the impression that he was sturdily in command of himself, and he did not want to do that. A man or woman in great distress, in need of support, likes to think that he is not alone in experiencing inner torment. The comforter, Crewson knew, has to be a little shaken himself—if he is to provide a wholly sympathetic kind of support.

He took a firm hold of Forbes's shoulder as he had of Helen Tanner's hand and cautioned: "Perhaps you'd better not try to talk. Suppose you just let me have a look at your side. The wound may not be as bad as you think."

Forbes made no attempt to rise. But he removed the hand that had been pressed to his side, exposing a dull red stain that was triangular in shape. His sport shirt was badly ripped, with pinpoints of glistening redness on the torn cloth where it clung to the wound in frayed strips.

He shook his head when Crewson bent to examine more closely one of the lacerations, which seemed the opposite of a superficial scratch.

"No sense in looking at it," Forbes said, quickly replacing his hand. "I know how bad it is. Its talons were like little knives. If they had been longer—"

"Its talons?"

"I tried to tell you. Why did you stop me? It was like a mist at first, and then it changed. It changed into some kind of animal. It was jet-black and had four limbs and a head. The head kept getting larger and there were eyes in it, and I think it had a beak. But I can't be sure, because something happened to my mind. I could see nothing clearly after that."

"Did you try to defend yourself when it attacked

you?" Crewson heard himself asking. "Did you struggle with it?"

Forbes let go of the rope he'd been gripping and pounded the deck with his fist, as if just remembering what had happened demanded some kind of emotional release.

"I couldn't move. I tried to back away from it, tried to get the rail behind me for support. But it rose up and flung itself at me while I was in a state of shock. There was a heaviness in my legs, and the deck looked warped, twisted up. It must have done something to my mind."

"It didn't attack Miss Tanner?"

"No, she tried to make it let go of me. She screamed and tugged at it. I don't know why it didn't turn on her. You can see what just the sight of it has done to her."

"It may have been the feel of it," Crewson said. "I didn't ask."

"Please don't," Forbes said, staring across the deck to where Helen Tanner was still sitting motionless, her shoulders now a little hunched, and her fingers pressed to both sides of her brow. "She's been through enough."

The salt sea air that had always meant so much to Crewson seemed suddenly an unhealthy kind of air to breathe.

He found that he could not take seriously a great deal of what Forbes had said. But something could have come flopping up out of the sea and landed on deck—probably had. A seal perhaps. They were not unheard of in New England waters. Then some kind of wild hysteria could have gripped both Forbes and Helen Tanner, and—

But how to explain the lacerations on Forbes's right side and his ripped shirt?

Could Helen Tanner have succumbed to so wild a fright that she had lost all contact with reality and lunged at him with a knife, mistaking him for whatever it was that had flopped over the rail to the deck? But if she had done that, what had happened to the knife?

Crewson came to a quick, firm decision. He bent and took steadying hold of Forbes's shoulder for the second time.

"We've got to get you to a hospital," he said. "I'll go ashore and come right back, and drive you both to East Windham. Miss Tanner needs immediate medical attention. The worst wounds are not always physical."

"You can say that again," Forbes muttered, with a slight upward tilt to his lips that didn't quite result in a smile.

It was past midnight when Crewson returned to the cottage after a two-way fifty-mile drive. He put the car back into the garage and walked wearily up the white gravel path to the door of the sun parlor, surprised by its lighted-up aspect.

The instant he passed through the door he was greeted by Timothy with an open book still in his hand.

"What happened, Dad?" he asked. "What did they say at the hospital? Were they surprised?"

"Naturally they were surprised," Crewson said. "A man with a bad wound in his side he can't readily explain away and a woman half out of her mind."

He looked steadily at his son for a moment, then demanded: "Why are you up so late? I hope you were worried about me."

"I never worry about you, Dad," Timothy assured him. "You can take care of yourself."

"I often wonder about that," Crewson said. "Going for a walk when supper was practically on the table wasn't such a bright idea—in view of what happened on the beach."

"Do you believe Mr. Forbes's story?" Timothy asked.

"I'm sorry I even mentioned what happened when I came back to get the car," Crewson said. "Now look. Forget about that excuse. What I want you to do is go straight upstairs to bed. You've done enough reading for today."

"The Grecian shop—" Timothy began.

Crewson suddenly became as angry as he was capable of becoming in the presence of his son.

"You heard me. Straight upstairs to bed. I'm very serious, Timothy."

"All right. But I just wanted you to know that what happened to Mr. Forbes wasn't my fault. I couldn't have stopped it. If I hadn't been reading about the Fall of Troy—"

It confirmed everything that Crewson had feared. Stories of heroes and mythical monsters and ancient cities famous in song and legend might or might not be just the right kind of reading for children living under the shadow of The Bomb. But even if that could be debated pro and con, it was the worst possible kind of reading for his son.

It was Timothy above every other child in the world that he had been seeking to safeguard in taking what his wife had considered a ridiculous stand.

Was it already too late? Had Timothy lost all

contact with the world of sobriety and common sense? Childhood schizophrenia—

It was a horror he refused to dwell on. Not tonight, not after all he had endured. It had been even worse at the hospital, in a way, than when he'd heaved himself up over the rail of Forbes's boat and looked into Helen Tanner's fathomless, terror-haunted eyes. At the hospital she had collapsed again and they had carried her, shrieking and raving, into the emergency ward. It had taken two strong interns to control her.

"Timothy," Crewson said.

"What is it, Dad?"

"Forgive me if I spoke a little harshly. Just go upstairs now and turn in. And try not to wake your mother. She may be needing all the sleep she can get."

"But don't you want to know why—"

"I don't want to hear anything more tonight," Crewson said, silencing his son with a look that Timothy would have been unwise to ignore. "We'll talk about it tomorrow."

As soon as Timothy had vanished in the darkness at the top of the staircase, Crewson took a slow turn up and down the sun parlor. The night beyond its wide-paned windows was inky black, and the instant Timothy had ceased to make the stairs creak, Crewson reached up and pulled the chain on the hanging electric bulb that his son had left blazing.

He had no particular desire to join his family upstairs. Anne, he knew, would go right on sleeping and not miss him at all unless she happened to wake up, and if she did she would take for granted that he'd chosen to spend the rest of the night on his favorite couch. Timothy would tell her that he'd returned safely even if she didn't come downstairs to make sure. Probably she wouldn't, because he'd made a habit of sleeping on the couch several times a month, where the air was cooler on hot nights. It was something Anne did herself at times, creep downstairs in the middle of the night and leave him to slumber on in the heat in their upstairs bedroom.

The couch was quite long and spacious and since it was on the side of the sun parlor, where a cool breeze from the sea blew in most strongly—if just one window remained raised—all Crewson had to do was stretch himself out at full length and relax.

It creaked a little as he eased himself down, making him decide to oil the springs in the morning. He sighed, turned on his side, and almost immediately fell asleep.

Just how deep a sleep it was he had no way of knowing. He knew only that he awoke once, aware of an unusually strong sea smell in the room, but was far too drugged with sleep to pay it much attention. In a deep, half-conscious way he remained aware of it for perhaps a full minute, but so overwhelming was his drowsiness that when it became no stronger he made no effort to resist the tug of slumber.

When he opened his eyes again, the sun parlor was no longer in total darkness. There was a faint glow in the eastern sky, and though the light that had crept in through the windows was too dim to enable him to see more than the shadowy outlines of the furniture—three chairs, a flower stand, and a small circular table—he could make out something huge and misshapen in a far corner that should not have been there at all.

It was too solid-looking to have been a shadow.

And there was nothing in the sun parlor that could have caused one of that shape and size.

For a moment Crewson wasn't in the least frightened. There were so many ways of explaining something like that—a big chunk of bark from the dead oak on the lawn, ripped from the trunk and blown through the open window by a fierce gust of wind in the night, or something Timothy had lugged downstairs in the small hours, being too restless to sleep and wanting something to do. Or just possibly—but no, it was far too large to be a cat or a woodchuck or a skunk.

The chill began when he realized that it might have been some animal that had climbed through the window while he slept. It got worse when the thing began to move about, sending so great a coldness lancing up through him that his lips began to shake.

He sat up abruptly, as wide awake as he had ever been, jolted by an awareness of danger so acute that it drove every vestige of slumber from his brain. Only the dimness of the light prevented him from seeing it clearly, for his vision had ceased to be even slightly blurred.

There was something vaguely parrotlike about it. But its body did not seem in the least birdlike and it moved with a scraping sound, as if its feet were claw-tipped.

Crewson was shaking violently and uncontrollably now. He knew that he possessed as much courage as most men. But when a breath from the unknown blew cold upon anyone, man or woman, courage became a relative thing. It had always been that way, from the rude beginnings of human life on earth.

There was a breath—sea-bottom fetid, as if some decaying shellfish had been stirred into a vaporized broth and sprayed into every corner of the sun parlor.

It was moving toward him more swiftly now, swaying as it advanced, and making a sound that he had never associated with an animal of land-dwelling habits. It was neither a growl nor a catlike whining, but a kind of blubbery smacking-together of what may or may not have been lips.

Suddenly it reared up and appeared to increase in bulk, and that abrupt change in its attitude seemed to do something to the light. There was a sudden brightness high up under the ceiling, bringing into view an enormous shining beak and two eyes as large as dinner plates that were trained so fiercely upon Crewson that he could feel the heat of them searing his pupils and burning its way into his brain.

There was an abrupt loud clattering on the stairs, followed by a thud. It brought about an instant dimming of the light again. The beak and the eyes hovered for the barest instant in the diminished glow and then whipped away out of sight. The high-rearing bulk of the monstrous shape began to dissolve as Crewson stared, growing more and more attenuated until nothing but a thin curtain of revolving mist lingered between the couch and the corner of the room from which it had emerged. And in another moment even the mist was gone.

Crewson's trembling had not stopped. But shaken as he was, he somehow managed to stand up and jerk at the chain of the hanging light bulb which he'd turned off long ago, in another age surely —some immeasurably remote period in time when his sanity had not yet deserted him in quite so total a way.

The instant the sun parlor became flooded with light he saw Timothy. He was lying at the foot of the stairs in a sprawled-out heap, with no trace of animation in his limbs or features. His eyes were tightly shut and he was pajama-clad, and there was a swelling, dark bruise on his forehead that was visible from where Crewson stood.

It was the bruise more than anything else that brought Crewson to his son's side with a concern so acute that he staggered and almost fell. He bent and gathered Timothy into his arms and started shaking him, not trusting himself to speak.

Timothy opened his eyes and stared up at him. "What happened, Dad? I was just starting to— Did I trip? Yeah, I must have taken a tumble. Everything went black."

"You had a very bad fall," Crewson heard himself muttering, his concern suddenly less acute. "Are you all right? Do you feel all right? Not dizzy or anything?"

"Maybe I'll feel dizzy if I stand up," Timothy said. "But I guess not. I feel pretty good."

"I'm glad of that, at least," Crewson said. "But I don't know why you should feel good, after giving me a scare like that. Why did you come downstairs at this hour? Tell me."

"I stayed up all night, Dad. I was reading in bed. Then I started worrying about what might happen if I kept thinking about what happened when the Greek ships—"

"Stop right there," Crewson ordered. "We're not going into that again. Not now—or ever again. Do you understand? I don't want to hear about it."

"All right, Dad. But that smell will keep coming back."

Crewson's heart skipped a beat. "What smell?" he demanded. "What are you talking about?"

Just the fact that he knew only too well what Timothy was talking about meant nothing, one way or the other. The last thing he wanted to do was let Timothy know that he knew.

"Susan smelled it, too," Timothy said defensively. "It woke her up. When Mom boils a lobster and when she steams clams, Susan can't stand the smell. She stays out on the lawn until supper's ready. You never get cross with her."

"She's allergic to seafood," Crewson said. "I've told you that many times. But it's mostly shellfish. That's why we never let her eat shellfish."

It was an irrelevant remark. But Crewson felt it would encourage his son to talk more freely, and he no longer wanted him to stop.

"It came right out of the sea again," Timothy said. "I can always tell. But when Susan smelled it I knew it was getting bad. It will be like that now even when it doesn't come back. Mom will smell it, too."

"Is that why you came rushing downstairs so fast—to find out if I smelled anything strange?"

Timothy shook his head. "I was scared you'd see it. That's worse than just smelling it. Mr. Forbes saw it, and was nearly killed."

Crewson had forgotten for a moment what Timothy had said about feeling dizzy if he tried to walk. But now all of his concern came back.

"Get up, son," he said. "Walk up and down a few times. We've got to make sure that bump on your head is nothing to worry about. Kids your age take so many tumbles, you get in the habit of giving it little thought. But sometimes you don't worry enough."

Timothy got up and walked back and forth until his father told him to stop.

"Any dizziness?" Crewson asked.

"No, Dad. I feel fine."

"I'm glad. There's just one more thing I want you to do. Go upstairs and wake your mother. Tell her I have to see her right away. And don't come back with her. Just go to your room and stay there. I've got to have a long, serious talk with her."

If Timothy had the slightest inclination to disobey, it was not apparent in his behavior. He turned slowly and went back up the stairs, dragging his feet a little as if in sullen protest against parental dominance.

Five minutes later Anne Crewson was sitting at her husband's side, listening to what he was saying without making any attempt to interrupt him. The creaking of the couch as she shifted her position almost continuously was more revealing of the way she felt than her expression, for she was a woman who could endure a great deal of inner torment with composed features.

Crewson carefully avoided so much as hinting at the torment that he had endured before his son's fall had made a horror beyond sane description waver and vanish. He started with Timothy's mishap, explaining that it was the crash that had awakened him. But he told her everything that their son had said, and when he had finished he was almost sure, from the long silence which ensued, that her concern was now as great as his, and perhaps even surpassed it.

Her voice, when she spoke, was slightly tremulous. "We're very lucky, in a way, Ralph. Dr. Moorehouse is not only a kindly and understanding man. He doesn't really belong in a town as small as East Windham, even though they have a quite large general hospital. I don't need to tell you how famous he has become. There are few child psychologists—"

"He started as a Jungian analyst," Crewson said before she could continue. "Most of his patients, in those days, were troubled adults. He's still a Jungian, I've been told, but yes—he's a good man. I've never had anything against Jung—or Freud, for that matter, except that I've never been a convert to any kind of analytical therapy."

"Most people are today," Anne said.

"No, I wouldn't say that exactly," Crewson said. "It's a big world and we make a mistake when we let ourselves forget it."

"You picked a strange time to interpose objections," Anne said. "Timothy is more than just troubled. There are few adults—"

"That's not what you said when Timothy was sprawled out on the floor reading about the Fall of Troy for the fiftieth time. I told you then that it was the wrong book. A very bad book for Timothy —even if a case could be made for letting that kind of reading fall into the hands of comparatively well-balanced children for a while longer."

"I've changed my mind, that's all," Anne said.

Crewson reached out and pressed his wife's hand. "I'm glad you have. I'll drive to East Windham and have a talk with Moorehouse just as soon as you can perk some strong coffee—make it three cups. Black, no cream."

"That's unusual for you," Anne said, trying very hard to smile. "You hate black coffee. Oh, hell—I'll boil you two eggs while I'm at it. It won't take more than ten minutes."

Under ordinary circumstances Crewson would have phoned Dr. Moorehouse to check on his availability before driving to East Windham at so early an hour. But he needed to get out into the open in a speeding car regardless of the hour; and no matter how soon he arrived in the town a period of waiting seemed inevitable, and he saw no reason for worrying about whether it would be long or comparatively short.

Possibly, he told himself, an appointment could be arranged as early as ten o'clock at Moorehouse's residence. And if it had to be later at the hospital, where the psychiatrist was a staff therapist, East Windham was a pleasant enough town to keep the dread that darkened his thoughts from becoming overwhelming for a few hours.

It turned out better than he had dared to hope and a phone call to Moorehouse's home on his arrival secured him an appointment at nine-thirty. The hour and a half of waiting which remained he spent roaming through the more ancient part of town, studying the old houses, some dating back to the sixteenth century, and talking for twenty minutes on the phone with Forbes, in his private room at the hospital.

The news he received was reassuring. Forbes's wound had been well attended to, and unless some complication developed, which seemed unlikely, he would be up and about again in a few days. Miss Tanner was no longer under sedation.

He arrived at Moorehouse's home ten minutes

ahead of time and was ushered into his quite large, tastefully furnished office facing the street by his wife. The quiet-spoken, attractive woman was quick to explain that the doctor's regular office hours were eleven to one, and were followed by his duties at the hospital that sometimes kept him occupied all night.

"Sometimes he sees patients earlier," she told Crewson. "He's been terribly busy in recent weeks. Everything's so uncertain today that people are taking up more and more of his time. I worry about the schedule he's imposed on himself."

She nodded and shut the door, and Crewson found himself staring across the sunlit room at a slightly stout, gray-haired man with thoughtful brown eyes, and rather small features that were finely chiseled and verged on the handsome. There was nothing particularly distinguished about him, but there was something in his expression that inspired confidence at first glance.

He arose from behind his desk, gestured to a chair drawn up opposite the desk, and sat down again. He did not offer his hand in greeting, but his first words put Crewson completely at ease.

"We have two mutual friends, it seems. But this is the first time I've had the pleasure of meeting you in person. I understand you wish to talk to me about your son."

Crewson had debated with himself the wisdom of telling the composed, widely experienced man who now sat facing him everything that had happened since the previous afternoon, starting with Timothy's wild talk and the angry scene with his wife that had made him decide to go for a walk on the beach.

He abruptly decided that he would be defeating his own purpose in seeking the psychiatrist's help if he kept anything back, including the appalling spectacle that had confronted him when he'd heaved himself over the rail of Forbes's boat.

Quite possibly Moorehouse had talked with Forbes at the hospital and already knew about that. The emergency had been an unusual one, and a staff psychiatrist could well have been summoned to provide some immediate help, particularly since Helen Tanner had undergone a dangerous kind of hysterical collapse.

It took Crewson close to half an hour to acquaint Moorehouse with a sequence of occurrences that went far beyond what the psychiatrist could have surmised from just talking with Forbes. And he was careful to stress that not only were they sanity-threatening, but seemed to bear some frightening relationship to Timothy's state of mind.

When he had finished, Moorehouse remained for a long moment staring at him with an inscrutable expression on his face. Then he arose quietly, walked to the window, and stared out, as if he needed an even longer moment to think over what he had been told.

When he returned to the desk and resumed his seat the inscrutable expression had vanished. It had been replaced by a look of restrained reassurance.

"Let me ask you something," he said. "Just what kind of boy is your son? Oh, I know. You've described him, but not sufficiently. Is he ever in the least outgoing, despite his tendency to engage in daydreaming a great deal of the time?"

"He can be," Crewson said. "With other kids at times. And I guess you could say he is with me. He talks back, gets aggressive, and disobeys. But most of the time he's obedient enough."

"Children are always a little outgoing with their own parents," Moorehouse said. "I wasn't really thinking of that. Is he the kind of boy who has a lot of bottled-up emotions he'd like to display in an aggressive way, despite his introspective tendencies? But he doesn't simply because daydreaming seems easier, and more emotionally satisfying to him except at rare intervals. But then, once in a while he really lets go. He blackens the eye of some kid he regards as a bully, and gives a damned good account of himself in other ways. Am I describing him accurately?"

"Very," Crewson said.

"Just how familiar are you with the Jungian hypothesis in general?" Moorehouse asked.

"Not too familiar," Crewson replied. "It covers so wide a territory. But I've dipped into Jung now and then. You refer to it as a hypothesis," he couldn't resist adding. "Are you implying you don't accept the whole of Jung?"

"Naturally, I don't," Moorehouse said. "If I did that I'd be a bum psychiatrist from the word go. No mathematical physicist in his right mind would, or could, accept the whole of Einstein. It's the last thing Einstein would have wanted anyone to do."

A very earnest, serious expression came into Moorehouse's eyes. "Only one aspect of the Jungian hypothesis in general concerns me now. I'll try to discuss it as briefly as I can. It's the very familiar one, the one that four people out of five—and that would take in the bartender at the café a block from here—would know what you were talking about if you mentioned it in casual conversation. I'm referring, of course, to man's collective unconscious, the repository of archetypal images that Jung was firmly convinced we all carry about with us in the depths of our minds."

He paused for a moment, and though Crewson had more than an inkling of what Moorehouse was about to say he waited patiently for him to go on.

Before doing so, Moorehouse removed a cigarette from the package at his elbow, lit it and took a few slow puffs.

"Those archetypal images," he resumed, "are often frightful—enormous snakes, tribal effigies with chalk-white faces, and legendary kings with scepters of fire who practiced cruelty night and day. All that we know. But Jung even suggested—since there is no way of knowing how far the collective unconscious goes back in time—that images from a reptile-stage or fish-stage period of evolution may form a part of man's buried ancestral heritage. And that would explain the frequent appearance as archetypes of fanged and flying lizards or even hideous monsters from the sea."

Moorehouse fell silent again, and Crewson found himself wondering, with some concern, if he had allowed the way he was staring at the psychiatrist to make him reluctant to say more.

Very quickly he ceased to stare, looking beyond Moorehouse to the glimmering patch of sunlight on the opposite wall.

"Just what are you trying to tell me?" he asked. "It would be very hard for me to believe—"

"Yes, I know," Moorehouse interposed. "It would be hard for me to believe it, too. But Jung once allowed himself to speculate—wait, put it this way. What if a very imaginative child—or an adult, for that matter—with the bottled-up aggressive drives we've discussed—became abnormally stimulated in some way by something he had read? I mean—you see—"

"I'm afraid I don't see."

"I'm sure you do. It's always a mistake to conceal from ourselves what we would prefer not to believe."

"Aren't you doing that yourself, right now? You just said—"

"I said it would be very hard for me to believe that visual images—even when they are not archetypal—can seem more real to us if we link them to something we've read. A book of mythology, for instance, or—if you were a child in the Victorian Age—the darkly frightening, even cruel world of fantasy conjured up by the Brothers Grimm."

"Are you trying to make me believe that an archetypal image in Timothy's mind took on form and substance and—"

Moorehouse raised a protesting hand. "I'm not asking you to believe anything. It's Timothy you're most concerned about, and so am I. You came here to consult me for no other reason. We've got to help Timothy, because when a sensitive, imaginative child with many fine qualities is in trouble—well, there's no greater tragedy."

"For God's sake," Crewson heard himself saying, "what do you suggest? What would you have me do?"

"Just listen carefully. Has Timothy ever spent the summer in a boys' camp, in everyday relaxed contact with other kids his age? Has he ever gone in for bird-watching and paddled around in a canoe, and played tennis and baseball and engaged in a half-dozen other sports? Very strenuous ones, guaranteed to make him feel so tired at night he'll just drop down exhausted and sleep like a log until he's caught up in another day of activity?"

"No, I'm afraid not," Crewson heard himself replying. "We never felt—it was partly his mother's fault. She couldn't bear the thought of not seeing him for six or eight weeks. And he never cared much for sports, aside from baseball."

"There's a camp right here in East Windham," Moorehouse said. "An excellent one, which I can personally recommend. I have a nephew Timothy's age, and he has spent three summers with the Wheltons. It's in the deep woods, by Sharon Lake —not twenty minutes drive from the center of town."

"That means we could see him—"

Dr. Moorehouse shook his head. "No—I wouldn't advise that. If you love your son, you'll make him understand that when once he's deposited in the camp he's staying there until fall. That will not prevent you from writing to him—as often as you wish."

Crewson got slowly to his feet and this time Moorehouse reached across the desk and firmly clasped his hand. "When Timothy comes back," Moorehouse said, "you may find that your worries are at an end."

There was a telephone handset on Moorehouse's desk and Crewson tapped it with his forefinger. "May I—call my wife on this phone? I'd like to get this settled as quickly as possible."

"By all means," Moorehouse said. "I was just about to suggest it."

A moment later Crewson was saying into the phone, "Anne, I want you to pack a few of Timothy's clothes—in that small brown leather suitcase in the hall closet. Just an extra pair of trousers, sneakers, two or three flannel shirts—you know, what you packed for him when he spent the weekend with your sister in Brookdale two summers ago. Everything he'll need for a few days away from home.

"What's that? No, darling, I can't go into it now, but he'll be going on a short visit. Yes, yes, I've talked with Dr. Moorehouse and I'm phoning from his home. It's something he felt was most urgent."

Anne's voice came so frantically over the line that he had to hold the receiver away from his ear for a moment. When the protests stopped he added: "Nothing to worry about, darling. Everything's fine. Timothy is going to be all right. I'll explain when I get back. I just want to be sure the suitcase is packed, and that Timothy will be ready to leave with me when I drive up in the car. Right away—that's most important."

He hung up before Anne could protest further.

"You handled that very well," Moorehouse said.

Driving home on a road that skirted the sea for a mile or so at frequent intervals, Crewson kept turning over in his mind everything that Moorehouse had said to him. It was hard for him to believe any part of it, and he very much doubted if Moorehouse took more than a tenth of it seriously.

But in one tenth of a far-out surmise there might reside just enough truth to make its dismissal an act of folly. What did the Jungians advise when a problem of that nature presented itself?

Dismiss nothing as absolutely unbelievable.

Watch every step you take, tread cautiously. There may well be some kind of tenuous connection between the logically untenable and the mysterious nature of ultimate reality.

Perhaps nothing so gross as a visual image, archetypal or otherwise, could be thought of as capable of separating itself from the mind, at least in part, and acquiring destructive physical attributes.

But terrifying occurrences had seemingly taken place that had come as no surprise to Timothy, and his wild talk had clearly established some kind of relationship between his thoughts and the occurrences. Perhaps Moorehouse had been all wrong about the nature of those relationships. But just the fact that they appeared to exist made caution mandatory.

The shape that had towered above the couch with its eyes malignantly trained on him had dwindled and vanished a few seconds after Timothy had tripped on the stairs and struck his head in falling. It seemed unlikely that the sudden blotting out of Timothy's consciousness could have been totally unrelated to the shape's disappearance. Unanticipated coincidences were perhaps common enough under ordinary circumstances. But when something happened that was both terrifying and unusual, how often did coincidence play a role as well? It was asking too much of the law of averages, was loading the dice in a totally unacceptable way.

Crewson tightened his hold on the wheel of the speeding car, wished the sea would not come into view so often. The breeze whipped at his hair, setting it to swirling on his brow and occasionally half blinding him.

Suddenly, the long ledge of rock where Forbes's boat was still bobbing about in the tide came into view and all of his apprehension vanished. It was close enough to the cottage now for him to bring the car flush with the garage, leap out, and cross the lawn in eight or ten long strides.

Twenty seconds later he was doing just that, the wind still whipping at his hair. He was almost at the door of the cottage, when the wind brought so strong an odor of decaying shellfish to his nostrils that he came to an abrupt halt.

He started to turn, to see if the odor became stronger when he faced the wharf. But before he'd swung completely around, he realized it could only be coming from the cottage. The tide was at its full, and there were no mud flats from which it could have been carried by the wind.

He remained for an instant motionless, facing the door without jerking it open, choosing to listen instead. The slightest sound from within the cottage—light, unhurried footsteps, Anne's voice or that of the children talking back and forth —would have dispelled the fear that had come upon him, and he desperately needed such reassurance. It was worth waiting for five, six, seven seconds. Waiting longer was unthinkable, and when no sounds came to his ears he grasped the doorknob, gave it a violent wrench, and entered the cottage in a kind of stumbling rush.

He almost stumbled over Anne. She was lying slumped on the floor just inside the door, her face drained of all color. He was instantly on his knees at her side, slipping one arm under her shoulder and raising her to a sitting position. She moaned and stirred a little, but he had to shake her and plead with her to say something—anything —before her terrible limpness vanished and she leaned heavily against him, her voice coming in choking gasps.

"Ralph, it—it's horrible! Half fish, half hairy animal. I tried to—make it let go of Timothy—and it hurled me across the room. Everything went hazy for a minute. I thought my back was broken. If you hadn't started shaking me—" Her hand went out and fastened on his wrist. "You've got to get to them. Timothy was screaming and Susan—"

"Both of the children!" Crewson couldn't seem to breathe. "Where are they? I don't see them."

"It dragged Timothy upstairs. And Susan ran after them. I couldn't stop her."

"All right—careful now," Crewson cautioned. "Just lean back against the wall when I take my arm away. Don't twist about. And don't try to get up."

"I won't. But hurry, darling! It may not be too late—"

Crewson got swayingly to his feet, and in another moment was mounting the stairs, ascending to the floor above, a nightmarish feeling of unreality making it hard for him to believe it wasn't happening to someone else.

Sunlight was streaming in through the two small windows in the upper hallway, but there was a swirling curtain of mist at the end of the hall which prevented him from seeing into Timothy's room. Since Timothy seldom closed the door on summer days, Crewson didn't expect to find it shut. But the thought that it might be gave him little concern. He felt fully capable of battering it down, and he moved now with a steadiness of purpose which, for an instant, had almost deserted him on the stairs.

The odor of decaying shellfish became sickening as the mist swirled up around him, forcing him to cover his face with his hand. Then he was inside the room, staring up with his hand lowered, feeling a wetness start up in his forehead and turn into a cold trickling that ran down both cheeks to his throat.

Timothy was suspended between the floor and the ceiling by long tendrils of mist that crisscrossed and held him enmeshed as if he had stumbled by accident into a vast, glowing spider web and been elevated to its exact center by his own furious struggles to escape.

Lower down in the web Susan Jane was also enmeshed. But she had seemingly given up struggling and dangled as limply as a calico doll tossed carelessly across a bedpost for the night.

Behind the bed a huge shape towered, beaked and taloned, faintly rimmed with sunlight from a window which its bulk had nine-tenths blocked out.

When Timothy saw his father, he stopped struggling so abruptly that his limbs seemed still in motion, for the web continued to tremble for a moment in the same violent way. Timothy could not have looked more frightened and despairing, and that seemed to be keeping him from surrendering to another kind of emotion.

It was only what he said that startled Crewson and made him stare unbelievably.

"If you don't go, it will kill you, Dad. I don't want you to die. Tell Mom good-bye. I love her very much. You too, Dad."

Timothy's voice seemed so startlingly calm and adult it was hard for Crewson to realize it was his own son speaking.

Crewson's throat had tightened up, and for an instant he could say nothing in reply. His mouth felt as dry as death, and that made speaking even more difficult. But he made a supreme effort, and when he heard himself saying "No one in this house is going to die, Timothy," his voice seemed even calmer than Timothy's had been.

"I can't get free, Dad," Timothy said. "And Susan can't either. But if you go right back downstairs it may not kill you."

"Listen to me," Crewson pleaded. "Stop thinking. Can you do that? Try—make your mind a total blank. I'm not here, you're not here. You're in a different place and you've stopped thinking about anything. You're just waiting for something to happen. It's so wonderful, so certain to happen, you don't even have to give it a thought."

Crewson suddenly realized that he'd let himself forget that Timothy was only nine. Could a trance-like state, with all immediate awareness blotted out, be self-induced by a boy that young and bring about a change in his conscious thinking? If he failed to comprehend exactly what he was being urged to do—

Timothy seemed to understand, for his expression changed, and although he continued to look directly at his father an unmistakable look of remoteness began to creep into his eyes.

"You're far away, Timothy," Crewson murmured. "There's nothing to be afraid of, and you're being protected from all harm and you're not letting anything frighten you. You're thinking about nothing at all because you know that thinking can make people unhappy for no reason."

It happened more quickly than Crewson had dared to hope. The beaked and darkly towering shape behind the web began to waver and dissolve. First the shining beak vanished and then the ghastly bulk of the creature dwindled and fell away, until nothing remained of it between the web and the window but a few floating filaments of mist that took just a little longer to disappear.

The web vanished then, in a sudden, almost blinding burst of light, and both children tumbled to the floor.

If Timothy had been shaken up by the fall or was still a little under the sway of the trance that had brought a look of remoteness into his eyes, he displayed no evidence of it. He was almost instantly on his feet, helping his sister to rise.

As soon as both children were on their feet Crewson hurried them out of the room without saying a word, gripping Timothy by the wrist and encircling Susan Jane's wrist almost fiercely with his free arm. His only thought was to keep Timothy from talking about any part of what had happened until they were downstairs and out of the house.

Timothy began remembering before they were halfway down the stairs.

"Dad, for a minute I didn't know where I was. What happened—?"

"You just now helped Susan to get up," Crewson told him. "You mean—you did that with your mind a blank?"

"I must have, Dad. How did we get away? It was

going to kill me and Susan, and I told you—"

"Your mother may be badly hurt," Crewson said. "Think about that—nothing else."

They were at the bottom of the stairs now and Crewson saw with relief that Anne was coming toward them across the sun parlor. She was holding herself very straight and had the look of a fully recovered woman whose only emotion was of overwhelming gratefulness.

She started to speak, but her voice broke and although Crewson knew how much time a family reunion could consume, he released his tight grip on Timothy and Susan Jane and let them run straight into Anne's outstretched arms.

He wasn't sure he had done a wise thing, and spoke almost harshly to make his wife realize that all rejoicing must be cut short.

"We're getting out of the house and into the car and driving to East Windham right now," he said. "Timothy won't be needing the suitcase I told you to pack. He'll be having the time of his life at a boys' camp—hiking, camping, swimming—well into October. We can buy him everything he'll need in East Windham tomorrow. We may even get there today before the stores close."

Anne looked at him out of eyes swimming with tears. "You got to them in time," she said. "Nothing else matters. I'll miss Timothy. You know that. But if a boys' summer camp is what you worked out for him with Dr. Moorehouse, I won't say a word."

"He couldn't be any more tanned than he's now," Crewson said. "But otherwise you won't know him when he comes back in October. He'll have a real rough-and-tumble look."

He gripped his wife's hand and pressed his lips to her cheek.

"Come on," he said, leading the way to the door. "We haven't a moment to lose."

The children followed.

"Thank you, darling," Anne said, as they passed out into the clear, bright sunlight.

AUTHOR'S NOTE

Selecting a story of one's choice for an important new anthology presents, for me at least, both a danger and an unusual kind of challenge. The danger consists in letting some early story gain preference, in the decision-making process, over a much later one, largely because it has been highly praised and remembered across the years.

In the supernatural fiction realm—or dark fantasy realm, as it is sometimes called—some forty of my short stories have appeared in major publisher anthologies, most of them in hard cover, and five of these, "The Hounds of Tindalos," "The Visitor from Egypt," "The Black Druid," "Second Night Out" and "Grab Bags Are Dangerous," I have no second thoughts about today. I would place them, without hesitation, among my very best stories, past or present. But in the course of the years it is not unusual for a writer to bring to his work something that surprises even himself a little—a kind of mutation in the creative growth department—and when I returned to short-story writing for a spell, after three decades of novel writing, I turned out a round dozen supernatural horror stories in which characterization seemed to walk more hand in hand with the darkly brooding atmosphere and suspense it had previously paced at a safer distance.

"Cottage Tenant" was the first of this new, quite recent twelvesome, and it is the one that I most fear to dwell on in the chill hours just preceding dawn.

—Frank Belknap Long

THE HOUNDS
Kate Wilhelm

ROSE ELLEN KNEW THAT MARTIN HAD BEEN LAID OFF, had known it for over a week, but she had waited for him to tell her. She watched him get out of the car on Friday, and she said to herself, "Now he's ready. He's got a plan and he'll tell me what we're going to do, and it'll be all right." There was more relief in her voice, that was in her mind only, than she had thought possible. Why, I've been scared, she thought, in wonder, savoring the feeling now that there was no longer any need to deny it. She knew Martin was ready by the way he left the car. He was a thin, intense man, not very tall, five nine. When worried, or preoccupied, or under pressure, he seemed to lose all his coordination. He bumped into furniture, moved jerkily, upsetting things within reach, knocked over coffee cups, glasses. And he forgot to turn things off: water, lights, the car engine once. He had a high domed forehead, thin hair the color of wet sand, and now, after twelve years at the cape, a very deep burned-in suntan. He was driven by a nervous energy that sought release through constant motion. He always had a dozen projects under way: refinishing furniture, assembling a stereo system, designing a space lab model, breeding toy poodles, raising hydroponic vegetables. All his projects turned out well. All were one-man efforts. This afternoon his motion was fluid as he swung his legs out of the car, followed through with a smooth movement, then slammed the door hard. His walk was jaunty as he came up the drive and around the canary date palm to where she waited at the poolside bar. Rose Ellen was in a bikini, although the air was a bit too cool, and she wouldn't dream of swimming yet. But the sun felt good when the wind died down, and she knew she looked as good in the brief red strips as she had looked fifteen or even twenty years ago. She saw herself reflected in his eyes, not actually, but his expression told her that he was seeing her again. He hadn't for the whole week.

He didn't kiss her; they never kissed until they were going to make love. He patted her bottom and reached for the cocktail shaker. He shook it once then poured and sat down, still looking at her approvingly.

"You know," he said.

"What, honey? I know what?" Her relief put a lilt in her voice, made her want to sing.

"And you've known all along. Well, okay, here's to us."

"Are you going to tell me what it is that I've known all along, or are you just going to sit there looking enigmatic as hell and pleased, and slightly soused?" She leaned over him, looking into his eyes, sniffing. "And how long ago did you leave the office?"

"Noon. Little after. I didn't go back after lunch. I

got the can, last Thursday." He put his glass down and pulled her to his lap. "And I don't care."

"May they all rot in hell," Rose Ellen said, "You! You've been there longer than almost anyone. And when they come to you beggin' you to come back, tell them to go to hell. Right?"

"Well, I don't think they'll come begging for me," Martin said, but he was pleased with himself. The worry was gone, and the circles under his eyes seemed less dark, although he still hadn't slept. Rose Ellen pushed herself away from him slightly in order to see him better.

"Anyway, you can get a job up in Jacksonville tomorrow. They know that, don't they? That you'll not be available if they let you go."

"Honey, they aren't Machiavellian, you know. The agency doesn't want to break up our team, but they had no choice, no money, no appropriation for more money. We did what they hired us to do. Now it's over. Let's go to bed."

"Uh-uh! Not until you tell me what's making you grin like that."

"Right. Look, doll, I'm forty-nine. And laid off. You know what the story is for the other guys who've had this happen. No luck. No job. Nothing. It wouldn't be any different with me, honey. You have to accept that."

She kissed his nose and stood up, hands on hips, studying him. "You! You're better than all the others put together. You know you are. You told me yourself a hundred times."

"Honey, I'm forty-nine. No one hires men who are forty-nine."

"Martin, stop this! I won't have it. You're a young man. Educated! My God, you've got degrees nobody ever even heard of. You've got education you've never even used yet."

He laughed and poured his second martini. She knew it pleased him for her to get indignant on his behalf. "I know what I'm talking about, honey. Simmer down, and listen. Okay?" She sat down again, on a stool on the other side of the bar, facing him. A tight feeling had come across her stomach, like the feeling she used to get just before the roller coaster started to go down the last, wildest drop. "I don't want another job, Rose. I've had it with jobs. I want to buy a farm."

She stared at him. He said it again. "We could do it, honey. We could sell the house and with the money left after we pay off the mortgage, the car, the other things, there'd be enough for a small farm. Ten, twenty acres. Not on the coast. Inland. West Virginia. Or Kentucky. I could get a job teaching. I wouldn't mind that."

"Martin? Martin! Stop. It's not funny. It isn't funny at all. Don't go on like this." Her playfulness evaporated leaving only the tight feeling.

"You bet your sweet ass it isn't funny. And I'm serious, Rose. Dead serious."

"A farm! What on earth would I do on the farm? What about the kids?"

"We can work out all those things. . . ."

"Not now, Martin. I have to go get Juliette. Later, later." She ran into the house without looking back at him. Bad strategy, she thought at herself, dressing. She should have gone to bed with him, and then talked him out of his crazy notion. That's all it was, a crazy notion. He was as scared as she was. He could get a job in Jacksonville. He could. It wasn't a bad drive. He could come home weekends, if he didn't want to drive it every day, although some people did. She thought about the house payments, and the insurance, and the pool maintenance, and the yard people, and the house-cleaning woman who came twice a week. And the lessons: piano, ballet, scuba, sailing. The clubs. The marina where they left the ketch. She thought of her dressmaker and her hairdresser, and his tailor, and the special shoes for Annamarie, and the kennel fees when they went away for the weekend and had to leave the three toy poodles. She thought of two thousand dollars worth of braces for Juliette in another two years.

She thought about the others it had happened to. Out of six close friends only one, Burdorf, had another job, advisor to an ad agency. But Burdorf had an in with them; his wife's father owned it.

Rose Ellen tried to stop thinking of the others who had been laid off. But Martin was different, she thought again. Really different. He had so many degrees, for one thing. She shook her head. That didn't matter. It hadn't mattered for any of the others.

She thought about being without him. She and the children without him. She shivered and hugged herself hard. She could go to work. She hadn't because neither of them had wanted her to before. But she could. She could teach, actually, easier than Martin could. He didn't have any of the education courses that were required now. So, she pursued it further, she would teach, at about seven thousand a year, and Martin would have to pay, oh, say four hundred a month. . . . And if he didn't, or couldn't? If he was on a farm somewhere without any money at all? Seven thousand. Braces, two thousand. House, two thousand. Some extras, not many, but some, like a car. In another year Annamarie would be driving, and junior insurance, and then Jeffrey would be wanting a car. . . .

More important, they wouldn't mind her. She knew it. Martin could control them with a word, a glower. She was easy and soft with them. It had always been impossible to tell them no, to tell them she wouldn't take them here or there, do this or that for them. They'd run all over her, she knew.

Martin bought a farm in May and they moved as soon as school was out. The farm was twelve acres, with a small orchard and a deep well and barn. The house was modern and good, and the children, surprisingly, accepted the move unquestioningly and even liked it all. They held a family council the day after moving into the house and took a vote on whether to buy a pool table for the basement rec room, or a horse. It would be the only luxury they could afford for a long time. Only Rose Ellen voted for the pool table.

Martin had to take three courses at the university in the fall semester, then he would teach, starting in mid-term, not his own field of mathematics, because they had a very good teacher already, he was told, but if he could brush up on high school general science . . .

Rose Ellen signed up as a substitute teacher for the fall semester. The school was only a mile and a half from their house; she could walk there when the weather was pleasant.

"It's going to be all right, honey," Martin said one night in early September. Everyone had started school, the whole move to the country had been so without trauma that it was suspicious. Rose Ellen nodded, staring at him. "What's wrong?" he asked. "Dirt on my face?"

"No. It's strange how much you looked like my father there for a moment. A passing expression, there and gone so fast that I probably imagined it."

"Your father?"

She picked up the magazine she had been looking at. "Yes. I told you I couldn't remember him because I didn't want to talk about him. It was a lie. He didn't die until I was eleven."

Martin didn't say anything, and reluctantly she lowered the magazine again. "I'm sorry. But after I told you that, back in the beginning, I was stuck with it. I'm glad it came out finally."

"Do you want to talk about him?"

"No. Not really. He drank a lot. He and mother fought like animals most of the time. Then he died in a car accident. Drunk driving, hit a truck head-on, killed himself, nearly killed the driver of the truck. Period. When I was fourteen she married again, and this time it was to a rich man."

"Did she love Eddie?"

"Eddie was the practical one," Rose Ellen said. "She married for love the first time, for practical reasons the second time. The second one was better. They've been peaceful together. No more fights. No more dodging bill collectors. Like that."

"Did she love him?"

"I don't know. I don't think so, but it didn't matter."

Martin didn't say any more, and she wondered about her mother and her second husband. Had it mattered? She didn't know. She turned pages of the magazine without looking at them, and Martin's voice startled her.

"Sometimes I think we should fight now and

then," he said. "I wonder sometimes what all you're bottling up."

"Me? You know we discuss everything."

"Discuss isn't what I mean. We discuss only after you get quiet and stay quiet long enough to come to a decision. I'd like to know sometimes what all goes on in that head of yours while you're in the process of deciding."

She laughed and stood up. "Right now all that's in my head is the fact that I want a bath and bed."

She was at the door to the kitchen when Martin asked, "What did your father do?"

She stopped. Without turning around again she said, "He had a small farm. Nothing else."

She soaked for a while and thought about his words. It was true that they never fought. He hadn't lived with two people who did fight, or he'd never say anything like that. She knew it was better to be civilized and give in. She was a good wife, she told herself soberly. A good wife. And she was adaptable. He had taken her from Atlanta to Florida, from there to Kentucky. So be it. She could get along no matter where they lived, or what they did. One of them had to, she said sharply in her mind. She had been a silent observer in her own house, then in her stepfather's house for years. It was better that way. She let the water out and rubbed herself briskly. At the bathroom door she saw that Martin had come up, their light was on. She paused for a few seconds, then went downstairs to read. She had been more tired than sleepy, she decided. Actually it was quite early.

October was still days of gold and red light, of blue skies that were endlessly deep, of russet leaves underfoot and flaming maples and scarlet poison ivy and sumac, yellow poplars and ash trees. She walked home from school with a shopping bag under her arm, alone on the narrow road that was seldom used, except by the half-dozen families that lived along it. Here one side was bordered by a fence line long grown up with blackberries and boysenberries and inhabited by small scurrying things that were invisible. The other side had a woods, not very dense, then a field of corn that had been harvested so that only skeletons remained. Behind the fence line was a pasture with a stream, peaceful cows that never once looked up as she passed them. The pasture ended, a stand of pine trees came up to the road. Then there was an outcropping of limestone and a hill with oak trees and some tall firs, and walnut trees. Walnuts had dropped over the road, along both sides of it.

She stopped at the walnuts and began to gather the heavy green hulls, hardly even broken by the fall. They would have to spread them out, let them dry. A scene from her childhood came to her, surprising her. There were so few scenes from her early years that sometimes she worried about it. They had gathered nuts one day. She, her mother, her father, out along a dirt road near their farm, gathering hickory nuts, and butternuts. They had taken a lunch with them, and had eaten it by a stream, and she had waded, although the water had been icy. Her father had made a fire and she had warmed her feet at it. She saw again his smiling face looking up at her as he rubbed her cold toes between his warm hands.

She finished filling her bag and picked up her purse again. Then she saw the dogs. Two of them stood on the other side of the road, behind the single strand of wire that was a fence. They were silver, and long legged, and very beautiful. They were as motionless as statues. She moved and their eyes followed her; they remained motionless. Their eyes were large, like deers' eyes, and golden. She turned to look at them again after passing them; they were watching her.

That night she tried to describe them to Martin. "Hunting dogs, I'd guess," she said. "But I've never seen any like them before. They were as skinny as possible to still have enough muscles to stand up with. All long muscles and bones, and that amazing silver hair."

Martin was polite, but not really interested, and she became silent about them. The children were upstairs in their rooms, studying. She realized that she saw very little of them anymore. They had adapted so well that they were busy most of the time, and the school days here were longer, the buses were later than they used to be, so that they didn't get home until four-fifteen. Then there were the things that teenagers always did: telephone; records; riding the horse, currying it, feeding it; Jeffrey out on his bike with other boys. . . . She sighed and began to look over the papers she had brought home to grade. She would have Miss Witner's fifth-grade class for another week. She decided that she detested geography.

The next afternoon the dogs were there again; this time they left the field as she came near, and stood just off the road while she passed them. She spoke to them in what she hoped was a soothing voice, but they seemed not to hear; they merely stared at her.

They were bigger than she had remembered. Their tails were like silver plumes, responding to the gentle breeze as delicately as strands of silk. Feathery silver hair stirred on their chests and the backs of their long, thin legs.

She slowed down, but continued to walk evenly until she was past them, then she looked back; they were watching her.

Her father had had a hound dog, she remembered suddenly. And her mother had let it loose one day. They never had found it. Sometimes at night she had thought she could hear its strange voice from the hills. It had a broken howl that distinguished it from the other hounds. It started high, rose and rose, then broke and started again on a different key.

She never had wondered why her mother let it go, but now she did. How furious her father had been. They had screamed at each other for hours, and just as suddenly they had been laughing at each other, and that had been all of the scene. She realized that they had gone to bed, that they always had gone to bed after one of their fights. Everything they had done together had been like that, fierce, wild, uninhibited, thorough. And now her mother was growing old in Eddie's fine house, with no one to yell at, no one to yell at her. No one to make up with. Rose Ellen resisted the impulse to look back at the dogs. She knew they would be watching her. She didn't want to see them watching her again.

The next day was Friday and she left school later than usual, after a short staff meeting about a football game. As a substitute she didn't have to attend the meeting, and certainly she wasn't required to go to the game, but she thought she might. If Jeffrey wanted to go, she would take him. Maybe they would all go. The sun was low and the afternoon was cooler than it had been all week. She walked fast, then stopped. The dogs were there. Suddenly she was terrified. And she felt stupid. They were polite, well-behaved dogs, very valuable from the looks of them. They must belong to John Renfrew. They were always at his property line anyway. She wondered if he knew they were loose. Or were they so well trained that they wouldn't leave his property? She started to move ahead again, but slowly. When she got even with them, they moved too. Not at her side, but a step behind her. She stopped and they stopped and looked at her.

"Scat," she said. "Go home." They stared at her. "Go on home!" She felt a mounting fear and shook it off with annoyance. They weren't menacing or frightening, not growling, or making any threatening movement at all. They were merely dumb. She pointed toward John Renfrew's field again. "Go home!" They watched her.

She started to walk again, and they accompanied her home. She couldn't make them go back, or stop, or sit, or anything. No matter what she said, they simply looked at her. She wondered if they were deaf and mute, and decided that she was being silly now. They would have followed her inside the house if she hadn't closed the door before they could.

"Martin!" The three champagne-colored poodles were ecstatic over her return. They jumped on her, and pranced, and got in the way, yapping. She hadn't noticed the car, but he could have put it in the garage, she thought, looking in the study, the kitchen, opening the basement door, stepping over poodles automatically. No one else was home yet. She looked out the window. They were sitting on the porch, waiting for her. She pulled back and found that she was shivering.

"This is ridiculous!" she said. "They are dogs!" She looked up Renfrew's number and called him. His wife answered.

"Who? Oh, yes. I've been meaning to come over there, but we've been so busy. You understand."

"Yes. Yes. But I'm afraid your dogs followed me home today. I tried to make them go back, but they wouldn't."

"Dogs? You mean Lucky? I thought I saw him a minute ago. Yes, he's here. I can see him out in the yard."

"These are hunting dogs. They are silver-colored, long tails . . ."

"Our Lucky is a border collie. Black and white. And he's home. I don't know whose dogs you have, but not ours. We don't have any hunting dogs."

Rose Ellen hung up. She knew they were still there. The back door slammed and Jeffrey and Annamarie were home. Presently Juliette would be there, and Martin would be back, and they could all decide what to do about the dogs on the porch. Rose Ellen went to the kitchen, ready to make sandwiches, or start dinner, or anything. She felt a grim satisfaction that she had successfully resisted looking at the dogs again. Let them wait, she thought.

"Hi, kids. Hungry?"

"Hi, Mom. Can I stay over at Jennifer's house tonight? She's a drum majorette and has to go to the game, and I thought I might go, too, with Frank and Sue Cox, and then go to Jennifer's house for hamburgers and Cokes after?"

Rose Ellen blinked at Annamarie. "I suppose so," she said. Jennifer was the daughter of the principal. She marveled at how quickly children made friends.

"I have to run, then," Annamarie said. "I have to get some pants on, and my heavy sweater. Do you think I'll need a jacket? Did you hear the weather? How cold will it get?" But she was running upstairs as she talked, and out of earshot already.

"Well, how about you?" Rose Ellen said to Jeffrey. "You going to the game too?"

"Yeah. We're ushers. That's our chore, you know. This month we do that, then we sell candy at the basketball games after Christmas. Is it okay if I have a hot dog and go? I told Mike I'd meet him at his house, and we'll catch the bus there."

Rose Ellen nodded. Martin and Juliette came home together then. He had picked her up at the bus stop.

They had dinner, and Juliette vanished to make one of her interminable phone calls to Betsy, her all-time closest friend. Rose Ellen told Martin about the dogs. "They're out on the porch," she said. "I'm sure they're very expensive. No collars."

With the three toy poodles dancing around him, Martin went to the door to look. The hounds walked in when the door opened. The poodles drew back in alarm; they sniffed the big dogs, and then ignored them. Rose Ellen felt tight in her stomach. The silly poodles were always panicked by another dog.

"Good God," Martin said. "They're beautiful!" He clicked his fingers and called softly, "Come on, boy. Come here." The dogs seemed oblivious of him. They looked at Rose Ellen. Martin walked around them, then reached down tentatively and put his hand on the nearer one's head. The dog didn't move. He ran his hand over the shoulders, down the flank, down the leg. The dog didn't seem to notice. Martin felt both dogs the same way. He ran his hand over the shoulders, down the lean sides of the dogs, over their bellies, again and again. A strange look came over his face and abruptly he pulled away. "Have you felt them?"

"No."

"You should. It's like silk. Warm and soft and alive under your fingers. My God, it's the most sensuous dog I've ever seen." He backed off and studied them both. They continued to watch Rose Ellen. "Come on and feel them. You can see how tame they are."

She shook her head. "Put them out, Martin."

"Rose? What's wrong with you? Are you afraid of them? You've never been afraid of dogs before. The poodles . . ."

"They're not dogs. They're animated toys. And I have always been afraid of dogs. Put them out!" Her voice rose slightly. Martin went to the door, calling the dogs. They didn't move. She had known they wouldn't. Slowly she walked to the door. They followed her. Martin watched, puzzled. She walked out on the porch, and the dogs went too. Then she went back inside, opening the door only enough to slip in, not letting them come with her. They sat down and waited.

"Well, they know who they like," Martin said. "You must be imprinted on their brains, like a duckling imprints what he sees first and thinks it's his mother." He laughed and went back to the table for his coffee.

Rose Ellen was cold. She wasn't afraid, she told herself. They were the quietest, most polite dogs she had ever seen. They were the least threatening dogs she had ever seen. Probably the most expensive ones she had ever seen. Still she was very cold.

"What will we do about them?" she asked, holding her hot coffee cup with both hands, not looking at Martin.

"Oh, advertise, I guess. The owner might have an ad in the paper, in fact. Have you looked?"

She hadn't thought of it. They looked together, but there was nothing. "Okay, tomorrow I'll put in an ad. Probably there'll be a reward. Could be they got away miles from here, over near Lexington. I'll put an ad in Lexington papers, too."

"But what will we do with them until the owner comes to get them?"

"What can we do? I'll feed them and let them sleep in the barn."

Even the coffee cup in her hands couldn't warm her. She thought of the gold eyes watching all night, waiting for her to come out.

"Honey, are you all right?"

"Yes. Of course. I just think they're . . . strange, I guess. I don't like them."

"That's because you didn't feel them. You should have. I've never felt anything like it."

She looked at her cup. She knew there was no power on earth that could induce her to touch one of those dogs.

Rose Ellen woke up during the night. The dogs, she thought. They were out there waiting for her. She tried to go to sleep again, but she was tense and every time she closed her eyes she saw the gold eyes looking at her. Finally she got up. She couldn't see the porch from her bedroom, but from Juliette's room she could. She covered Juliette, as if that was what she had entered the room for, then she started to leave resolutely. It was crazy to go looking for them, as crazy as it was for them to keep watching her. At the hall door she stopped, and finally she turned and went back to the window. They were there.

The hall night light shone dimly on the porch, and in the square of soft light the two animals were curled up with the head of one of them on the back of the other. As she looked at them they both raised their heads and looked up at her, their eyes gleaming gold. She stifled a scream and dropped the curtain, shaking.

On Saturday morning, Joe MacLaughton, the county agent, came over to help Martin plan for a pond that he wanted to have dug. He looked at the dogs admiringly. "You sure have a pair of beauties," he said. "You don't want to let them loose in those hills. Someone'll sure as hell lift them."

"I wish they would," Rose Ellen said. She was tired; she hadn't slept after going back to bed at three-thirty.

"Ma'am?" Joe said politely.

"They aren't ours. They followed me home."

"You don't say?" He walked around the dogs thoughtfully. "They don't come from around here," he said finally.

"I'm going to call the paper and put an ad in the Lost and Found," Martin said.

"Waste of time in the locals," Joe said stubbornly. "If those dogs belonged around here, I'd know about it. Might try the kennel club over in Lexington, though.''

Martin nodded. "That's a thought. They must know about such valuable dogs in this area.''

They went out to look at the proposed pond site. The dogs stayed on the porch, looking at the door.

After the agent left, Martin made his calls. The kennel club president was no help. Weimaraners? Martin said no, and he named another breed or two, and then said he'd have to have a look at the dogs, didn't sound like anything he knew. After he hung up, Martin swore. He had an address in Lexington where he could take the dogs for identification. He called the newspaper and placed the ad.

All day the sound of hammering from the barn where Martin was making repairs sounded and resounded. Annamarie and Jennifer came in and volunteered to gather apples. Jeffrey helped his father, and Juliette tagged with one pair, then the other. She tried to get the dogs to play with her, but they wouldn't. After patting them for a few minutes she ignored them as thoroughly as they ignored all the children. Rose didn't go outside all day. She started to leave by the back door once, but they heard her and walked around the corner of the house before she got off the steps. She returned to the kitchen. They returned to the porch.

They wouldn't stay in the barn. There were too many places where creatures as thin as they were could slip through, so Martin didn't even try to make them stay there. They seemed to prefer the porch. No one wanted to go to town to buy collars for them in order to tie them up. Martin didn't like the idea of tying them up anyway. "What if they decide to go back to where they came from?" he asked. Rose didn't press the idea after that.

At dinner she said, "Let's go over to Lexington to a movie tonight?"

Martin sagged. "What's playing?"

She shrugged. "I don't know. Something must be playing that we'd like to see."

"Another night? Tomorrow night?" Martin said. "Tell you what, I'll even throw in dinner."

"Oh, never mind. It was a sudden thought. I don't even know what's on." Rose and Annamarie cleared the table and she brought in apple pie, and coffee. She thought of the dogs on the porch.

"Next February I'll spray the trees," Martin said. "And I'll fertilize under the trees. Watch and see the difference then. Just wait."

Rose Ellen nodded. Just wait. Martin was tired, and thinner than usual. He worked harder here than he ever had anywhere, she was sure. Building, repairing, planting, studying about farming methods, and his school courses. She wondered if he was happy. Later, she thought, later she would ask him if he was happy. She wondered if that was one of those questions that you don't ask unless you already know the answer. Would she dare ask if she suspected that he might answer no? She hoped he wouldn't ask her.

Martin was an inventive lover. It pleased him immensely to delight her, or give her an unexpected thrill, or just to stay with her for an hour. They made love that night and afterward, both drowsy and contented, she asked if he was happy.

"Yes," he said simply. And that was that. "I wish you were, too," he said moments later. She had almost fallen asleep. She stiffened at his words. "Sorry, honey. Relax again. Okay?"

"What did you mean by that?"

"I'm not sure. Sometimes I just feel that I've got it all. You, the kids, the farm now, and school. I can't think of anything else I want."

"I've got all those things too, you know."

"I know." He stretched and yawned and wanted to let it drop.

"Martin, you must have meant something. You think I'm not happy, is that it?"

"I don't know. I don't know what it takes to make you happy."

She didn't reply and soon he was asleep. She didn't know either.

She dozed after a while, and was awakened by a rhythmic noise that seemed to start in her dream, then linger after the dream faded. She turned over, but the noise didn't go away. She turned again and snuggled close to Martin. The bedroom was chilly. A wind had started to blow, and the window was open too much. She felt the air current on her cheek, and finally got up to close the window. The noise was louder. She got her robe on and went into the hall, then to the window in Juliette's room. The dogs were walking back and forth on the porch, their nails clicking with each step. They both stopped and looked at her. She ran from the room shaking and, strangely, weeping.

At breakfast she said to Martin, "You have to get them out of here today. I can't stand them any longer."

"They really got to you, didn't they?"

"Yes, they got to me! Take them to Lexington, leave them with the kennel club people, or the dog pound, or something."

"Okay, Rose. Let's wait until afternoon. See if

anyone answers our ad first."

No one called about them, and at one Martin tried to get them into the car. They refused to leave the porch. "I could carry them," he said doubtfully. They weren't heavy, obviously. Anything as thin as they couldn't be heavy. But when he tried to lift one, it started to shiver, and it struggled and slipped through his arms. When he tried again, the dog growled, a hoarse sound of warning deep in its throat, not so much a threat as a plea not to make it follow through. Its gold eyes were soft and clear and very large. Martin stopped. "Now what?" he asked.

"I'll get them to the car," Rose said. She led the two dogs to the car and opened the door for them. They jumped inside. When she closed the door again, they pressed their noses against the window and looked at her. "See if they'll let you drive," she said.

They wouldn't let Martin get inside the car at all, not until Rose was behind the wheel, and then they paid no attention to him. "I'll drive," she said tightly. Her hands on the wheel were very stiff and the hard feeling in her stomach made it difficult to breathe. Martin nodded. He reached out and put his hand on her knee and squeezed it gently.

He was saying it was all right, but it wasn't, she thought, driving.

The kennel club was run by Colonel Owen Luce, who was a Kentucky colonel, and wanted the title used. "Proud of it, you know," he said genially. "Got mine the hard way, through service. Nowadays you can buy it, but not back when I got mine." He was forty, with blond wavy hair, tall and too good looking not to know it. He posed and swaggered and preened, and reminded Rose of a peacock that had stolen bread from their picnic table at Sunken Gardens in Florida once.

"They're handsome dogs," Colonel Luce said, walking around the hounds. "Handsome. Deerhounds? No. Not with that silky hair. Hm. Don't tell me. Not wolfhounds. Got it! Salukis!" He looked at Rose, waiting for approval. She shrugged. "I'm not certain," he said, as if by admitting his fallibility, he was letting her in on a closely guarded secret that very few would ever know. He didn't ignore Martin as much as bypass him, first glancing at him, then addressing himself to Rose. Obviously he thought she was the dog fancier, since the hounds clung to her so closely.

"We don't know what they are," she said. "And they aren't ours. They followed me home. We want to return them to their owner."

"Ah. You should get quite a reward then. There aren't many salukis in this country. Very rare, and very expensive."

"We don't want a reward," Rose said. "We want to get rid of them."

"Why? Are they mean?" It was a ridiculous question. He smiled to show he was joking. "I always heard that salukis were more nervous than these seem to be," he said, studying them once more. "And the eyes are wrong, I think, if memory serves. I wonder if they could be a cross?"

Rose looked at Martin imploringly, but he was looking stubborn. He disliked the colonel very much. "Colonel Luce, can you house these dogs?" Rose asked. "You can claim the reward, and if no one shows up to claim them, then they'd be yours by default, wouldn't they? You could sell them."

"My dear lady, I couldn't possibly. We don't

know anything about a medical history for them, now do we? I would have to assume that they've had nothing in the way of shots, obviously not true, but with no records." He spread his hands and smiled prettily at Rose. "You do understand. I would have to isolate them for three weeks, to protect my own dogs. And give them the shots, and the examinations, and then have an irate owner show up? No thank you. Owners of valuable dogs tend to get very nasty if you doctor their hounds for them without their approval."

"Christ!" Martin said in disgust. "How much would you charge to board them then?"

"In isolation? Eight dollars a day, each."

Rose stared at him. He smiled again, showing every tooth in his head. She turned away. "Let's go, Martin." She took the dogs to the car and opened the door for them. She got behind the wheel and Martin got in, and only then did the dogs sit down. The dog pound was closed. "They won't get in the car again," Rose said dully. "Can you think of anyplace else?" He couldn't and she started for home.

The blue grass country that they drove through was very lovely at that time of year. The fields rose and fell gently, delineated by white fences, punctuated in the distance by dark horses. Stands of woods were bouquets in full bloom, brilliant in the late afternoon sunlight. A haze softened the clear blue of the sky, and in the far distance hazy blue hills held the sky and land apart. Rose looked at it all, then said bitterly, "I shouldn't have let you do this."

"What?"

"Come here. Bring me here."

"Honey, what's wrong? Don't you like the farm?"

"I don't know. I just know I should have told you no. We should have tried to work it out without this."

"Rose, you didn't say anything about not wanting to come here. Not a word."

"You might have known, if you hadn't closed your eyes to what I wanted. You always close your eyes to what I want. It's always what you want. Always."

"That isn't fair. How in God's name was I supposed to know what you were thinking? You didn't say anything. You knew we had to do something. We couldn't keep the house and the boat and everything, we had to do something."

"You didn't even try to get a job!"

"Rose. Don't do this now. Wait until we get home."

She slowed down. "Sorry. But, Martin, it's like that with us. You say you want to do this or that, and we do it. Period. It's always been like that with us. I never had a voice in anything."

"You never spoke out."

"You wouldn't let me! It was always decided first, then you told me. You always just assumed that if you wanted something then I would too. As if I exist only in your shadow, as if I must want what you want without fail, without question."

"Rose, I never thought that. If I made the decisions it was only because you wouldn't. I don't know how many times I've brought something up for us to talk about and decide on, only to have you too busy, or not interested, or playing helpless."

"Playing helpless? What's that supposed to

mean? You mean when you tell me we're moving I should chain myself to a tree and say no? Is that how I could have a voice? What can I do when you say we're doing this and you have the tickets, the plans, the whole thing worked out from beginning to end? When have you ever said how about doing this, before you already had it all arranged?"

He was silent and she realized that she had been speeding again. She slowed down. "I didn't want children right away. But you did. Bang, children. I didn't want to move to Florida, but you had such a great job there. What a great job! Bang, we're in Florida. I might have been a teacher. Or a success in business. Or something. But no, I had to have children and stay home and cook and clean and look pretty for you and your friends."

"Rose." Martin's voice was low. He looked straight ahead. "Rose, please stop now. I didn't realize how much of this you had pent up. But not now. Or let me drive. Pull off the road."

She hit the brakes hard, frightened suddenly. Her hands were shaking. She saw the dogs in the rear-view mirror. "They wouldn't let you drive," she said. "Will you light me a cigarette, please?"

He gave it to her wordlessly, staring ahead. She reached for the radio and he said, "Let me do it." He tuned in country music and she reached for it again. He changed the station to a press interview with someone from HEW.

Rose stubbed the cigarette out. "Martin, I'm frightened. We've never done that before. Not in the car anyway, not like that."

"I know," he said. He still didn't look at her.

She drove slowly and carefully the last ten minutes and neither of them spoke again until they were inside the house, the dogs on the porch. "Why'd you bring them back?" Jeffrey asked disgustedly. He thought that dogs as big as they were should be willing to retrieve, or something.

Martin told them about the colonel and Rose went upstairs to wash her face and hands. Halfway up the stairs she turned and called, "Martin, will you put some coffee on, please." And he answered cheerfully.

It was the dogs, she told herself in the bathroom. They had made the quarrel happen, somehow. She couldn't really remember what they had quarreled about, only that it had been ugly and dangerous. Once when she had glanced at the speedometer, it had registered eighty-five. She shivered thinking of it. It had been the dogs' fault, she knew, without being able to think how they had done it, or why, or what the argument had been about.

Annamarie had made potato salad, and they had ham with it, and baked apples with heavy cream for dessert. Throughout dinner Rose was aware of Martin's searching gaze on her, and although she smiled at him, he didn't respond with his own wide grin, but remained watchful and quiet.

After the children went to bed, Martin wanted to talk about it, but she wouldn't. "Not now," she said. "I have to think. I don't know what happened, and I have to think."

"Rose, we can't just leave it at that. You said some things I never had thought of before. I had no idea you felt left out of our decisions. I honestly believed you wanted it like that."

She put her hands over her ears. "Not now! Please, Martin, not now. I have to think."

"And then hit me with it again, that I don't talk things over with you?"

"Shut up! Can't you for the love of God just shut up?"

He stared at her and she took a deep breath, but didn't soften it at all. "Sure," he said. "For now."

That night she finally fell asleep breathing in time to the clicking of the dogs' nails on the porch floor. She dreamed. She floated downstairs with a long pale silk negligee drifting around her, like a bride of Dracula. She could see herself, a faint smile on her lips, her hair long and loose. It didn't look very much like her, but that was unimportant. The air was pleasantly cool on her skin, and she glided across the yard, beckoning to her dogs to come. There was a moon that turned everything into white and black and gray and the world now was not the same one that she had known before. Her horse was waiting for her and she floated up to mount it. Then they were flying across the fields, she on the horse, the dogs at one side. They were painfully beautiful running, their silver hair blowing; stretched out they seemed not to touch the ground at all. They looked like silver light flowing above the ground. Her horse ran easily, silently, and there was no sound at all in this new world. The field gave way to the forest, where the light from the moon came down in silver shafts, aslant and gleaming. The dogs disappeared in the shadows, appeared, dazzling bright in the moonlight, only to vanish again. They ran and ran, without a sound and she had no fear of hitting anything. Her horse knew its way. They reached the end of the motionless woods, and there was a meadow sprinkled with spiderwebs that were like fine lace glistening with dew that caught the moonlight like pearls. They slowed down now. Somewhere ahead was the game that they chased. Now the dogs were fearful to her. The golden eyes gleamed and they became hunting machines. First one, then the other sniffed the still air, and then with a flicker of motion they were off again, her horse following, not able to keep up with them. They were on the trail. She saw the deer then, a magnificent buck with wide spread antlers. It saw the dogs and leaped through the air, twenty feet, thirty feet, an impossible leap executed in slow motion. But the dogs had it, and she knew it, and the buck knew it. It ran from necessity; it was the prey, they the hunters, and the ritual forced it to run. She stopped to watch the kill, and this was as silent as the entire hunt had been. The dogs leaped and the deer fell and presently the dogs drew away from it, bloody now, and stood silently watching her.

She woke up. She was shivering as if with fever.

Martin took her to school, and when she got out of the car, he said, "I'll be back before you're through. I'll pick you up." She nodded. The dogs were on the porch when they got home that afternoon.

That night he asked her if she was ready to talk. She looked at him helplessly. "I don't know. I can't think of anything to say."

"How about what's bugging you?"

"The dogs. Nothing else."

"Not the dogs."

"That's all, Martin. They're haunting me."

"Live dogs can't haunt anyone." He picked up his book and began to make notes.

Tuesday he met her after school again. The dogs were on the porch when they got home. She didn't look at them.

On Wednesday Martin had a late class and wouldn't be home until after six. "Will you be all right?" he asked when he dropped her off.

"Yes. Of course."

He reached for her arm, and holding it, looked at her for a moment. He let her go. "Right. See you later."

When she turned into the county road after school the dogs were there waiting for her. She felt dizzy and faint, and stopped, steadying herself with one hand on a tree. She looked back toward the school, a quarter of a mile down the highway. She shook her head. Stupid! Stupid! She started to walk, trying not to look at the golden eyes that watched her. For three nights they had shared a common dream, and she felt suddenly that they knew about it, and that was the link that bound them together. She walked too fast and began to feel winded and hot. It was as quiet on the little road as it was in the fields and woods of her dream. No wind blew, no leaves stirred, even the birds were silent. She picked up a stick, and looked quickly at the dogs, slightly behind her, so that in order to see them she had to turn her head slightly. They trotted silently, watching her.

Each night in the dream she got closer to the deer before the kill, and that night she was afoot, standing close enough to touch it when the dogs leaped. In her hand was a knife, and when the dogs felled the animal, she braced herself to leap also.

"No!" She sat up, throwing off the covers, thrashing about frantically, moaning now. Martin caught her and held her still until she was wide awake.

"Honey, you've got to tell me. Please, Rose. Please."

"I can't," she moaned. "It's gone now. A nightmare."

He didn't believe her, but he held her and stroked her hair and made soothing noises. "I love you," he said over and over. "I love you. I love you."

And finally she relaxed and found that she was weeping. "I love you, Martin," she said, sobbing suddenly. "I do. I really do."

"I know you do," he said. "I'm glad that you know it too."

On Thursday she learned that the teacher she was subbing for was well and would return the following day. Martin picked her up after school and she told him.

"I don't want you to stay home all day with those dogs," he said. "I'll get them in the car somehow and take them to the pound. No one is going to claim them."

She shook her head. "You can't," she said.

"I can try."

But he couldn't. They refused to budge from the porch on Friday morning. Rose watched from inside the house. She hadn't slept at all during the night. She had been afraid to, and she felt dopey and heavy-limbed. All night she had sat up watching television, drinking coffee, eating cheese and apples and cookies, reading. Listening to the clicking nails on the porch.

"I'll stay home, then," Martin said when they both knew that the dogs were not going to go with him. "Or, maybe you could trick them into getting in the car."

But they knew she couldn't. The dogs wouldn't move for her either. He approached them with the idea of trying to carry them, and they both growled, and the hairs on their necks bristled.

"Martin, just go. We'll have all weekend to decide what to do with them. They'll sit out there and I'll stay in here. It's all right. You'll be late."

He kissed her then, and she felt surprise. He never kissed her when he left. Only when they were going to go to bed, or were in bed already. "Stay inside. Promise?"

She nodded and watched him drive away. The dogs looked at her. "What do you want from me?" she demanded, going out to the porch, standing before them. "Just what do you want?" She took a step toward them. *"What do you want?"* She realized that the screaming voice was her own and she stopped. She was very near them now. She could touch them if she reached out. They waited for her to touch them, to stroke them. Suddenly she whirled around and ran back inside the house. They didn't try to get in this time. They knew she would be back.

She went to the kitchen feeling dull and blank and heavy. She poured coffee and sat down at the kitchen table with it, and then put her head down on her arms. Drifting, drifting, the warmth of sleep stealing over her. Suddenly she jumped up, knocking over her coffee. No! She knew she must not sleep, must not dream that dream again. She made more coffee and cleaned up the mess she had made, then washed the dishes. She put clothes in the washer, made the beds, peeled apples to make jelly, and all the time the clicking back and forth went on. She turned on the radio, and found herself listening over the music for the noise of their nails. She turned it off again. At noon she looked at them from Juliette's room. They turned to watch her, stopping in their tracks when she lifted the curtain. The light caught in the gold eyes, making them look as if they were flashing at her. Signals flashing at her. She let the curtain fall and backed away.

Then she went to Martin's study and took down his rifle. She loaded it carefully and walked out the back door, letting it slam behind her. She didn't turn to see if they were coming. She knew they were. At the back of the barn she waited for them. She thought of how beautiful they were running, how silky and fine their hair was, alive and blowing in the wind. They came around the corner of the barn, walking quietly, very sure of her. She raised the rifle, aiming it carefully, as Martin had taught her. The large gold eyes caught the sun and flashed. She shot. The first dog dropped without a whimper. The other one was transfixed. He hadn't believed she would do it. Neither of them had believed her capable of doing it. She aimed again and shot. She was looking into the golden eyes as she pulled the trigger. She saw the light go out in them.

She dropped the rifle and hid her face in her hands. She was shaking violently. Then she vomited repeatedly and after there was nothing left in her, she retched and heaved helplessly. Finally she staggered to the house and washed out her mouth, and washed her face and hands. She didn't look at herself in the mirror.

She put the rifle back and went out to the barn again, this time with a spade. She dug the grave big enough for them both, behind the barn where she could cover it with straw so that it wouldn't show. And when she was ready for them, she stopped. She would have to touch them after all. But the hair was just hair now, the silkiness and aliveness was gone. Just gray hair. She dragged them to the grave and covered them and hid the place with straw.

The children asked about the dogs, and she said they had run off just as mysteriously as they had come. Jeffrey said he was glad, they had been spooky. Juliette said she dreamed of them last night, and she was sorry they were gone. Annamarie didn't comment at all, but ran to the phone to call Jennifer.

Martin didn't believe her story. But he didn't question her. That night she told him. "I killed them."

A tremor passed over him. He nodded. "Are you all right?"

"I'm all right." She looked at him. "You're not surprised or shocked or disgusted? Something?"

"Not now. Maybe later. Now, nothing."

She nodded too. That was how she felt. They didn't talk about it again that night, but sat quietly, with the television off, neither of them reading or doing anything. They went to bed early and held each other hard until they fell asleep.

AUTHOR'S NOTE

We all have different thresholds for humor, for compassion, and for terror. What has one person rolling in helpless laughter often leaves another yawning. One weeps with sympathy and another mutters, "Sentimental tripe." And what pass for tales of terror very often leave me bored. An excess of body parts and blood strikes me as gross, even childish, like junior high school boys trying to outdo each other by adding yet one more gory detail. I grew up with brothers and have sons, and, I'm afraid, creepy-crawlies under the bed are giggle affairs.

But there is terror. When something comes along that strips away humanity from people, that exposes the gloss of civilization as a very thin patina, easily removed, that draws forth reactions atavistic and archetypal from sophisticated moderns—that something can only be called terror.

I have read that people experiencing a severe earthquake react with terror again and again. It is the ultimate betrayal when the earth itself changes the rules. We know and fear the wind when it mounts to hurricane force; we know and fear lightning storms; or blizzards; or a number of natural occurrences. We feel terror when the earth shakes.

We spend years learning the rules of our world, becoming acculturated, fitting into our society, adapting to nature, adapting it to ourselves. We don't expect to have the rules changed without warning. We especially don't expect to be stranded with no new rules to replace those that have been violated.

Can there be terror when there is no overt threat, when there is nothing grotesquely out of the ordinary? I think so. I think we rely on those accepted rules, stated or not, much more than we realize. This story came to my head and stayed exactly the way the hounds came and stayed. I found it disturbing and haunting and finally had to write it. For me, this is a story of terror.

—Kate Wilhelm

ZOMBIQUE
Joseph Payne Brennan

YOU MAY HAVE HEARD OF THE TYLER MARINSONS. He'd made a fortune on "the Street" before he was thirty. Finally he tired of the stock market shuffle, bought a superb country house, with fifty acres, in Barsted, Connecticut, closed his New York office and began leading the life of a country gentleman.

He still had investments, of course, and he watched them closely, but his market maneuvers became little more than a hobby. If all of his remaining stock investments had been wiped out, it wouldn't have mattered much. He had enough real estate, municipal bonds, notes, trust funds, cash and personal property to survive almost anything except revolution or a nuclear attack.

He stayed on several boards of directors to "keep a hand in," as he expressed it.

His wife, Maria, was delighted with her new life. She'd hated New York and she loved the country. For nearly a year the Marinsons lived almost like recluses. They seldom entertained; they went to New York only twice in ten months.

At length, however, Maria felt that her husband was getting restless. She began having house parties and frequent weekend guests. Tyler, off the tight-rope of tension which he had walked in New York, slipped easily into the new scheme of things. The Marinson house parties became "musts" and Tyler himself turned into something of a raconteur.

They were a handsome couple, mid-thirties and childless but not a bit maladjusted. Tyler, tall and dark with fine chiseled features; Maria, small and blond with the kind of arresting blue eyes that look unreal.

They met Kemley through the Paulmanns. Kemley had made it in oils. He spent most of his time poking around the Caribbean. He became the Marinsons' "pet." He was a bachelor nearing fifty and Maria, with a persistence which amused him, kept steering various women friends—widows mostly—in his direction. It became a standing joke between them. Kemley adored her and respected Tyler. He never returned from one of his jaunts without bringing back some souvenir for the two of them.

It wasn't easy. You don't buy typical tourist baubles for people like the Marinsons. Kemley concentrated on curios which, while not always expensive, were hard to get. Tyler appreciated them and Maria always received them with the wide-eyed enthusiasm of a child.

It was one of Kemley's curio gifts which precipitated the business. Or maybe it was all coincidence. You'll have to judge for yourself.

Shortly after a trip to Haiti, Kemley brought the Marinsons a Haitian voodoo doll. About four inches high, it was carved out of hard native wood, tufted with feathers and mounted on a thick wooden base. Branching from each side of it were narrow metal rods ending in carved wooden cylinders which resembled drums. The figure was so attached to the base that when you gave one of the rods or drums a push, the doll would execute a grotesque dance atop the base, twirling, bobbing and swaying as if suddenly animated with a life of its own.

Kemley told the Marinsons that if you wanted to bring bad luck to an enemy, someone you hated, you twirled the doll, spoke its name—*Zombique*—and told it what you wanted.

Tyler was fascinated by it but, for once, Maria's enthusiasm seemed forced. After Kemley had left, she admitted to her husband that she didn't like the figure. She confessed, in fact, that she was afraid of it.

Tyler joshed her about it, twirled the doll, spoke its name and asked that old Harrington's steel stocks drop twenty points.

The next day Harrington's steel stocks moved up two points. Tyler duly brought this to Maria's attention.

She frowned. "You didn't actually fulfill the conditions," she pointed out. "Harrington was never your enemy; you were just rivals. You never *hated* him. And you didn't *really* want his steel to drop twenty points."

Tyler laughed. "Maybe you're right at that. Anyhow it's all a bag of nonsense."

The Haitian doll remained on the mantel and Maria gradually forgot about it.

And then Tyler had a furious row with Jake Seff, owner of the local Atlas Garage. What it amounted to, in brief, was that the Atlas had done a shoddy repair job on Tyler's favorite sports car and then had grossly overcharged him for the inferior work. Jake Seff stubbornly refused to do the work over and just as stubbornly refused to reduce his bill.

Tyler came home swearing like a whole platoon of troopers. Maria tried to placate him, but he sulked and brooded the entire evening.

"But darling," she pleaded as they prepared for bed, "it's only a few hundred dollars!"

Tyler scowled. "That's not the point. I don't like being made a fool of because I have money. I accumulated that money by my wits and it wasn't easy. I took some pretty risks. Seff thinks he can clip me and get away with it. Thinks I'll just shrug it off. Well—I won't!"

The next day he made telephone calls during the morning and left after lunch. He returned in time for cocktails, still furious but more self-contained than on the previous day.

Over drinks he told Maria that he had checked into the financial status of the Atlas Garage. Jake Seff, he revealed, was nearing the brink of bankruptcy. He was so desperate for cash he had even allowed his insurance on the garage to lapse.

Tyler refilled his glass. "He's not only unscrupulous—he's plain stupid. That insurance should get priority over everything. He wouldn't get a dime if the garage burned down; he'd be finished."

Maria tried to change the subject, but Tyler wasn't listening. He paced around the room. By chance he stopped near the mantel, feet away from Kemley's Haitian voodoo doll.

He set down his glass. "By God, I'm going to try it!"

Maria came over. "Tyler! That's childish!"

He ignored her. Flicking a finger against one of the drums, he triggered the feathered doll into its twirling, bobbing dance.

"Zombique!" he commanded. "Burn down Jackie Seff's Atlas Garage!"

Maria sighed and sat down. "Tyler, I don't *like* this. You shouldn't hate anyone like that. Let's get rid of that horrid thing!"

Tyler picked up his glass. "What? Get rid of it? Old Kemley would never forgive us. He looks to see if it's still on the mantelpiece every time he comes."

The next morning when Maria came down to breakfast, Tyler was already reading an area newspaper as he sipped his orange juice.

Pointing to a brief paragraph, he handed her the paper without a word.

She read the caption—*Seff's Garage Burns; Total Ruin*—and turned white.

"Tyler! You didn't—?"

"What? Set fire to Seff's junkyard garage? Don't be a silly goose! And that doll had nothing to do with it either. It's all just a crazy coincidence."

Ignoring her orange juice, Maria poured a cup of coffee. She sipped it black. "Tyler, please take that voodoo thing out of the house and burn it—or throw it in the woods."

Tyler looked across at her. "You're talking like a ten-year-old. These things happen once in a while. Pity you can't see the humor in it. We could both have a good laugh."

Maria shook her head. "Somebody's bankruptcy is nothing to laugh about—even if he is dishonest. And now I'm *really* afraid of that nasty little puppet."

Tyler finished his coffee and stood up. "Well, I think I'll take a spin to the village. Need a few things from Carson's store."

Maria watched as he slipped on his coat. "You just want to drive past Seff's and look at the smoking ruins!" she commented with a vehemence which surprised him.

He shrugged and went out the door.

The voodoo doll remained on the mantel shelf but it was weeks before Maria appeared to throw off her uneasiness concerning it. On several occasions Tyler almost yielded to an impulse to destroy the doll, but each time, a certain implacable element in his nature, grounded, it seemed, in the very bedrock of his being, asserted itself. The Haitian doll stayed on the mantel.

And then Tyler got arrested by Sergeant Skepley. Maria was home, bedded down with the flu, and Tyler had to make one of his infrequent trips to New York. The directors' meeting was late; it was already dusk by the time he reached the parkway.

He traveled well over the limit all the way up to Hartford and nobody bothered him. He slowed down for the cutoff but by the time he reached the outskirts of Barsted he was way over the posted limit again. The roads in Barsted were narrow and winding. You were reasonably safe at thirty-five, but definitely not at fifty-five.

Tyler was fretting about Maria and inwardly cursing Templeton, whose long, tedious spiel had held up the directors' meeting, when he saw the flashing red lights in his rearview mirror.

Momentarily he pressed the accelerator a bit farther toward the floor. He thought better of it, however, slowed up and finally braked to a stop.

The police car pulled up behind him, red signal lights still flashing. He had his license and registration cards ready by the time the sergeant came abreast of his own car window.

As the sergeant studied the documents, he studied the sergeant. Young. Officious-looking. Already a sergeant. No sense telling him he had a sick wife at home alone.

The sergeant pulled a printed form out of his pocket. "I'm placing charges, Mr. Marinson, for reckless driving, for exceeding the speed limit and for attempting to evade arrest."

Marinson felt the blood rush to his face. "Now wait a minute! Maybe I was over the limit, but you can't throw the whole book at me! What's this about evading?"

The sergeant's humorless eyes stared back at him. "When you first noticed my lights, Mr. Marinson, you hit your gas pedal. That's 'attempting to evade.'"

He turned toward the patrol car.

"I'll need about ten minutes to fill out this arrest form, Mr. Marinson."

Marinson sat waiting, flushed with rage. Twenty minutes passed before the sergeant returned with the completed form.

He started to explain something about circuit court in Meriden but Marinson snatched the form out of his hand, threw it on the car seat and turned the ignition key.

"It's on the form, isn't it?" he asked furiously. "I can read!"

When he got around the next curve in the road, he experienced an impulse to press the gas pedal down to the floor. He glanced in the rearview mirror. The sergeant's prowl car was already coming around the curve.

When he reached home, he was trembling with fury. He drove into the garage and sat for a few minutes before going inside.

Maria said she felt better but she hadn't eaten and she still looked feverish. He wanted to call Dr. Clane again but she shook her head.

"I called him this afternoon. He said to go on with the medication, stay in bed and drink a lot of fluids. He said it runs its course and I'll be better in a few days."

Tyler sat with her for an hour before going down to get an improvised dinner snack. He had told her about the tedious directors' meeting but not about his arrest.

The kitchen looked uninviting. He decided he wasn't hungry and went into the living room. Pouring a stiff scotch and soda, he took out the arrest form.

The form indicated that he had to appear in circuit court in Meriden on a specified date, unless he chose to plead not guilty. In that case, he had to so notify the court and he would be informed of a subsequent date for appearance.

The arresting officer was a Sergeant Skepley.

Swearing, he threw down the form. He was well known in the town. Any other member of the force, he told himself, would have given him a simple warning or, at worst, a summons which could be mailed in with a nominal fine. Skepley, he remembered, had a reputation for toughness. Recalling the sergeant's steady, somewhat bulging eyes and compressed lips, Marinson concluded that he was not merely tough but actually sadistic.

After another drink, he decided to fight the case. He'd call Boatner's law firm tomorrow morning. They had a branch in nearby Hartford. He knew young Millward who was in charge of it. Millward would get him off the hook if anybody could.

He felt better after the third drink. He poured a fourth, sprawling back in his chair with a sigh of relative contentment. As he glanced toward the mantel, he noticed the Haitian doll.

He set down his drink and crossed the room.

Flicking his forefinger against one of the wooden drums attached to the figure, he triggered the feathered doll into motion. Bobbing, nodding and swaying, it performed a macabre little dance.

"Zombique," he commanded, "make Sergeant Skepley drop dead!"

"Dead, dead, dead!" he repeated as the dance slowed and the puppet came to rest.

Returning to his chair, he decided to finish off the bottle of scotch.

He woke up with a nagging hangover the next morning. Maria was fretful and feverish and didn't want to eat.

He telephoned Boatner's law office in Hartford before ten o'clock. Millward hadn't arrived yet. He left no message but said he'd call back.

He tried again shortly before eleven. Millward had arrived but was in conference and couldn't be disturbed. Did he want to leave a message? Muttering, he hung up.

After pacing the floor for a few minutes, he went up to see Maria.

She was reading in bed and seemed somewhat better. He told her he had to talk to Millward but hadn't been able to reach him by telephone.

Maria laid down her book. "Tyler, you're so restless, you're making me nervous! Why don't you just drive into Hartford and see Millward?"

When he murmured something about leaving her alone, she scoffed. "The phone's next to my bed and anyway, I'm better. You've been wound up tight ever since that directors' meeting. You don't need to fuss over me. Go and talk to Millward. Something's making you positively jumpy!"

Picking up her book, she waved a mock good-bye.

He kissed her and grinned. "If I were a doctor, you'd be my favorite patient! All right. I'll see you later then."

He drove to Hartford, taking his time down Farmington Avenue. When he arrived at Boatner's, Millward had already left for lunch. He went out for a cocktail and a sandwich and came back an hour later.

This time Millward was in. Tyler told his story, getting angry all over again.

Millward sat back, put his fingertips together and pushed up his glasses. Marinson observed that he was beginning to get paunchy.

Millward's smile held a tinge of deprecation. "Things aren't the way they used to be, Tyler. At least not here in Connecticut. To quash something like this is almost impossible. The best we can do is get some delays and stall for the right judge. With luck, you'll hang on to your license. This Skepley must have a reputation and you did have a sick wife at home. We'll see what we can do."

Marinson thanked him and stood up. He felt a keen sense of disappointment. A few years ago, in New York, Millward would have taken the ticket

and torn it up in front of him. Then there'd be a
slap on the back and a drink from Millward's
private flask.

He started homeward in a thoughtful mood,
vaguely troubled and apprehensive. His money and
presence, he reflected, no longer seemed to matter
as much as formerly.

He drove through the small center of Barsted,
noticing that it appeared nearly deserted.

As he swung into Postgate Road, which led to his
house, an ambulance pulled into view. It wasn't
going very fast and the siren wasn't on. He stared
into it as it passed. A figure lay in the back, covered
with a blanket.

He stopped, hesitated and very nearly backed
around to follow the ambulance. He changed his
mind and drove on, feeling his stomach constrict.
Postgate Road lay in a relatively isolated area.
There were only two houses besides his own on the
entire length of it.

Ten minutes later he topped the rise which led to
his house and the bottom fell out of his world.

There was no house—only a smoking sprawl of
blackened timbers, brick chimneys and collapsed
pipes, sagging crazily in every direction.

He managed to stop the car.

As he sat transfixed, a man in a corduroy suit
came over. It was someone he recognized but he
couldn't recall who it was.

"Take it easy, Mr. Marinson. We did all we
could. I'm sorry, awful sorry."

Staring around, Marinson saw the Barsted Vol-
unteer Fire Company trucks, police cars and at
least a dozen civilian cars. His lawn, he decided,
would be a frightful mess.

Abruptly, he started the car. "I'm going after my wife," he said. "She was in that ambulance."

People were hovering around the car. A hand closed on his wrist.

Someone stood there, looking mournful, shaking his head.

"Your wife wasn't in the ambulance, Mr. Marinson."

He got out of the car, suddenly furious. "What *is* this? Of course it was my wife. What are you telling—?"

He stopped and stared toward the smoking ruins of his house. His eyes sought the others' eyes. Not a single pair of them would meet his own.

A sob shook him. He ran toward the twisted, blackened debris. "Maria!"

Someone put an arm around his shoulder. He looked up dully and turned away, then stopped, puzzled. "My wife's body . . . You say— Who was in the ambulance?"

A familiar voice replied. "That was Sergeant Skepley in the ambulance. He's dead. He came by here on patrol, far as we can figure out, saw the place on fire and ran to see if anyone was inside. He never made it. He dropped dead halfway between his car and the house. Heart attack, we think. Massive. Shortly after, I guess, the Confords saw flames shooting over the trees and called the fire volunteers. They got here in record time but too late. Your wife must have been overcome with smoke. She never—got out."

Marinson stumbled toward the ruins. He stopped, staring.

The living room's brick chimney and its attached marble mantel were still standing.

Although its feathers had been burned off, the Haitian doll remained on the mantel shelf. The fine-grained wood from which it was carved had somehow survived the sudden inferno of flames.

A wind had risen, buffeting against the miniature drums fastened to the tiny figure.

Bobbing, swaying and bowing, it executed a bizarre little dance of death.

AUTHOR'S NOTE

When I was asked to submit a story for *Masters of Darkness II*, three immediately came to mind: "Canavan's Back Yard," "Levitation" and "Slime." Stephen King wrote that he considered "Canavan's Back Yard" "one of the dozen best stories of the macabre ever written by an American." All three stories have demonstrated enduring popularity—but all three have been anthologized time and again. I decided that readers of a new anthology deserved a different story. I chose "Zombique" which, to my knowledge at least, was included in an anthology only once, and that over ten years ago.

I think "Zombique" is one of my best stories. I don't know which is my *very best* story. How can such a thing be determined? Some readers would vote for "Canavan's Back Yard," others for "Slime," "Levitation," "The Horror at Chilton Castle," "Zombique," etc. There are several hundred to choose from.

Footnote on "Zombique": The story possesses an element of fact. A friend of ours actually gave us the Haitian figure described in the story. My wife, Doris, hates it. She is firmly convinced it has brought us nothing but bad luck. She wants it tossed in the trash. I would consider this a rash act. If the doll were subjected to such ignominy and it *does* possess strange powers—what terrible revenge might it not wreak?

I am unwilling to find out. . . .

—Joseph Payne Brennan

TAKING THE NIGHT TRAIN
Thomas F. Monteleone

IT WAS AFTER 3:00 A.M. WHEN RALPHIE LOGGINS scuttled down the stairs, into the cold sterility of his special world.

Holding the railing carefully so that he would not slip, as the November night wind chased him, he entered the Times Square subway station. Ralphie always had to be watchful on steps because the elevated heel on his left shoe was constantly trying to trip him up. He fished a token from the pocket of his Navy pea jacket and dropped it into the turnstile, passing through and easing his way down the last set of stairs to the platform.

Ralphie walked with his special clump-click-slide to a supporting girder by the tracks and waited for the Broadway–Seventh Avenue local, noticing that he was not alone on the platform. There were few travelers on the subways in the middle of such winter nights, and he could feel the fear and paranoia hanging thickly in the air. Turning his head slowly to the left, Ralphie saw a short, gray man at the far end of the station. He wore a tattered, thin corduroy jacket insulated with crumpled sheets of the *Daily News*.

To Ralphie's right, he heard footsteps approaching.

Just as he turned to look, he felt something sharp threatening to penetrate his coat and ultimately his kidneys. At the limits of his peripheral vision he was aware of someone tall and dark-skinned looming over him, the stranger's breath heavy and warm on his neck.

"Okay, suckah!" came a harsh whisper, the words stinging Ralphie's ear. "You move and you *dead*! Dig?"

Ralphie nodded, relaxing inwardly since he knew what would come next. When he did not move, the man pressed his knife blade a little more firmly into the fabric of the coat, held it there.

"Now, real easy like . . . get out your bread, and give it up. . . ."

Ralphie slipped his left hand into his back pocket, pulling out his wallet, and passed it back over his shoulder to the mugger. It was snatched away and rifled cleanly and quickly. The tip of the blade retreated, as did the tall, dark presence of the thief. His footsteps described his flight from the station, and Ralphie was alone again. He looked to the end of the platform where the gray old man still stood in a senile, shivering daze.

A growing sense of loss and anger swelled in Ralphie. He felt violated, defiled, *hurt* in some deeply psychic manner. The mugger had reinforced his views of life in the city and all the dead hours within it. A silence pervaded the station, punctuated by a special kind of sadness and futility. Stifling his anger and his pain, Ralphie smiled ironically—it was most fitting that he be robbed in the subway, he thought.

Time seemed to lose its way beneath the streets of Manhattan, flowing at a rate completely its own, and it seemed to Ralphie that there might be a reason for it. He felt that there was something essentially *wrong* about the subways. As though man had somehow violated the earth by cutting these filthy pathways through her, and that the earth had reacted violently to it. Ralphie believed this, because there was a feeling of evil, of fear, and of something lurking beneath the depths of the city that *everyone* felt in the subways. Ralphie knew that others had sensed it, felt it, as they descended into the cold, tomblike stations.

His thoughts were shattered by the approaching roar of the train. A gust of warmer air was pushed into the station as the local surged out of the tunnel, jerked to a halt, opened its doors. The old man shuffled into a distant car; Ralphie entered the one closest to him. As he sat on the smooth plastic seat, the doors sighed shut, and the train rattled off into the darkness, under the belly of the beast, the city. The only other passenger in Ralphie's car, an old woman in a ragged coat, a pair of stuffed shopping bags by her high-topped shoes, looked at him with yellow eyes. Her face was a roadmap of wrinkles, her lips so chapped and cracked they looked orange and festering.

Ralphie kept watching the old woman, wondering the usual thoughts about members of her legion. Where did she live? What did she carry in those mysterious bags? Where did she come from? Why was she out riding the night trains? The rocking motion of the cars was semi-hypnotic, soothing, and Ralphie felt himself unwinding from the tension of the robbery. He allowed himself to smile, knowing that the mugger had gotten nothing of value—his left pants pocket still held his money clip and bills, whereas the wallet had contained only some pictures, business cards, and his library card. He had not been counting the local's stops, but he had been riding the train for so many years that he had an instinctive feeling for when his station would be coming up. It was not until the train reached Christopher Street–Sheridan Square that Ralphie began staring through the dirty glass into the hurtling darkness. Houston Street would be next.

Then it happened.

The lights in the car flickered and the motion of the car slowed. The old shopping-bag lady seemed to be as still as a statue, and even the sound of the wheels clattering on the tracks seemed softer, *slower*. The warm air in the car became thicker, heavier, and Ralphie felt it was becoming difficult to breathe. He stood up, and it felt as if he were underwater, as though something were restraining him. Something was *wrong*. The train seemed to be slowing down, and he looked out the windows, past the reflection of the interior lights, to see something for the briefest of moments—a platform, a station with no sign, no passengers, only a single overhead bulb illuminating the cold beige tiles of its walls.

For a second, Ralphie imagined the train was trying to stop at the strange station, or that something was trying to stop the train. There was a confluence of forces at work, and time itself had seemed to slow, and stretch, while the train struggled past the place. Then it was gone, replaced by the darkness, and the train was gathering speed, regaining its place in the time flow.

The air thinned out, the old lady moved her head, gripped her bags more tightly, and Ralphie could move without interference. The train was loud and full of energy once again. Ralphie felt a shudder pass through him. It was as though something back there had been reaching out, grasping for the train, and just barely failing. The image persisted and he could not stop thinking about it. He knew that the image of the stark, pale platform and the single naked bulb would prey upon him like a bad dream. He knew he had passed a place that no one ever saw, that no one even knew existed; yet he had *seen* it, felt its power. . . .

The local lurched to a halt, its doors slamming open. Ralphie looked up and saw the Houston Street sign embedded in the wall tiles. Jumping from the car, he hobbled across the deserted platform, wedged through the turnstile, and pulled himself up the steps. The cold darkness of the street embraced him as he reached the sidewalk, and he pulled his collar tightly about his neck. The street was littered with the remnants of people's lives as he threaded his way past the overturned trash cans, discarded toys, heaps of eviction furniture, stripped cars, and empty wine bottles. This was the shabby reality of his neighborhood, the empty shell that surrounded his life. He walked to the next corner, turned left, and came to a cellarway beneath a shoe repair shop. Hobbling down the steps, he took out his key and unlocked the door to his one-room apartment. He flipped on the light switch and a single lamp illuminated the gray, tired room. Ralphie hated the place, but knew that he would never escape its prison-cell confines. Throwing his coat over a straight-backed chair, he walked to a small sink and medicine chest, which had been wedged into the corner of the room. His hands were trembling as he washed warm water over them, chasing the stinging cold from his bones. In the spotted mirror he saw an old face, etched with the lines of defeat and loneliness. Only thirty-one and looking ten years older: his sandy hair was getting gray on the edges, his blue eyes doing the same. He tried to smile ironically, but could not manage it. There was little joy left in him, and he knew it would be better to simply crawl beneath his quilt on the mildewed couch and sleep.

That night he dreamed of subway trains.

It was late in the afternoon before he awakened, feeling oddly unrefreshed. He could not forget the baleful image of the empty station, and he decided that he would have to investigate the place. When he took a train up to midtown, he asked the trainman about it. The IRT employee said he had never heard of that particular platform, but that there were countless places like that beneath the city: maintenance bays, abandoned stations, old tunnels that had been sealed off. Somebody must have left a light on, that's why Ralphie had seen it at all. The trainman seemed unimpressed, but Ralphie had not told him how he had felt something reaching out from that place, trying to take hold of the train. . . .

After having coffee in a small shop off Fifty-second Street, Ralphie walked the streets aimlessly. He knew that he should go to the public library and get a new card, but he felt too restless today. His mind was too agitated to read, even though it was one of his only pleasures. When he had been a

child, living with his uncle, the old man had taught
him the wonders of books, and Ralphie had educated himself in his uncle's library. When the old
man died without a will or an heir, Ralphie was
turned out on the street, a victim of New York State
Probate Court at the age of seventeen, with nothing. A string of odd jobs leading nowhere, com-
bined with his crippled leg, had beaten him down
until he didn't seem to care anymore. He identified
with the desperation of characters from Dostoevski
and Gogol, the self-inflicted terror and pain of
characters from Hawthorne and Poe. The world
had been different when those writers had lived, he
often thought, and people knew how to *feel*, and
think, and *care*. In the city, Ralphie wondered if
people even cared about themselves anymore.

Evening crept into the streets, and Ralphie
worked his way toward Times Square, watching the
faces of those he passed on the crowded sidewalks.
Some said that it was an unwritten law that you did
not look at anyone you passed in the city, but
Ralphie knew that was untrue. *Everyone* looked at
everyone else. Only they did it furtively, secretly,
stealing glances at one another like thieves. They
walked behind masks of indifference, like Gogol's
"dead souls," playing the parts assigned them in
the mindless dollhouse of the city. It was like a
disease, thought Ralphie, which had infected us all.

Down Broadway, he turned left at Forty-second
Street, already ablaze with the flashing lights and
colors of the theaters and porn shops. The crowds
of tourists and theatergoers mingled with the pan-
handlers, the hustlers, and the legions of blacks and
Puerto Ricans carrying suitcase-sized radios at full
volume. Dealers hung in doorways or strutted and

leered at passersby. The sidewalks were speckled with trash and dark wet patches that could be any number of things. In the middle of the block, Ralphie entered the glass, satin-lined doors of the Honey Pot, to be swallowed up in the sweaty darkness and loud music of the bar. The lyrics of a song pounded at him, and he listened to the words without wanting to:

> *I want to grab your thighs . . .*
> *I want to hear your sighs . . .*
> *M-m-m-make luuuuuv to you! . . .*

Ralphie shook his head sadly to himself, took off his coat, and walked past the bar, which was already half-filled with patrons. Behind the bar was a light-studded runway, backed by a floor-to-ceiling mirror, where the girls could watch themselves while they danced. Brandy was strutting back and forth across the runway, wearing only a pair of spike heels and a silver-sequined G-string. She was short and lithe, with stringy dark hair, boyish hips, and pendulous, stretch-marked breasts that seemed absurdly large for her small frame. She half walked, half pranced to the beat of the music, causing her breasts to bounce and loll in what to Ralphie was a most unerotic manner. Once in a while she would smile at the patrons, or lick her lips and pout, but it was an empty, hollow gesture. Ralphie had seen all the girls pretending to like the customers and he hated the whole game, hated that they were trapped in it, as was he. Empty exchanges, devalued emotions, flensed of meaning and feeling.

When he reached the end of the bar, his boss, Mr.

Maurice, spotted him. "Hey, Ralphie boy! You're early tonight.... ."

"Hello, Mr. Maurice. You want me to start anyway?"

Maurice, a broad-shouldered, overweight, and balding man, smiled and shook his head. "Naw, there ain't nothin' out there yet. Go on in the back and get a coffee. I'll call ya when I need ya."

He dismissed Ralphie with a turn of the head, resuming his conversation with one of the new dancers, who was sitting on a barstool by her boss, clothed only in a bra and panties.

"Okay," said Ralphie, walking into the darkness beyond the bar, and through a door to the girls' "dressing" rooms, to a small alcove where a coffee maker and Styrofoam cups could be found. As he poured the black liquid into his cup, someone entered behind him. Turning, he saw it was Brandy, completely nude, going to the dressing room.

"Hi, Brandy. . . . How are you?"

The girl looked at him and smiled, but said nothing, then disappeared behind the door. She treated him as all the girls did—like a mascot or a pet dog. Funny, he thought, but he had never grown accustomed to the way people treated him. Just because he was a short, dough-faced cripple didn't mean that he had less of a need for warmth and a little caring. . . . Ralphie shook his head slowly, embarrassed that he could indulge so easily in self-pity. He walked from the back room to one of the vacant tables farthest away from the bar, sat down, and sipped his coffee. A half hour passed under the haze of cigarette smoke and the sheets of loud music as Ralphie ignored the laughter and the whistles from the bar patrons. His thoughts kept returning to the Broadway local, and that abandoned station—there was something about the place that would not leave him. It was as though there were something down there, waiting. Waiting for him, perhaps. . . . He knew it was a crazy thought, but it felt so strong in him that he could not get rid of the idea. He had *felt* something, damn it, and he had to know what it had been.

Maurice appeared by his shoulder, slapping him in mock friendliness. "S'after eight . . . ya better get out there and bring in some rubes, huh? Whaddaya say, Ralphie boy?" Another slap on the arm.

"Yeah, okay, Mr. Maurice." He stood up from the table and pulled on his coat, wrapped his scarf about his neck. Ralphie hated his job, but it was by far the best-paying gig he'd ever had. If he didn't need the money so badly, he would have quit long ago.

Walking past the bar, he saw that Chrissie was dancing now. She had long legs which seemed too thin when she wore a dress, but looked all right when she was nude. Her face was long and thin, making her eyes look large and forlorn. She was not what you would call pretty, but she had, as Maurice phrased it, "a big rack," and that was what the guys liked.

He pushed through the glass doors and felt the wind sting his face, the brilliance of the lights cut his eyes. Even in the cold November night, there were thousands of people, mostly men, out looking for warmth—or whatever could be passed off as the same. Ralphie held open the door to the Honey Pot and began his spiel, the words so automatic that he never thought of them anymore: "All right, fellas! No cover, no minimum! Take a peek inside! We got the best show in town! Young girls for *you*! All nude, and that means *na*ked!"

He would pause for a moment, and then repeat his message to the ever-changing surge of topcoated bodies. Sometimes he would stare into the men's faces, especially the ones who listened to his patter, the ones who slipped through the open door with heads bowed as if entering a church. He always saw the same things in their eyes. Our eyes betray us always, he thought, and he saw in their expressions a searching for something, for something lost and becoming unrecognizable. He also saw sadness. Sadness and shame.

On and on, he repeated his litany of the flesh, until the night had whipped past him and the traffic thinned out, the pedestrians disappearing. Maurice came up behind him and tapped his shoulder. "Okay, Ralphie. Nice job, let's pack it in, baby."

He entered the bar, walked past the hunched row of men. They were the hangers-on, the ones who closed the bars, the loneliest of the lonely. This last crowd watched Jessie work through her final number, wearing only a pair of gold-glitter platform heels as she swished her hips and played with her blond pubic hair. She had an attractive face, but it was flawed by her empty-eyed stare, her artlessly constructed smile.

Ralphie sat at the back table after getting a cup of coffee from the back room. As he used its heat to warm his hands before sipping it, more thoughts of the Broadway local ripped through his mind, and he feared that he was becoming obsessed with it. There were whispers and giggles behind him as the girls were emerging from the dressing room, putting on their coats, and preparing to leave. They filed past him, ignoring him as they always did, but this night the gesture seemed to eat at him more than usual. He knew that he should have become accustomed to the treatment, but he never did. The strange thing about it was that for the first time he felt himself disliking them, almost hating them for their lack of compassion, of simple, honest feeling. And that scared him.

Finishing his coffee, he left the bar, not saying good night to anyone, and no one seeming to notice his departure. Out in the Broadway night, fleets of cabs battled for one last fare, and the fringe people of the dark hours huddled in doorways and on street corners. Ralphie descended into the Times Square station, dropped a token through the stile, and held the railing as he went down to the platform. He was thinking that he should quit the Honey Pot, knowing that he had hung on there so long only because it was easier than looking for something better, or even taking courses during the day so that he could be qualified for something with more of a future. But that would mean getting out and interacting with the people of the day, and that might mean more pain and indignation. At least the people of the night considered him almost invisible, and did not actively hurt him. But they *did* hurt him, he thought, only to a lesser degree. To everyone, Ralphie was a loser, a hunched-up, bummy-looking clubfoot. He was one of the semi-human things that inhabited the shadowy parts of all cities, one who did not think or feel, but only slinked and scrabbled and hustled for an empty existence.

He would show them someday how wrong they were, he thought.

A rattling roar filled the station as the local rumbled to a stop. The train was a sooty, speckled nightmare covered with spray-paint graffiti—an old, dying beast. Its doors opened and Ralphie stepped inside, moving to a hideously colored turquoise seat. The air in the car was heavy with the smell of cheap wine and vomit, but the only other passenger, a dozing, fur-coated pimp in a droopy-brimmed hat, did not seem to notice. Ralphie took a seat near the doors and stared at his reflection in the smeared glass window across the aisle.

Penn Station. Twenty-eighth Street. Twenty-third. The night train hurtled down the tunnel, and Ralphie felt his pulse quickening. Would it happen again? Would he see that station with no name? The questions dominated his thoughts. Eighteenth Street. Then Fourteenth. Sheridan Square was next, and the train seemed to be going slower already. He hoped that it was not just his imagination.

When the train stopped at the Square, several passengers boarded. Two were teenaged girls wearing almost identical suede jackets with fur collars and Calvin Klein jeans with butterflies embroidered down the legs. Rich girls out slumming, thought Ralphie, as one of them looked into his eyes and smiled. He felt something stir in his heart, and smiled back at the pretty young girl.

"You're kind of cute," said the girl. "Come here often?"

Ralphie couldn't believe what she said. He could only stare for a moment. "What?" he asked dumbly.

The girl giggled and nudged her friend, who looked at Ralphie, then whispered loudly to the first girl, "Hey, watch it, you're getting Quasimodo excited!"

They both laughed, and Ralphie looked away, feeling something shatter inside, breaking and turning to dust. The train was moving again, and he wanted to ask them why they had acted that way, but his thoughts were racing ahead as he sensed the train approaching that secret place once again. There was something new smoldering in his heart; it was a new feeling, still unrecognized. He looked past the reflections in the glass into the rumbling darkness, and suddenly it was happening again.

He felt a *slowness* come over him, and he looked to the other passengers, the pimp and the two girls. Why didn't *they* feel it too!? He could feel the train itself struggling to get past that place, that station with no name. Watching and waiting, Ralphie sensed something tugging at the fibers of time itself. There came a flicker of light beyond the car and, for an instant, an illuminated rectangle. The image burned into his mind: the single bulb, the cold yellow tiles, the empty platform.

And then it was gone.

The train seemed to be regaining its speed, the sound of the girls giggling and the wheels clacking. How could they not have *seen* it? *Felt* it? He stood up, grabbing the center pole as his vision fogged for a moment, and he fought the sensation that he was going to black out. He swayed drunkenly, fighting it, still looking out the windows. Then the train was jerking to a halt, its doors opening at Houston Street.

Forcing his legs to move, Ralphie limped from the car and stood on the concrete platform, rubbing his forehead. The vertigo had passed and the cooler air of the station seemed to help. The doors whooshed shut, and the local clattered from the station, leaving him alone, staring down the black shaft from which he had just come. It was so close, he thought. It could not be far from where he now stood. . . .

There would be no trains for fifteen minutes. He had the time. He was alone in the station, and no one saw him ease off the platform and slip down to the tracks. The electrified rail was across the road-bed and he could easily avoid it, but ahead of him the black tunnel hung open like a mouth waiting to devour him. Driven by the need to find the abandoned station, he walked forward into the darkness, trying not to think of what it would be like if a train rushed him ahead of schedule.

The tracks curved to the left and soon the lights from the Houston Street station were completely obscured and Ralphie was moving in total darkness. There was not even the dim eye of a signal semaphore to give him direction, and he felt his stomach tightening as he moved clumsily, keeping his left hand in touch with the cold, slightly moist, slightly slimy wall of the tunnel. He lost all sense of time, becoming engrossed with the darkness, the uneven roadbed, and the dead touch of the wall. He felt more terribly alone than he had in his entire life, and he knew in his gut that he was walking to a place where no man had ever walked before.

Something was taking shape ahead of him, rimmed by faint light: he saw that it was the outline of a support girder along the wall. Another came into view, and then another. With each step the light grew stronger, and he could see the shine of the rails ahead of him. The wall curved to the left again, and he was upon the place: a rectangle of light suspended in the darkness. It looked unreal, like a stage devoid of props and actors.

He pressed forward and pulled himself up over the edge of the platform, instantly aware of a *coldness* about the place which transcended temperature. It was a chilling sense of timelessness that touched his mind rather than his flesh. Looking about, Ralphie saw that the platform was not deep, nor were there any exit stairs. Only a seamless wall of cold tiles trailing off into the shadows beyond the perimeters of light from the solitary bulb.

He knew that it was into the shadows he must walk, and as he did so, he became more acutely aware of the silence of the place. The mechanical clop of his elevated heel seemed so loud, so obscenely loud. He should have felt fear in this place, but it was replaced by a stronger emotion, a *need* to know this place for whatever it was. Then there was something touching his face. Out of the shadows it languished and played about his cheek like fog. It became a cold, heavy mist that swirled and churned with a glowing energy of its own, and it became brighter the deeper he probed it. He could sense a barrier ahead of him, but not anything that would stop him, but rather a portal through which he must pass.

He stepped forward . . .

. . . to find himself standing upon a narrow,

rocky ledge, which wound across the sheer face of a
great cavern. Above him, like the vault of a cathe-
dral, the ceiling arched, defined by the phosphores-
cent glow of mineral veins. To his right a sheer cliff
dropped off into utter darkness; to his left was a
perfectly vertical wall. Ralphie followed the narrow
winding path, each step bringing him closer to an
eerie sound. At first it was like a gently rising wind,
whispering, then murmuring, finally screaming
through the cavern. An uncontrollable, eternal
wailing.

Ralphie recognized the sound—it was the sound
of utter loneliness. It was a sound made by something totally alien, and simultaneously all too
human. It was a sound that, until now, he had
heard only in the depths of his own mind. Such a
primal, basic sound. . . . He became entranced by
it, moving closer to its source, until he saw the
thing.

The ledge had widened ahead of him, becoming
a ridge that sloped gently upward to another sheer
cliff face. Affixed to the face of the cliff, upon a
jagged outcropping of rock, by great shining chains
was the thing. Even from a distance it looked
monstrously huge. Its arms and legs gave it a
vaguely human form, but its true shape was amorphous, indistinct. There was a shimmering, almost
slimy aspect to its body as it writhed and strained
against the chains that bound it to the rock.

Moving closer, Ralphie now saw a bird thing
perched upon a piece of the jagged rock, balancing
and swaying, and batting the air with its leathery
wings. It was skeletal, reptilian, its head hideously
out of proportion to its thin body. All curved beak
and yellow, moon-pool eyes.

The creature paid no attention to Ralphie's approach, continuing with its task in dead earnest —savagely tearing out the chained one's entrails. With each rooting thrust of the bird's beak, Ralphie heard the wailing fill the chamber louder than the last. One foul creature feeding upon the other. Ralphie watched the nightmare for a moment and knew it for what it was.

The thing on the rock must have perceived Ralphie's recognition, for it turned away from the cause of its agony long enough to look down at Ralphie with fierce white eyes. It regarded him with a coldness, a calmness, which seemed to say: *So you have come at last. . . .*

Ralphie looked into its eyes, human and yet inhuman, seeing the eons of suffering, millennia of pain and loneliness. And deep within the eyes he could also see the disillusionment, the brooding coals of hate and retribution waiting to be unleashed.

There was a sensation of betrayal which radiated from those monstrous eyes, and Ralphie could feel a bond with the tortured figure on the rock. Watching it, Ralphie saw it change. Less amorphous now, a head and face appeared vaguely. The emotions in its eyes seemed to alter.

When the bird swung its beak savagely into the thing's middle once again, it flinched, but there was no sound of pain this time, no agony in its eyes, which remained fixed upon Ralphie, as though speaking to him.

Set me free, said its eyes. *And I shall right the wrongs.*

Ralphie understood, nodding, almost smiling. Slowly he approached the bird on its perch, seeing that it was almost equal in size to him and could tear him to ribbons with razorlike talons. A man would normally fear this thing from the myth time, but Ralphie was beyond fear now. He had peered into the eyes of the thing on the rock, sharing the greatest pain, the hate, and the betrayal. Ralphie could feel these things pulsing out of the creature, especially the hate, which had been bubbling like lava for untold ages. It raged to be free upon the world that had twisted its gift, forgotten its sacrifice. It reached out and touched Ralphie, suffusing him with strength, and he stepped closer to the bird, his left foot sliding upon the cavern floor.

Hearing the sound, the bird paused, turning its skullish head, cocking it to the side, to regard the odd little creature that stood below it. As it watched, Ralphie bent to pick up a fist-sized rock. In one motion he stood and hurled it at its head, striking one of its great yellow eyes, puncturing it like the delicate yolk of an egg. The bird screamed as its empty socket oozed, then launched itself upward with a furious beating of its thick wings. It shrieked as it hovered for a moment above Ralphie, then it rose up into the darkness, leaving only the echo of its wings smacking the dead air.

Once again, Ralphie looked up to the figure on the rock, transfixed by its ravaged entrails and the stains on the stone below, where the excess of its torture had dripped for millennia. Stepping forward, he touched one of the chains; it was hot to his touch. There was a large pin holding the chain to a hasp cut into the rock, and Ralphie pulled upon it. He could hear a chinking sound as the chain fell free, and the great thing with the eyes that spoke to him surged against the remaining bonds. Its wailing had ceased, replaced by a gathering vortex of excitement and power. The sensation grew like an approaching storm, filling the cavern with a terrible static charge.

Ralphie reached up and loosed another pin; the chain fell away from the harnessed body as it moved against the last two restraints. It gave out a great cry—a cry born of eons of humiliation and defeat, but now almost free. The cavern walls shook from the power of the cry and the remaining chains exploded in a shower of metallic fragments. Ralphie backed away, for the first time awed by the power he had unleashed, seeing that its face had changed into something dark and nameless. For an instant, the thing's eyes touched him, and he felt immediately cold. Then there was an eruption of light and a clap of thunder. Ralphie fell backward as the great thing leaped from its prison rock, past him, and toward the exit from the depths.

Darkness and cold settled over Ralphie as he lay in the emptiness of the cavern. He knew where the thing would be going, and he knew what terrible lessons it would wreak upon the world, what payments would be exacted upon the dead souls. All the centuries of twisted vision would soon be put aright. His thoughts were coming slower and his limbs were becoming numb as he surrendered to the chilling darkness. He knew that he was going to fall asleep, despite the rumblings in the earth, despite the choirlike screams that were rising up from the city.

And when he awoke, he was not surprised to find himself upon a rock, bound by great chains of silver light, spread-eagled and suspended above the cavern floor. The air was filled with the smells of death and burning, of unrelenting pain, but he did not mind.

Out of the darkness, up from Gehenna, there came a deliberate flapping. It was the sound of wings, beating against the darkness, closer, and closer, until Ralphie could see the skull-like face, the beak, and the one good eye.

AUTHOR'S NOTE

The idea for this story hit me when I saw a guy who looked a lot like Ralphie barkering in front of a topless joint off 42nd Street near Times Square. He looked like hell on the half shell, and you could tell that all systems were shutting down with this guy. Everything was dying inside him except for an insistent light which sparked behind his eyes. As I walked past him, our gazes locked for an instant, and I felt in that instant that I *knew* this guy, and that I could feel his pain. The moment passed, the eye-contact broken, but as I headed east towards the Avenue of the Americas, I knew I had the beginnings of a story taking shape in my head.

If I had known then how much hassle I would endure in getting the story published, I might have never written it. Like Ralphie Loggins, my tale became an outcast.

When I finally wrote it as "Taking the Night Train," I sent it off to Dave Hartwell who was editing a magazine called *Cosmos*. Dave bought it and the story sat in inventory for about six months, and then *Cosmos* folded, ushering my story out into the street.

I then sent it to Ramsey Campbell in England,

who bought it for a horror anthology (I forget the name) he was doing. About six months later, he wrote to tell me that his publisher balked at printing his anthology at its present length, and insisted on cutting several stories from the batch. Guess whose story was one of the casualties?

And so, homeless again, I sent the story to Roy Torgeson, who was editing the *Chrysalis* series of anthologies for Doubleday. Roy bought the story not long after I had sold my short story collection, *Dark Stars and Other Illuminations,* to Doubleday. Deciding I had suffered enough indignity in trying to place "Taking the Night Train," I had included it in my collection just to see it in print. But this just brought on more trouble. Doubleday told Torgeson they didn't want my story appearing in *his* anthology because it was going to be published in *my* collection *first.* That would technically make the *Chrysalis* appearance a *reprint,* and Doubleday hawked Roy's anthology as "all new, original stories." Which meant, when you flensed away all the blubber, my story was "un-bought" again.

I had just about given up when I received a nice letter from Gerald Brown, who was the editor of a magazine called *Night Voyages*. Mike Bracken had sold him an interview he'd done of me, and Gerald wanted a story to accompany the piece. I smiled and asked him if he could beat the deadline appearance of my short story collection. When he promised me he could, I sent him "Taking the Night Train," and it finally saw print in the Spring 1981 issue of *Night Voyages*.

About a year later, I met an editor at Fawcett, Michaela Hamilton, who had read the story, and liked it so much, she suggested I do a novel based on some of the ideas and images in the story. I followed her advice, publishing *Night Train* in October 1984, a book which was optioned for a film, and ended up doing very well for me.

There's probably an object lesson in all this, but I'd rather not think about it.

—Thomas F. Monteleone

BLACK CORRIDOR

Fritz Leiber

HE SAT HUNCHED IN A CORRIDOR HEAD-HIGH AND about two doors wide, trying to remember who he was.

He felt very weary in his legs, as if he'd been walking the corridor a long, long time.

The corridor was of a black shimmering metal cool to his skin. He couldn't spot the source of the shimmer, which dimly lit the corridor though leaving the metal black, but he was pretty sure that was a minor problem.

He heard a faint steady whining, but he thought that was minor too.

He was hunched so that his heels pressed his buttocks and his elbows his sides, while his hands and the lower half of his face rested on his knees. Like a big rangy fetus sitting up, or the corpse in an early Egyptian hole-burial. There droned in his mind, "Naked I came into the world and naked I go out."

The corridor was literally two doors wide, for it ended ten yards away in two doors which faced him squarely. Each door had a glowing button on it and below the button a short word he couldn't quite read, though now and then he lifted his face to squint at them.

After a while he might go and read the two words, but now it seemed important to sit hunched all together, as if that helped him concentrate, and try to remember who he was.

Moreover, though he tried to keep it out of his mind, he really shrank from investigating the two doors. There was something about them that daunted and sickened him.

Instead, he chased memories in the inner darkness of his mind, but they turned and fled like tiny moonlit fish from a nighttime skin diver.

He had the feeling that he'd taken a wrong fork somewhere behind him in the corridor, and that as he'd taken that curving turn, his name and all that had ever happened to him had slipped away, as if dragged out of his mind by centrifugal force.

Maybe when he had rested a little more he should go back and find the fork and this time take the straight branch.

As he had that thought, cool metal touched his back.

He threw out his arms, and they struck cool metal, even with his back, to either side.

The movement jerked his torso erect. His head, neck, and shoulders touched cool metal too.

He scrambled to his feet and turned around. Where there had stretched an endless corridor, there was now a wall about a yard away. A black wall with no doors or door in it.

Instead of being in a corridor open-ended one way, he was in a glimmering black box ten yards long.

He realized that the faint steady whining had

stopped only when it started up again.

The wall that had touched him began moving toward him very slowly, at about the normal walking speed of an ant.

He stood stiffly erect, facing it. His arms hanging at his sides began to tremble, then his legs. His breath came and went between his teeth in little shuddering gusts. His eyes slowly converged. The wall touched the ends of his big toes, then nudged them. Without stepping back, he threw up his hands beside his shoulders and pressed against the wall.

The whining stopped, but after he had taken two more breaths, softly sighing ones through his nose, he could feel the wall begin to press back. Holding his breath and without changing his stance, he pressed harder. The wall pressed harder still and with a sudden little scream threw him back.

He saved himself from falling and then took another backward jump.

The wall's little scream sank immediately to a whine, but the whine was a little louder now, and the wall came on a little faster, like a cockroach in a hurry.

This time he readied himself carefully for the wall's approach, taking a position somewhat like that of a wrestler but also a fencer. His right leg, bent slightly at the knee, was thrust almost straight behind him, and that foot pointed back too. His left leg was bent under him, left foot pointing straight forward. The soles of both feet, toes gripping, were planted flat on the floor, which compared to the smooth walls was a trifle gritty, firming his stance.

When the wall reached him, the box he was in being then seven yards long, he met the wall simultaneously with his spread-fingered right hand, his left shoulder and his whole left arm doubled up clench-fisted against his chest, the left side of his head, and his left knee.

The wall stopped dead. In fact, it gave back a little, or seemed to. He pressed a little harder, but it gave no more. He did not waste his strength then, but only maintained the same relatively light pressure which had stopped the wall, trying to relax as much as he dared. His teeth were lightly clenched, but through his nostrils he drew and expelled deep breaths, as a climber does before tackling a difficult stretch of rock face.

After what seemed a long time, the wall began to push at him again. He contented himself with matching its pressure, guessing that if he put out his full strength, the wall would do the same, shortening the contest.

What point there was in prolonging the contest for as long a time as possible, he couldn't define, but he was sure there was one.

Naturally he was pushing at the wall to keep himself from being crushed when the glimmering black box shortened to nothing. Yet surely the sane thing to do would be to inspect the two doors behind him and escape by way of one of them, instead of pouring out his remaining strength here. But no, he had such a deep if undefined horror of the two doors that he was determined to have nothing to do with them unless absolutely forced to. Whether sane or not, the preferable course now was to oppose the wall with all his might.

Slowly his muscles began to bulge and his heartbeat and respiration to speed up, though he made himself take the same deep, even, controlled breaths. A bead of sweat stung the inside corner of

his left eye. He had to keep reminding himself not
to waste energy grinding his teeth and on no
account to yield to the temptation to shove out
with sudden violence or begin to shout curses. *I
mustn't let the wall trick me*, he thought fiercely.

His muscles began to ache, his breaths were now
deep snorts. He became aware of his heartbeat and
felt the blood throbbing in his temples and wrists.
He heard little creakings here and there in his body,
or thought he did. Despite himself, his teeth began
to clench tighter and tighter.

The pain in his muscles increased. There was fire
in his joints. He broke wind, and that rattled him
and almost threw him off guard. He could feel the
sweat trickling down his back and legs. He prayed
that it wouldn't make him slip. It was running into
his eyes now, so that he blinked constantly. Under
his chin it pooled in the tiny cup between the bent
thumb and curled forefinger of his clenched left fist.

But he knew the wall still hadn't budged him,
chiefly because it was silent—no whine, no scream.

In the midst of his near agony, there flashed up in
his mind one sane reason for keeping up his seemingly insane struggle: the hope that a connection
might burn out in the engine powering the wall, or
something in it break, or its fuel run out, or the
creature or creatures pushing the wall from the
other side tire before he did. Then he might be able
to push the wall back, even as far as the fork in the
tunnel, making it unnecessary to investigate the
two doors ahead.

His heart and head were pounding now, there
was a roaring in his ears, he was breathing in deep,
open-mouthed gasps, his body was one flame,

through his sweat-smarting eyes the wall seemed dazzling one moment, dead black the next, he felt consciousness ebbing, but still he stuck to his labor.

With a scream like a hunting leopard close by, the wall gave a mighty shove that sent him staggering back. The scream sank to a loud whine, and the wall came on at the speed of ungoaded oxen.

Though his mind was swimming and he could barely stand, and while he was still breathing in great, wide-mouthed, acid gasps, he turned at once and walked in long strides toward the two doors. And though he reeled from side to side, his legs cramping and his arms hanging like fiery bars of lead, he nevertheless went on tiptoe, fearing that any extra sound he made might speed up the wall.

He was burning when he started that five-stride journey. When he finished it he was shivering and the sweat on him was icy and his teeth were chattering.

By the time he was within touching distance of the doors, his mind and body had steadied, but he still had to blink twice before he could read the short words under the two buttons.

The one said WATER, the other AIR.

With the eager whine coming swiftly closer and closer, he lashed himself to think. *Let's see, air could mean emptiness and height, a great fall. He couldn't fly, hell, he could hardly stand.*

But he could swim. Water was necessary to life. Life came originally from the seas.

Yet he could also drown.

Acrophobia versus hydrophobia.

As the wall struck his heels and pushed him on, this time with a merciless lack of hesitation, and as he zigged a finger toward the button on the WATER door, an afterthought came to him in a flash.

Air was also necessary to life. He still had enough water in him, even after his sweating, to live at least a day. But he would be dead without air, or his brain would be dead, in about five minutes.

He zagged his finger to the AIR button. That door opened away from him, and he stumbled through it, pushed by the wall, and it slammed shut behind him.

He wasn't falling through emptiness, or standing in the open either, for that matter. He was simply in another section of black corridor.

He staggered forward a few steps and then between relief and exhaustion collapsed to his knees and hands. His roaring head slumped, his eyes staring dully at the faintly gritty metallic floor while he gulped oxygen.

After a short time he looked around him. The corridor wall on the WATER-door side wasn't shimmering black metal as he had taken for granted, but must be heavy glass or some other transparent amorphous substance, for in it were small silvery fish, a few small squid jetting about, and some speeding faintly-phosphorescent veils he couldn't identify, all lodged in dark water which rose at least to the roof of that other corridor.

He congratulated himself that he'd made the right choice, even on a last-minute hunch.

By right (except that the universe doesn't recognize rights) the corridor he was in should have been halved in width, but it was as broad as before. He deduced that it had acquired extra width on the side away from the water.

He looked ahead, and there were two more

doors, each with a glowing button and a short word he couldn't make out.

With a feeling of "This is too much," he sprawled full length on the floor, as if to sleep. One of his feet touched the transparent wall, while the elbow of the arm pillowing his head touched the wall opposite. He closed his eyes.

It was only then he realized that the sound in his ears wasn't the roaring and ringing in his head dying away, but the wail of the oncoming wall.

Such was his weariness and sudden fatalistic disinterest that he didn't tense, let alone jump up. He didn't even open his eyes.

Cool metal struck him along leg and side, gently but inflexibly. He let the wall roll him over twice before he resignedly scrambled to his feet. There was no sign in the advancing wall of the doorway by which he had entered. Stepping backward evenly, he swept a fingernail across the wall without hearing or feeling the faintest tick. Then he turned and trotted on to the next two doors.

They were marked FIRE and EARTH, and he punched the button of the second almost without physical hesitation, though there was the flash of a wondering whether EARTH might not be the name of a star or moon.

The main course of his nearly instantaneous reasoning had been: *Fire will kill me—and don't give me any tricky plays on meaning that there is a slow "fire" in my flesh and in all life. While earth —hell, even if it packed the next corridor to the top, I could scramble my way into it before the wall caught up.*

Tucked into that flash of reasoning there had

even been the crafty though qualified deduction: *If this door opens inward like the first, there's bound to be some space behind it. Though who says doors have to obey rules? This one might slide sideways.*

The door did open inward, and he trotted through almost without a break in his step, and it slammed shut behind him.

For a moment he thought he had been cruelly tricked. The whole corridor ahead glared with an irregularly pulsing red like a forest fire.

Then he realized he couldn't smell a speck of burning or feel any radiant heat. All the flaring red was coming through the transparent wall on the FIRE-door side. There, great flames writhed crowdedly from ceiling to floor. Here, it was cool, while the floor had changed from slightly gritty metal to even cooler packed earth, the dry and faintly sour smell of which now came to him. He reached out and gingerly brushed the transparent wall. It was barely warm, but he supposed it could be double, with insulating vacuum between. Why radiant heat didn't still come through, he didn't know.

It did not surprise him to discover that his corridor was as broad as ever and ended in two more labeled doors. Without hesitation he trotted toward them. This time he read the labels by the red glare of the flames. They were DEMONS and TIGERS.

At each word he felt a different quiver of fear. Easy enough to laugh at the concept of demons when in the midst of a wise and scientifically sophisticated civilization. Or to smile warily at tigers, for that matter, when cradling in your arms some potent energy weapon. But alone down here in this labyrinth, naked and unarmed, it was another matter.

Also the change in pace of the choice he had to make rattled him. This one had almost a fairy-tale quality. But there had been nothing of light fantasy, so far, in his experiences down here. Everything had been implacably real, especially the wall. Even demons would be real down here, probably. It occurred to him, too, that he had been lucky until now and had survived by playing hunches. The AIR door could have plunged him into emptiness. EARTH might have smothered or instantly blocked him, while he seemed to recall creatures who could walk through fire, at least for ten yards. This time he must really analyze.

But how? His mind felt useless. He even thought of digging a hole for himself in the dirt, so the wall would pass over him. But the earth was hard as adobe.

A mounting hungry snarl made him glance hurriedly back. The wall was coming on at a speed greater than that to which he had provoked it by his all-out attempt to hold it back, and it was barely five yards away, the same distance as when he had made his split-second EARTH choice in the last section of the corridor. It had more than canceled the time advantage that quick decision had gained him; it had given him no credit for it at all. The wall wasn't fair!

The thoughts started as he whirled around. *Demons don't exist, are superstitions. Everywhere? Outside this red-lit tightening tomb is a universe incomprehensibly vast. Somewhere there may be demons, and the mere word symbolizes a power greater than that of creatures.*

Tigers are real. But I remember someone killing a tiger barehanded. A leopard, anyhow. But tigers, plural?

The wall struck him. With the thought that *demons may exist and be able to kill me, but only an idiot takes on tigers, plural, where there's an alternative,* he jabbed the DEMONS button and was through that door and in turn locked in by it before he could think again.

Again he believed he'd been cruelly tricked. Facing him a few yards away in the glimmering black corridor were two huge felines with silky black fur and green eyes glinting with evil intelligence. They lashed their great tails. They writhed their powerful shoulders. Their claws scraped the gritty metal floor like chalk rasping on slate. They carried their white-fanged heads low, their green eyes glaring up at him. While from their throats issued snarls louder and more menacing than that of the wall.

But at that moment the wall once more struck him. Almost before he knew it, he was running toward the magnified black panthers, his eyes squinted, his shoulders hunched.

They reared up, unsheathing their scimitar claws, fully baring their fangs, and screaming like black trumpets in a satanic symphony. To keep himself from stopping, he had to remind himself: *They're not black panthers bigger than tigers, they're only demons.*

As he ran between them, he felt their hot breath, their bristly fur, but nothing more. Through eyes squinting sideways toward the TIGERS-door wall, he glimpsed glassed-in moonlit jungle and gliding through it, palely and darkly striped, flat-sided felines a little smaller than his demons.

Then he was facing doors glow-labeled REAL and UNREAL, while the wall, not demons, snarled at his heels.

Last time I picked the unreal and won, he thought. *Maybe I should again. But demons are only a tiny sub-branch of the small branch of the unreal labeled "supernatural beings." In the realm of the unreal are also insanity, psychosis, the innumerable delusions of locked-up minds completely out of touch with reality and lacking even internal organization, a sea of locked-in microcosms adrift and lost, never to know each other, even the nearest. While the realm of the real holds a hell of a lot besides tigers.*

He was pressing the REAL button as the wall slammed him. Then he was through the REAL door and this time running fast as he could down the black corridor toward the next pair. He kept his eyes averted from the UNREAL side of the corridor, for through its transparency he glimpsed a psychedelic churning of colors and forms, constantly patterning and unpatterning, which he sensed might derange any mind behind eyes that stared very long.

The next two doors were labeled INSTANT PAINLESS DEATH and TORTURE.

Now they've quit playing around with me, he thought. *They're slamming it at me, but good. Something's reached down deep, deep inside me and brought up the slimiest black noggin of them all.*

Let's see, they say even torture comes to an end.

Yes, in death. Why not pick painless death to start with? Makes sense. But back there I picked the real. Torture is a part of the real. While death is unreality squared, cubed and to the nth *power. With torture, there's a chance of survival, with death no chance at all. Tautology.*

As the wall came screaming up behind him and he pushed the TORTURE button, he thought, *Well, at least I'm not strapped down yet, and to stop that I'll fight as hard as I pushed against the wall.*

He was in another section of corridor, all glimmering black this time, no transparent wall, and coming toward him was an anthropoid being or machine, the shape and size of a gorilla, except it had no head. It kept swinging apart its long arms and then bringing them together, as if to embrace someone tightly, while its stubby legs planted and replanted themselves firmly.

It was made of metal and covered with sharp spikes that were stubby except for five long, curving talons ending each arm. An iron maiden turned inside out.

Choosing a moment when its arms were swinging apart, he punched it with all his might high in the center of its chest.

It slowly toppled over backwards, landed with a sharp crash, and lay there on its back with its stubby legs planting and replanting themselves in air and its long arms swinging apart and closing together, clashing the floor of the corridor each time they were parted widest.

The screaming wall struck him from behind. Choosing the next time the metal arms swung inward, he darted past the thing and sprinted to the next pair of doors, noting there was more lettering below one button than he'd ever seen before.

That door was labeled PERPETUAL SOLITARY CONFINEMENT IN HAPPY COMFORT. The other said only DEATH OR LIFE.

He thought, *Last time I opted against death. Shouldn't I do so again?*

Behind him, a scraping and clashing mixed with the scream of the wall. Of course, it was the wall pushing the spiked automaton before it.

He thought, *Solitary confinement in happy comfort. That sounds like being drunk forever, without hangovers. All alone with an infinity of glorious, glowing thoughts and unending wonderful dreams.*

But all alone.

An even chance at life is better than that. Any chance of life is better than that.

With the screaming and scraping and clashing just behind him, he frantically jabbed the DEATH OR LIFE button and plunged out into a wide, long patio roofed by a fabric through which violet light filtered onto a smoothly tiled floor, and he stood there gasping and shaking. Behind a table nearby, a woman in the professional whites of a nurse was working quietly at some charts. When his breathing had evened out, she looked up at him and, lifting a gray looseleaf folder, said, "Hello. Here are your name and personal history, to read when you wish." After a faintly smiling pause she added, "Do you have any immediate questions?"

After a while he said, frowning, "I think I get it about the last four pairs of buttons. But about the first two, would I have died if I'd picked water or fire?"

She replied, "I am not at liberty to answer that.

There are many branchings in the corridors."

He still frowned as he moved slowly toward the table.

"Is something else bothering you?" she asked.

He nodded somewhat surlily and said, "When I punched the torture button, I didn't really get any. There was only that witless robot."

"You are difficult to please," she replied. "Wasn't it torture enough, what happened to your hand?"

He lifted it, still balled in a fist, and studied the eight circular wounds, from which blood slowly dripped, and felt the dull pain. Then he reached for the gray folder in her hand, noting that her other was a gleaming gray metal prosthetic with eight slim many-jointed fingers like a spider's legs.

As he touched the folder he felt a surge of frantic curiosity and started to flip it open but caught himself and instead, carrying it half rolled, began to walk slowly down the patio, then more rapidly as he neared the balustrade of gray metal marking its end.

Resting his hands on the warm smooth rail, he looked out at the prospect dropping gently away.

In a pale yellow sky, a violet sun was sinking behind rounded hills ten miles away. Its purpling beams shone on a valley half filled with cultivated reddish fields and scarlet trees and half with evenly ranked transparent tubes, through which rushed fluids shading from pink to crimson of some sort of algae farming. Midway to the hills, beside a meandering river, was a town with irregularly spaced round pastel roofs, mostly low. Here and there he made out the figures of two-legged beasts and six-legged ones, the latter carrying their foremost limbs high, like centaurs. From somewhere came a faint piping and a fainter, complexly rhythmic drumming. It looked like a good planet.

After a while he could learn its name and all about it, just as after a while he could learn from the folder, reassuringly bulked between his fingers, his own name and what he'd feared and flinched away from into the black inner corridor which had become the black therapeutic corridor from which he'd now emerged. And after a while he could go back to the nurse and have her fix his hand, the dull pain of which was oddly reassuring.

For the moment it was enough to know he was alive and a man.

AUTHOR'S NOTE

The dark story fits better the supernatural horror field (dire encounters with the mysterious unknown, the cosmos in its malevolent mode) than the field of science fiction, where problems are usually solved and mysteries unraveled. Of course there are exceptions to the latter, tales of natural disaster and cautionary ones of atomic doom. And then there are mood-mixing yarns of an individual sort, such as "Black Corridor."

I wrote the story while living in Venice, California, that romantical-grotesque beach town with its canals, arching little bridges, porticoed central sidewalks, and other amiable copyings of her Adriatic big sister, but also her oil wells and picturesque squalors, half swallowed by sprawling Los Angeles. The place was in one of its quiet periods: the beatniks had faded down after their Gashouse burned, but the colorful roller-skaters and skateboard folk had not yet taken over Ocean Front Walk. She'd already given me "The Black Gondolier," but now I was in another mood.

In my mind I dedicated the new tale to Robert Heinlein, whose stories and books have always been both an inspiration and a science-fiction education to me.

—Fritz Leiber

STRANGERS ON PARADISE
Damon Knight

PARADISE WAS THE NAME OF THE PLANET. ONCE IT HAD been called something else, but nobody knew what.

From this distance, it was a warm blue cloud-speckled globe turning in darkness. Selby viewed it in a holotube, not directly, because there was no porthole in the isolation room, but he thought he knew how the first settlers had felt a century ago, seeing it for the first time after their long voyage. He felt much the same way himself; he had been in medical isolation on the entryport satellite for three months, waiting to get to the place he had dreamed of with hopeless longing all his life: a place without disease, without violence, a world that had never known the sin of Cain.

Selby (Howard W., Ph.D.) was a slender, balding man in his forties, an Irishman, a reformed drunkard, an unsuccessful poet, a professor of English literature at the University of Toronto. One of his particular interests was the work of Eleanor Petryk, the expatriate lyric poet who had lived on Paradise for thirty years, the last ten of them silent. After Petryk's death in 2156, he had applied for a grant

from the International Endowment to write a definitive critical biography of Petryk, and in two years
of negotiation he had succeeded in gaining entry to
Paradise. It was, he knew, going to be the peak
experience of his life.

The Paradisans had pumped out his blood and
replaced it with something that, they assured him,
was just as efficient at carrying oxygen but was not
an appetizing medium for microbes. They had
taken samples of his body fluids and snippets of his
flesh from here and there. He had been scanned by
a dozen machines, and they had given him injec-
tions for twenty diseases and parasites they said he
was carrying. Their faces, in the holotubes, had
smiled pityingly when he told them he had had a
clean bill of health when he was checked out in
Houston.

It was like being in a hospital, except that only
machines touched him, and he saw human faces
only in the holotube. He had spent the time reading
and watching canned information films of happy,
healthy people working and playing in the golden
sunlight. Their faces were smooth, their eyes bright.
The burden of the films was always the same: how
happy the Paradisans were, how fulfilling their
lives, how proud of the world they were building.

The books were a little more informative. The
planet had two large continents, one inhabited, the
other desert (although from space it looked much
like the other), plus a few rocky, uninhabitable
island chains. The axial tilt was seven degrees. The
seasons were mild. The planet was geologically
inactive; there were no volcanoes, and earthquakes
were unknown. The low, rounded hills offered no
impediment to the global circulation of air. The

soil was rich. And there was no disease.

This morning, after his hospital breakfast of orange juice, oatmeal, and toast, they had told him he would be released at noon. And that was like a hospital, too; it was almost two o'clock now, and he was still here.

"Mr. Selby."

He turned, saw the woman's smiling face in the holotube. "Yes?"

"We are ready for you now. Will you walk into the anteroom?"

"With the greatest of pleasure."

The door swung open. Selby entered; the door closed behind him. The clothes he had been wearing when he arrived were on a rack; they were newly cleaned and, doubtless, disinfected. Watched by an eye on the wall, he took off his pajamas and dressed. He felt like an invalid after a long illness; the shoes and belt were unfamiliar objects.

The outer door opened. Beyond stood the nurse in her green cap and bright smile; behind her was a man in a yellow jumpsuit.

"Mr. Selby, I'm John Ledbitter. I'll be taking you groundside as soon as you're thumbed out."

There were three forms to thumbprint, with multiple copies. "Thank you, Mr. Selby," said the nurse. "It's been a pleasure to have you with us. We hope you will enjoy your stay on Paradise."

"Thank you."

"Please." That was what they said instead of "You're welcome"; it was short for "Please don't mention it," but it was hard to get used to.

"This way." He followed Ledbitter down a long corridor in which they met no one. They got into an elevator. "Hang on, please." Selby put his arms through the straps. The elevator fell away; when it stopped, they were floating, weightless.

Ledbitter took his arm to help him out of the elevator. Alarm bells were ringing somewhere. "This way." They pulled themselves along a cord to the jump box, a cubicle as big as Selby's hospital room. "Please lie down here."

They lay side by side on narrow cots. Ledbitter put up the padded rails. "Legs and arms apart, please, head straight. Make sure you are comfortable. Are you ready?"

"Yes."

Ledbitter opened the control box by his side, watching the instruments in the ceiling. "On my three," he said. "One . . . two . . ."

Selby felt a sudden increase in weight as the satellite decelerated to match the speed of the planetary surface. After a long time the control lights blinked; the cot sprang up against him. They were on Paradise.

The jump boxes, more properly Henderson-Rosenberg devices, had made interplanetary and interstellar travel almost instantaneous—not quite, because vectors at sending and receiving stations had to be matched, but near enough. The hitch was that you couldn't get anywhere by jump box unless someone had been there before and brought a receiving station. That meant that interstellar exploration had to proceed by conventional means: the Taylor Drive at first, then impulse engines; round trips, even to nearby stars, took twenty years or more. Paradise, colonized in 2056 by a Geneite sect from the United States, had been the first Earthlike planet to be discovered; it was still the only one, and it was off-limits to Earthlings except on special occasions. There was not much the governments of Earth could do about that.

A uniformed woman, who said she had been assigned as his guide, took him in tow. Her name was Helga Sonnstein. She was magnificently built, clear-skinned and rosy, like all the other Paradisans he had seen so far.

They walked to the hotel on clean streets, under monorails that swooped gracefully overhead. The passersby were beautifully dressed; some of them glanced curiously at Selby. The air was so pure and fresh that simply breathing was a pleasure. The sky over the white buildings was a robin's-egg blue. The disorientation Selby felt was somehow less than he had expected.

In his room, he looked up Karen McMorrow's code. Her face in the holotube was pleasant, but she did not smile. "Welcome to Paradise, Mr. Selby. Are you enjoying your visit?"

"Very much, so far."

"Can you tell me when you would like to come to the Cottage?"

"Whenever it's convenient for you, Miss McMorrow."

"Unfortunately, there is family business I must take care of. In two or three days?"

"That will be perfectly fine. I have a few other people to interview, and I'd like to see something of the city while I'm here."

"Until later, then. I'm sorry for this delay."

"Please," said Selby.

That afternoon Miss Sonnstein took him around the city. And it was all true. The Paradisans were happy, healthy, energetic, and cheerful. He had never seen so many unlined faces, so many clear eyes and bright smiles. Even the patients in the hospital looked healthy. They were accident victims for the most part—broken legs, cuts. He was just beginning to understand what it was like to live on a world where there was no infectious disease and never had been.

He liked the Paradisans—they were immensely friendly, warm, outgoing people. It was impossible not to like them. And at the same time he envied and resented them. He understood why, but he couldn't stop.

On his second day he talked to Petryk's editor at the state publishing house, an amiable man named Truro, who took him to lunch and gave him a handsomely bound copy of Petryk's *Collected Poems*.

During lunch—lake trout, apparently as much a delicacy here as it was in North America—Truro drew him out about his academic background, his publications, his plans for the future. "We would certainly like to publish your book about Eleanor," he said. "In fact, if it were possible, we would be even happier to publish it here first."

Selby explained his arrangements with Macmillan Schuster. Truro said, "But there's no contract yet?"

Selby, intrigued by the direction the conversation was taking, admitted that there was none.

"Well, let's see how things turn out," said Truro. Back in the office, he showed Selby photos of Petryk taken after the famous one, the only one that had appeared on Earth. She was a thin-faced woman, fragile-looking. Her hair was a little grayer, the face more lined—sadder, perhaps.

"Is there any unpublished work?" Selby asked.

"None that she wanted to preserve. She was very selective, and of course her poems sold quite well here—not as much as on Earth, but she made a comfortable living."

"What about the silence—the last ten years?"

"It was her choice. She no longer wanted to write poems. She turned to sculpture instead—wood carvings, mostly. You'll see when you go out to the Cottage."

Afterward Truro arranged for him to see Potter Hargrove, Petryk's divorced husband. Hargrove was in his seventies, white-haired, and red-faced. He was the official in charge of what they called the New Lands Program: satellite cities were being built by teams of young volunteers—the ground cleared and sterilized, terrestrial plantings made. Hargrove had a great deal to say about this.

With some difficulty, Selby turned the conversation to Eleanor Petryk. "How did she happen to get permission to live on Paradise, Mr. Hargrove? I've always been curious."

"It's been our policy to admit occasional immigrants, when we think they have something we lack. *Very* occasional. We don't publicize it. I'm sure you understand."

"Yes, of course." Selby collected his thoughts. "What was she like, those last ten years?"

"I don't know. We were divorced five years before that. I remarried. Afterward, Eleanor became rather isolated."

When Selby stood up to leave, Hargrove said, "Have you an hour or so? I'd like to show you something."

They got into a comfortable four-seat runabout and drove north, through the commercial district, then suburban streets. Hargrove parked the runabout, and they walked down a dirt road past a cluster of farm buildings. The sky was an innocent blue; the sun was warm. An insect buzzed past Selby's ear; he turned and saw that it was a honeybee. Ahead was a field of corn.

The waves of green rolled away from them to the horizon, rippling in the wind. Every stalk, every leaf, was perfect.

"No weeds," said Selby.

Hargrove smiled with satisfaction. "That's the beautiful part," he said. "No weeds, because any Earth plant poisons the soil for them. Not only that, but no pests, rusts, blights. The native organisms are incompatible. We can't eat them, and they can't eat us."

"It seems very antiseptic," Selby said.

"Well, that may seem strange to you, but the word comes from the Greek *sepsis*, which means 'putrid.' I don't think we have to apologize for being against putrefaction. We came here without bringing any Earth diseases or parasites with us, and that means there is *nothing* that can attack us. It will take hundreds of thousands of years for the local organisms to adapt to us, if they ever do."

"And then?"

Hargrove shrugged. "Maybe we'll find another planet."

"What if there aren't any other suitable planets within reach? Wasn't it just luck that you found this one?"

"Not luck. It was God's will, Mr. Selby."

* * *

Hargrove had given him the names of four old friends of Petryk's who were still alive. After some parleying on the holo, Selby arranged to meet them together in the home of Mark Andrevon, a novelist well known on Paradise in the seventies. (The present year, by Paradisan reckoning, was A.L. 102.) The others were Theodore Bonwait, a painter; Alice Orr, a poet and ceramicist; and Ruth-Joan Wellman, another poet.

At the beginning of the evening, Andrevon was pugnacious about what he termed his neglect in the English-Speaking Union; he told Selby in considerable detail about his literary honors and the editions of his works. This was familiar talk to Selby; he gathered that Andrevon was now little read even here. He managed to soothe the disgruntled author and turn the conversation to Petryk's early years on Paradise.

"Poets don't actually like each other much, I'm sure you know that, Mr. Selby," said Ruth-Joan Wellman. "We got along fairly well, though—we were all young and unheard of then, and we used to get together and cook spaghetti, that sort of thing. Then Ellie got married, and . . ."

"Mr. Hargrove didn't care for her friends?"

"Something like that," said Theodore Bonwait. "Well, there were more demands on her time, too. It was a rather strong attachment at first. We saw them occasionally, at parties and openings, that sort of thing."

"What was she like then, can you tell me? What was your impression?"

They thought about it. Talented, they agreed, a little vague about practical matters ("which was why it seemed so lucky for her to marry Potter," said Alice Orr, "but it didn't work out"), very charming sometimes, but a sharp-tongued critic. Selby took notes. He got them to tell him where they had all lived, where they had met, in what years. Three of them admitted that they had some of Petryk's letters, and promised to send him copies.

After another day or so, Truro called him and asked him to come to the office. Selby felt that something was in the wind.

"Mr. Selby," Truro said, "you know visitors like yourself are so rare that we feel we have to take as much advantage of them as we can. This is a young world, we haven't paid as much attention as we might to literary and artistic matters. I wonder if you have ever thought of staying with us?"

Selby's heart gave a jolt. "Do you mean permanently?" he said. "I didn't think there was any chance—"

"Well, I've been talking to Potter Hargrove, and he thinks something might be arranged. This is all in confidence, of course, and I don't want you to make up your mind hurriedly. Think it over."

"I really don't know what to say. I'm surprised —I mean, I was sure I had offended Mr. Hargrove."

"Oh, no, he was favorably impressed. He likes your spice."

"I'm sorry?"

"Don't you have that expression? Your, how shall I say it, ability to stand up for yourself. He's the older generation, you know—son of a pioneer. They respect someone who speaks his mind."

Selby, out on the street, felt an incredulous joy.

Of all the billions on Earth, how many would ever be offered such a prize?

Later, with Helga Sonnstein, he visited an elementary school. "Did you ever have a cold?" a serious eight-year-old girl asked him.

"Yes, many times."

"What was it like?"

"Well, your nose runs, you cough and sneeze a lot, and your head feels stuffy. Sometimes you have a little fever, and your bones ache."

"That's *awful*," she said, and her small face expressed something between commiseration and disbelief.

Well, it *was* awful, and a cold was the least of it—"no worse than a bad cold," people used to say about syphilis. Thank God she had not asked about that.

He felt healthy himself, and in fact he was healthy—even before the Paradisan treatments, he had always considered himself healthy. But his medical history, he knew, would have looked like a catalog of horrors to these people—influenza, mumps, cerebrospinal meningitis once, various rashes, dysentery several times (something you had to expect if you traveled). You took it for granted —all those swellings and oozings—it was part of the game. What would it be like to go back to that now?

Miss Sonnstein took him to the university, introduced him to several people, and left him there for the afternoon. Selby talked to the head of the English department, a vaguely hearty man named Quincy; nothing was said to suggest that he might be offered a job if he decided to remain, but Selby's instinct told him that he was being inspected with that end in view.

Afterward he visited the natural history museum and talked to a professor named Morrison, who was a specialist in native life forms.

The plants and animals of Paradise were unlike anything on Earth. The "trees" were scaly, bulbous-bottomed things, some with lacy fronds waving sixty feet overhead, others with cup-shaped leaves that tilted individually to follow the sun. There were no large predators, Morrison assured him; it would be perfectly safe to go into the boonies, providing he did not run out of food. There were slender, active animals with bucket-shaped noses climbing in the forests or burrowing in the ground, and there were things that were not exactly insects; one species had a fixed wing like a maple seedpod—it spiraled down from the tree-tops, eating other airborne creatures on the way, and then climbed up again.

Of the dominant species, the aborigines, Morrison's department had only bones, not even recon-structions. They had been upright, about five feet tall, large-skulled, possibly mammalian. The eye-holes of their skulls were canted. The bones of their feet were peculiar, bent like the footbones of horses or cattle. "I wonder what they looked like," Selby said.

Morrison smiled. He was a little man with a brushy black mustache. "Not very attractive, I'm afraid. We do have their stone carvings, and some wall pictures and inscriptions." He showed Selby an album of photographs. The carvings, of what looked like weathered granite, showed angular crea-tures with blunt muzzles. The paintings were the same, but the expression of the eyes was startlingly human. Around some of the paintings were columns of written characters that looked like clusters of tiny hoofprints.

"You can't translate these?"

"Not without a Rosetta Stone. That's the pity of it—if only we'd gotten here just a little earlier."

"How long ago did they die off?"

"Probably not more than a few centuries. We find their skeletons buried in the trunks of trees. Very well preserved. About what happened there are various theories. The likeliest thing is plague, but some people think there was a climatic change."

Then Selby saw the genetics laboratory. They were working on some alterations in the immune system, they said, which they hoped in thirty years would make it possible to abandon the allergy treatments that all children now got from the cradle up. "Here's something else that's quite interesting," said the head of the department, a blond woman named Reynolds. She showed him white rabbits in a row of cages. Sunlight came through the open door; beyond was a loading dock, where a man with a Y-lift was hoisting up a bale of feed.

"These are Lyman Whites, a standard strain," said Miss Reynolds. "Do you notice anything unusual about them?"

"They look very healthy," said Selby.

"Nothing else?"

"No."

She smiled. "These rabbits were bred from genetic material spliced with bits of DNA from native organisms. The object was to see if we could enable them to digest native proteins. That has been only partly successful, but something completely unexpected happened. We seem to have interrupted a series of cues that turns on the aging process. The rabbits do not age past maturity. This pair, and those in the next cage, are twenty-one years old."

"Immortal rabbits?"

"No, we can't say that. All we can say is that they have lived twenty-one years. That is three times their normal span. Let's see what happens in another fifty or a hundred years."

As they left the room, Selby asked, "Are you thinking of applying this discovery to human beings?"

"It has been discussed. We don't know enough yet. We have tried to replicate the effect in rhesus monkeys, but so far without success."

"If you should find that this procedure is possible in human beings, do you think it would be wise?"

She stopped and faced him. "Yes, why not? If you are miserable and ill, I can understand why you would not want to live a long time. But if you are happy and productive, why not? Why should people have to grow old and die?"

She seemed to want his approval. Selby said, "But, if nobody ever died, you'd have to stop having children. The world wouldn't be big enough."

She smiled again. "This is a very big world, Mr. Selby."

Selby had seen in Claire Reynolds's eyes a certain guarded interest; he had seen it before in Paradisan women, including Helga Sonnstein. He did not know how to account for it. He was shorter than the average Paradisan male, not as robust; he had had to be purged of a dozen or two loathsome diseases before he could set foot on Paradise. Perhaps that was it: perhaps he was interesting to women because he was unlike all the other men they knew.

He called the next day and asked Miss Reynolds to dinner. Her face in the tube looked surprised, then pleased. "Yes, that would be very nice," she said.

An hour later he had a call from Karen McMorrow; she was free now to welcome him to the Cottage, and would be glad to see him that afternoon. Selby recognized the workings of that law of the universe that tends to bring about a desired result at the least convenient time; he called the laboratory, left a message of regret, and boarded the intercity tube for the town where Eleanor Petryk had lived and died.

The tube, a transparent cylinder suspended from pylons, ran up and over the rolling hills. The crystal windows were open; sweet flower scents drifted in, and behind them darker smells, unfamiliar and disturbing. Selby felt a thrill of excitement when he realized that he was looking at the countryside with new eyes, not as a tourist but as someone who might make this strange land his home.

They passed mile after mile of growing crops —corn, soybeans, then acres of beans, squash, peas; then fallow fields and grazing land in which the traceries of buried ruins could be seen.

After a while the cultivated fields began to thin out, and Selby saw the boonies for the first time. The tall fronded plants looked like anachronisms from the Carboniferous. The forests stopped at the borders of the fields as if they had been cut with a knife.

Provo was now a town of about a hundred thousand; when Eleanor Petryk had first lived there, it had been only a crossroads at the edge of the boonies. Selby got off the tube in late afternoon. A woman in blue stepped forward. "Mr. Selby."

"Yes."

"I'm Karen McMorrow. Was your trip pleasant?"

"Very pleasant."

She was a little older than she had looked on the holotube, in her late fifties, perhaps. "Come with me, please." No monorails here; she had a little impulse-powered runabout. They swung off the main street onto a blacktop road that ran between rows of tall maples.

"You were Miss Petryk's companion during her later years?"

"Secretary. Amanuensis." She smiled briefly.

"Did she have many friends in Provo?"

"No. None. She was a very private person. Here we are." She stopped the runabout; they were in a narrow lane with hollyhocks on either side.

The house was a low white-painted wooden building half-hidden by evergreens. Miss McMorrow opened the door and ushered him in. There was a cool, stale odor, the smell of a house unlived in.

The sitting room was dominated by a massive coffee table apparently carved from the cross section of a tree. In the middle of it, in a hollow space, was a stone bowl, and in the bowl, three carved bones.

"Is this native wood?" Selby asked, stooping to run his hand over the polished grain.

"Yes. Redwood, we call it, but it is nothing like the Earth tree. It is not really a tree at all. This was the first piece she carved; there are others in the workroom, through there."

The workroom, a shed attached to the house, was cluttered with wood carvings, some taller than Selby, others small enough to be held in the palm of the hand. The larger ones were curiously tormented shapes, half human and half tree. The smaller ones were animals and children.

"We knew nothing about this," Selby said. "Only that she had gone silent. She never explained?"

"It was her choice."

They went into Petryk's study. Books were in glass-fronted cases, and there were shelves of books and record cubes. A vase with sprays of cherry blossoms was on a windowsill.

"This is where she wrote?"

"Yes. Always in longhand, here, at the table. She wrote in pencil, on yellow paper. She said poems could not be made on machines."

"And all her papers are here?"

"Yes, in these cabinets. Thirty years of work. You will want to look through them?"

"Yes. I'm very grateful."

"Let me show you first where you will eat and sleep, then you can begin. I will come out once a day to see how you are getting on."

In the cabinets were thousands of pages of manuscript—treasures, including ten drafts of the famous poem *Walking the River*. Selby went through them methodically one by one, making copious notes. He worked until he could not see the pages, and fell into bed exhausted every night.

On the third day, Miss McMorrow took him on a trip into the boonies. Dark scents were all around them. The dirt road, such as it was, ended after half a mile; then they walked. "Eleanor often came out here, camping," she said. "Sometimes for a week or more. She liked the solitude." In the gloom of the tall shapes that were not trees, the ground was covered with not-grass and not-ferns. The silence was deep. Faint trails ran off in both directions. "Are these animal runs?" Selby asked.

"No. She made them. They are growing back now. There are no large animals on Paradise."

"I haven't even seen any small ones."

Through the undergrowth he glimpsed a mound of stone on a hill. "What is that?"

"Aborigine ruins. They are all through the boonies."

She followed him as he climbed up to it. The cut stones formed a complex hundreds of yards across. Selby stooped to peer through a doorway. The aborigines had been a small people.

At one corner of the ruins was a toppled stone figure, thirty feet long. The weeds had grown over it, but he could see that the face had been broken away, as if by blows of a hammer.

"What they could have taught us," Selby said.

"What could they have taught us?"

"What it is to be human, perhaps."

"I think we have to decide that for ourselves."

Six weeks went by. Selby was conscious that he now knew more about Eleanor Petryk than anyone on Earth, and also that he did not understand her at all. In the evenings he sometimes went into the workroom and looked at the tormented carved figures. Obviously she had turned to them because she had to do something, and because she could no longer write. But why the silence?

Toward the end, at the back of the last cabinet, Selby found a curious poem.

XC

Tremble at the coming of the light,
Hear the rings rustle on the trees.
Every creature runs away in fright;
Years will pass before the end of
    night;
Woe to them who drift upon the
    seas.
Erebus above hears not their pleas;
Repentance he has none upon his
    height—
Earth will always take what she
    can seize.

Knights of the sky, throw down
    your shining spears.
In luxury enjoy your stolen prize.
Let those who will respond to what
    I write,
Lest all of us forget to count the
    years.
Empty are the voices, and the eyes
Dead in the coming of that night.

Selby looked at it in puzzlement. It was a sonnet of sorts, a form that had lapsed into obscurity centuries ago, and one that, to his knowledge, Petryk had never used before in her life. What was more curious was that it was an awkward poem, almost a jingle. Petryk could not possibly have been guilty of it, and yet here it was in her handwriting.

With a sudden thrill of understanding, he looked at the initial letters of the lines. The poem was an acrostic, another forgotten form. It concealed a message, and that was why the poem was awkward —deliberately so, perhaps.

He read the poem again. Its meaning was incredible but clear. They had bombed the planet —probably the other continent, the one that was said to be covered with desert. No doubt it was, now. Blast and radiation would have done for any aborigines there, and a brief nuclear winter would have taken care of the rest. And the title, "XC" —Roman numerals, another forgotten art. Ninety years.

In his anguish, there was one curious phrase that he still did not understand—"Hear the rings rustle," where the expected word was "leaves." Why rings?

Suddenly he thought he knew. He went into the other room and looked at the coffee table. In the hollow, the stone bowl with its carved bones. Around it, the rings. There was a scar where the tree had been cut into, hollowed out; but it had been a big tree even then. He counted the rings outside the scar: the first one was narrow, almost invisible, but it was there. Altogether there were ninety.

The natives had buried their dead in chambers cut from the wood of living trees. Petryk must have found this one on one of her expeditions. And she had left the evidence here, where anyone could see it.

That night Selby thought of Eleanor Petryk, lying sleepless in this house. What could one do with such knowledge? Her answer had been silence: ten years of silence, until she died. But she had left the message behind her, because she could not bear the silence. He cursed her for her frailty; had she never guessed what a burden she had laid on the man who was to read her message, the man who by sheer perverse bad fortune was himself?

In the morning he called Miss McMorrow and told her he was ready to leave. She said good-bye to him at the tube, and he rode back to the city, looking out with bitter hatred at the scars the aborigines had left in the valleys.

He made the rounds to say good-bye to the people he had met. At the genetics laboratory, a pleasant young man told him that Miss Reynolds was not in. "She may have left for the weekend, but I'm not sure. If you'll wait here a few minutes, I'll see if I can find out."

It was a fine day, and the back door was open. Outside stood an impulse-powered pickup, empty.

Selby looked at the rabbits in their cages. He was thinking of something he had run across in one of Eleanor Petryk's old books, a work on mathematics. "Fibonacci numbers were invented by the thirteenth-century Italian mathematician to furnish a model of population growth in rabbits. His assumptions were: 1) it takes rabbits one month from birth to reach maturity; 2) one month after reaching maturity, and every month thereafter, each pair of rabbits will produce another pair of rabbits; and 3) rabbits never die."

As if in a dream, Selby unlatched the cages and took out two rabbits, one a buck, the other a doe heavy with young. He put them under his arms, warm and quivering. He got into the pickup with them and drove northward, past the fields of corn, until he reached the edge of the cultivated land. He walked through the undergrowth to a clearing where tender shoots grew. He put the rabbits down. They snuffed around suspiciously. One hopped, then the other. Presently they were out of sight.

Selby felt as if his blood were fizzing; he was elated and horrified all at once. He drove the pickup to the highway and parked it just outside town. Now he was frozen and did not feel anything at all.

From the hotel he made arrangements for his departure. Miss Sonnstein accompanied him to the jump terminal. "Good-bye, Mr. Selby. I hope you have had a pleasant visit."

"It has been most enlightening, thank you."

"Please," she said.

It was raining in Houston, where Selby bought, for sentimental reasons, a bottle of Old Space Ranger. The shuttle was crowded and smelly; three people were coughing as if their lungs would burst. Black snow was falling in Toronto. Selby let himself into his apartment, feeling as if he had never been away. He got the bottle out of his luggage, filled a glass, and sat for a while looking at it. His notes and the copies of Petryk's papers were in his suitcase, monuments to a book that he now knew would never be written. The doggerel of "XC" ran through his head. Two lines of it, actually, were not so bad:

*Empty are the voices, and the eyes
Dead in the coming of that night.*

AUTHOR'S NOTE

A couple of editors told me I should not have written this story. (I am paraphrasing and distorting a little to make a point.) One said, more or less, "There are too many stories about how bad we are; if I published them the magazine wouldn't be any fun." The other, "Come on, Damon, you live in the Pacific Northwest where something just about like this happened, and how often do you feel a twinge?"

I admit the strength of these arguments, but it seems to me that they leave something out. It is true that all of us are the beneficiaries of crimes committed by our ancestors, and it is true that nothing can be done about that now because the victims are dead and the survivors are innocent. These are good reasons for keeping our mouths shut about the past: but tell me, what are our reasons for silence about atrocities still to come?

—Damon Knight

The Bell

BY THE OVAL WINDOW A BELL RINGS.

"Nine seven," I say, because it keeps me a unit still, and not a person. Who knows? This might be a wrong number.

Beyond the window, the glass city stretches away.

"Hallo?" asks a voice. "Is that you, Geminna?" it asks me.

And the turquoise hills, and the blue hills.

"Yes. This is Geminna," I say, and inside me, *It* stirs.

"Why, Geminna, we haven't seen you for so long. We're going to the sea, Geminna. Come with us."

And the pale blue hills, like hyacinths.

"I can't," I say. "I'm sorry."

And the palest blue hills, like sky.

"Oh, but, oh, Geminna—I know there's your reading and your studies—can't you study with us at the beach, by the sea? Can't you, Geminna?"

"Another time," I say, "it would be wonderful."

"Oh." Rebuffed, the voice of a forgotten friend hangs adrift in the wires. I don't have many of these calls now. Soon they will stop forever. "If you're

sure, then. Some other time."
And the pale silver sea.
But I can't go out.
It won't let me.

The House

This is an old house, stone and brick and stucco,
a long ramble of a house, with many rooms and
inner courts, and a long, wild garden with a high
wall. Here I may do what I want. As long as I am
alone. In the garden are mulberry trees and twisted
hawthorn, and tall pines, and old stone urns from
which spill beautiful rank weeds. Halfway, a river
runs, several feet across, where fish glitter. A stone
bridge crosses the river, and on the other side the
wilderness rises in terraces to a faded white summer house. Beyond the summer house is the tower.
This is the highest point, and from the tower-roof,
ringed by the crumbling parapet, I can see all the
city, the hills, even the sea, restless in the distance.
Above, the stars turn and burn. In winter everything is white, and the sea opaque with ice-floes.

The Sea

Sometimes *It* will let me go to the sea, for a little
while. Then I walk barefoot in the cool water and
the sand, smelling the old fish smell that the sea
carries with it. I bring back shells and stones, and
pictures I have drawn, or clicked with the eye of my
little camera. Once a big dog found me, and we
played by the sea's edge, in the salty froth. We ran
backwards and forwards, laughing, until a man
came.

I thought I would stay and speak to the man. He
was young and handsome and the dog loved him,
but *It* wouldn't let me. So I went away.

Dawn is the best time for the sea, or early in the morning, before the moon sets. There are not many people then.

The House

There is a lot to do in the house. It cleans itself twice in every ten days, and I help it. I like to cook from the deliveries that are brought to the service door. There's no problem there, of course. The door takes in what I need and pays the men, who then go away. They mutter and look up at the windows, blind with sunlight. Does anyone really live here? Books come, too. I have already a vast library; poetry, drama, novels, works of science and philosophy and magic. I don't always understand, but I try. My mind is opening little by little, like a rusty flower. I can play five instruments, the ancient pianos of the house, the harp, all the range of guitars which hang from mahogany pegs in the music room, the reed flute whose sound is uneasy, green, and my own voice which I have trained now to an extensive range. I also paint and sculpt, embroider, study the stars—I have much to do.

Often, very late or early, I walk through the city.

I have seen drunks lying in the road, or lovers in the parks. In winter the parks are empty except for the swans.

But people still remember me.

If only people would leave me alone.

Before

When I was a child, before *It* came, I knew many people, and children, but I was always more adult than child, and had no understanding with my own kind. They were like wild animals to me, but without the beauty of wild animals. They had to grow before understanding came between us, and then it was too late.

I was a born child, but my mother soon tired of me.

I don't remember her, only my guardians, who were kind and did not stay long. And, of course, I remember the name she chose for me. She called me Geminna, after the golden twins of the zodiac, but she didn't know how apt that name would be.

At sixteen I received this house, an ancestral possession, and my citizen's pension, enough to keep me. I have all I need, and more.

Service

But there is no complete escape.

Every three months come the ten days of Service, my duty to the city.

It is my spring fear, my summer terror, my autumn horror, my winter despair.

This is where I meet these people who linger and cling.

I seem to fascinate them because I am remote.

They want me because I am always moving away.

The Bell

The bell rings.

"Nine seven."

"Ah, yes. Am I speaking to Sol. Geminna Mavern?"

"Yes."

"Sol. Mavern, I am to inform you that your three-monthly period of service is due."

"Thank you."

"We have on record your request for isolated

labor. This time we suggest you report to the Library of Inanimate Beauty. This is more or less a solitary post, where your studies may be continued and also used to profit the establishment."

"Thank you."

"You will commence Service the morning of the day after tomorrow. The twenty-fifth of the month. Your stated working time will be ten in the morning until sixteen hours. Your instructor will meet you in the outer hall."

I have often wanted to visit the Library of Inanimate Beauty, but I couldn't. And now—fear.

Darkness.

The Day Is Here

The day is here.

I rise, bathe and dress in inconspicuous pale black, a dress reaching almost to my ankles, and a wig to hide my hair. The wig is a dull but pleasant brown. My own hair, the golden hair of the golden Twins, attracts too much attention.

Hypnotized by the pale green of the breakfast grapefruit, I can hardly eat it. I drink wine with my coffee, and then more wine without coffee. And then . . .

And now I must go.

I leave the house.

The succession of old doors clang to behind me, shutting me out. Will I be able to return?

There is never this panic when I leave for my lonely walks. This panic is only because I am going where *It* does not like me to go.

The streets surge with people.

Their teeth glint like eyes; their eyes, like teeth, bite my peeled face. A river rushing nowhere sweeps me along. The crowded public cars, the dust, and morning slapping the city across the face. I look back. On the hill, an old mansion. Mine.

There are cascading trees in Palmer Street which leads to the Library of Inanimate Beauty. I think I have come this way before.

White steps, tall slender Martian pillars, each wound round with a bronze snake.

The doors, having recognized me from my Service card, slip open and close behind me.

Now.

Now *It* begins. How can I explain what happens, this intangible terror, the great waves of thick silence beating at my head.

But my instructor is coming.

"Good morning," we say to each other.

He guides me, gliding through the roaring chasms of fear he does not see.

"Sitting room . . . garden . . . food is brought in . . . these books . . ."

He is telling me all manner of things I shall have to discover for myself, later.

He is a big man, like an overfed dog, but plain. Because of this, *It* does not torture me too much. Any sense of quickening at a new presence, and *It* would wring me from end to end with agonized jealousy.

Half an hour has passed.

We drink thin delicate tea, and now he is going. He is gone.

A Sort of Peace

It washes back into *It*self but I can feel *It*, waiting, watchful. *It* will never let me be completely at ease in this new place. There is no guarantee that others may not come, even though I have been told I shall be alone.

But compared to what I was before, now I am liberated. I take off the hot wig and *It* pangs in me: "Be careful."

I wander from room to priceless room, among the ice-limbs of statues, the turning harps, playing, the mosaics and paintings, glass and books. Today people will not come in until fourteen in the afternoon, and by then I will be in my own apartment with my work. Tomorrow the Library will be shut, and mine all day. After that it will be open all the time, and I shall hide, quite safely, but out of reach of this beauty.

There is a golden sun, inside the sun a crystal, inside the crystal a lion of some black glossy material. It sings at the touch of a switch.

The apartment where I am to work is cool and lofty, lined with books, and looks out on to a small walled garden. My instructor has left me a list of instructions, despite our meeting.

I catalogue the books and the music tapes, reading some and listening to some. It is leisurely and enjoyable work. I have been very lucky this time. On the great plaster sheet, four feet by six, I plan the painting they have suggested I might try for them. It will be a panel in one of the walls of the Library, something rich for the whiteness of the room.

Of course, I will make it the Twins.

Slight, muscular, white-bodied beauty in yellow robes, their long hair like marigolds. They are so alike that it is only their sexes, male and female, that makes the slight difference between them, but her breasts are very small, and he has no beard.

Around them are paler yellow leaves and darker
ocher leaves, copper flowers, and the enormous
limbs of old trees. Geminna and Geminni, in their
mind forest, hand in hand, a golden incest of the
soul.

My meal break comes, an optional hour
—shorter or longer if I wish. I sit in the garden, hot
with sun, eating a peach. I am almost, almost at
peace. It is still. Quietness.

A Voice

A bell rings.

I look up, and see it singing in a niche in the
garden wall. I stare at it. It rings and rings. It occurs
to me that I must answer.

I answer.

"L.I.A. three five."

"May I speak to Sol. Mavern? I believe she's
working there."

"Yes, this is Sol. Mavern."

"Geminna!" The voice tells me a name, and says
she met me three months before, when I worked in
the Gallery of Light. "May I come to see you? Now,
perhaps."

"I have a lot of work to do," I say.

"Oh, now, Geminna. You know no one expects
you to work *hard* at anything. You always were so
conscientious. I shall be there at fifteen, after the
Library opens."

The Trap

I put on the brown wig and wait, in my trap, as
the sun slants down the sky. At fourteen the doors
open, and people wander in. Distantly I hear the
extra activity as things whirr and sing, shapes

dance, and colors musically change. I put away the books and continue with the Geminni, but my hands are trembling.

She comes early.

Her dress is a scarlet that hurts my eyes, her movements, fluttery and agitated as a bird's, hurt my eyes. *It* hates her. She flickers into a chair. I summon tea for her and slices of orange, and she smokes long silver cigarettes which make her an aura of silver perfumed smoke.

"Ah, yes . . . So long . . . The party, a simple thing—you never came . . . You promised us you would. This place . . . Old . . . Boring for you . . . Dinner . . . You must come then. Oh, you *must*. So many men, dying to meet you. It *is* a *man* that you'd be interested in? I have other friends. . . . Such a recluse! Geminna, you are so *elusive!*"

I say, I think, the correct things. I hope she will go soon. She does not. She is suggesting that we walk to a café or wine house at sixteen to celebrate our reunion.

"I'm afraid I can't," I say. "It's impossible."

"Oh, it always is!"

She laughs. *I* am impossible.

At last sixteen comes and we leave together. My apartment locks itself behind me. She walks beside me in the open street, where every shaft of sunshine is too brilliant, brittle like glass (we may crack the light by moving through it too quickly), and her voice is splintering the air.

At a corner she leaves me, amused sourly at my rejection. I am white and drained. But I am going home. I seem to run the last yards. My doors fly open, shut fast behind me.

The vise *It* has held me in all day relaxes.

I

I am looking at my face.

It is looking at my face.

Small, pale, tapering, all color drawn out of it into the gold hair. Sometimes plain, sometimes ugly, sometimes beautiful. A changing face, a face like a year, with seasons, days and nights. When I am beautiful, *It* feeds on me, staring out of my own eyes into my own eyes. I have sat half an hour before a mirror, hypnotized, till *It* had had enough.

This is the morning of my fifth day of Service.

Tomorrow and the day after are my rest period, and I may stay at home if I want. After that, another five days and then freedom. Until the next time. It has not been so terrible after all. The girl in scarlet rang me again, but she didn't come to see me.

The Intruder

I walk through the streets, half shut against the noise and movement, and come to the Library of Inanimate Beauty.

Inside I find my instructor. A brief shock. *It* grasps me hard as if I had betrayed *It* and must be punished—as though this unexpected intruder were my fault.

"You look surprised, Sol. Mavern," I hear him saying. "Don't be alarmed. Your work is excellent, I must say. The mural-panel is"—he spreads his hands—"I wish we could attach you to our staff permanently."

In the book-lined room, he summons tea which we drink. He is talking and talking. I wonder why he waits. Suddenly he takes my hand. The touch is electric but horrifying. Alien contact. As if he had burnt me, I snatch away, and *It* writhes in me like a serpent.

He laughs, uneasily.

"A quiet dinner," he says, part of a sentence I have missed.

"No," I say.

I think he has seen *It* in my eyes, hating him. Now it is his turn to recoil. He clears his throat, gets up.

"Someone else will be joining you this afternoon, Sol. Mavern. I hope you'll be kind enough to show them the work that must be done."

Icebergs are splintering and clashing in my head as he goes.

Always I have hated to be touched, because *It* has hated it, furious at my violation. Now I cannot be calm. *It* will not let me be. Once a man, long ago in one of the periods of Service . . . He pulled me to him. He was a handsome man, and *It* detested him more than most. The dark room was red with blood color as he forced my mouth toward the chasm of his mouth, and *It* was a cobra smashing my spine. If I cannot get away, *It* will kill me, kill me rather than let another being have me, even for an instant. I am not very tall or particularly strong, but I thrust the man away from me. *It*s strength worked through me.

Now *It* would like to kill the instructor, and cannot, and so *It* hurts me instead.

When calm comes back, I recall what he has said.

Another one is coming.

Another outsider, another alien.

And I must—

The Young Man

I am painting now, and while the color and the pattern absorb me, I can almost ignore *It*'s iron grip, tightening, as we wait.

I look into the face of Geminni. He looks at me. His face is beautiful and cruel. He holds Geminna tightly by the hand, his other hand stealing towards her breast; claiming her and holding her tight.

The brown wig is very hot. I can't take it off.

Outside, the hum as people move between the statues and the music.

Another sound.

The door of my apartment slides open.

I can't turn. I stare into the face of Geminni, who lashes me with thorns across the old scars of other lashings.

"Can I come in?"

Almost the voice of Geminni, young, male, a beautiful voice.

"Of course."

I must look round now.

I look round.

Damn them, damn them. They have sent me a handsome man.

No, a beautiful man. Young, sapling, lion's hair, eyes like blue knife blades.

It leaps. Like a sea dragon *It* leaps.

I see him staring at me, this young beautiful man. He looks—delightedly amazed.

"I'm sorry," he says, "I expected an old hag. A woman working alone among books and objets d'art—I'm not sure how I formed such a ridiculous impression. And you're not."

He flushes slightly, giving so much away at once to my silence. His skin is clear, pale, the tough gold male hair along his jaw a surprise after the smooth hard softness, almost metallic, across his cheek bones.

I consult the name on his Service card.

Sol. Cyprian.

I can't see the name, but I have memorized the name previously.

"Sol. Cyprian?" I ask him.

He grins.

"Oh yes. Very formal. Try David."

It is eating me alive as I tell him I am called Geminna. He looks from me to the panel, but I whisk him towards the books and music tapes. I have learned my lines for two hours. Now I am word perfect. I see him staring at me as I explain the work he must do. He is puzzled by me. Friendly and attractive, he is used to any response but this. He looks curious, quizzical. When I finish, he wanders back towards the Geminni, wanting to talk to me about it. But I go away. I close myself in the rest room, and sit on the long couch, and the beating sea retreats, leaving me cast up like a dried-out shell on the beach of despair.

Far off, unreal, I hear a flight of planes pass overhead.

Later

Later, it comes to me I must go back. I walk into the room, every sure step the creeping of a terrified insect. I cannot seem to focus as I balance before my painting. I am aware that he sits reading, looks up at me from time to time, still curious. He does no work at all. Ignore me, grow bored with me. You are so beautiful I cannot be quiet. The whole room is full of your presence as if of the sound of the sea, or of some incense burning. I am burning. My hands, my lungs, my eyes are scorched out.

What is the time? Tension has stretched minutes into a thin bright sharpened stake to pierce me. Only fourteen. I cannot bear two more hours of sharp crystal. Where is escape? There must be escape. Sea waves gurn and turn and roar through the hollows of my body, until I am blind, deaf, numb, defeated, caring for nothing except release. I do not even question *It*'s cruelty any longer. I accept all, all, only find me some way to obey you, and so be free.

"Tell me," he says. I hear him from a great distance. It occurs to me that he is not real, a nightmare only. "Do you disapprove of me as much as you seem to? I mean, if you like, I can really do some work."

"Please do what you want," I say.

He smiles, gets up, takes his book into the little walled garden. The sun shines on him. Golden. He is no longer in the room. The transparent doors close softly, dividing us. I will go now. Nothing matters. Excuses can be made later—I am ill, perhaps, or have forgotten some vital personal errand. . . . I slip out of the room, make a way through the people in the Library. The streets are full. Sunlight bursts on the white glass towers of the city, the million windows. There is so much *light*.

The House

Evening purples the oval windows of the house into stained glass. Cool garden darkness hangs over the river. I watch the fish and think of nothing. There is a great calm in me, like the sweet cool peace which follows the cessation of great physical pain. Deliberately, I do not think back over the afternoon, or forward, ahead of the next two days which are mine, for both these avenues of thought are sharpened to hurt me. My image evolves like a ghost on the dark water, disturbed a little by the fish. This is how it is with me, to stand forever, disturbed a little, wavering, distorted, forming again, but always transparent. But there is a reason. There must be a reason. Am I special? Yes, yes, *It* whispers in me. Unique, singled out from the rest—the ones who run in herds. Am I? For what purpose then? The purpose is myself. Why then? There must be some answer, hidden—where? And what?

Dreaming

I am dreaming. I know I am dreaming, because when I am asleep, *It* is no longer with me. Asleep, I am often with people, and it does not seem strange or impossible then, neither am I afraid. David Cyprian is waiting for me in Wilton Square, before the marble portico of the airport. I see very clearly the blue and white flagstones laid out in patterns under our feet. He takes my hand. His touch is familiar yet wonderful. My hand is delighted at its contact with his hand, which is so much larger, dry and cool as a leaf. We walk under the portico. My hair is the color of his, though lighter. I see our reflection in the long mirrors of the walls and, though we are different, we are similar, like brother and sister. Music tinkles through the airport, as I have heard it sometimes, awake, standing outside in the star-frosted dark. A page of the dream turns. Now we are in a little plane, lifting straight into the blue air above the city, rising and rising. He turns and kisses me on the mouth and his mouth is like the world all brought together and given to me in one moment.

I open my eyes and am awake. *It* grips me at once, strongly, fills me and bursts me open. Betrayed, vengeful, *It* rips every memory of pleasure from me, and leaves me empty in the silence.

The House

Two days pass very swiftly. I have done many things, played much music late into the night, finished the embroidered hanging that I shall put up on this wall which faces the garden. Dusk brings uneasiness. I wander across the lawns, the river, the terraces, around the summer house. I climb the steps of the old tower. The city stretches to the hills, a net of neon stars spread over it.

Tomorrow.

I will not think about tomorrow.

Morning

It is morning. I rise, linger over bathing, linger over breakfast without eating. Now is the time to leave. I do not leave. I walk from room to room. An ivory clock-face shows itself, threatening eleven o'clock. I will not think.

Now it is almost twelve. It is impossible that I should see him again. The very *thought* of seeing him again—is impossible. I go to the wall and touch the bell. I ask for the Committee. I explain. I am ill, but very willing to complete my period of Service when I am well once again—in ten days, perhaps? They agree, are sympathetic. I will have to sign a form, of course, which they will send me. But I must not distress myself. They will arrange for my duties to be resumed once I am completely recovered, and everything is perfectly all right. Relief is wonderful. Breathtaking. It was so easy, I am suddenly ashamed. I will not think of this. I am safe. This is all that matters. And whoever else will be there in ten days time, it will not be him. He will be gone, his Service over. It was so easy.

Will he wonder where I am? Will he wonder why I am not there? Will he remember me at all?

I

The day of unexpected freedom is full of an exciting refinding. I read a great deal, and it seems to me my progress is accelerating. In the sunset I dress in the long white dress with its winding embroidery of yellow flowers which are the same shade as my hair. We stand before the mirror. I touch my own hand in the glass, and seem to feel the contact of flesh. We are one. I am whole. *It* lights up my heart like a warm flame. What does anything else matter?

The Door

There is a sound. I recognize the sound as the noise which the door makes when someone comes to it to be admitted. The noise is rare yet full of menace. I sit frozen among the white roses, the candles, the wineglass frozen into my hand. Seconds skitter away. The noise comes again. The core of me holds itself tightly. Go away, whoever you are, go away. I wait. The noise comes. I rise, look about me. Will they stare in at the windows? Will they see the lower rooms where I have sat and walked and lived? Will they climb the walls by some incredible means, stare through into this room and see me imprisoned here in the vivid candlelight, a fly in amber? The door sounds again. So persistent. Who is it that is so persistent? Anyone else would have gone away, thinking me out. I wait.

The door is silent. I count the seconds, then the minutes, standing still at the center of the room. Slowly the core of me relaxes. My hands unfreeze from the glass which breaks in pieces on the floor. They have gone.

It comes to me suddenly that I must check the lower doors of the house—particularly the glass doors to the garden. I cannot remember that I have locked them—these doors which in this old house must still be bolted and barred. And yet, how seldom it is that I forget . . . I take a candlebranch, afraid of the harsh revealing ceiling lights. I go down the stairs, across the hall, into the room where the candles touch gold on the embroidered hanging. I go to the glass doors, and beyond them, in the dusk garden, I see a man's figure.

The Visitor

He has climbed the garden wall after all, its delapidation providing dangerous but successful footholds. He is dusting himself down after his jump from the top into the patch of purple weeds at the side of the house. He looks up and meets my eyes, and comes to the doors. He opens them before I can move, and is in the room with me.

"I really am sorry," he says. "God knows what you must think. You don't even remember who I am, do you? David Cyprian—we met three days ago—look, when you didn't come back, I thought something might be wrong. Then this girl arrived —she said she was a friend of yours. She mentioned where you lived, and it's an out-of-the-way sort of place, isn't it? I dropped by after work—just on a sudden impulse—to see if you needed anything—you're on your own, aren't you? Then you didn't answer the bell. I thought, well, I thought you might be ill. Hence the rescue act over the wall." Suddenly he stops explaining. He takes in my appearance. "But I can see you're quite all right," he says. His eyes narrow slightly. "My apologies. I'll be going then. Can I use your front door, or would you rather I went back the way I came?"

I shut and lock the doors behind him. My hands are trembling; the situation is so strange I don't know what to do with it. I walk out of the room and he follows me.

In the hallway I hear him stop behind me. I too stop, as if at a signal.

"Tell me," he says, and his voice has changed again, "you *are* all right, aren't you?"

He is young and he is concerned. Unafraid of his own kind, he has an interest in them, an affection for them; he does not even understand that I am *not* of his kind. I turn to him, and become all pain and terror as *It* lashes *It's* serpent coils into my heart and brain. I stand and look up at him out of the vortex of my individual and special agony.

The Word

"No," I hear myself say.

One word. One word of betrayal for which *It* will never forgive me. There is nothing more *It* can do to me than *It* will do to me now, for now *It* will kill me. And yet. I am looking into his face still, seeing in his face the lost world drifting away, out of my reach forever, which is foolish, for how can one lose that which one has never possessed? And then I am angry. Anger comes like a biting howling thing; never before have I experienced this madness which exalts in its own extremities.

I run towards the stairs, up them, and he runs after me.

"Wait!"

I run into the music room. The candles smoke. He stands at the open door. I run to the pianos and my fingers sparkle over the decaying keys like scurrying diamond rats in the erratic light. I pull the guitars from their pegs and break their hearts open in brief insanities of song. I run out, and he lets me past. I run into the library. I pull the books in showers of white and scarlet from the shelves. Science and philosophy, poetry and magic lie like severed flower-heads at my feet. I turn and look at him, and I see he is startled, afraid almost of what I have become. It gladdens me. Now *I* am fear also.

And the fear in me, the never-slackening vise, becomes his fear, not mine, so that I glory in it. I run out, down the stairs across the house. My fingers fumble at the locks of the glass doors, and then I am running in the silent darkness of the garden. Pines, the tortured hawthorns, over the stone bridge, the river below me. The summer-house—a white clock-face deprived of hands, timeless—is forever. The terraces, the tower. And then comes stillness, for there is nowhere else to run.

Below, the city. Beyond, the hills fading into the sea. Stars blink at the brightness of the city's stars beneath.

By the Parapet

I stand by the parapet, listening. He is gone. No. I hear him come out onto the tower roof behind me. He is afraid of me. Why has he followed me?

He comes to stand beside me. Why is he here? He is at a loss. I can't grasp his sense of obligation. If only he would leave me alone. In that moment he reaches towards me. A second later I understand that he meant only to touch my arm, guide me back from the edge of the tower roof. But in the moment when I feel the pressure of his hand, I am certain that he will kiss me, and his mouth will become the world. And *It* leaps in me. Like a sea dragon *It* leaps. Always I have hated to be touched, because *It* has hated it. Once, a man, long ago . . . If I cannot get away, *It* will kill me, kill me rather than let another being have me, even for an instant. I am not tall or particularly strong, but I thrust him away from me. *It* thrusts him away from me.

And, losing his balance, the crumbling parapet is

all that can support him. And the parapet does not. In an incredible little burst of snow-white breath, the old stucco-work falls apart like the mummy-dust in a violated tomb.

Death

I accept because I must.

I accept my difference. Understanding follows acceptance. Understanding of the defenses I must not allow to be breached. Nothing else matters. Preservation is the foremost instinct. Ultimately, we kill to survive. Even so, the responsibility is not mine, could never be mine. *It* knew the threat against *It*self. *It* acted. The blade, the bullet, the bomb are not assassins, it is the hand which uses them. I also have been put to use. *It* did what *It* must.

When I think of death, it does not offend me. Death can be beautiful. There need be no stigma of any kind attached to it. Grass and rank flowers, the powder of old stone, the silence, hold all the elements of the wreath, the grave, the monument, the requiem.

The garden reclaims all things into itself.

I put the books back, and the guitars on their pegs. I have begun a new embroidery, larger than the last. Soon I shall have to complete my period of Service, but not yet. There is a lot to do. I shall have no time to go to the tower for many weeks, but the stars are very patient and enduring.

The house is full of peace.

The Bell

By the oval window a bell rings.

"Nine seven," I say, because it keeps me a unit still, and not a person. Who knows? This might be a wrong number.

Beyond the window the glass city stretches away.

"Sol. Mavern?" asks a voice.

And the turquoise hills and the blue hills.

"Yes," I say, and inside me, *It* stirs.

"Sol. Mavern, I'm speaking on behalf of the Committee. We're making inquiries about a young man—a David Cyprian. I understand you worked a Service period with him quite recently?"

And the pale blue hills, like hyacinths.

"It's possible," I say, "but I don't remember. I'm sorry."

And the palest blue hills, like sky.

"I see. In fact, it was your last Service period—I think you left some days early because you were unwell?"

"Yes. Perhaps that's why I don't remember. There was a young man, I believe. I can't recall his name."

"Then you wouldn't have seen him at all since the third of the month?"

"Oh, no," I say. "I didn't really know him."

"I see, Sol. Mavern. Well, I'm sorry to have troubled you."

And the pale silver sea.

But I can't go out.

It won't let me.

Perhaps *It* will never let me again.

AUTHOR'S NOTE

Most of us, with a madman's knife at our throats, would be afraid. Or if we woke up in the night to smoke and a smell of burning. Or if, captured in some out-of-the-way place, we had just been sentenced to be shot in the morning. Or when, opening a familiar door, a clammy tentacle emerged to clasp our wrists. Yes, we would be very afraid indeed, and in the eyes of the world, we should have every right to be.

But there are other kinds of fear, aren't there. Rogue fears, silly fears, that come on us for "no good reason." Most of us have felt their touch, and some of us their taloned grasp. The amateur theatrical we got involved in and, as the curtain rose, wished we hadn't. The first college dance. That dinner party. Even less in focus . . . the crowded store . . . the empty house . . . the car journey two hours long—what's there to be afraid of? These are the things that don't threaten with a knife, a bullet, fire or fiend. Why get so nervous?

Gemini is not a story about devilish possession. It is a story about a case of bad nerves. The human creature concerned, tortured beyond sanity by her own phobias, has morally distanced them, giving them another name and a partially masculine persona—the symbol of her terror of, among other matters, men, the intrusion of the "male" force of vitality and life. Worst of all, perhaps, she has poetically rationalized her subjugation, allied herself to the unacceptable. She has forgotten, too, and so never reveals, where these horrors began. But they are almost always with her, and always waiting in the wings. Only in her dreams, consciousness freed from a body that has become fear's instrument, is she ever at liberty.

Anyone who ever had a nervous moment, for "no good reason," may sense an echo in *Gemini*. It is the monster within who is so terrible. Not the death sentence, or the Thing from the black swamp. We, ourselves, *us*.

And that is, for me, what makes *Gemini* one of the darkest pieces I ever wrote.

—Tanith Lee

GLIMMER, GLIMMER
George Alec Effinger

ROSA TOMCZIK WATCHED HER HUSBAND BUILD UP THE campfire. He dropped on a double handful of sticks and branches, and the flame blazed brighter, sending sparks up toward the evergreen boughs overhead. As the fire died back, while the daylight creatures slipped away and the nighttime animals made their first tentative cries of the evening, Rosa waited for contentment. She waited five minutes. She waited five minutes more, and she realized that she did, after all, feel something, but it wasn't contentment.

What she felt was an anxious suspense, like that moment after a nurse swabbed Rosa's skin and before she stuck in the needle. Rosa had felt that way for most of the vacation.

Her husband, Joey, hadn't taken a single day off from work in the twelve years they'd been married. The whole notion of this bicycle trip had sounded peculiar ever since Joey had suggested it. Joey had started out as a sales clerk in his father's small dress shop. Now Joey owned more than three hundred fashion outlets in shopping malls across the country. Whenever Rosa brought up the subject of a

231

vacation, he always said he had his empire to protect. He'd been tempted, but he had always resisted.

Until now. Of course, it had been Joey's decision to bike around the countryside. Rosa knew that he wouldn't put up with all the discomforts under normal conditions. She wondered where Joey was taking them. She felt lost, completely cut off from civilization. She didn't like discomfort, either. Joey was bearing up under all the hardships, and he didn't complain. That, too, wasn't like him. He was behaving like a totally different person. It was enough to make Rosa harbor suspicions.

Rosa took a can of insect repellent out of her pack and sprayed her arms, hands, and face. She walked around the fire and offered the can to Joey. He sprayed himself and gave the can back to her. She went back to her pack and stowed the can. Then she looked across the campfire at her husband. "So tell me, Joey," she said softly, "is this trip saving our marriage or what?"

"Don't you think things are better?" He sounded surprised.

"Sure, right now things are better. But will they still be better when we get back home? You know, back to the real world. When I go back to my white lab coat and clipboard and you go back to being the boy wonder of ready-to-wear."

In the twilight she saw him shrug. "It's too early to tell. This may all be some big mistake."

She started to reply, closed her mouth, then laid down in her sleeping bag and turned to face away from him. She didn't get to sleep for a long time. As she drifted finally into dreams, she thought of Melinda, Joey's girlfriend. He said that Melinda meant nothing at all to him. He claimed to have no deep feelings for Melinda, and Melinda didn't seem to need or want them. After all, Joey Tomczik bought her things and took her places; what more could a woman ask for?

In the morning they shared coffee, bacon, and eggs. Fifteen minutes later, Rosa repacked the food and Joey scrubbed out the skillet. Joey and Rosa on a vacation. As soon as they got home, he'd throw his things together and leave her. That's the way his mind worked. The question of asking for a divorce would never come up. A divorce would mean that Joey would lose half his wealth. A whole fortune is better than a divided fortune.

Joey rubbed his eyes, then looked up at the sun. "We could put in a short day, get a really good night's sleep tonight. No sense killing ourselves. I figure we're at least two days ahead of schedule anyway."

Rosa nodded. "That's okay," she said. "Where do you figure we are?"

He took out a creased and torn map. "There's a state forest less than a day's ride from here. We'll make the campground by suppertime. We can spend a little while looking at flowers and butterflies and stuff." Rosa was irritated by his condescending assessment of her life's work in biochemical research: flowers and butterflies and stuff.

They pedaled at an easy pace and the land changed gradually from farms and empty fields to thick stands of pine and spruce, and then there was a wooden sign saying the state forest was fifteen miles farther. Less than an hour later they were there. A profound and unbreakable hush wrapped them almost immediately. Rosa looked deeper into the forest from the path. The trees were straight and tall, and the light that sifted down among them was reassuring in its gentleness. Rosa found it peaceful. She stared at Joey's sweat-streaked back and wondered what he, the blouse-monger, her off-the-rack tycoon husband, was seeing. If anything.

The forest was so lovely that neither Rosa nor Joey knew where they should stop for the night. They had already passed several areas set aside for campers in their recreational vehicles. Joey had made it clear that he didn't want to use these campsites. He said they were like camping out in the back yard, with their electrical outlets, running water, and cooking facilities. He'd rather go out into the dense woods themselves, the virgin forest, far away from all the conveniences. Joey liked to pitch camp near a stream, build a small but efficient cooking fire, fix a nice hot supper, watch the dying coals, grow sleepy, shake out the sleeping bags, and settle down on the ground beneath a silent old giant of the forest.

Rosa didn't get a vote in the matter.

Suddenly he announced, "We'll stop here." He pushed his bike off the trail and into the forest, and Rosa followed. They moved slowly through the fresh pine kitchen-floor scent of the air. The evergreen needles crunched beneath their feet. They heard bird twitterings and the buzzing of invisible insects. They steered their bicycles around patches of wildflowers and little shrubs whenever they could. After several minutes, they found a stream and decided they had come far enough. Rosa didn't like the spot at all. They were too far from the trail, too far into the deep forest. What if something should happen to them? It might be years before someone stumbled upon this place. She glanced at Joey, who seemed unusually elated. Rosa's vague suspicions were beginning to take a solid and ominous form.

She took two clean Clorox bottles down to the stream and filled them with water while Joey started clearing the ground for the fire. When Rosa returned, she asked, "Are you nearly ready?"

"Fire's burned down almost enough," said Joey.

"We still have this package of freeze-dried beef stroganoff," she said. "And a couple of packages of hot chocolate and cookies for dessert. We'll need to pick up some more supplies tomorrow or the next day. And refill the drinking water at one of the bathhouses."

"No problem," he said. He sat down beside Rosa and stared into the fire. They didn't say anything for a long while. Rosa thought the whole vacation had been arranged to get her here, alone, for some reason. She didn't want to think about why. It was probably only her imagination, she told herself. Still, from the very beginning Joey had done one uncharacteristic thing after another. She couldn't deny all that. But what did it add up to?

An hour later, after supper had been prepared, eaten, and washed up after, they stared again into the flickering flames. Rosa studied Joey. What was he looking for? Joey: the real man, the adventurer, the bold leader always in control. It was always Joey who chose the day's route. Through the farmland, over the hills, along the forest trail, it was the little two-bike parade with Joey as the grand marshal and Rosa pedaling along behind.

She understood that what galled Joey was asking for a divorce. He knew how she felt. First he would threaten, then plead, then bribe. He would do anything but succeed. Rosa knew that Joey would do anything to avoid the distractions to his work, to avoid paying attorneys their fat fees, to avoid the publicity. He would not be able to bear Rosa's ending up with most of what he'd created and built up the hard way. Which she would demand. It would be a long, arduous legal battle, or it would be a short, murderous one.

So, Rosa thought, Joey was probably toying with the idea of an easier though violent solution. An idyllic bike vacation was not natural or logical at this point in their marriage. Rosa was well aware of this, and it made her tense, wary.

"Look," said Joey. "Lightning bugs."

"Fireflies."

"Yeah. I love lightning bugs. You're the science expert—what makes them light up?"

"It's a chemical reaction," said Rosa. "Bioluminescence. And they're not bugs. The only insects that are true bugs belong to the order Hemiptera. Fireflies belong to the order Coleoptera."

"So big deal." Joey stared into the darkness. "Look," he said, pointing. "Look how it's shining underneath that bush, like a flashlight under those leaves. I don't believe how bright it is."

"The females. Glowworms, people call them."

"Look how many there are," said Joey. "You just don't see so many lightning bugs at home. They're beautiful. It's really beautiful. My God. I've never seen so many."

"You couldn't even describe this to anybody," she said. "They wouldn't understand how gorgeous it is. Everybody's seen fireflies, but not many people have seen them like this." She stood up, went to her pack, and took out a spray can marked insect repellent. "It's getting late, the humidity's gone up, and the mosquitoes will be murder."

"Hey, Rosa, look over there." Joey had walked farther into the woods.

Rosa looked where he was pointing. "What about it?" she asked.

"I've never in my life seen so many lightning bugs, not so bright. It looks like there's a shopping center glowing behind these trees."

"You've discovered the fireflies' burial ground, Joey," said Rosa, laughing. "They come from all over the world to die here. You'll be famous."

"I mean it, Rosa." He walked through the blackness far from the campfire.

"Where are you going? The water's starting to boil. Don't you want your tea? But if you're going out there, better spray yourself some more. Remember how you bitched the last two nights about the way the mosquitoes bit you up?"

"Yeah, and I remember that you were bitten even worse than I was." He came back to her and took the spray can. He covered all his exposed skin, then tossed the can back to Rosa. She made a fumbling attempt to catch it, but she missed.

"Aw, come on. Leave the fire for now. Let's enjoy the night, Rosa. The weather is perfect, and I'm feeling good."

She followed her husband a few yards farther into the forest. Joey had suddenly become awed by nature. It might be genuine, but Rosa thought he might just be pretending, trying to lure her even deeper into the wilderness. His childlike curiosity was more menacing than anything he'd said or done so far.

She stopped beside a slender tree. Joey moved on ahead of her. The fireflies flashed and flickered around him. He was surrounded by thousands of yellow-green points of light. Rosa watched, fascinated.

"There are even more of them here now," called Joey. "Away from the glare of our fire. It looks like a swarm or something."

"Maybe it's mating season for them," said Rosa.

"Just enjoy it, honey," he said, annoyed. "You can leave all that stuff back at the lab."

"You may not want your tea, but I do," said Rosa, and she turned back, looking over her shoulder.

Ten or twenty yards deeper into the woods, the fireflies were now flashing brighter and faster. The insects were so luminous, they seemed like a bonfire burning. "My God," Joey murmured. He moved slowly toward the light. "At home we've got lightning bugs, but I've never, never seen anything like this. It's crazy."

As Joey drew closer, the insects flared brighter, melding their lights into a constant, fierce, greenish glow. "Rosa."

"I'm having a nice cup of tea," she called to him. "I may even save you some." She watched her husband and just shook her head.

He stood among them, his face weirdly contorted by the pulsing greenish light of the fireflies. She heard him laugh, then choke. He spat and gagged. Rosa imagined what it must feel like to have a large insect wriggling in her mouth. She shuddered in revulsion.

Fireflies brushed Joey's face. Rosa thought with disgust of the fireflies creeping into his ears, his eyes, his mouth, his nostrils. Joey tried to fling them away, but they were endless in their numbers. Rosa saw him fall to his knees. "Rosa!" he called weakly. She stood up to watch.

He was kneeling on the ground, his arms around his head. He seemed to Rosa to be clothed now in a thick, persistent cloud of throbbing yellow-green. The fireflies covered his face completely, his neck, too, and his arms and hands. A mass of insects crawled up his chest. She heard Joey whimper, and even more fireflies forced their way into his mouth. He retched and tried to clear his throat, but he was choking, smothering. He thrashed and vainly flung himself about, hoping to roll clear of the fireflies, but he couldn't escape them. He couldn't see because the insects were gathered thickly over his eyelids. Rosa saw him crack his head painfully on the rough trunk of a tree. She was sickened by the sight, but at the same time she was compelled to watch.

Joey's panic rose; Rosa pictured herself in his place, and she knew she might go crazy if she couldn't end the torment. The terrible feeling of thousands of insects crawling, creeping, buzzing, violating his entire body overcame him at last. Joey fell prone on the forest floor. The fireflies in his mouth and throat had suffocated and strangled him. His body fell not far from the campsite. Rosa stared at her husband's contorted, still-glowing body. In a few moments he was unrecognizable in the vast greenish aura.

Rosa realized that her muscles were cramped and stiff from tension. Her exposed skin had been ravaged by mosquitoes. She went to her pack and took out the safe can of repellent—the one with the gray lid—and sprayed herself thoroughly. Using a plastic glove, she picked up the other can of repellent—the one with the black lid—from the ground where she had let it fall when Joey had tossed it to her. She dropped the can, the one she'd filled with firefly sex pheromone, into a plastic bag. She unpeeled the glove, put that in the bag, too, and sealed the bag with a twist-tie. She'd dispose of it later. She left all the camping gear behind, just as a terrified and grief-stricken wife would.

Joey hadn't asked for a divorce because that would mean splitting everything he had. It never occurred to him that the sword cut both ways. Rosa allowed herself a wry smile: a whole fortune was definitely better than half, Joey had been right about that. As she pedaled easily through the forest, she began rehearsing what she would say to the park rangers and how she would act.

AUTHOR'S NOTE

I got the idea for "Glimmer, Glimmer" while camping one night a while ago. I saw a cloud of fireflies, and I realized that it had been a good number of years since I'd seen them in an urban setting, the way they used to be in my backyard in Cleveland when I was a child. We used to catch them and keep them in glass jars, with a few leaves of grass for them to "eat." They'd die fast. We were always sorry, because we all loved fireflies.

The character of the tycoon husband came from an article in *New York* magazine I had read just a couple of days before I sat down to work on the story. I drew the husband from that article, gave the wife a professional understanding of biochemistry, and the story took over and told me what sort of marriage they would end up with. Before I knew it, the plot had worked itself out for me. The final shape of the story was refined by Alice Turner, the fiction editor of *Playboy*, who suggested a few imaginative ways to tighten the prose and increase the suspense. I'm glad to acknowledge her help.

My aim was to write a story in the manner of Roald Dahl or John Collier, two great masters of the very short, very powerful suspense story. "Glimmer, Glimmer" is a thriller, a horror story, or a science fiction story, depending on your point of view. I think it's a black humor piece, with one of the world's most unlikely murder weapons.

—George Alec Effinger

PERVERTS
Whitley Strieber

FRANK WAS SICK OF LIVING ONLY AFTER DARK, SICK OF always being dirty and afraid and so godawful tired. And hungry. As usual he needed something more than the single doughnut he had been able to afford. He needed a hamburger or a steak or a Chateaubriand—or even more, the softest of caresses. He sipped his coffee, watching the waitress move back and forth behind the long white counter. She was as pale as the marble countertop, her hair ash-blond, her eyebrows made visible only by the droplets of sweat gleaming in the hairs. When the screen door creaked she glanced up for an instant. A smile of recognition flickered across her face and she tossed a curl out of her eyes with a carefully manicured finger. "Hiya, Becky," she said to the tall woman who had entered.

Small-town people. Everybody knows people. Frank looked down into his cup. He knew that the two deputy sheriffs at the corner table were aware of him, and that they'd jump at any excuse to put a dirty hobo on the county gang for a couple of weeks. One of the two men had an elaborately bandaged upper lip, and eyes as hard and bright as ball bearings.

The waitress came and went, flashing like a shaft of sunlight up and down the counter. Two prim little girls sat together drinking Postum. They also knew the waitress, and nodded to the tall woman as she pulled up to the counter. Funny that kids would be allowed out this late and nobody seeming to mind.

The tall woman, not quite young, her face dense with makeup, her fingernails cracked by hard work, ordered sausage and eggs. The waitress was also the chef, and she slung the meal together over the grill, adding plenty of home fries and even a half of a tomato. Frank knew he wouldn't get extras if he ordered a meal. When the plate was put in front of her the tall woman hung over it, eating steadily.

For midnight in the middle of the dust bowl this was a pretty lively place. But around it, in the dark, Frank knew that there was nothing but vast Texas space, miles of weevil-ridden cotton and houses with rattling shutters, sweaty beds and wind, wind without end.

Frank mourned. There had been a time when he wouldn't even have glanced at such a girl as this waitress. He had been made so rich by the 1928 runup in shares that he had gone to the Continent on the *Berengaria*, the world's most luxurious liner. The hiss of the water, the icy, tinkling chatter of Rebecca Landauer, the roses and the whispering sheets . . .

Rebecca Landauer, dark where this girl was light, her eyes full of fire and complication. What did the waitress offer? Lust, for her friends. For the likes of a hobo, absolutely nothing.

Which was okay by him. He understood. He didn't want to make trouble. He had come in here to rest his bones and take advantage of the endless coffee pot, and that was all.

"Hey, kid." He nodded toward his mug.

"You got it." She swung past, gave him his refill. He watched the faint blue veins on the back of her hand as she poured, then looked up into her eyes. He was startled by something unexpected there, a fierceness that confused him, and he quickly glanced away. Her full lips, slightly parted, were touched by a complex smile.

A man with a dollar and seven cents in his pocket does not come on to a decent woman, not even a counter girl. He pushed his old porkpie back on his head and wished for roses and calling cards and his enormous car. But life is loss, the green becomes brown, the dancers go home.

And Octobers come, like for example, the October of two years ago when men strutting in broadcloth one day were penniless the next. He had known what it was to take his last ride in his Duesenberg, to smell the maroon leather interior for a final time, to cancel his massage at the Athletic Club and his last date with Rebecca Landauer, to leave his splendid apartments in the Majestic and find himself, blinded by tears, clumsily learning in the middle of the night the trick of hopping a freight.

Rebecca Landauer. If only, only, only she had not convinced him to put so very much money in the Commercial Solvents pool. If only. She had murdered him with her innocent tip.

The Depression was a boon for Rebecca

Landauer. She had gone short a few days before the crash.

And she had said: "The race goeth to the swift, Frankie." Her indifference was so vast that it was a kind of affliction, like a withered limb or the inability to laugh.

He had discovered how dark the land gets after moonset, and the way hobos in boxcars smell, and the taste of the truncheon and the rifle stock. He had been beaten and threatened and made to crouch for two days in a cell that had been a chicken coop. The freights and the other 'bos and the bulls had become too much for him, and he had abandoned the rails in Waco, and taken to the road. He was just another Okie now, and he had learned all there is to know about dust and getting left behind and wishing to almighty God that you would just keel over and die.

Frank was a man who had given a girl a two-thousand dollar necklace on her birthday, but now he cared only for the lingering taste of his doughnut and this steaming mug of java.

He had listened to wind in prairie grass, and found that night was his best time, because darkness is the friend of desperate men. He had walked the roads, stopping to examine Hershey wrappers and corn shucks, and longing for just five minutes of riding in one of the old flivvers that occasionally chugged by. He had slept away this past afternoon in a culvert because he didn't dare enter Waco during daylight hours. If he did he would end up doing a stretch chained to other stinking unfortunates, hacking at roadside brush with a sickle or hauling shoulder gravel.

Two weeks ago a woman had given him three dollars to tear down a barn. He had slaved ten hours a day for five days, and finally gotten the job done—and in the process learned a lot about how to use sledgehammer and crowbar with hands that had touched little more than narrow waists and bearer bonds and silver service.

The front door of the diner slammed as the two deputy sheriffs left. They started up their Ford and drove off, their single tail light glowing red beyond the diner's dark windows.

Frank was halfway finished with his second mug of coffee. He sipped it slowly. The overhead fans cooled him, and the smell of bacon and steak and frying eggs brought back creamy memories. He contemplated yet again the ten cent breakfast, but dared not drop below that critical dollar that kept him from committing the crime of vagrancy. He could not face jail again. Men died on the chain gangs all the time.

"You kids better get goin', y'all're up so late," the waitress said to the prim little girls. "Y'all sure you know what to do, now?"

"Yes ma'am," said the eldest of the girls, a child of sullen and extraordinary beauty. There was about her, with her straw-blond hair pulled back into a bun, a sense of severe energy. And her eyes were cold.

As the girls got up the middle-aged woman suddenly stretched and yawned expansively. "Now you got me yawnin', Pearl. I think maybe I'll turn in." She glanced in Frank's direction and he knew that her eyes were asking the waitress if she felt safe alone with the hobo.

Pearl laughed. "You go on. I'm gonna close down

in about fifteen minutes. Ain't nobody else comin' in now you vaudevilles and the sheriffs're done."

Frank watched the waitress set about cleaning the counter with a big gray cloth. The whirring of the fan and the snapping of the cloth were the only sounds until she spoke. "Give you one more cup, 'bo, then you're off. And don't you go sleepin' out behind this place. There's a fella comes in on the mornin' shift killed a 'bo back there last month. Stove in his head. Don't like you 'bos."

He thought: my name is Franklin Waring III. I am the grandson four times removed of General Augustus Waring of the Continental Army, who ate his boots at Valley Forge.

And then, as the fall of rain from an October sky, he was crying. The sobs poured out of him. When he fought them they became hacking, choked gnarls of sound, but they would not stop.

She put her hand under his chin and raised his face. He did not want her to see the distortion of his tears and tried to turn away. "No," she said, "you got a right, 'bo." And he revealed the humble truth of his grief to her. When he looked into her bland country prettiness he saw there something that had no limit and no end.

She asked, "You ridin' or walkin'?" and his heart began to pound.

He thought to ask, to beg her—deliver me from the evil poem of my life. But he said only: "Walkin'."

"Me, I'd ride. The freights are slow coming around Eight-Mile Bend and there's no bulls. Easy hop, if you want to do it. Get you to L.A. in eight days.

"The Katy Railroad is safe. But you've got to

change to the Santa Fe in San Antonio, and Santa Fe bulls shoot to kill.

"You aren't a regular 'bo. You talk too nice."

"I'm from back East."

She leaned across the counter to pick up his doughnut plate, and he thought she might have the most milk-white cleavage that had ever been granted mortal woman. He scented the promise of the breasts, and saw little jewels of sweat. "You want that coffee, Back East? Last chance."

"Frank."

"Hi, Frank. I'm Pearl."

"'Lo, Pearl."

"I come from the Garden of the Gods, Frank. I'm an actress. This is just fill-in work."

"Nightclub hereabouts?"

"Not the Garden of the Gods. It's vaudeville. Runs real late night. They got a place down along the Brazos. People come in all the way from New York and places to see the Garden of the Gods."

"Roadhouse? I'd like to go in one of those places and just say to the waiter, you give me the biggest and the best steak you've got. I'd eat myself to death and die a happy man."

"You won't die of overeating." Their eyes connected, and Frank felt almost as if she were touching him, but in a place so intimate that it didn't even have a name. He was repelled, like the time in the boxcars when the little boy had offered to "help him get to sleep" for a nickel. The kid had evoked this same cloying uneasiness, as if he had been stroked in a way that he could not bear, but could not resist. "I have the second sight," Pearl said. She took his hand and opened his palm. "You'll die in a fire. And not long from now. Not long at all."

Her words affected him as a sudden flash where no light should be. He laughed, of course. "You've got a lot to learn about fortune telling. Nobody'll ever pay you for news like that."

"It's what I see."

"I've suffered enough!" The vehemence of his own words astonished him. It was not his practice to speak intensely to women. When she smiled saucy and confident, he felt an urge to hit her, to slam his knuckles into that pale skin. He suddenly knew how men came to commit murder, and why they had to be executed for it.

"Gawd, gawd," a tremendous black man had said in a Kansas holding tank—big catchall cage in the Perry County jail—"Gawd, gawd, they gonna 'lectrocute me." He had just come back from his sentencing and was on his way to the state prison. A big illiterate man, with a Kirk fountain pen he conceived of as a kind of magic wand, he stood at the edge of the cage and fingered the bars.

You could get fifteen years for stealing a nickel, life for robbing a storekeeper of a dollar, or death for threatening a woman, if you were a 'bo.

Little places do not like wanderers, they bring too much of the tang of the road with them. For the crime of having less than a dollar to his name Frank had broken rocks on the Perry County gang for a month, watched by an indifferent trusty and hounded by summer-bored kids who liked to torture the convicts by tossing stones at their heads.

"You're remembering," Pearl said. "You left a fine life. And you miss it awful bad." She had come around the counter and now stood behind him.

"Not much to remember. Losing all my money. Hitting the road. Breaking rocks."

Her eyes seemed almost to haze. "Look, if you need a place to get some shut-eye—"

She lapsed to silence, slowly and carefully placing her coffee pot on the counter. Afraid even to whisper such wild, improbable, dangerous hopes, Frank questioned her with his eyes. When she smiled his heart started once more to pound. "Miss, if you've got a bed I could lie down in, I'll do anything in the world to get to it."

Her hand came and touched his temple, a gentle, motherly gesture. The night wind moaned around the corner of the diner. "Well, you can come along with me."

He felt stirring in his loins. "Thank you," he managed to breathe. Gratitude rushed over him, surged as a drowning tide, forcing more tears and downcast eyes.

Once again her hand lifted his chin. "There's no shame in hard times, Frank."

She cut off the fans one by one, then the grill and the coffee pot and she emptied the till into the floor safe. She looked around, sighed. "Diners are a hard business." Then she regarded Frank, who was still seated at the counter. If he got up his body was going to reveal his desire. His overalls were thin. He had no underwear to contain him. Her eyes became warmer, and she turned out the lights. "Might as well get going," she said. "The place is a little ways off from here."

He followed her stiffly down the unpaved street, watching her white uniform glowing like a baleful lantern ahead. They moved down toward the Brazos, in among the dark shacks of the poor, until they came to an enormous bulk of a house surrounded by huge chinaberry trees. The Brazos muttered in the blackness, the stars gave only enough light to edge the shadows. Frank was aware of their feet crunching on gravel and then tapping on granite pavements. He was a little perplexed in his mind, but his blood sang: woman, woman, woman. Along with the fragrance of laurel, the wind brought the dense perfume of her sweat.

Inside the house was steaming hot, the air absolutely still, absolutely black. There was a sense of large, dense space. And there were more perfumes here, even some he remembered: Arpège, Lanvin, and Rebecca's favorite, La Nuit.

He could no longer see even Pearl's uniform.

Then her hands touched both his cheeks, with such assurance that he knew she could see, and see well. For a moment she pressed her body against his, and he felt what a full, strong woman she was, not fragile like the fashionable girls of Manhattan. His flesh was tense with desire for these heavy cornbread hips. Her finger touched his lips. "You're scared," she said. Then a giggle came out of the darkness. "I think that's the bee's knees."

He heard the hiss of cotton against skin and thought she might be undressing. Then her hand came around his wrist. "Come," she said, and her tone seemed odd, as if she were calling a pet. "Come." Her fingers were too firm. Had he not been certain that this was the hand of a kind and gentle woman he would have recoiled.

She drew him through the house to a back room. He had an impression of curtained hallways, and once he thought he might have heard a whisper. "What is this place?"

"An abandoned mansion. Joringel, it's called. It belongs to a bankrupt cotton planter. Lots of those in this part of Texas."

He heard a faint click. She had locked the door. The darkness was absolute and impalpable. He couldn't see even the suggestion of a shape. When she laid his hand against her own cool thigh, he knew that she was indeed naked. "Come on over here," she said, "the bed's right here." There was a creak. "Lemme get you naked, 'bo, then you lie right down." He did not resist her quick fingers, and soon felt the intimacy of night air against his own stone skin. "Whatever I do, 'bo, you just lie still."

"I won't move, Pearl." No indeed. He felt her weight as she straddled him, and thought he must be beneath the very body of kindness.

She spoke to him in a voice that recalled the comforts of childhood. The bed was narrow and hard but she was neither, and he lay in the luxurious pillows of her flesh, and remembered how blond she was, and kissed her where he could, on her belly. She swung off him, then took his head and guided it down to the unknown regions of her body, where he grazed as contentedly as a herded steer.

As he touched and held and kissed her soft skin, he sensed that he was close to the border of passion, that this might very well become his deepest entry yet into love.

They rode on through the night, steaming in a sweated jungle of their own limbs and lips, while the heavens changed and the tiny room grew close with more breath than their own.

A sense of largeness came into the air, and it grew subtly cooler. He was confused. What was this greater dark, this soft, huge movement as if the wall itself was rising? "I told you, 'bo, just keep right on."

"Holy God, we're on a stage!"

"'Bo, I'm gonna give you whatfor if you don't shut up." Her voice was shrill, excited. "Right in front of all these people. You won't like it, 'bo."

One of the little girls from the diner was lighting candles around the bed, candles that burned with low, red flames.

Beyond the proscenium Frank could just see the first rows of the audience, their faces as rigid as wax.

"Welcome, ladies and gentlemen," said a voice that sounded very much like one of the deputies from the diner, "to the Garden of the Gods, where we offer you the spectacle of love and death, ladies and gentlemen, for your delight and your enlightenment."

Frank realized that he had heard of this place before, and what he had heard made his mouth go dry. He remembered rumors spoken in hushed whispers in the parlor car of the Century, in the smoking room of the Union Club . . . of a house somewhere in the South where frightful things were done, where it was possible to be witness to love, and to death. Rebecca had known of it. "Reality is the final entertainment there," she had said. "The farthest outpost of civilization, where art is death." Rebecca Landauer could be pompous. But she had also lured Frank into the extraordinary pleasures of absinthe and opium, on long, languid afternoons in her rooms at the Astor. Afternoons of nakedness, while Rebecca whispered all the twists of her imagination, then spoke them aloud: astonishing perversions, games of tasting what must not be tasted and touching what could not bear caress, of pleasure so extreme that it was harder to endure than pain.

He realized that she must have been to the Garden of the Gods. In a sense, perhaps, she had lured him here, not with artifice, but with a spider's patience.

"Rebecca," he called into the rows of uplifted faces. But of course she did not answer.

Pearl lay flat upon him as the quick-fingered girls from the diner tied his wrists to the bedframe.

"Let them," Pearl said, "you could get hurt if you resist."

He was surprised at how little afraid he was.

The deputies, in evening dress now, stood like sentinels at the edges of the stage. High above a skylight was cranked open. Night air flowed down, cool and rich. Frank fixed his gaze on the stars, and tried not to notice what Pearl was doing to him.

But his body noticed, and flexed with the pleasure her hands brought it. Each gasping spasm brought a flurry of applause from the audience.

The world was a very different place from what it seemed. The rows of houses, the Fords, the men in straw hats, the cherry phosphates of summer and the hot toddies of winter were not real at all, nor the mothers in their shawls, nor the Princeton crew, nor the trimotor airplane, nor the Graf Zeppelin, nor the old general store at Cox's Corner in Maine, where he and Rebecca had stopped for spoons to prepare opium, and she had said, "It deserves doing in silver."

And then his body noticed how very rough she was being with him. In a reedy voice the deputy said, "The crime of the Hindoo priestess Lopashlong!" The laughter came like knives, and a sudden white torment between his legs left him stunned and choking.

The trophy, his own self, was laid on a silver tray and taken through the aisles by the deputy with the wounded lip.

When it came back the bloody flesh was covered with tips: fifty-dollar gold pieces, hundred-dollar bills, jeweled trinkets, even the keys to a car. Pearl jangled the keys at the audience and then left the girls to pick the other tips from the bloody pile.

Frank supposed that he must be in shock. He understood the disaster that had befallen him, and felt the agony, but he was curiously unmoved by it all. He gazed at the stars, and listened to his own blood trickling into a can. Pearl caressed his face with a moist cloth. "You could kiss me," he said.

"My brother got his lip bitten off that way last week, kissing a client. She lost a breast, and she was madder than you."

"I'm not mad." He stared into the pale, soft features and longed for this one more touch of sex, this last meaningful contact of lip to lip. But she withdrew from him, lightly touching her fingers to his mouth. "Pearl, is this how everybody dies?"

She smiled. "Don't you trouble yourself about that. You just close your eyes now, 'bo."

"I want to look at the stars."

"If you see what we're about to do, you'll suffer. You've earned a peaceful death, 'bo."

"Who are the people in the audience?"

"Hush now, 'bo." Something scratched and flickered. Then she was cradling a match. Almost lazily, Frank tested his bonds. His hands and feet were tied tight to the bedframe.

The girls cuddled Frank tightly in the sheets as

Pearl knelt down beside the bed. She leaned far under it and busied herself there for a few moments.

He could see the fire she had set flickering on the faces of the audience.

A needle seemed to penetrate his left thigh, then another, then another. Then one came up between his shoulders. He squirmed. A band began to play, a tenor to sing, "Con-stan-ti-no-ple, C-o-n-s-t-a-n-t-i-n-o-p-l-e!" He had danced to that song when the decks of the *Berengaria* were washed by rain, and the sea beyond the portholes rode furious with mystery.

The stars flickered and danced in a vortex of heat, and he heard his own voice crying out with distant agony.

She remained as close to him as she could, shielding her eyes from the flames, letting him look upon her.

The audience was silent, awed by the suffering of the twisting, bouncing figure on the red-hot bed-stead.

Frank's heart swooned forth into great distances, striving upward with his smoke, seeking the freedom of the night. Behind him all was silence. Before him, also silence.

He felt himself no more than a vapor at the far limit of dream, although he was in fact the ruined, blackened victim of an obscene show, a lost hobo dying to amuse others no less lost, his heart swelling with awe and joy when it should have been breaking. But there was to be no repeat of last week, when the victim had struggled so, and died in fury and bitterness.

No, this was a place of luxury, where death

should fall like dew, where even savage torments should cause rapture.

It was thus, in a sense, a shrine of the triumph of man. Certainly Rebecca Landauer viewed it as such as she sifted the fine dust of the world, seeking and preparing her victims. And Pearl too, so raptured by what she had just done that her whole body was at this moment a tingling web of pleasure.

As for Frank, he saw nothing, but his corpse had the most delicate of smiles upon its blackened face.

AUTHOR'S NOTE

I am always shocked when I discover that I have written a story. It seems to me to be an unlikely thing to do, and while I am doing it I feel more as if I am living in a little world of restricted but incredibly energetic possibilities than conducting some sort of "work."

When I wrote "Perverts" I was living in an illusional version of my own reality. I was trying to find a way to express an inner fury that I could not then name. Now that I can name it, and have done so in *Communion*, another aspect of the relationship has come to be primary to my personality.

In all of my work there is a furious, ecstatic relationship to the female. This female is not the modern idealization of "womanhood," but a far older form. It is the raging, wise and kindly form of Ishtar, Astarte, Athene, the great triune goddess whose allies now cleave to the Virgin Mary in the West and to Kali in the East. My stories are about the melding of these two alliances in the fire of pure acceptance. This is why the tormented suffer such ecstasy in *The Hunger*, "Pain," "Perverts," and

The Night Church, and why Jamshid in *Black Magic* is such a sexually nebulous figure.

Here is a creation myth: As the Goddess whirled about, struck by the light of the universe, she cast off one by one all of her identities, and when she had whirled away to her final purity, each identity lay lambent in the earth, thus filling it with the whole potential that became the created world.

For me, search is a matter of rowing back toward this being. It is finding the madness of pleasure that hides in a flower or the cast of late light upon smooth skin, or in the surrender of the flesh to the flames.

—Whitley Strieber

ON ICE

Barry N. Malzberg

I GIVE IT TO MY MOTHER. ISN'T THIS WHAT I ALWAYS wanted? What else was always on my mind? It is extraordinary, absolutely extraordinary to do it in this way: I did not know the old bitch had so much drive in her.

"Do it son!" she shrieks, her wrinkled hands beating away at my neck, her thighs urging me into a more profound pace and I yield her literally everything that I have got, yards and yards of need or so it seems at this point, my genitals uncoiling like rope within her . . . and I shoot deep into her murky abcesses the load I have held back for decades, weeping I sent her the load I have always carried within me . . . and my sobs and shrieks could be mistaken for agony as she holds me against her and murmurs comfort, soothes me, advises me to be calm. "These things happen," she murmurs, still twitching against me, "you've got to learn to take them in stride."

"I don't have to be calm, you bitch!" I shouted, springing from her, the weapon of my necessity still shrieking hard to the touch as I stuff it away in my

pants. "I have a perfect right to do anything I want
to do and you can't touch me. You don't even
understand me!" I add which, although a perfectly
justifiable complaint and an old one, sounds somewhat thin under the circumstances and so, disgusted within myself, disgusted with my perversity,
I go away from there quite hurriedly, seeking a
different direction as once again they pull me to the
surface. It always ends this way; I am *yanked* from
situations. There is no dignity in any of this.
Something has got to be done.

II

"I'm sure you found that fascinating," the girl at
the desk says to me on the way out. "I can always
tell, telling's my job and I can see from your face
that you really enjoy that. When should I schedule
your next appointment?" and she takes a card from
the file rack behind her (my card!), holds a pen,
looks at me expectantly, and some aspect of taunt-
ing in her eyes makes me want to shout, brutalize,
tell her that whatever my condition she has no
right, this wretched parasite, to sit in judgment of
me . . . but then I remember that this is the Clinic
and the Clinic is impersonal and that once again I
have stumbled into the old habit of personal refer-
ent. So I only tell her that I will make two more
appointments, one for later this week and one at
the beginning of the next and then, giving her the
money in advance as always, hold back my fingers
from intimation of a caress . . . then stagger out the
door, as they say, a free man, purged for the time
being of these old resentments and obsessions, only
mildly interested in the weather and situations
outside so absorbed am I in my sense of release.

The Clinic is purgation, Purgation is release. Release is freedom. Free, free! . . . but already I am dreaming of my next appointment.

III

Going under I hold my desires until the last moment, meditating. Then I tell the technician who I want to do it to and how. I whisper it into the transceiver like a horrid confidence which perhaps it is although I long since thought that I had forsaken shame . . . and then, not a moment too soon, the drugs begin to ripple. They overtake and I am under.

IV

And so I do it to the receptionist, the bitch receptionist at the Clinic. Naked she lies under me, dreadful passions sifting and shimmering between her cheekbones and then her mouth opens and she whispers the inexpressible. "Because I want it," she adds with delicacy, "I want it and it must be done in this way." She touches the back of my neck, fingers claw, I gasp, convulse, mount her.

"Yes," I say, "yes, you deserve it," and lower myself slowly into her then, as if from a great height and she works me over patiently, lovingly. I feel her smooth tongue wind its way in and out of my mouth and then she lowers herself making loose, clucking sounds, gasps and takes my engorged prick between her teeth. I straddle the bed sweating, considering her helplessness, my dominance, her submission, my power, her emptiness, my fulfillment, her need, my control. "You think," I say, "you think you're so godamned superior to me out there but it's all the same you cunt, isn't it now?" talking, talking some more, talking inexhaustibly as she works on me with her bovine competence. "You see us come in and out, you think you know what's in our heads, you make the appointments and set the tapes but let me tell you this, you have *nothing* to hold over us because who's paying the bills? Think about this; think about it bitch: people like *me* are putting up the price and anyway I'm keeping my antisocial tendencies under check thanks to this which is more than you can say. What's *your* excuse?" I mumble, feeling the come rising and billowing, I am furious, try to disengage so that I can stick it deep into her but too late, too late—

—And so I come into the receptionist's mouth then, drained of the last drop. Her eyes close to the force of my come, then they open with a look of perfect contentment, she smiles around my prick . . . and swallows everything.

She cleans me out and then releases, shaking her head, clenching her little hands. Hovering over her as I do, I see at last her helplessness, I know that I have got her exactly where she deserves to be . . . but before I can take advantage of this new insight I feel myself going out of there, rising quickly at right angles to the situation, disappearing . . . and try as I may to hold on to this scene it is definitely too late. I surface gasping.

My last image is of the receptionist of the dream superimposed upon the receptionist herself as I leave, the look on her face as she sees me go (does she know what I elected to do?) and as I stop there to make two more appointments she can surely tell from my eyes exactly what has been going on and what use I have made of her but it is too late. There is nothing she can do. She is only an employee.

As I leave I cast her a single wink from the door which breaks through the mask and she gives me then a look of perfect astonishment which, mingled with my own satisfaction, serves well to get me through the afternoon.

V

In the mandatory monthly before the next treatment, my therapist says that he is disturbed by certain aspects of my behavior.

"You're not getting along quite as we had hoped," this therapist, a bland, rosy little man with a nametag says. "Not exactly." Under the law, the treatments, as I understand, can be given only under the guise of "therapy" but even though I know this and am willing to accept the charade, it is hard, often hard, to remain patient.

"That's none of your business," I say. "I'm paying the price. I inherited a fortune and so can pay you what you ask. Your responsibility should stop right there."

"Oh *no*," the therapist says with patent shock and the slightest intimation of a lisp. We have been through this before. "You know that this isn't the aim at all. The treatments are a temporary application, they are to be used therapeutically and they are not in any way to be thought of as an end in themselves. They are for treatment purposes; the institution is a curative program. Why, if the treatments were given without discrimination," he says, "that would be addictive; if we weren't moving toward therapeutic goals we would be misleading you terribly. And we just aren't very satisfied. I'm afraid that the monitors we inspect have shown some very distressing things. You're beginning to incorporate people from your present, ongoing life in the treatment and that isn't what we wanted at all. You must try to stay in the past and clear out the tensional memories."

"Just leave me alone," I say. "You let me do what I want." Under statute, the mandatory monthlies last half an hour and are supposed, I understand, to deal with "progress" and "goals." This is bad enough but what is even worse is that they are to be considered "appointments" as well and we must pay for them at the same rate as for use of the machines. This is all part of the swindle, of course, but there is hardly anywhere else to go. One can hardly cross the street to visit the competition: the Institute, as its promotional program has made quite clear, controls every possible patent on its marvelous device.

Knowing this, however, is little help. The mandatories are impossible. I have heard rumors of subjects who bribed their therapists into silence and of others who attacked them physically without retaliation but the treatments are too important to me (I am willing to admit this) to take any risks and so I have tried to take the tactic of patient listening without becoming involved. "If you say so," I say to him. "I can't argue with that."

"But that's the point," the therapist says. His eyebrows rise; his lisps seem more prominent. "This withdrawal of yours, the refusal to recognize that you may have a serious problem which you're evading. Now, our monitors indicate that instead of combing through your *past* and using the treatment as a well, *purgative*, you're beginning to indulge yourself in fantasies." He seems to blush.

"Fantasies with not only the, uh, people you may know in your present but with some of the institutional staff itself and—"

"I'm paying," I say. "I'm paying your price. I'm meeting all of the fee schedules and doing it promptly which I'm sure is more than most of the others can say. I inherited a lot of money so you can suck me dry. So—"

"Oh come now," he says, "you don't think that the motives of our Institute are purely mercenary now do you? We've got other purposes rather than profit and loss. That's the kind of thinking pattern you possess which we want to break. You regard everything in purely exploitative terms but we really want to *help*, we want to see you *grow*, we want to enable you to *overcome* your psychic deficiencies because only in that way—"

"Enough!" I say. The half hour is over; I can see the clock above us. "Enough, enough of this!" and rise from the chair, zooming then, as if in intercourse, to great height and a feeling of control. "I won't listen to any of this from you now. I can do anything I want to do because I can meet the price and furthermore I'm not hurting anyone, not a soul and furthermore, the only interest you people have in me or in any of us is purely the *money* so you leave me alone now. It's time for my treatment and I'm going there." It makes sense to schedule the mandatory monthly right before a treatment. "If you don't let me go," I say, leaning over the little therapist, moving forehead to forehead against him, "I'll stop the treatments." I hate to be threatening (it is pure bluff anyway) and we have been this way before but on the other hand, this seems to be the only way in which the monthlies can end for me. "I'll stop them because you and I both know that I can if I say so and think of all the money the Institute will lose and all of it will be *your* fault. Three appointments a week, that's four hundred and fifty dollars. Almost twenty-five thousand a *year*: do you make half of that?" and feint a little punch at him. He pushes the chair back, loses control, his tiny legs pump and skitter and he goes rolling across the room colliding with a *click!* against the wall (is he metal?) and quickly I am on top of him, seizing his thin shoulders.

"You know you can't make me," I shout, "now don't give me any of that therapeutic bullshit, don't talk to me anymore, just sign the godamned authorization and send me through or I'm finished with all of you!" and his little eyes roll in his head, his eyes dance and glaze, his delicate forehead twitches and mumbling, muttering, he picks himself from the chair piece by piece, by handhold, staggers across the room to his desk, signs the paper and gives it to me. Twelve more treatments approved.

"You're making a mistake," he whines, a tiny forefinger subtly moving toward his nostril to pick and squeeze but now, my purpose accomplished, I am insulated from him again and so I laugh. I giggle mercilessly at the ignorant therapist (is this too a dream?) and spring from the room toward the release of the corridors and the machine that I know will always await me.

VI

I think of a cousin who teased and taunted me to coitus interruptus when I was fifteen, I think of my father whose sallow cheeks (let me face this) I have always wanted to bugger but they bore me. I have been there before and if not I can always get there toward predictable ends. Instead, I whisper a more exciting order to the technician as the levers in the helmet close and then I—

—Well I do it to the therapist. I dream that I am standing over his naked body in a room hung with whips and garrotes. In the midst of all this armament, I order him to kneel, turning the other way and as he does so I seize a dull sword from its pocket on the wall and begin to beat him over the shoulders. The blood runs, his shoulders shake, he commences to weep, opening himself to vulnerability and pain as he does so and then I mount him violently from the rear, an *aaah!* of surprise and delight pouring from him and so I do it to him then, mounted, riding him, still holding the sword.

"You son of a bitch," I say, "I can do anything I want for the rest of my life because I inherited this money and this wonderful process has been invented and there is nothing, now there is absolutely *nothing* which can stop me from doing what I want to do."

"Yes," he says, "all right, you can, please don't hurt me, I'm at your mercy you see, just get it over with," and I get it over with, savage and quick strokes pouring into him, pouring into the receptionist, pouring into my mother and father, holding on to myself at the summit and screaming with epiphany. Enough insight and power here to be sure, enough to get me through at least forty-eight hours until the next session and I know in my heart that this has been the best ever as I struggle off his dead body. New territory opened up, the best ever, and the treatment, like my own soul and possibilities is endless, infinite.

"Free!" I shout to the technician as I surface. "Free!" I shout to the receptionist as I leave. "Free, free, free!" I call to a young girl on the street, pausing to seize her by the shoulders and stare so that I will have her features memorized for the next session when (I decided with my new and profound sense of release) I will surely, surely possess her.

Because that is what it is all about.

AUTHOR'S NOTE

This is a tough story and did me no good. Written for Tom Scortia's *Strange Bedfellows* (Random House, 1972), an anthology of science fiction stories about sex or vice versa, it was swiftly rejected and no surprise either, not so much for the sexual content as for the astonishingly grim use to which that content was put. I didn't even think of offering it elsewhere, sent it off to Ted White at *Amazing*, took my thirty-five dollars gratefully (I had already realized with how many taboos this story had contended) and prepared to forget about it.

It was published in the January 1973 issue of that useful journal, so usefully edited by Ted White for a decade, and several months after that a letter appeared in the vox populi section by someone who, not fearful of disclosing his identity, I will call X. X said that "On Ice" was shocking, loathsome, and disgusting; pure hackwork on a controversial theme; why he and his fan club had devoted two hours of their monthly meeting to a panel on the story and they had agreed to a panelist that it was a loathsome work and, besides, it was of no interest whatsoever. Many months after *that* I made the mistake of suggesting somewhere that perhaps "On Ice" dealt with certain acts which fascinated X and which desires he could not stand to see within himself and that was really a mistake; X declared war on your faithless little undersigned in various journals and fora and I have not, alas, heard the last of him yet nor, since he is younger by many years than I, do I expect to hear the last of him in (or out of, perhaps) this lifetime.

The story, X to the contrary, is in my humble opinion genuinely shocking, *genuinely* (as opposed to frivolously, which is the case with too many of us too much of the time) disturbing and I am happy to have it back in print; it did appear in *The Best of Malzberg* (Pocket Books, 1976) but nowhere else after original publication and everyone except your courageous editor and your faithless undersigned has avoided it sedulously as the plague, religiously as the vestry.

—Barry N. Malzberg

THE MONKEY TREATMENT
George R. R. Martin

KENNY DORCHESTER WAS A FAT MAN.

He had not always been a fat man, of course. He had come into the world a perfectly normal infant of modest weight, but the normalcy was short-lived in Kenny's case, and before very long he had become a chubby-cheeked toddler well swaddled in baby fat. From then on it was all downhill and upscale so far as Kenny was concerned. He became a pudgy child, a corpulent adolescent, and a positively porcine college student all in good turn, and by adulthood he had left all those intermediate steps behind and graduated into full obesity.

People become obese for a variety of complex reasons, some of them physiological. Kenny's reason was relatively simple: food. Kenny Dorchester loved to eat. Often he would paraphrase Will Rogers, winking broadly, and tell his friends that he had never met a food he didn't like. This was not precisely true, since Kenny loathed both liver and prune juice. Perhaps, if his mother had served them more often during his childhood, he would never have attained the girth and gravity that so haunted him at maturity. Unfortunately, Gina Dorchester was more inclined to lasagne and roast turkey with stuffing and sweet potatoes and chocolate pudding and veal cordon bleu and buttered corn on the cob and stacks of blueberry pancakes (although not all in one meal) than she was to liver and prune juice, and once Kenny had expressed his preference in the matter by retching his liver back onto his plate, she obligingly never served liver and prune juice again.

Thus, all unknowing, she set her son on the soft, suety road to the monkey treatment. But that was long ago, and the poor woman really cannot be blamed, since it was Kenny himself who ate his way there.

Kenny loved pepperoni pizza, or plain pizza, or garbage pizza with everything on it, including anchovies. Kenny could eat an entire slab of barbecued ribs, either beef or pork, and the spicier the sauce was, the more he approved. He was fond of rare prime rib and roast chicken and Rock Cornish game hens stuffed with rice, and he was hardly the sort to object to a nice sirloin or a platter of fried shrimp or a hunk of kielbasa. He liked his burgers with everything on them, and fries and onion rings on the side, please. There was nothing you could do to his friend the potato that would possibly turn him against it, but he was also partial to pasta and rice, to yams candied and un-, and even to mashed rutabagas.

"Desserts are my downfall," he would sometimes say, for he liked sweets of all varieties, especially devil's food cake and cannelloni and hot apple pie with cheese (Cheddar, please), or maybe cold strawberry pie with whipped cream. "Bread is my downfall," he would say at other times, when it seemed likely that no dessert was forthcoming, and so saying he would rip off another chunk of sour-dough or butter up another crescent roll or reach for another slice of garlic bread, which was a particular vice.

Kenny had a lot of particular vices. He thought himself an authority on both fine restaurants and fast-food franchises, and could discourse endlessly and knowledgeably about either. He relished Greek food and Chinese food and Japanese food and Korean food and German food and Italian food and French food and Indian food, and was always on the lookout for new ethnic groups so he might "expand my cultural horizons." When Saigon fell, Kenny speculated about how many of the Vietnamese refugees would be likely to open restaurants. When Kenny traveled, he always made it a point to gorge himself on the area's specialty, and he could tell you the best places to eat in any of twenty-four major American cities, while reminiscing fondly about the meals he had enjoyed in each of them. His favorite writers were James Beard and Calvin Trillin.

"I live a tasty life!" Kenny Dorchester would proclaim, beaming. And so he did. But Kenny also had a secret. He did not often think of it and never spoke it, but it was there nonetheless, down at the heart of him beneath all those great rolls of flesh, and not all his sauces could drown it, nor could his trusty fork keep it at bay.

Kenny Dorchester did not *like* being fat.

Kenny was like a man torn between two lovers, for while he loved his food with an abiding passion, he also dreamed of other loves, of women, and he knew that in order to secure the one he would have to give up the other, and that knowledge was his secret pain. Often he wrestled with the dilemmas posed by his situation. It seemed to Kenny that while it might be preferable to be slender and have a woman than to be fat and have only a crawfish bisque, nonetheless the latter was not entirely to be spurned. Both were sources of happiness, after all, and the real misery fell to those who gave up the one and failed to obtain the other. Nothing depressed or saddened Kenny so much as the sight of a fat person eating cottage cheese. Such pathetic human beings never seemed to get appreciably skinnier, Kenny thought, and were doomed to go through life bereft of both women and crawfish, a fate too grim to contemplate.

Yet despite all his misgivings, at times the secret pain inside Kenny Dorchester would flare up mightily, and fill him with a sense of resolve that made him feel as if anything might be possible. The sight of a particularly beautiful woman or the word of some new, painless, and wonderfully effective diet were particularly prone to trigger what Kenny thought of as his "aberrations." When such moods came, Kenny would be driven to diet.

Over the years he tried every diet there was, briefly and secretly. He tried Dr. Atkins's diet and Dr. Stillman's diet, the grapefruit diet and the brown rice diet. He tried the liquid protein diet, which was truly disgusting. He lived for a week on nothing but Slender and Sego, until he had run through all of the flavors and gotten bored. He joined a Pounds-Off club and attended a few meetings, until he discovered that the company of fellow dieters did him no good whatsoever, since all they talked about was food. He went on a hunger strike that lasted until he got hungry. He tried the fruit juice diet, and the drinking man's diet (even though he was not a drinking man), and the martinis-and-whipped-cream diet (he omitted the martinis).

A hypnotist told him that his favorite foods tasted bad and he wasn't hungry anyway, but it was a damned lie, and that was that for hypnosis. He had his behavior modified so he put down his fork between bites, used small plates that looked full even with tiny portions, and wrote down everything he ate in a notebook. That left him with stacks of notebooks, a great many small dishes to wash, and unusual manual dexterity in putting down and picking up his fork. His favorite diet was the one that said you could eat all you wanted of your favorite food, so long as you ate nothing *but* that. The only problem was that Kenny couldn't decide what was really his one true favorite, so he wound up eating ribs for a week, and pizza for a week, and Peking duck for a week (that was an expensive week), and losing no weight whatsoever, although he did have a great time.

Most of Kenny Dorchester's aberrations lasted for a week or two. Then, like a man coming out of a fog, he would look around and realize that he was absolutely miserable, losing relatively little weight, and in imminent danger of turning into one of those cottage-cheese fatties he so pitied. At that point he would chuck the diet, go out for a good meal, and be restored to his normal self for another six months, until his secret pain surfaced again.

Then, one Friday night, he spied Henry Moroney at the Slab.

The Slab was Kenny's favorite barbecue joint. It specialized in ribs, charred and meaty and served dripping with a sauce that Kenny approved of mightily. And on Fridays the Slab offered all the ribs you could eat for only fifteen dollars, which was prohibitively high for most people but a bargain for Kenny, who could eat a great many ribs. On that particular Friday, Kenny had just finished his first slab and was waiting for the second, sipping beer and eating bread, when he chanced to look up and realized, with a start, that the slim, haggard fellow in the next booth was, in fact, Henry Moroney.

Kenny Dorchester was nonplussed. The last time he had seen Henry Moroney, they had both been unhappy Pounds-Off members, and Moroney had been the only one in the club who weighed more than Kenny did. A great fat whale of a man, Moroney had carried about the cruel nickname of "Boney," as he confessed to his fellow members. Only now the nickname seemed to fit. Not only was Moroney skinny enough to hint at a rib cage under his skin, but the table in front of him was absolutely littered with bones. That was the detail that intrigued Kenny Dorchester. All those bones. He began to count, and he lost track before very long, because all the bones were disordered, strewn about on empty plates in little puddles of drying sauce. But from the sheer mass of them it was clear that Moroney had put away at least four slabs of ribs, maybe five.

It seemed to Kenny Dorchester that Henry "Boney" Moroney knew the secret. If there were a way to lose hundreds of pounds and still be able to consume five slabs of ribs at a sitting, that was something Kenny desperately needed to know. So he rose and walked over to Moroney's booth and squeezed in opposite him. "It *is* you," he said.

Moroney looked up as if he hadn't noticed

Kenny until that very second. "Oh," he said in a thin, tired voice. "You." He seemed very weary, but Kenny thought that was probably natural for someone who had lost so much weight. Moroney's eyes were sunk in deep gray hollows, his flesh sagged in pale, empty folds, and he was slouching forward with his elbows on the table as if he were too exhausted to sit up straight. He looked terrible, but he had lost so much *weight*. . . .

"You look wonderful!" Kenny blurted. "How did you do it? How? You must tell me, Henry, really you must."

"No," Moroney whispered. "No, Kenny. Go away."

Kenny was taken aback. "Really!" he declared. "That's not very friendly. I'm not leaving until I know your secret, Henry. You owe it to me. Think of all the times we've broken bread together."

"Oh, Kenny," Moroney said, in his faint and terrible voice. "Go, please, go, you don't want to know, it's too . . . too . . ." He stopped in mid-sentence, and a spasm passed across his face. He moaned. His head twisted wildly to the side, as if he were having some kind of fit, and his hands beat on the table. "Oooooo," he said.

"Henry, what's wrong?" Kenny said, alarmed. He was certain now that Boney Moroney had overdone this diet.

"Ohhhh," Moroney sighed in sudden relief. "Nothing, nothing. I'm fine." His voice had none of the enthusiasm of his words. "I'm wonderful, in fact. Wonderful, Kenny. I haven't been so slim since . . . since . . . why, never. It's a miracle." He smiled faintly. "I'll be at my goal soon, and then it will be over. I think. Think I'll be at my goal. Don't know my weight, really." He put a hand to his brow. "I am slender, though, truly I am. Don't you think I look good?"

"Yes, yes," Kenny agreed impatiently. "But how? You must tell me. Surely not those Pounds-Off phonies. . . ."

"No," said Moroney weakly. "No, it was the monkey treatment. Here, I'll write it down for you." He took out a pencil and scrawled an address on a napkin.

Kenny stuffed the napkin into a pocket. "The monkey treatment? I've never heard of that. What is it?"

Henry Moroney licked his lips. "They . . ." he started, and then another fit hit him, and his head twitched around grotesquely. "Go," he said to Kenny, "just go. It works, Kenny, yes, oh. The monkey treatment, yes. I can't say more. You have the address. Excuse me." He placed his hands flat on the table and pushed himself to his feet, then walked over to the cashier, shuffling like a man twice his age. Kenny Dorchester watched him go, and decided that Moroney had *definitely* overdone this monkey treatment, whatever it was. He had never had tics or spasms before, or whatever that had been.

"You have to have a sense of proportion about these things," Kenny said stoutly to himself. He patted his pocket to make sure the napkin was still there, resolved that he would handle things more sensibly than Boney Moroney, and returned to his own booth and his second slab of ribs. He ate four that night, figuring that if he was going to start a diet tomorrow he had better get in some eating while the eating was good.

The next day being Saturday, Kenny was free to pursue the monkey treatment and dream of a new, slender him. He rose early, and immediately rushed to the bathroom to weigh himself on his digital scale, which he loved dearly because you didn't have to squint down at the numbers, since they lit up nice and bright and precise in red. This morning they lit up as 367. He had gained a few pounds, but he hardly minded. The monkey treatment would strip them off again soon enough.

Kenny tried to phone ahead, to make sure this place was open on Saturday, but that proved to be impossible. Moroney had written nothing but an address, and there was no diet center at that listing in the Yellow Pages, nor a health club, nor a doctor. Kenny looked in the white pages under "Monkey," but that yielded nothing. So there was nothing to do but go down there in person.

Even that was troublesome. The address was way down by the docks in a singularly unsavory neighborhood, and Kenny had a hard time getting a cab to take him there. He finally got his way by threatening to report the cabbie to the commissioner. Kenny Dorchester knew his rights.

Before long, though, he began to have his doubts. The narrow little streets they wound through were filthy and decaying, altogether unappetizing, and it occurred to Kenny that any diet center located down here might offer only dangerous quackery. The block in question was an old commercial strip gone to seed, and it put his hackles up even more. Half the stores were boarded closed, and the rest lurked behind filthy dark windows and iron gates. The cab pulled up in front of an absolutely miserable old brick storefront, flanked by two vacant lots full of rubble, its plate glass windows grimed over impenetrably. A faded Coca-Cola sign swung back and forth, groaning, above the door. But the number was the number that Boney Moroney had written down.

"Here you are," the cabbie said impatiently, as Kenny peered out the taxi window, aghast.

"This does not look correct," Kenny said. "I will investigate. Kindly wait here until I am certain this is the place."

The cabbie nodded, and Kenny slid over and levered himself out of the taxi. He had taken two steps when he heard the cab shift gears and pull away from the curb, screeching. He turned and watched in astonishment. "Here, you can't . . ." he began. But it did. He would most definitely report that man to the commissioner, he decided.

But meanwhile he was stranded down here, and it seemed foolish not to proceed when he had come this far. Whether he took the monkey treatment or not, no doubt they would let him use a phone to summon another cab. Kenny screwed up his resolution, and went on into the grimy, unmarked storefront. A bell tinkled as he opened the door.

It was dark inside. The dust and dirt on the windows kept out nearly all the sunlight, and it took a moment for Kenny's eyes to adjust. When they did, he saw to his horror that he had walked into someone's living room. One of those gypsy families that moved into abandoned stores, he thought. He was standing on a threadbare carpet, and around and about him was a scatter of old furniture, no doubt the best the Salvation Army had to offer. An ancient black-and-white TV set crouched in one corner, staring at him blindly. The

room stank of urine. "Sorry," Kenny muttered
feebly, terrified that some dark gypsy youth would
come out of the shadows to knife him. "Sorry." He
had stepped backward, groping behind him for the
doorknob, when the man came out of the back
room.

"Ah!" the man said, spying Kenny at once from
tiny bright eyes. "Ah, the monkey treatment!" He
rubbed his hands together and grinned. Kenny was
terrified. The man was the fattest, grossest human
being that Kenny had ever laid eyes on. He had
squeezed through the door sideways. He was fatter
than Kenny, fatter than Boney Moroney. He literally dripped with fat. And he was repulsive in other
ways as well. He had the complexion of a mush-
room, and minuscule little eyes almost invisible
amid rolls of pale flesh. His corpulence seemed to
have overwhelmed even his hair, of which he had
very little. Bare-chested, he displayed vast areas of
folded, bulging skin, and his huge breasts flopped
as he came forward quickly and seized Kenny by
the arm. "The monkey treatment!" he repeated
eagerly, pulling Kenny forward. Kenny looked at
him in shock, and was struck dumb by his grin.
When the man grinned, his mouth seemed to
become half of his face, a grotesque semicircle full
of shining white teeth.

"No," Kenny said at last, "no, I have changed my
mind." Boney Moroney or no, he didn't think he
cared to try this monkey treatment if it was admin-
istered by such as this. In the first place, it clearly
could not be very effective, or else the man would
not be so monstrously obese. Besides, it was probably dangerous, some quack potion of monkey hor-
mones or something like that. "*NO!*" Kenny

repeated more forcefully, trying to wrest his arm free from the grasp of the grotesquerie who held it.

But it was useless. The man was distinctly larger and infinitely stronger than Kenny, and he propelled him across the room with ease, oblivious to Kenny's protests, grinning like a maniac all the while. "Fat man," he burbled, and as if to prove his point, he reached out and seized one of Kenny's bulges and twisted it painfully. "Fat, fat, fat, no good. Monkey treatment make you thin."

"Yes, but . . ."

"Monkey treatment," the man repeated, and somehow he had gotten behind Kenny. He put his weight against Kenny's back and pushed, and Kenny staggered through a curtained doorway into the back room. The smell of urine was much stronger in there, strong enough to make him want to retch. It was pitch black, and from all sides Kenny heard rustlings and scurryings in the darkness. *Rats*, he thought wildly. Kenny was deathly afraid of rats. He fumbled about and propelled himself toward the square dim light that marked the curtain he had come through.

Before he was quite there, a high-pitched chittering sounded suddenly from behind him, sharp and rapid as fire from a machine gun. Then another voice took it up, then a third, and suddenly the dark was alive with the terrible hammering noise. Kenny put his hands over his ears and staggered through the curtain, but just as he emerged he felt something brush the back of his neck, something warm and hairy. "Aieeee!" he screamed, dancing out into the front room where the tremendous bare-chested madman was waiting patiently. Kenny hopped from one foot to the other, screeching, "Aieeee, a rat, a rat on my back. Get it off, get it *off*!" He was trying to grab for it with both hands, but the thing was very quick, and shifted around so cleverly that he couldn't get ahold of it. But he felt it there, alive, moving. "Help me, help me!" he called out. "A rat!"

The proprietor grinned at him and shook his head, so all his many chins went bobbing merrily. "No, no," he said. "No rat, fat man. Monkey. You get the monkey treatment." Then he stepped forward and seized Kenny by the elbow again, and drew him over to a full-length mirror mounted on the wall. It was so dim in the room that Kenny could scarcely make out anything in the mirror, except that it wasn't wide enough and chopped off both his arms. The man stepped back and yanked a pull-cord dangling from the ceiling, and a single bare light bulb clicked on overhead. The bulb swung back and forth, back and forth, so the light shifted crazily. Kenny Dorchester trembled and stared at the mirror.

"Oh," he said.

There was a monkey on his back.

Actually it was on his shoulders, its legs wrapped around his thick neck and twined together beneath his triple chin. He could feel its monkey hair scratching the back of his neck, could feel its warm little monkey paws lightly grasping his ears. It was a very tiny monkey. As Kenny looked into the mirror, he saw it peek out from behind his head, grinning hugely. It had quick darting eyes, coarse brown hair, and altogether too many shiny white teeth for Kenny's liking. Its long prehensile tail swayed about restlessly, like some hairy snake that had grown out of the back of Kenny's skull.

Kenny's heart was pounding away like some great air hammer lodged in his chest, and he was altogether distressed by this place, this man, and this monkey, but he gathered all his reserves and forced himself to be calm. It wasn't a rat, after all. The little monkey couldn't harm him. It had to be a trained monkey, the way it had perched on his shoulders. Its owner must let it ride around like this, and when Kenny had come unwillingly through that curtain, it had probably mistaken him. All fat men look alike in the dark.

Kenny grabbed behind him and tried to pull the monkey loose, but somehow he couldn't seem to get a grip on it. The mirror, reversing everything, just made it worse. He jumped up and down ponderously, shaking the entire room and making the furniture leap around every time he landed, but the monkey held on tight to his ears and could not be dislodged.

Finally, with what Kenny thought was incredible aplomb under the circumstances, he turned to the gross proprietor and said, "Your monkey, sir. Kindly help me remove it."

"No, no," the man said. "Make you skinny. Monkey treatment. You no want to be skinny?"

"Of course I do," Kenny said unhappily, "but this is absurd." He was confused. This monkey on his back seemed to be part of the monkey treatment, but that certainly didn't make very much sense.

"Go," the man said. He reached up and snapped off the light with a sharp tug that sent the bulb careening wildly again. Then he started toward Kenny, who backpedaled nervously. "Go," the man repeated, as he grabbed Kenny's arm again.

"Out, out. You get monkey treatment, you go now."

"See here!" Kenny said furiously. "Let go of me! Get this monkey off me, do you hear? I don't want your monkey! Do you hear me? Quit pushing, sir! I tell you, I have friends with the police department, you aren't going to get away with this. Here now . . ."

But all his protestations were useless. The man was a veritable tidal wave of sweating, smelling pale flesh, and he put his weight against Kenny and propelled him helplessly toward the door. The bell rang again as he pulled it open and shoved Kenny out into the garish bright sunlight.

"I'm not going to pay for this!" Kenny said stoutly, staggering. "Not a cent, do you hear!"

"No charge for monkey treatment," the man said, grinning.

"At least let me call a cab," Kenny began, but it was too late, the man had closed the door. Kenny stepped forward angrily and tried to yank it back open, but it did not budge. Locked. "Open up in there!" Kenny demanded at the top of his lungs. There was no reply. He shouted again, and grew suddenly and uncomfortably aware that he was being stared at. Kenny turned around. Across the street three old winos were sitting on the stoop of a boarded-up store, passing a bottle in a brown paper bag and regarding him through wary eyes.

That was when Kenny Dorchester recalled that he was standing there in the street in broad daylight with a monkey on his back.

A flush crept up his neck and spread across his cheeks. He felt very silly. "A pet!" he shouted to the winos, forcing a smile. "Just my little pet!" They went on staring. Kenny gave a last angry look at the locked door, and set off down the street, his legs pumping furiously. He had to get to someplace private.

Rounding the corner, he came upon a dark, narrow alley behind two gray old tenement buildings, and ducked inside, wheezing for breath. He sat down heavily on a trash can, pulled out his handkerchief, and mopped his brow. The monkey shifted just a bit, and Kenny felt it move. "Off me!" he shouted, reaching up and back again to try to wrench it off by the scruff of its neck, only to have it elude him once more. He tucked away his handkerchief and groped behind his head with both hands, but he just couldn't get ahold of it. Finally, exhausted, he stopped, and tried to think.

The legs! he thought. The legs under his chins! That's the ticket! Very calmly and deliberately, he reached up, felt for the monkey's legs, and wrapped one big fleshy hand around each of them. He took a deep breath and then savagely tried to yank them apart, as if they were two ends of a giant wishbone.

The monkey attacked him.

One hand twisted his right ear painfully, until it felt like it was being pulled clean off his head. The other started hammering against his temple, beating a furious tattoo. Kenny Dorchester yelped in distress and let go of the monkey's legs—which he hadn't budged for all his efforts. The monkey quit beating on him and released his ear. Kenny sobbed, half with relief and half with frustration. He felt wretched.

He sat there in that filthy alley for ages, defeated in his efforts to remove the monkey and afraid to go back to the street where people would point at him and laugh, or make rude, insulting comments under their breath. It was difficult enough going through life as a fat man, Kenny thought. How much worse, then, to face the cruel world as a fat man with a monkey on his back. Kenny did not want to know. He resolved to sit there on that trash can in the dark alley until he died or the monkey died, rather than face shame and ridicule on the streets.

His resolve endured about an hour. Then Kenny Dorchester began to get hungry. Maybe people would laugh at him, but they had always laughed at him, so what did it matter? Kenny rose and dusted himself off, while the monkey settled itself more comfortably on his neck. He ignored it, and decided to go in search of a pepperoni pizza.

He did not find one easily. The abysmal slum in which he had been stranded had a surfeit of winos, dangerous-looking teenagers, and burned-out or boarded-up buildings, but it had precious few pizza parlors. Nor did it have any taxis. Kenny walked down the main thoroughfare with brisk dignity, looking neither left nor right, heading for safer neighborhoods as fast as his plump little legs could carry him. Twice he came upon phone booths, and eagerly fetched out a coin to summon transportation, but both times the phones proved to be out of order. Vandals, thought Kenny Dorchester, were as bad as rats.

Finally, after what seemed like hours of walking, he stumbled upon a sleazy café. The lettering on the window said JOHN'S GRILL, and there was a neon sign above the door that said, simply, EAT. Kenny was very familiar with those three lovely letters, and he recognized the sign two blocks off. It called to him like a beacon. Even before he entered, he knew it was rather unlikely that such a place would include pepperoni pizza on its menu, but by that time Kenny had ceased to care.

As he pushed the door aside, Kenny experienced a brief moment of apprehension, partially because he felt very out of place in the café, where the rest of the diners all appeared to be muggers, and partially because he was afraid they would refuse to serve him because of the monkey on his back. Acutely uncomfortable in the doorway, he moved quickly to a small table in an obscure corner, where he hoped to escape the curious stares. A gaunt gray-haired waitress in a faded pink uniform moved purposefully toward him, and Kenny sat with his eyes downcast, playing nervously with the salt, pepper, ketchup, dreading the moment when she arrived and said, "Hey, you can't bring that thing in here!"

But when the waitress reached his table, she simply pulled a pad out of her apron pocket and stood poised, pencil in hand. "Well?" she demanded. "What'll it be?"

Kenny stared up in shock, and smiled. He stammered a bit, then recovered himself and ordered a cheese omelet with a double side of bacon, coffee and a large glass of milk, and cinnamon toast. "Do hash browns come with?" he asked hopefully, but the waitress shook her head and departed.

What a marvelous, kind woman, Kenny thought as he waited for his meal and shredded a paper napkin thoughtfully. What a wonderful place! Why, they hadn't even mentioned his monkey! How very polite of them.

The food arrived shortly. "Ahhhh," Kenny said

as the waitress laid it out in front of him on the Formica tabletop. He was ravenous. He selected a slice of cinnamon toast, and brought it to his mouth.

And a little monkey darted out from behind his head and snatched it clean away.

Kenny Dorchester sat in numb surprise for an instant, his suddenly empty hand poised before his open mouth. He heard the monkey eating his toast, chomping noisily. Then, before Kenny had quite comprehended what was happening, the monkey's great long tail snaked in under his armpit, curled around his glass of milk, and spirited it up and away in the blink of an eye.

"*Hey!*" Kenny said, but he was much too slow. Behind his back he heard slurping, sucking sounds, and all of a sudden the glass came vaulting over his left shoulder. He caught it before it fell and smashed, and set it down unsteadily. The monkey's tail came stealthily around and headed for his bacon. Kenny grabbed up a fork and stabbed at it, but the monkey was faster than he was. The bacon vanished, and the tines of the fork bent against the hard Formica uselessly.

By then Kenny knew he was in a race. Dropping the bent fork, he used his spoon to cut off a chunk of the omelet, dripping cheese, and he bent forward as he lifted it, quick as he could. The monkey was quicker. A little hand flashed in from somewhere, and the spoon had only a tantalizing gob of half-melted cheese remaining on it when it reached Kenny's mouth. He lunged back toward his plate, and loaded up again, but it didn't matter how fast he tried to be. The monkey had two paws and a tail, and once it even used a little monkey foot to snatch something away from him. In hardly any time at all, Kenny Dorchester's meal was gone. He sat there staring down at the empty, greasy plate, and he felt tears gathering in his eyes.

The waitress reappeared without Kenny noticing. "My, you sure are a hungry one," she said to him, ripping off his check from her pad and putting it in front of him. "Polished that off quicker than anyone I ever saw."

Kenny looked up at her. "But I *didn't*," he protested. "The monkey ate it all!"

The waitress looked at him very oddly. "The monkey?" she said uncertainly.

"The monkey," Kenny said. He did not care for the way she was staring at him, like he was crazy or something.

"What monkey?" she asked. "You didn't sneak no animals in here, did you? The board of health don't allow no animals in here, mister."

"What do you mean, *sneak*?" Kenny said in annoyance. "Why, the monkey is right on my—" He never got a chance to finish. Just then the monkey hit him, a tremendous hard blow on the left side of his face. The force of it twisted his head half-around, and Kenny yelped in pain and shock.

The waitress seemed concerned. "You OK, mister?" she asked. "You ain't gonna have a fit, are you, twitching like that?"

"*I didn't twitch!*" Kenny all but shouted. "The goddamned monkey hit me! Can't you see?"

"Oh," said the waitress, taking a step backward. "Oh, of course. Your monkey hit you. Pesky little things, ain't they?"

Kenny pounded his fists on the table in frustration. "Never mind," he said, "just never mind." He snatched up the check—the monkey did not take that away from him, he noted—and rose. "Here," he said, pulling out his wallet. "And you have a phone in this place, don't you? Call me a cab, all right? You can do that, can't you?"

"Sure," the waitress said, moving to the register to ring up his meal. Everyone in the café was staring at him. "Sure, mister," she muttered. "A cab. We'll get you a cab right away."

Kenny waited, fuming. The cab driver made no comment on his monkey. Instead of going home, he took the cab to his favorite pizza place, three blocks from his apartment. Then he stormed right in and ordered a large pepperoni. The monkey ate it all, even when Kenny tried to confuse it by picking up one slice in each hand and moving them simultaneously toward his mouth. Unfortunately, the monkey had two hands as well, both of them faster than Kenny's.

When the pizza was completely gone, Kenny thought for a moment, summoned over the waitress, and ordered a second. This time he got a large anchovy. He thought that was very clever. Kenny Dorchester had never met anyone else beside himself who liked anchovy pizza. Those little salty fishes would be his salvation, he thought. To increase the odds, when the pizza arrived Kenny picked up the hot pepper shaker and covered it with enough hot peppers to ignite a major conflagration. Then, feeling confident, he tried to eat a slice.

The monkey liked anchovy pizza with lots of hot peppers. Kenny Dorchester almost wept.

He went from the pizza place to the Slab, from the Slab to a fine Greek restaurant, from the Greek restaurant to a local McDonald's, from McDonald's to a bakery that made the most marvelous chocolate éclairs. Sooner or later, Kenny Dorchester thought, the monkey would be full. It was only a very little monkey, after all. How much food could it eat? He would just keep on ordering food, he resolved, and the monkey would either reach its limits or rupture and die.

That day Kenny spent more than two hundred dollars on meals.

He got absolutely nothing to eat.

The monkey seemed to be a bottomless pit. If it had a capacity, that capacity was surely greater than the capacity of Kenny's wallet. Finally he was forced to admit defeat. The monkey could not be stuffed into submission.

Kenny cast about for another tactic, and finally hit on it. Monkeys were stupid, after all, even invisible monkeys with prodigious appetites. Smiling slyly, Kenny went to a neighborhood supermarket, and picked up a box of banana pudding (it seemed appropriate) and a box of rat poison. Humming a spry little tune, he walked on home, and set to work making the pudding, stirring in liberal amounts of the rat poison as it cooked. The poison was nicely odorless. The pudding smelled wonderful. Kenny poured it into some dessert cups to cool, and watched television for an hour or so. Finally he rose nonchalantly, went to the refrigerator, and got out a pudding and a nice big spoon. He sat back down in front of the set, spooned up a generous glob of pudding, and brought it to his open mouth. Where he paused. And paused. And waited.

The monkey did nothing.

Maybe it was full at last, Kenny thought. He put aside the poisoned pudding and rushed back to his kitchen, where he found a box of vanilla wafers hiding on a shelf, and a few forlorn Fig Newtons as well.

The monkey ate all of them.

A tear trickled down Kenny's cheek. The monkey would let him have all the poisoned pudding he wanted, it seemed, but nothing else. He reached back halfheartedly and tried to grab the monkey once again, thinking maybe all that eating would have slowed it down some, but it was a vain hope. The monkey evaded him, and when Kenny persisted the monkey bit his finger. Kenny yowled and snatched his hand back. His finger was bleeding. He sucked on it. That much, at least, the monkey permitted him.

When he had washed his finger and wrapped a Band-Aid around it, Kenny returned to his living room and seated himself heavily, weary and defeated, in front of his television set. An old rerun of *The Galloping Gourmet* was coming on. He couldn't stand it. He jabbed at his remote control to change the channel, and watched blindly for hours, sunk in despair, weeping at the Betty Crocker commercials. Finally, during the late late show, he stirred a little at one of the frequent public service announcements. That was it, he thought; he had to enlist others, he had to get help.

He picked up his phone and punched out the Crisis Line number.

The woman who answered sounded kind and sympathetic and very beautiful, and Kenny began to pour out his heart to her, all about the monkey that wouldn't let him eat, about how nobody else seemed to notice the monkey, about . . . but he had barely gotten his heart-pouring going good when the monkey smashed him across the side of the head. Kenny moaned. "What's wrong?" the woman asked. The monkey yanked his ear. Kenny tried to ignore the pain and keep on talking, but the monkey kept hurting him until finally he shuddered and sobbed and hung up the phone.

This is a nightmare, Kenny thought, a terrible nightmare. And so thinking, he pushed himself to his feet and staggered off to bed, hoping that everything would be normal in the morning, that the monkey would have been nothing but part of some wretched dream, no doubt brought on by indigestion.

The merciless little monkey would not even allow him to sleep properly, Kenny discovered. He was accustomed to sleeping on his back, with his hands folded very primly on his stomach. But when he undressed and tried to assume that position, the monkey fists came raining down on his poor head like some furious hairy hail. The monkey was not about to be squashed between Kenny's bulk and the pillows, it seemed. Kenny squealed with pain and rolled over on his stomach. He was very uncomfortable this way and had difficulty falling asleep, but it was the only way the monkey would leave him alone.

The next morning Kenny Dorchester drifted slowly into wakefulness, his cheek mashed against the pillows and his right arm still asleep. He was afraid to move. It was all a dream, he told himself, there is no monkey—what a silly thing that would be, monkey indeed!—it was only that Boney

Moroney had told him about this "monkey treatment," and he had slept on it and had a nightmare. He couldn't feel anything on his back, not a thing. This was just like any other morning. He opened one bleary eye. His bedroom looked perfectly normal. Still he was afraid to move. It was very peaceful lying here like this, monkeyless, and he wanted to savor this feeling. So Kenny lay very still for the longest time, watching the numbers on his digital clock change slowly.

Then his stomach growled at him. It was very upset. Kenny gathered up his courage. "There is no monkey!" he proclaimed loudly, and he sat up in bed.

He felt the monkey shift.

Kenny trembled and almost started to weep again, but he controlled himself with an effort. No monkey was going to get the best of Kenny Dorchester, he told himself. Grimacing, he donned his slippers and plodded into the bathroom.

The monkey peered out cautiously from behind his head while Kenny was shaving. He glared at it in the bathroom mirror. It seemed to have grown a bit, but that was hardly surprising, considering how much it had eaten yesterday. Kenny toyed with the idea of trying to cut the monkey's throat, but decided that his Norelco electric shaver was not terribly well suited to that end. And even if he used a knife, trying to stab behind his own back while looking in the mirror was a dangerously uncertain proposition.

Before leaving the bathroom, Kenny was struck by a whim. He stepped on his scale.

The numbers lit up at once: 367. The same as yesterday, he thought. The monkey weighed nothing. He frowned. No, that had to be wrong. No doubt the little monkey weighed a pound or two, but its weight was offset by whatever poundage Kenny had lost. He had to have lost *some* weight, he reasoned, since he hadn't been allowed to eat anything for ever so long. He stepped off the scale; then got back on quickly, just to double-check. It still read 367. Kenny was certain that he had lost weight. Perhaps some good would come of his travails after all. The thought made him feel oddly cheerful.

Kenny grew even more cheerful at breakfast. For the first time since he had gotten his monkey, he managed to get some food into his mouth.

When he arrived at the kitchen, he debated between French toast and bacon and eggs, but only briefly. Then he decided that he would never get to taste either. Instead, with a somber fatalism, Kenny fetched down a bowl and filled it with corn flakes and milk. The monkey would probably steal it all anyway, he thought, so there was no sense going to any trouble.

Quick as he could, he hurried the spoon to his mouth. The monkey grabbed it away. Kenny had expected it, had known it would happen, but when the monkey hand wrenched the spoon away he nonetheless felt a sudden and terrible grief. "No," he said uselessly. "No, no, no." He could hear the corn flakes crunching in that filthy monkey mouth, and he felt milk dripping down the back of his neck. Tears gathered in his eyes as he stared down at the bowl of corn flakes, so near and yet so far.

Then he had an idea.

Kenny Dorchester lunged forward and stuck his face right down in the bowl.

The monkey twisted his ear and shrieked and pounded on his temple, but Kenny didn't care. He was sucking in milk gleefully and gobbling up as many corn flakes as his mouth could hold. By the time the monkey's tail lashed around angrily and sent the bowl sailing from the table to shatter on the floor, Kenny had a huge wet mouthful. His cheeks bulged and milk dribbled down his chin, and somehow he'd gotten a corn flake up his right nostril, but Kenny was in heaven. He chewed and swallowed as fast as he could, almost choking on the food.

When it was all gone he licked his lips and rose triumphantly. "Ha, ha, ha." He walked back to his bedroom with great dignity and dressed, sneering at the monkey in the full-length bedroom mirror. He had beaten it.

In the days and weeks that followed, Kenny Dorchester settled into a new sort of daily routine and an uneasy accommodation with his monkey. It proved easier than Kenny might have imagined, except at mealtimes. When he was not attempting to get food into his mouth, it was almost possible to forget about the monkey entirely. At work it sat peacefully on his back while Kenny shuffled his papers and made his phone calls. His co-workers either failed to notice his monkey or were sufficiently polite so as not to comment on it. The only difficulty came one day at coffee break, when Kenny foolhardily approached the coffee vendor in an effort to secure a cheese Danish. The monkey ate nine of them before Kenny could stagger away, and the man insisted that Kenny had done it when his back was turned.

Simply by avoiding mirrors, a habit that Kenny

Dorchester now began to cultivate as assiduously as any vampire, he was able to keep his mind off the monkey for most of the day. He had only one difficulty, though it occurred thrice daily: breakfast, lunch, and dinner. At those times the monkey asserted itself forcefully, and Kenny was forced to deal with it. As the weeks passed, he gradually fell into the habit of ordering food that could be served in bowls, so that he might practice what he termed his "Kellogg maneuver." By this stratagem, Kenny usually managed to get at least a few mouthfuls to eat each and every day.

To be sure, there *were* problems. People would stare at him rather strangely when he used the Kellogg maneuver in public, and sometimes make rude comments on his table manners. At a chili emporium Kenny liked to frequent, the proprietor assumed he had suffered a heart attack when Kenny dove toward his chili, and was very angry with him afterward. On another occasion a bowl of soup left him with facial burns that made it look as though he were constantly blushing. And the last straw came when he was thrown bodily out of his favorite seafood restaurant in the world, simply because he plunged his face into a bowl of crawfish bisque and began sucking it up noisily. Kenny stood in the street and berated them loudly and forcefully, reminding them how much money he had spent there over the years. Thereafter he ate only at home.

Despite the limited success of his Kellogg maneuver, Kenny Dorchester still lost nine-tenths of every meal to the voracious monkey on his back. At first he was constantly hungry, frequently depressed, and full of schemes for ridding himself of his monkey. The only problem with these schemes was that none of them seemed to work. One Saturday, Kenny went to the monkey house at the zoo, hoping that his monkey might hop off to play with others of its kind, or perhaps go in pursuit of some attractive monkey of the opposite sex. Instead, no sooner had he entered the monkey house than all the monkeys imprisoned therein ran to the bars of their cages and began to chitter and scream and spit and leap up and down madly. His own monkey answered in kind, and when some of the caged monkeys began to throw peanut husks and other bits of garbage Kenny clapped his hands over his ears and fled.

On another occasion he allowed himself to visit a local saloon, and ordered a number of boilermakers, a drink he understood to be particularly devastating. His intent was to get his monkey so blind-drunk that it might be easily removed. This experiment, too, had rather unfortunate consequences. The monkey drank the boilermakers as fast as Kenny could order them, but after the third one it began to keep time to the disco music from the jukebox by beating on the top of Kenny's head. The next morning it was Kenny who woke with the pounding headache; the monkey seemed fine.

After a time, Kenny finally put all his scheming aside. Failure had discouraged him, and moreover the matter seemed somehow less urgent than it had originally. He was seldom hungry after the first week, in fact. Instead he went through a brief period of weakness, marked by frequent dizzy spells, and then a kind of euphoria settled over him. He felt just wonderful, and even better, he was losing weight!

To be sure, it did not show on his scale. Every morning he climbed up on it, and every morning it lit up as 367. But that was only because it was weighing the monkey as well as himself. Kenny knew he was losing; he could almost feel the pounds and inches just melting away, and some of his co-workers in the office remarked on it as well. Kenny owned up to it, beaming. When they asked him how he was doing it, he winked and replied, "The monkey treatment! The mysterious monkey treatment!" He said no more than that. The one time he tried to explain, the monkey fetched him such as wallop it almost took his head off, and Kenny's friends began to mutter about his strange spasms.

Finally the day came when Kenny had to tell his cleaner to take in all his pants a few inches. That was one of the most delightful tasks of his life, he thought.

All the pleasure went right out of the moment when he exited the store, however, and chanced to glance briefly to his side and see his reflection in the window. At home Kenny had long since removed all his mirrors, so he was shocked at the sight of his monkey. It had grown. It was a little thing no longer. Now it hunched on his back like some evil deformed chimpanzee, and its grinning face loomed above his head instead of peering out behind it. The monkey was grossly fat beneath its sparse brown hair, almost as wide as it was tall, and its great long tail drooped all the way to the ground. Kenny stared at it with horror, and it grinned back at him. No wonder he had been having backaches recently, he thought.

He walked home slowly, all the jauntiness gone

out of his step, trying to think. A few neighborhood dogs followed him up the street, barking at his monkey. Kenny ignored them. He had long since learned that dogs could see his monkey, just like the monkeys at the zoo. He suspected that drunks could see it as well. One man had stared at him for a very long time that night he had visited the saloon. Of course, the fellow might just have been staring at those vanishing boilermakers.

Back in his apartment Kenny Dorchester stretched out on his couch on his stomach, stuck a pillow underneath his chin, and turned on his television set. He paid no attention to the screen, however. He was trying to figure things out. Even the Pizza Hut commercials were insufficiently distracting, although Kenny did absently mutter "Ah-h-h-h" like you were supposed to when the slice of pizza, dripping long strands of cheese, was first lifted from the pan.

When the show ended, Kenny got up and turned off the set and sat himself down at his dining room table. He found a piece of paper and a stubby little pencil. Very carefully, he block-printed a formula across the paper, and stared at it.

ME + MONKEY = 367 POUNDS

There were certain disturbing implications in that formula, Kenny thought. The more he considered them, the less he liked them. He was definitely losing weight, to be sure, and that was not to be sneered at—nonetheless, the grim inflexibility of the formula hinted that most of the gains traditionally attributed to weight loss would never be his to enjoy. No matter how much fat he shed, he would continue to carry around 367 pounds, and the strain on his body would be the same. As for

becoming svelte and dashing and attractive to
women, how could he even consider it so long as he
had his monkey? Kenny thought of how a dinner
date might go for him, and shuddered. "Where will
it all end?" he said aloud.

The monkey shifted, and snickered a vile little
snicker.

Kenny pursed his lips in firm disapproval. This
could not go on, he resolved. He decided to go
straight to the source on the morrow, and with that
idea planted firmly in his mind, he took himself to
bed.

The next day, after work, Kenny Dorchester
returned by cab to the seedy neighborhood where
he had been subjected to the monkey treatment.

The storefront was gone.

Kenny sat in the back seat of the taxi (this time
he had the good sense not to get out, and moreover
had tipped the driver handsomely in advance) and
blinked in confusion. A tiny wet blubbery moan
escaped his lips. The address was right, he knew it,
he still had the slip of paper that had brought him
there in the first place. But where he had found a
grimy brick storefront adorned by a faded Coca-
Cola sign and flanked by two vacant lots, now there
was only one large vacant lot, choked with weeds
and rubbish and broken bricks. "Oh, no," Kenny
said. "Oh, no."

"You OK?" asked the lady driving the cab.

"Yes," Kenny muttered. "Just . . . just wait,
please. I have to think." He held his head in his
hands. He feared he was going to develop a splitting
headache. Suddenly he felt weak and dizzy. And
very hungry. The meter ticked. The cabbie whis-
tled. Kenny thought. The street looked just as he

remembered it, except for the missing storefront. It was just as dirty, the old winos were still on their stoop, the . . .

Kenny rolled down the window. "You, sir!" he called out to one of the winos. The man stared at him. "Come here, sir!" Kenny yelled.

Warily, the old man shuffled across the street.

Kenny fetched out a dollar bill from his wallet and pressed it into the man's hand. "Here, friend," he said. "Go and buy yourself some vintage Thunderbird, if you will."

"Why you givin' me this?" the wino said suspiciously.

"I wish you to answer me a question. What has become of the building that was standing there" —Kenny pointed—"a few weeks ago?"

The man stuffed the dollar into his pocket quickly. "Ain't been no buildin' there fo' years," he said.

"I was afraid of that," Kenny said. "Are you certain? I was here in the not-so-distant past and I *distinctly* recall . . ."

"No buildin'," the wino said firmly. He turned and walked away, but after a few steps he paused and glanced back. "You're one of them fat guys," he said accusingly.

"What do you know about . . . ahem . . . overweight men?"

"See 'em wanderin' round over there, all the time. Crazy, too. Yellin' at thin air, playin' with some kind of animals. Yeah. I 'member you. You're one of them fat guys, all right." He scowled at Kenny, confused. "Looks like you lost some of that blubber, though. Real good. Thanks for the dollar."

Kenny Dorchester watched him return to his stoop and begin conversing animatedly with his colleagues. With a tremulous sigh, Kenny rolled up the window, glanced at the empty lot again, and bid his driver take him home. Him and his monkey, that is.

Weeks went dripping by and Kenny Dorchester lived as if in a trance. He went to work, shuffled his papers, mumbled pleasantries to his co-workers, struggled and schemed for his meager mouthfuls of food, avoided mirrors. The scale read 367. His flesh melted away from him at a precipitous rate. He developed slack, droopy jowls, and his skin sagged all about his middle, looking as flaccid and pitiful as a used condom. He began to have fainting spells, brought on by hunger. At times he staggered and lurched about the street, his thinning and weakened legs unable to support the weight of his growing monkey. His vision got blurry.

Once he even thought that his hair had started to fall out, but that at least was a false alarm; it was the monkey who was losing hair, thank goodness. It shed all over the place, ruining his furniture, and even daily vacuuming didn't seem to help much. Soon Kenny stopped trying to clean up. He lacked the energy. He lacked the energy for just about everything, in fact. Rising from a chair was a major undertaking. Cooking dinner was impossible torment—but he did *that* anyway, since the monkey beat him severely when it was not fed. Nothing seemed to matter very much to Kenny Dorchester. Nothing but the terrible tale of his scale each morning, and the formula that he had scotch-taped to his bathroom wall.

ME + MONKEY = 367 POUNDS

He wondered how much was ME anymore, and how much was MONKEY, but he did not really want to find out. One day, following the dictates of a kind of feeble whim, Kenny made a sudden grab for the monkey's legs under his chin, hoping against hope that it had gotten slow and obese and that he would be able to yank it from his back. His hands closed on nothing. On his own pale flesh. The monkey's legs did not seem to be there, though Kenny could still feel its awful crushing weight. He patted his neck and breast in dim confusion, staring down at himself, and noting absently that he could see his feet. He wondered how long that had been true. They seemed to be perfectly nice feet, Kenny Dorchester thought, although the legs to which they were attached were alarmingly gaunt.

Slowly his mind wandered back to the quandary at hand—what had become of the monkey's hind legs? Kenny frowned and puzzled and tried to work it all out in his head, but nothing occurred to him. Finally he slid his newly discovered feet into a pair of bedroom slippers and shuffled to the closet where he had stored all of his mirrors. Closing his eyes, he reached in, fumbled about, and found the full-length mirror that had once hung on his bedroom wall. It was a large, wide mirror. Working entirely by touch, Kenny fetched it out, carried it a few feet, and painstakingly propped it up against a wall. Then he held his breath and opened his eyes.

There in the mirror stood a gaunt, gray, skeletal-looking fellow, hunched over and sickly. On his back, grinning, was a thing the size of a gorilla. A very obese gorilla. It had a long, pale, snakelike tail, and great long arms, and it was as white as a maggot and entirely hairless. It had no legs. It was . . . attached to him now, growing right out of his back. Its grin was terrible, and filled up half of its face. It looked very like the gross proprietor of the monkey treatment emporium, in fact. Why had he never noticed that before? Of course, of course.

Kenny Dorchester turned from the mirror, and cooked the monkey a big rich dinner before going to bed.

That night he dreamed of how it all started, back in the Slab when he had met Boney Moroney. In his nightmare a great evil white thing rode atop Moroney's shoulders, eating slab after slab of ribs, but Kenny politely pretended not to notice while he and Boney made bright, sprightly conversation. Then the thing ran out of ribs, so it reached down and lifted one of Boney's arms and began to eat his hand. The bones crunched nicely, and Moroney kept right on talking. The creature had eaten its way up to the elbow when Kenny woke screaming, covered with a cold sweat. He had wet his bed, too.

Agonizingly, he pushed himself up and staggered to the toilet, where he dry-heaved for ten minutes. The monkey, angry at being wakened, gave him a desultory slap from time to time.

And then a furtive light came into Kenny Dorchester's eyes. "Boney," he whispered. Hurriedly, he scrambled back to his bedroom on hands and knees, rose, and threw on some clothes. It was three in the morning, but Kenny knew there was no time to waste. He looked up an address in his phone book, and called a cab.

Boney Moroney lived in a tall, modern high-rise by the river, with moonlight shining brightly off its silver-mirrored flanks. When Kenny staggered in, he found the night doorman asleep at his station, which was just as well. Kenny tiptoed past him to the elevators and rode up to the eighth floor. The monkey on his back had begun stirring now, and seemed uneasy and ill-tempered.

Kenny's finger trembled as he pushed the round black button set in the door to Moroney's apartment, just beneath the eyehole. Musical chimes sounded loudly within, startling in the morning stillness. Kenny leaned on the button. The music played on and on. Finally he heard footsteps, heavy and threatening. The peephole opened and closed again. Then the door swung open.

The apartment was black, though the far wall was made entirely of glass, so the moonlight illuminated the darkness softly. Outlined against the stars and the lights of the city stood the man who had opened the door. He was hugely, obscenely fat, and his skin was a pasty fungoid white, and he had little dark eyes set deep into crinkles in his broad suety face. He wore nothing but a vast pair of striped shorts. His breasts flopped about against his chest when he shifted his weight. And when he smiled, his teeth filled up half his face. A great crescent moon of teeth. He smiled when he saw Kenny, and Kenny's monkey. Kenny felt sick. The thing in the door weighed twice as much as the one on his back. Kenny trembled. "Where is he?" he whispered softly. "Where is Boney? What have you done to him?"

The creature laughed, and its pendulous breasts flounced about wildly as it shook with mirth. The monkey on Kenny's back began to laugh, too, a higher, thinner laughter as sharp as the edge of a knife. It reached down and twisted Kenny's ear cruelly. Suddenly a vast fear and a vast anger filled Kenny Dorchester. He summoned all the strength left in his wasted body and pushed forward, and

somehow, somehow, he barged past the obese co-
lossus who barred his way and staggered into the
interior of the apartment. "Boney," he called,
"where are you, Boney? It's me, Kenny."

There was no answer. Kenny went from room to
room. The apartment was filthy, a shambles. There
was no sign of Boney Moroney anywhere. When
Kenny came panting back to the living room, the
monkey shifted abruptly, and threw him off balance. He stumbled and fell hard. Pain went shooting up through his knees, and he cut open one
outstretched hand on the edge of the chrome-and-
glass coffee table. Kenny began to weep.

He heard the door close, and the thing that lived
here moved slowly toward him. Kenny blinked
back tears and stared at the approach of those two
mammoth legs, pale in the moonlight, sagging all
around with fat. He looked up and it was like
gazing up the side of a mountain. Far, far above
him grinned those terrible mocking teeth. "*Where
is he?*" Kenny Dorchester whispered. "What have
you done with poor Boney?"

The grin did not change. The thing reached down
a meaty hand, fingers as thick as a length of
kielbasa, and snagged the waistband of the baggy
striped shorts. It pulled them down clumsily, and
they settled to the ground like a parachute, bunch-
ing around its feet.

"Oh, no," said Kenny Dorchester.

The thing had no genitals. Hanging down between its legs, almost touching the carpet now that
it had been freed from the confines of the soiled
shorts, was a wrinkled droopy bag of skin, long and
gaunt, growing from the creature's crotch. But as
Kenny stared at it in horror, it thrashed feebly, and

stirred, and the loose folds of flesh separated briefly into tiny arms and legs.

Then it opened its eyes.

Kenny Dorchester screamed and suddenly he was back on his feet, lurching away from the grinning obscenity in the center of the room. Between its legs, the thing that had been Boney Moroney raised its pitiful stick-thin arms in supplication. "Oh, nooooo," Kenny moaned, blubbering, and he danced about wildly, the vast weight of his monkey heavy on his back. Round and round he danced in the dimness, in the moonlight, searching for an escape from this madness.

Beyond the plate glass wall the lights of the city beckoned.

Kenny paused and panted and stared at them. Somehow the monkey must have known what he was thinking, for suddenly it began to beat on him wildly, to twist at his ears, to rain savage blows all around his head. But Kenny Dorchester paid no mind. With a smile that was almost beatific, he gathered the last of his strength and rushed pell-mell toward the moonlight.

The glass shattered into a million glittering shards, and Kenny smiled all the way down.

It was the smell that told him he was still alive, the smell of disinfectant, and the feel of starched sheets beneath him. A hospital, he thought amidst a haze of pain. He was in a hospital. Kenny wanted to cry. Why hadn't he died? Oh, why, oh, why? He opened his eyes and tried to say something.

Suddenly a nurse was there, standing over him, feeling his brow and looking down with concern. Kenny wanted to beg her to kill him, but the words would not come. She went away, and when she came back she had others with her.

A chubby young man stood by his side and touched him and prodded here and there. Kenny's mouth worked soundlessly. "Easy," the doctor said. "You'll be all right, Mr. Dorchester, but you have a long way to go. You're in a hospital. You're a very lucky man. You fell eight stories. You ought to be dead."

I want to be dead, Kenny thought, and he shaped the words very, very carefully with his mouth, but no one seemed to hear them. Maybe the monkey has taken over, he thought. Maybe I can't even talk anymore.

"He wants to say something," the nurse said.

"I can see that," said the chubby young doctor. "Mr. Dorchester, please don't strain yourself. Really. If you are trying to ask about your friend, I'm afraid he wasn't as lucky as you. He was killed by the fall. You would have died as well, but fortunately you landed on top of him."

Kenny's fear and confusion must have been obvious, for the nurse put a gentle hand on his arm. "The other man," she said patiently. "The fat one. You can thank God he was so fat, too. He broke your fall like a giant pillow."

And finally Kenny Dorchester understood what they were saying, and he began to weep, but now he was weeping for joy, and trembling.

Three days later, he managed his first word. "Pizza," he said, and it came weak and hoarse from between his lips, but the sound elated him and he repeated it, louder, and then louder still, and before long he was pushing the nurse's call button and shouting and pushing and shouting. "Pizza, pizza,

pizza, pizza," he chanted, and he would not be calm until they ordered one for him. Nothing had ever tasted so good.

AUTHOR'S NOTE

One of the nicest things about life is that so much of it is unexpected. One of the worst things about art is that so much of it isn't.

I grew up loving the horror genre, everything from creature features to H. P. Lovecraft. I used to sell monster stories to the other kids in the projects where I lived, and for their nickel they got not only the story but also my dramatic reading. But it must be admitted, there was a period where I drifted away. Horror fiction seemed to have lost its savor. The stories began to seem too much alike. I got bored.

With the benefit of hindsight, I now understand why. I was bored by the sheer predictability of the stories I was reading, bored by horror stories that were *only* horror stories.

All good fiction, it seems to me, is about more than what it's about. Like life, it is full of many different things, and flavored with the full range of human emotion and experience. The modern publishing industry markets fiction as if it were ice cream, as if love and horror and laughter and lust and suspense could be put in little cartons like butter brickle and rocky road and peanut butter chocolate. Come on in, readers, here we have 31 Emotions, no waiting.

Well, I've always been the sort who gets scoops of two or even three different flavors on my sugar cones. Which brings me to the story you just read.

I wanted to write a story that was genuinely funny and genuinely horrifying. In life, horror and humor are not all that far apart. When we rise in the morning, we don't know if the day will be full of fear, or laughter, or both. That ought to be true when we pick up a book too.

Ergo "The Monkey Treatment." A lot of editors didn't know quite what to make of this story. Some thought it was funny, some thought it was horrible, some thought it was disgusting. Some thought it was funny and horrible and disgusting, but told me I couldn't *do* that, at least not in their ice cream store. Ed Ferman of *F&SF* thought it was a good story, and bought it. Enough readers agreed with him to make the story a Hugo and Nebula finalist.

I don't know about you, but I found that very encouraging. It's nice to know that there are other people out there, like me and Kenny, who appreciate a wide range of flavors.

—George R. R. Martin

CASEY AGONISTES

Richard McKenna

You can't just plain die. You got to do it by the book.

That's how come I'm here in this TB ward with nine other recruits. Basic training to die.

You do it by stages. First a big ward, you walk around and go out and they call you mister. Then, if you got what it takes, a promotion to this isolation ward and they call you charles. You can't go nowhere, you meet the masks, and you get the feel of being dead.

Being dead is being weak and walled off. You hear car noises and see little doll-people down on the sidewalks, but when they come to visit you they wear white masks and nightgowns and talk past you in the wrong voices. They're scared you'll rub some off on them. You would, too, if you knew how.

Nobody ever visits me. I had practice being dead before I come here. Maybe that's how I got to be charles so quick.

It's easy, playing dead here. You eat your pills, make out to sleep in the quiet hours and drink your milk like a good little charles. You grin at their phony joshing about how healthy you look and feel. You all know better, but them's the rules.

Sick call is when they really make you know it. It's a parade—the head doctor and nurse, the floor nurse Mary Howard and two interns, all in masks and nightgowns. Mary pushes the wheeled rack with our fever charts on it. The doc is a tall skinhead with wooden eyes and pinchnose glasses. The head nurse is fat, with little pig eyes and a deep voice.

The doc can't see, hear, smell or touch you. He looks at your reflection in the chart and talks about you like you was real, but it's Mary that pulls down the cover and opens your pajama coat, and the interns poke and look and listen and tell the doc what they see and hear. He asks them questions for you to answer. You tell them how good you feel and they tell him. He ain't supposed to get contaminated.

Mary's small, dark and sweet and the head nurse gives her a bad time. One intern is small and dark like Mary, but with soft black eyes and very gentle. The other one is pink and chubby.

The doc's voice is high and thin, like he ain't all there below decks. The head nurse snaps at Mary, snips at the interns, and puts a kind of dog wiggle in her voice when she talks to the doc.

I'm glad not to know what's under any of their masks, except maybe Mary's, because I can likely imagine better faces for them than God did. The head nurse makes rounds, writing the book. When she catches us out of line, like smoking or being up in a quiet hour, she gives Mary hell.

She gives us hell too, like we was babies. She kind of hints that if we ain't respectful to her and obey her rules maybe she won't let us die after all.

Christ, how I hate this hag! I hope I meet her in hell.

That's how it struck me, first day or two in isolation. I'd looked around for old shipmates, like a guy does, but didn't see any. On the third day one recognized me. I thought I knew that gravel voice, but even after he told me I couldn't hardly believe it was old Slop Chute Hewitt.

He was skin and bones and his blue eyes had a kind of puzzled look like I saw in them once years ago when a big limey sucker punched him in Nagasaki Joe's. When I remembered that, it made me know, all right.

He said glad to see me there and we both laughed. Some of the others shuffled over in striped bathrobes and all of a sudden I was in like Flynn, knowing Slop Chute. I found out they called the head doc Uncle Death. The fat nurse was Mama Death. The blond intern was Pink Waldo, the dark one Curly Waldo, and Mary was Mary. Knowing things like that is a kind of password.

They said Curly Waldo was sweet on Mary, but he was a poor Italian. Pink Waldo come of good family and was trying to beat him out. They were pulling for Curly Waldo.

When they left, Slop Chute and me talked over old times in China. I kept seeing him like he was on the *John D. Edwards,* sitting with a cup of coffee topside by the after fireroom hatch, while his snipes turned to down below. He wore bleached dungarees and shined shoes and he looked like a lord of the earth. His broad face and big belly. The way he stoked chow into himself in the guinea pullman —that's what give him his name. The way he took aboard beer and samshu in the Kongmoon Happiness Garden. The way he swung the little ne-sans dancing in the hotels on Skibby Hill. Now . . . Godalmighty! It made me know.

But he still had the big jack-lantern grin.

"Remember little Connie that danced at the Palais?" he asked.

I remember her, half Portygee, cute as hell.

"You know, Charley, now I'm headed for scrap, the onliest one damn thing I'm sorry for is I didn't shack with her when I had the chance."

"She was nice," I said.

"She was green fire in the velvet, Charley. I had her a few times when I was on the *Monocacy*. She wanted to shack and I wouldn't never do it. Christ, Christ, I wish I did, now!"

"I ain't sorry for anything, that I can think of."

"You'll come to it, sailor. For every guy there's some one thing. Remember how Connie used to put her finger on her nose like a Jap girl?"

"Now, Mr. Noble, you mustn't keep arthur awake in quiet hour. Lie down yourself, please."

It was Mama Death, sneaked up on us.

"Now rest like a good boy, charles, and we'll have you home before you know it," she told me on her way out.

I thought a thought at her.

The ward had green-gray linoleum, high, narrow windows, a sparcolor overhead, and five bunks on a side. My bunk was at one end next to the solarium. Slop Chute was across from me in the middle. Six of us was sailors, three soldiers, and there was one marine.

We got mucho sack time, training for the long

sleep. The marine bunked next to me and I saw a lot of him.

He was a strange guy. Name of Carnahan, with a pointed nose and a short upper lip and a go-to-hell stare. He most always wore his radio earphones and he was all the time grinning and chuckling like he was in a private world from the rest of us.

It wasn't the program that made him grin, either, like I thought first. He'd do it even if some house-wife was yapping about how to didify the dump-lings. He carried on worst during sick call. Sometimes Uncle Death looked across almost like he could hear it direct.

I asked him about it and he put me off, but finally he told me. Seems he could hypnotize himself to see a big ape and then make the ape clown around. He told me I might could get to see it too. I wanted to try, so we did.

"He's there," Carnahan would say. "Sag your eyes, look out the corners. He won't be plain at first.

"Just *expect* him, he'll come. Don't want him to do anything. You just *feel.* He'll do what's natural," he kept telling me.

I got where I could see the ape—Casey, Carnahan called him—in flashes. Then one day Mama Death was chewing out Mary and I saw him plain. He come up behind Mama and—I busted right out laughing.

He looked like a bowlegged man in an ape suit covered with red-brown hair. He grinned and made faces with a mouth full of big yellow teeth and he was furnished like John Keeno himself. I roared.

"Put on your phones so you'll have an excuse for

laughing," Carnahan whispered. "Only you and me can see him, you know."

Fixing to be dead, you're ready for God knows what, but Casey was sure something.

"Hell, no he ain't real," Carnahan said. "We ain't so real ourselves any more. That's why we can see him."

Carnahan told me okay to try and let Slop Chute in on it. It ended we cut the whole gang in, going slow so the masks wouldn't get suspicious.

It bothered Casey at first, us all looking at him. It was like we all had a string on him and he didn't know who to mind. He backed and filled and tacked and yawed all over the ward not able to steer himself. Only when Mama Death was there and Casey went after her, then it was like all the strings pulled the same way.

The more we watched him the plainer and stronger he got till finally he started being his own man. He came and went as he pleased and we never knew what he'd do next except that there'd be a laugh in it. Casey got more and more there for us, but he never made a sound.

He made a big difference. We all wore our earphones and giggled like idiots. Slop Chute wore his big sideways grin more often. Old Webster almost stopped griping.

There was a man filling in for a padre came to visitate us every week. Casey would sit on his knee and wiggle and drool, with one finger between those strong, yellow teeth. The man said the radio was a godsend to us patient spirits in our hour of trial. He stopped coming.

Casey made a real show out of sick call. He kissed Mama Death smack on her mask, danced with her and bit her on the rump. He rode piggy back on Uncle Death. He even took a hand in Mary's romance.

One Waldo always went in on each side of a bunk to look, listen and feel for Uncle. Mary could go on either side. We kept count of whose side she picked and how close she stood to him. That's how we figured Pink Waldo was ahead.

Well, Casey started to shoo her gently in by Curly Waldo and then crowd her closer to him. And, you know, the count began to change in Curly's favor. Casey had something.

If no masks were around to bedevil, Casey would dance and turn handsprings. He made us all feel good.

Uncle Death smelled a rat and had the radio turned off during sick call and quiet hours. But he couldn't cut off Casey.

Something went wrong with Roby, the cheerful black boy next to Slop Chute. The masks were all upset about it and finally Mary come told him on the sly. He wasn't going to make it. They were going to flunk him back to the big ward and maybe back to the world.

Mary's good that way. We never see her face, of course, but I always imagine for her a mouth like Venus has, in that picture you see her standing in the shell.

When Roby had to go, he come around to each bunk and said goodbye. Casey stayed right behind him with his tongue stuck out. Roby kept looking around for Casey, but of course he couldn't see him.

He turned around, just before he left the ward, and all of a sudden Casey was back in the middle and scowling at him. Roby stood looking at Casey with the saddest face I ever saw him wear. Then Casey grinned and waved a hand. Roby grinned back and tears run down his black face. He waved and shoved off.

Casey took to sleeping in Roby's bunk till another recruit come in.

One day two masked orderlies loaded old Webster the whiner onto a go-to-Jesus cart and wheeled him off to X-ray. They said. But later one came back and wouldn't look at us and pushed Webster's locker out and we knew. The masks had him in a quiet room for the graduation exercises.

They always done that, Slop Chute told me, so's not to hurt the morale of the guys not able to make the grade yet. Trouble was, when a guy went to X-ray on a go-to-Jesus cart he never knew till he got back whether he was going to see the gang again.

Next morning when Uncle Death fell in for sick call, Casey come bouncing down the ward and hit him a haymaker plumb on the mask.

I swear the bald-headed bastard staggered. I know his glasses fell off and Pink Waldo caught them. He said something about a moment of vertigo, and made a quick job of sick call. Casey stayed right behind him and kicked his stern post every step he took.

Mary favored Curly Waldo's side that day without any help from Casey.

After that Mama Death really got ugly. She

slobbered loving care all over us to keep us from knowing what we was there for. We got baths and back rubs we didn't want. Quiet hour had to start on the dot and be really quiet. She was always reading Mary off in whispers, like she knew it bothered us.

Casey followed her around aping her duck waddle and poking her behind now and again. We laughed and she thought it was at her and I guess it was. So she got Uncle Death to order the routine temperatures taken rectally, which she knew we hated. We stopped laughing and she knocked off the rectal temperatures. It was a kind of unspoken agreement. Casey give her a worse time than ever, but we saved our laughing till she was gone.

Poor Slop Chute couldn't do anything about his big, lopsided grin that was louder than a belly laugh. Mama give him a real bad time. She arthured the hell out of him.

He was coming along first rate, had another hemorrhage, and they started taking him to the clinic on a go-to-Jesus cart instead of in a chair. He was supposed to use ducks and a bedpan instead of going to the head, but he saved it up and after lights out we used to help him walk to the head. That made his reflection in the chart wrong and got him in deeper with Uncle Death.

I talked to him a lot, mostly about Connie. He said he dreamed about her pretty often now.

"I figure it means I'm near ready for the deep six, Charley."

"Figure you'll see Connie then?"

"No. Just hope I won't have to go on thinking about her then. I want it to be all night in and no reveille."

"Yeah," I said, "me too. What ever become of Connie?"

"I heard she ate poison right after the Reds took over Shanghai. I wonder if she ever dreamed about me?"

"I bet she did, Slop Chute," I said. "She likely used to wake up screaming and she ate the poison just to get rid of you."

He put on his big grin.

"You regret something too, Charley. You find it yet?"

"Well, maybe," I said. "Once on a stormy night at sea on the *Black Hawk* I had a chance to push King Brody over the side. I'm sorry now I didn't."

"Just come to you?"

"Hell, no, it come to me three days later when he give me a week's restriction in Tsingtao. I been sorry ever since."

"No. It'll smell you out, Charley. You wait."

Casey was shadow boxing down the middle of the ward as I shuffled back to my bunk.

It must've been spring because the days were longer. One night, right after the nurse come through, Casey and Carnahan and me helped Slop Chute walk to the head. While he was there he had another hemorrhage.

Carnahan started for help but Casey got in the way and motioned him back and we knew Slop Chute didn't want it.

We pulled Slop Chute's pajama top off and steadied him. He went on his knees in front of the bowl and the soft, bubbling cough went on for a long time. We kept flushing it. Casey opened the door and went out to keep away the nurse.

Finally it pretty well stopped. Slop Chute was too weak to stand. We cleaned him up and I put my pajama top on him, and we stood him up. If Casey hadn't took half the load, we'd'a never got him back to his bunk.

Godalmighty! I used to carry hundred-kilo sacks of cement like they was nothing.

We went back and cleaned up the head. I washed out the pajama top and draped it on the radiator. I was in a cold sweat and my face burned when I turned in.

Across the ward Casey was sitting like a statue beside Slop Chute's bunk.

Next day was Friday, because Pink Waldo made some crack about fish to Curly Waldo when they formed up for sick call. Mary moved closer to Curly Waldo and gave Pink Waldo a cold look. That was good.

Slop Chute looked waxy, and Uncle Death seemed to see it because a gleam come into his wooden eyes. Both Waldos listened all over Slop Chute and told uncle what they heard in their secret language. Uncle nodded, and Casey thumbed his nose at him.

No doubt about it, the ways was greased for Slop Chute. Mama Death come back soon as she could and began to loosen the chocks. She slobbered arthurs all over Slop Chute and flittered around like women do when they smell a wedding. Casey give her extra special hell, and we all laughed right out and she hardly noticed.

That afternoon two orderly-masks come with a go-to-Jesus cart and wanted to take Slop Chute to X-ray. Casey climbed on the cart and scowled at them.

Slop Chute told 'em shove off, he wasn't going.

They got Mary and she told Slop Chute please go, it was doctor's orders.

Sorry, no, he said.

"Please, for me, Slop Chute," she begged.

She knows our right names—that's one reason we love her. But Slop Chute shook his head, and his big jaw bone stuck out.

Mary—she had to then—called Mama Death. Mama waddled in, and Casey spit in her mask.

"Now, arthur, what is this, arthur, you know we want to help you get well and go home, arthur," she arthured at Slop Chute. "Be a good boy now, arthur, and go along to the clinic."

She motioned the orderlies to pick him up anyway. Casey hit one in the mask and Slop Chute growled, "Sheer off, you bastards!"

The orderlies hesitated.

Mama's little eyes squinted and she wiggled her hands at them. "Let's not be naughty, arthur. Doctor knows best, arthur."

The orderlies looked at Slop Chute and at each other. Casey wrapped his arms around Mama Death and began chewing on her neck. He seemed to mix right into her, someway, and she broke and run out of the ward.

She come right back, though, trailing Uncle Death. Casey met him at the door and beat hell out of him all the way to Slop Chute's bunk. Mama sent Mary for the chart, and Uncle Death studied Slop Chute's reflection for a minute. He looked pale and swayed a little from Casey's beating.

He turned toward Slop Chute and breathed in deep and Casey was on him again. Casey wrapped his arms and legs around him and chewed at his mask with those big yellow teeth. Casey's hair bristled and his eyes were red as the flames of hell.

Uncle Death staggered back across the ward and fetched up against Carnahan's bunk. The other masks were scared spitless, looking all around, kind of knowing.

Casey pulled away, and Uncle Death said maybe he was wrong, schedule it for tomorrow. All the masks left in a hurry except Mary. She went back to Slop Chute and took his hand.

"I'm sorry, Slop Chute," she whispered.

"Bless you, Connie," he said, and grinned. It was the last thing I ever heard him say.

Slop Chute went to sleep, and Casey sat beside his bunk. He motioned me off when I wanted to help Slop Chute to the head after lights out. I turned in and went to sleep.

I don't know what woke me. Casey was moving around fidgety-like, but of course not making a sound. I could hear the others stirring and whispering in the dark too.

Then I heard a muffled noise—the bubbling cough again, and spitting. Slop Chute was having another hemorrhage and he had his head under the blankets to hide the sound. Carnahan started to get up. Casey waved him down.

I saw a deeper shadow high in the dark over Slop Chute's bunk. It came down ever so gently and Casey would push it back up again. The muffled coughing went on.

Casey had a harder time pushing back the shadow. Finally he climbed on the bunk straddle of Slop Chute and kept a steady push against it.

The blackness came down anyway, little by little.

Casey strained and shifted his footing. I could hear him grunt and hear his joints crack.

I was breathing forced draft with my heart like to pull off its bed bolts. I heard other bedsprings creaking. Somebody across from me whimpered low, but it was sure never Slop Chute that done it.

Casey went to his knees, his hands forced almost level with his head. He swung his head back and forth and I saw his lips curled back from the big teeth clenched tight together. . . . Then he had the blackness on his shoulders like the weight of the whole world.

Casey went down on hands and knees with his back arched like a bridge. Almost I thought I heard him grunt . . . and he gained a little.

Then the blackness settled heavier, and I heard Casey's tendons pull out and his bones snap. Casey and Slop Chute disappeared under the blackness, and it overflowed from there over the whole bed . . . and more . . . and it seemed to fill the whole ward.

It wasn't like going to sleep, but I don't know anything it was like.

The masks must've towed off Slop Chute's hulk in the night, because it was gone when I woke up.

So was Casey.

Casey didn't show up for sick call and I knew then how much he meant to me. With him around to fight back I didn't feel as dead as they wanted me to. Without him I felt deader than ever. I even almost liked Mama Death when she charlesed me.

Mary came on duty that morning with a diamond on her third finger and a brighter sparkle in her eye. It was a little diamond, but it was Curly Waldo's and it kind of made up for Slop Chute.

I wished Casey was there to see it. He would've danced all around her and kissed her nice, the way he often did. Casey loved Mary.

It was Saturday, I know, because Mama Death come in and told some of us we could be wheeled to a special church hooraw before breakfast next morning if we wanted. We said no thanks. But it was a hell of a Saturday without Casey. Sharkey Brown said it for all of us—"With Casey gone, this place is like a morgue again."

Not even Carnahan could call him up.

"Sometimes I think I feel him stir, and then again I ain't sure," he said. "It beats hell where he's went to."

Going to sleep that night was as much like dying as it could be for men already dead.

Music from far off woke me up when it was just getting light. I was going to try to cork off again, when I saw Carnahan was awake.

"Casey's around somewhere," he whispered.

"Where?" I asked, looking around. "I don't see him."

"I feel him," Carnahan said. "He's around."

The others began to wake up and look around. It was like the night Casey and Slop Chute went under. Then something moved in the solarium. . . .

It was Casey.

He come in the ward slow and bashful-like, jerking his head all around, with his eyes open wide, and looking scared we was going to throw something at him. He stopped in the middle of the ward.

"Yea, Casey!" Carnahan said in a low, clear voice.

Casey looked at him sharp.

"Yea, Casey!" we all said. "Come aboard, you hairy old bastard!"

Casey shook hands with himself over his head and went into his dance. He grinned . . . and I swear to God it was Slop Chute's big, lopsided grin he had on.

For the first time in my whole damn life I wanted to cry.

NOTES ON THE CONTRIBUTORS

JOSEPH PAYNE BRENNAN began submitting stories to the legendary pulp magazine *Weird Tales* while still in his teens, and soon joined the ranks of H. P. Lovecraft, Robert E. Howard, Clark Ashton Smith, Manly Wade Wellman, Robert Bloch, Frank Belknap Long, Ray Bradbury and other distinguished authors of the dark and fantastic to emerge from its pages. He has since seen some eighteen books of his own published, including *9 Horrors and a Dream, The Dark Returners, Scream at Midnight, Stories of Darkness and Dread, The Shapes of Midnight,* and a series about one Lucius Leffing, psychic detective. He is also a renowned poet, his verses having appeared in *The New York Times Commonweal,* etc. and collected in several volumes. In 1982 Brennan was appropriately presented with the Life Achievement Award of the World Fantasy Convention, which gathering had earlier provided the setting for a Leffing adventure (*Act of Providence*). In 1985 he retired from Yale University Library after more than forty years, suggesting that further new titles, like the recent *Sixty Selected Poems* and *The Borders Just Beyond,* are soon to be seen.

GEORGE ALEC EFFINGER has the reputation of ironist in a field not well known for its ability to laugh at itself. That he is often a satirist is true enough, but for too many years his sense of humor has obscured a full assessment of his unique intelligence. For underlying Effinger's cosmic laughter is a keenly observant and unsparingly analytical mind which has no peer in sf. A member of the Milford and Clarion workshops, his first short fiction appeared in 1971; he has since published another 125 stories as varied as his own restless and unpredictable interests. Some of these stories have been collected in the volumes *Dirty Tricks, Irrational Numbers, Idle Pleasures* and *Mixed Feelings*. He also co-edited the magazine *Haunt of Horror* and wrote the novels *Felicia, Relatives, Nightmare Blue* (with Gardner Dozois), *Those Gentle Voices, What Entropy Means to Me, Heroics, The Wolves of Memory, The Nick of Time* and *The Bird of Time*. His most recent, *When Gravity Fails*, is equally unlikely: a science fiction mystery told in the hard-boiled manner of Raymond Chandler. Next up: a sequel, *A Fire in the Sun*, and *Shadow Money*.

CHARLES L. GRANT is one of several contributors whose work defies facile categorization. The novels *The Shadow of Alph* (1976) and *Ascension* (1977) and many short stories, two of which have won the Nebula Award, would seem enough to convince any career-minded professional that he ought to continue as a science fiction writer. During the same years, however, Grant was also busy writing horror: novels like *The Curse, The Hour of the Oxrun Dead* and *The Sound of Midnight*. His successes in that field, including multiple World Fantasy Awards, should have been sufficient to drive a left-brain type into schizophrenia. What, then, to do with a highly visible third career as editor (*Nightmares, Horrors, Fears, Midnight, Shadows, The Dodd, Mead Gallery of Horror,* et al.)? Well, why not write another twenty or so books under various pseudonyms, including gothics by "Felicia Andrews" and "Deborah Lewis"? At this point the protean impulse appears to have taken over; what Grant publishes next will probably be as much of a surprise to him as to his readers. Recently: *Night Songs, The Tea Party, The Long Night of the Grave, The Pet* and *The Orchard.*

DAMON KNIGHT is the man without whom modern science fiction would probably not exist in anything like the form we now know it. As a member of the Futurians, he was a crucial figure in the early days of fandom. As an editor, he discovered fresh talent and did much to influence the New Wave movement that changed the course of sf. As a critic, he introduced standards previously unknown in the field. As a teacher, his workshops produced an inordinate number of the finest and most honored writers now practicing. As founder and first president of the Science Fiction Writers of America, he was instrumental in creating the most effective organization yet for literary authors. And as author himself of novels and collections like *Hell's Pavement, A for Anything, Far Out, In Deep, Off Center* and *Turning On,* and such classic stories as "To Serve Man," "Babel II," "The Country of the Kind," "Stranger Station" and "Masks," he has earned a reputation as one of the most important names in the history of speculative fiction. He is the recipient of numerous awards, including the Hugo and Nebula. Upcoming: a sequel to his novel *CV.*

TANITH LEE won the World Fantasy Award for Best Short Story two years running—with "The Gorgon" in 1983 and "Elle Est Trois (La Mort)" in 1984—which accomplishment establishes for the record that she is one of today's most gifted practitioners of dark fantasy. What fans of the terror tale may not realize is that she is also the author of several books for children and young adults. One wonders what the parents of some of her juvenile readers might make of Lee's indisputably adult yarns, such as the disturbing example reprinted in these pages; sophisticated readers, however, will take much enjoyment from *The Dragon Hoard, Princess Hynchatti and Some Other Surprises, Animal Castle, Companions on the Road, The Winter Players* and *East of Midnight.* Her adult novels include *The Birthgrave, Vazkor, Son of Vazkor, Volkhavaar, Quest for the White Witch, Don't Bite the Sun, Drinking Sapphire Wine, The Storm Lord, Night's Master,* and *The Silver Metal Lover.* Her short stories may be found in most of the major anthologies. Recent and forthcoming books: *Days of Grass, Delirium's Mistress,* the collection *Night's Daughter,* and a novel about the French Revolution.

FRITZ LEIBER is credited with coining the term Sword-and-Sorcery, now used universally to describe a popular branch of fantasy fiction. Not surprisingly his Fafhrd and the Gray Mouser series skillfully avoids clichés found in heroic adventures created by lesser talents. Leiber's achievements in science fiction and horror are also universally appreciated, having cast a seminal influence over the entire world of imaginative literature. After six Hugos, four Nebulas and two World Fantasy

Awards (one for Life Achievement), his contribution is indisputable. *Gather, Darkness!, Destiny Times Three, The Green Millennium, The Big Time, The Wanderer, A Specter Is Haunting Texas, Conjure Wife* and *Our Lady of Darkness* is only a partial list of his famous novels; classic stories include "Two Sought Adventure," "Ill Met in Lankhmar," "Smoke Ghost," "The Man Who Made Friends with Electricity," "Coming Attractions," "Damnation Morning," "Belsen Express," "Gonna Roll the Bones" and "Catch That Zeppelin!" Most recent books include *The Mystery of the Japanese Clock* and *The Ghost Light*, with *The Knave and Knight of Swords* soon to be completed.

FRANK BELKNAP LONG is another true Grand Master by any standards. Born in 1903, he is a direct descendant of one of the *Mayflower* crewmen, and it was none other than his grandfather who raised the Statue of Liberty's platform in 1883. Long began as a poet, sold his first fantasy in 1924, appeared regularly in *Weird Tales* and many other periodicals, and has continued to publish through the 1980s in *Twilight Zone Magazine, Year's Best Horror Stories, Whispers III & IV, Writers of Supernatural Fiction*, etc., for a total of more than three hundred stories to date. One may only speculate as to what deal was struck with Cthulhu himself way back when to account for a career of such longevity and productivity. Books include *The Man from Genoa, The Goblin Tower, The Hounds of Tindalos, The Horror from the Hills, The Rim of the Unknown, The Early Long, So Dark a Heritage, Night Fear,* and a study of his friend and mentor, *Howard Phillips Lovecraft: Dreamer on the Nightside*. In 1978 he received the Life

Achievement Award of the World Fantasy Convention. He is presently at work on a new novel.

BARRY N. MALZBERG is the name that comes most immediately to mind as an antidote to comments by illiterates to the effect that science fiction, fantasy and horror constitute fare more appropriate to children and irresponsible sensationalists than to respectable members of the upscale intelligentsia. Had they read *The Destruction of the Temple*, *The Cross of Fire*, *Guernica Night*, *Herovitz's World*, *The Falling Astronauts*, *Revelations*, *Beyond Apollo*, or any of Malzberg's many other novels and hundred-plus short stories, they would know as profound a social conscience tortured by as relentless a struggle to come to terms with life in the twentieth century as can be found in the most widely praised French existentialists and American post-moderns. They would also learn that there is a darker side to science fiction, one that does not necessarily worship the scientific method as the best hope for our redemption. A winner of the John W. Campbell Award, Malzberg is additionally known as a fine editor. His nonfiction *The Engines of the Night* was a Hugo finalist in 1983, and the novel *The Remaking of Sigmund Freud* a Nebula finalist in 1986.

GEORGE R. R. MARTIN, a member of the baby-boom generation, has become one of the most respected postwar writers of science fiction, fantasy and horror, thereby sparing America the embarrassment of yet another yuppie. His first story, "The Hero," was sold to *Galaxy* at the age of twenty-one; since then he has accumulated three Hugos and two Nebulas (Nebulae?), the Japanese Daikon award, and more nominations than we have room to list. Books include the novels *Dying of the Light, Windhaven* (with Lisa Tuttle), *Fevre Dream* and *The Armageddon Rag;* the collections *A Song for Lya, Songs of Stars and Shadows, Sandkings, Songs the Dead Men Sing* and *Nightflyers;* and, as editor, several anthologies, among them various editions of *New Voices in Science Fiction* and *The John W. Campbell Awards.* Recent and forthcoming titles include a novel, *Black and White and Red All Over*, the collections *Tuf Voyaging* and *Twice as Tuf,* and the anthologies *Night Visions 3, Wild Cards, Aces High,* and *Jokers Wild.* His "Remembering Melody" became the most memorable episode of the HBO television series *The Hitchhiker;* and a feature, *Nightflyers,* based upon his story, was released in 1987.

RICHARD McKENNA served a twenty-two-year stint in the Navy before embarking on a second career. "Casey Agonistes" in *The Magazine of Fantasy and Science Fiction* gave him instant status as a major voice in the field. He wrote more science fiction stories while researching a massive novel about the U.S. Asiatic Fleet; chapters were published in *Harper's* and *The Saturday Evening Post,* and in 1962 *The Sand Pebbles* became a best seller. In 1964, only six years into a brilliant literary career, McKenna died. He left several stories and essays and an uncompleted novel, portions of which eventually appeared in *The Left-Handed Monkey Wrench,* a volume about Naval life. It would be inaccurate to say that he did not live long enough to achieve success—all of his works are considered classics. But he was clearly destined for greater rewards. *The Sand Pebbles* was adapted into an important motion picture, and several stories were published posthumously to great acclaim, including the Nebula Award-winning "The Secret Place." *New Eyes for Old: Nonfiction Writings by Richard McKenna* was edited by Eva Grice McKenna and Shirley Graves Cochrane in 1972.

THOMAS F. MONTELEONE began as a science fiction writer in 1972, and has not stopped producing the tight poetic short stories (some sixty to date) that won him early acclaim. A number of the best of these have been collected as *Dark Stars and Other Illuminations*. He has also published sixteen novels; *The Time Connection, The Time Swept City* and others are sf, but later books have expanded to encompass fantasy, suspense and, notably, horror (*Night Train*). Highly regarded by his contemporaries, Monteleone served as secretary to the SFWA for three years and has received many justly deserved award nominations. He has edited two outstanding anthologies, *The Arts and Beyond: Visions of Man's Aesthetic Future* and *Random Access Messages,* has written teleplays, and has seen his own short stories dramatized on *Tales from the Dark Side*. New and forthcoming books are horror novels *Lyrica, The Magnificent Gallery, Crooked House* (with John DeChancie), *Fantasma* and *Dragonstar Destiny,* the concluding volume of a trilogy with David Bischoff that began with *Day of the Dragonstar* and *Night of the Dragonstar*.

WHITLEY STRIEBER is the author of one of the most famous of all modern novels about vampirism; stringent, humane and highly moral, *The Hunger* is also remarkable for its conscious refusal to prejudice readers by using the word "vampire" anywhere in its pages. His *The Wolfen*, an earlier best seller and equally challenging in its ethical stance, was likewise made into a major motion picture, introducing an even larger audience to a writer whose purposes transcend commercial fashion. A former production assistant and underground filmmaker now living in New York City, Strieber employs horror as nothing less than a crucible for testing the farther reaches of philosophy and conscience. *The Night Church, Black Magic* and *Catmagic* explore religion, mythology and the paranormal in ways designed to provoke rather than to offer easy answers to the question of evil. The award-winning *Wolf of Shadows* concerns ethology; *War Day* (written with James Kunetka) addresses the issue of survival in the nuclear age. His latest books are *Nature's End* and *Communion*, a true account of an extraordinary experience.

LISA TUTTLE, author of such powerful stories as "Sun City," "Stone Circle," "Where the Stones Grow" and "Woman Waiting," as well as this volume's "The Other Room," is one of the newer masters represented here—and like most of the others has forged a career that includes science fiction, fantasy and horror in almost equal measure and without apparent favoritism. Her work tends to explore the darker implications of what lies below the calm, well-behaved surface of everyday life; could this concern with the skull beneath the skin result from a childhood informed by the Eisenhower years? Born in Houston, Texas, in 1952, Tuttle earned a degree from Syracuse University (1973) and a John W. Campbell Award for the best new science fiction writer of 1974 before moving in 1981 to England, where from all reports she continues to live quite happily as an expatriate.

In addition to more than fifty short stories, she has published the novels *Windhaven* (with George R. R. Martin) and *Familiar Spirit.* Most recently: the novel *Gabriel,* the collections *A Nest of Nightmares* and *A Spaceship Built of Stone,* and the nonfiction *Encyclopedia of Feminism.*

MANLY WADE WELLMAN (1903–1986) was also Gans T. Field, Hampton Wells, Levi Crow, Gabriel Barclay, Will Garth and a number of other popular authors during a career that spanned six decades. Football player, reporter, first lieutenant, teacher, scholar, biographer, historian, master storyteller and husband to *Weird Tales* writer Frances Garfield, he won fame in science fiction, fantasy and horror before a good many of the rest of the people in this book were born. Two hundred stories and nearly eighty books, such as *Who Fears the Devil?, Twice in Time, Sherlock Holmes's War of the Worlds* (with his son, Wade Wellman), *Island in the Sky, The Solar Invasion, The Old Gods Waken,* the World Fantasy Award–winning *Worse Things Waiting, Lonely Vigils, What Dreams May Come,* etc., ensure that his reputation will loom large as long as the art of fiction endures. He was finally presented with this field's highest honor, the Life Achievement Award of the World Fantasy Convention, in 1980. "My name is Manly Wade Wellman," he once told an admiring writer who will never forget shaking his hand, "and I'm a man." That he was.

KATE WILHELM works at the leading edge of contemporary fiction with the kind of deeply felt, precisely executed and refreshingly uncategorizable stories and novels that inspire the eclecticism of the present volume. Co-director (with her husband, Damon Knight) of the Milford Science Fiction

Writers Conference from 1963 to 1972, Wilhelm has exerted a profound influence on the development of speculative literature. *The Downstairs Room, The Infinity Box, Let the Fire Fall, Margaret and I, The Clewiston Test, Where Late the Sweet Birds Sang, Fault Lines* and *Somerset Dreams* have encouraged a generation of imaginative writers to seek levels of literary excellence beyond the formulaic minimums of the genre. "The Hounds" explores the uneasy intersection between dream and reality that is so often the subject of our peculiarly syncretic field—and never more exquisitely described than in the stories of Kate Wilhelm. A winner of the Hugo, Nebula and Jupiter awards, her latest books are *Huysman's Pet, The Hills Are Dancing* (with her son, Richard B. Wilhelm), and *Crazy Time.*